O9-BHK-539

HURON COUNTY LIBRARY

3 6492 00506052 7

A MAN IN A
DISTANT FIELD

FIC Kishk

Kishkan, T.
A man in a distant field.

PRICE: $21.99 (3559/wi)

THERESA KISHKAN

A MAN
IN A
DISTANT
FIELD

| A NOVEL |

SIMON & PIERRE FICTION
A MEMBER OF THE DUNDURN GROUP
TORONTO

Copyright © Theresa Kishkan, 2004

All rights reserved. No part of this publication may be reproduced, stored in a retrieval system, or trans-mitted in any form or by any means, electronic, mechanical, photocopying, recording, or otherwise (except for brief passages for purposes of review) without the prior permission of Dundurn Press. Permission to photocopy should be requested from Access Copyright.

Editor: Barry Jowett
Copy-editor: Andrea Pruss
Design: Jennifer Scott
Printer: Webcom

Library and Archives Canada Cataloguing in Publication

Kishkan, Theresa, 1955-
    A man in a distant field / Theresa Kishkan.

ISBN 1-55002-531-7

I. Title.

PS8571.I75M35 2004   C813'.54   C2004-905467-8

1   2   3   4   5   08   07   06   05   04

We acknowledge the support of the **Canada Council for the Arts** and the **Ontario Arts Council** for our publishing program. We also acknowledge the financial support of the **Government of Canada** through the **Book Publishing Industry Development Program** and **The Association for the Export of Canadian Books**, and the **Government of Ontario** through the **Ontario Book Publishers Tax Credit** program.

Care has been taken to trace the ownership of copyright material used in this book. The author and the publisher welcome any information enabling them to rectify any references or credits in subsequent editions.

J. Kirk Howard, President

Printed and bound in Canada. ♺
Printed on recycled paper.
www.dundurn.com

Dundurn Press
8 Market Street, Suite 200
Toronto, Ontario, Canada
M5E 1M6

Gazelle Book Services Limited
White Cross Mills
Hightown, Lancaster, England
LA1 4X5

Dundurn Press
2250 Military Road
Tonawanda, NY
U.S.A. 14150

A MAN IN A
DISTANT FIELD

Acknowledgements

Although this novel is a work of fiction, it is set in two actual places — Oyster Bay on B.C.'s Sechelt Peninsula and Delphi, in County Mayo, Ireland. I've tried to make the landscapes as accurate and real as possible, but the characters are products of my imagination, as are their stories, and any resemblance to those living or dead is pure coincidence.

The list of people who helped me with research and encouragement is too long to reproduce here, but I trust that they know who they are and I thank them all. Specific mention must be made of my husband and children, who provide love and good humour in necessary amounts. This book is for them. I would also like to thank Diana Davidson for reading the manuscript at a difficult time in its development and in turn her friend Gwyneth Evans for reading the passages about the harp and correcting a few errors. My editor, Barry Jowett, has been helpful but not intrusive, and I am grateful for that. And I would like to acknowledge the Canada Council for the Arts and the B.C. Arts Council, whose generous support made much of the work of this novel possible.

I am not a Greek scholar but tried to figure out the kind of translation a passionate but amateur reader of the *Odyssey* in a late-nineteenth-century edition might come up with. I used the Loeb edition of the *Odyssey* as a model and the Liddell and Scott standard Greek-English lexicon as well as *Cunliffe's Lexicon of the Homeric Dialect*. Any mistakes of grammar and usage are mine entirely.

Nil aon tintean mar do thintean fein.
There is no fireside like your own fireside.

(Irish proverb)

A man in a distant field, no hearthfires near,
will hide a fresh brand in his bed of embers
to keep a spark alive for the next day:
so in the leaves Odysseus hid himself ...

(*The Odyssey*, Book Five, lines 487–90,
trans. Robert Fitzgerald)

Part One

Oyster Bay,
Sechelt Peninsula, British Columbia,
Spring to Fall 1922

Chapter One

He was drifting on the tide, curled up small on the bottom of the skiff, feeling a chill through the thin slats of wood separating him from the waters of Oyster Bay. He could not rise to grasp the oars in their locks, to keep the skiff heading in the direction of his cabin, at ease in the current of strong water. Without lifting his head, he knew that the tides would take him back eventually because the bay ended at his steps, fed by the quick tea-coloured water of the creek that ran by his cabin and the other creeks that ran down off the mountain to the east and entered the chuck at the mud flats.

This was not the way he'd intended to return to the cabin, after a day and a night of hand-trolling out beyond the mouth of the bay. He'd sold his salmon to the pot scow — nice bluebacks that he'd wrapped in damp burlap potato sacks — and then begun the hard row home, feeling each pull of the oars right into the muscles of his back. Once he'd come through into the bay, he'd felt he could row until tomorrow at that rate, his shoulder joints oiled by the sweat that dripped down from under his cap into the collar of his pullover. It was seeing the moon in the eastern sky, still visible, though it must've been nearly noon by the position of the sun, that had slowed him. A new moon, delicate in the watery spring sky. There had been just such a moon on that other morning, hanging in the western Connemara sky like a sailmaker's needle, and seeing this one, he was pierced with such intense pain that he had to gather his limbs into his body and rock himself, crying, on the bottom of the skiff.

He must have fallen asleep. He couldn't remember the craft being pushed onto the shingle, round stones rolling under it, but found himself looking up from the carvel planks into the branches of the apple tree that grew between World's End and the water. A bird — he'd have called it a thrush, but here they were robins — was singing for all it was worth. Declan O'Malley knew the song had everything to do with territory. The robin had a mate and a nest in the apple tree, a fine construction of sticks and soft moss, a single strand of red wool woven into the sides like a sign to all that this was home. He supposed the bird hadn't known the wool was so bright, but perhaps it had and had chosen it for that reason, plucking it from a bramble where a garment of someone passing had snagged and then been eased away, leaving a thread behind. After all, in a momentary fit of consolation at having arrived at Oyster Bay, having decided to get himself as far as reasonably possible from the bloody Delphi soil, Declan had scratched "World's End" on a piece of cedar shake with a bit of charcoal and hammered it over his door.

No one named their habitations here, no farm had the descriptive notion secured to it as in Ireland, where a place might be known by its weather, its placement on a hill, or by a deeper meaning, mostly lost to memory but traceable, as though on a map, if one took the time. The cashels and bailes, the raths and crocs, piercing a place like a nail and fastening it to the long scan of history. His own farm, Tullaglas, named for its small green hill; the neighbouring Ardmor; the dark lake, Dhulough, below. A map of any Irish county would be busy with names, and not just for towns and villages — a countenance of promontories, rocks, wide space softened by sedges and hawthorns, ancient ground containing the remains of a fort, a battle.

And if a robin sang for territory, who could blame it, the poor bugger, because wasn't that what begetting and working your land and raising your children was about? Making a place for them in the world where they could be safe and grow like trees? He wished he'd done that in any country but the troubled one he'd been born in because he might yet be walking home to Tullaglas from the Bundorragha schoolhouse, a daughter on each side of him, looking forward to the thin plume of smoke in their chimney and Eilis greeting them with hot tea and a bit of barmbrack. It came again, the terrible sorrow, and he wept as he brought the skiff up above the high tide line, fastening its rope to the apple tree. He wept as he took the green cotton line from his boat to remove the strands of seaweed and to repair the breaks, took the little box of spinners to clean, took the oars, which he carefully leaned against the shake-clad wall of his cabin, along with the herring rake, and he was still weeping as he went in to start a fire so he could cook himself a meal, draping his sweat-damp pullover on a rock to dry. Some days were like this, the tears a river he could not for the life of him control.

In the distance, he could hear children, the children of the man who let him use the cabin; often they could be seen doing the work of men and women, ploughing a rough field behind a steady grey horse, washing clothing in the creek, leading a cow from one pasture to another. Encountered in this way, they looked to the ground or averted their eyes as they passed, a polite hello coaxed from the older ones. But he could tell, this time, that they were playing, their voices sounding so far away in the weather, though he knew they were only around the cove, at the mouth of a quick creek, where long grass hid the nests of geese and the passing of deer in the morning. Their voices were full of joy and youth, and he wept as he listened, for himself and for all the children of the world who would learn that no amount of love could keep grief from the door.

"Ma, the man's crying again. I didn't leave the milk because he looked too sad to bother with only a jug of milk."

The child looked to his mother, who was washing a tin bucket with scalding water from a kettle sitting on a stump. "Take this to the barn, Jack, and I'll take the milk myself. Did you spill any? I thought I'd filled the jug more than this."

"I tripped on a root and some splashed out. I didn't mean to. Duke licked it up before it had a chance to soak into the path, so it weren't really wasted."

His mother smiled at him. "That's one way to look at it, Jack. Now, take this bucket and mind you cover it with one of the clean rags on the bench so that it'll be ready for the evening milking. I'll be back soon."

She wiped her hands dry on her apron, which she then untied and hung on the pump. The trail to the cabin their tenant called World's End led through salal and oregon grape, dipping down at one place into a reedy marsh where her husband had made a corduroy walk of young cedars stripped of their branches and scored with an axe for traction. She was careful with her footing, balancing the jug of milk in her right hand and using her left to steady herself on the logs, which were slippery despite their scorings. Up a little hill, along a bluff of arbutus in full creamy bloom this middle of April, past the midden of clam and oyster shells, and along the muddy shore to World's End.

Declan O'Malley was inside by now, she could see smoke coming out of his chimney, the blue smoke that indicated he'd just lit a fire, using cedar kindling from the pile in the shelter of a big tree. The old oars they'd given him were standing under his eaves, sanded and oiled, and a herring rake she had seen before, too, a few strands of kelp between its tines. She knocked once on his weathered door. He came immediately.

"Jack brought this earlier but didn't want to trouble you. I'm sorry he spilled a bit on the trail. If you need more, we can let you have another jug after the evening milking, but I've used the earlier milk for my baking. Fishing, were you?"

"I'm much obliged, Mrs. Neil. Aye, I'd the boat out since yesterday morning, over to Outer Kelp by the point. Caught a few, too, now that I've the knack of it. I'm sorry a second trip had to be made with the milk. Will ye have a cup of tea?"

She looked past him into the cabin, wondering again at the fact that he had so little with which to make a life. Nearly two months he'd been there, a shadowy presence seen occasionally from her kitchen window, rowing out to fish or for provisions. With all the work of a stump farm and five children, she had no time to seek him out in a neighbourly way as she might have liked, yet was surprised to find him still camping (that was all you could call it) in the cabin, without anything much more than had been there when he'd arrived. A table, two rough benches he'd made from stumps. A blanket laid out neatly on the old mattress that had been in the cabin since the beginning of time, or at least the beginning of the century. And there were books, a big canvas bag with paper and ink, several bottles of it she'd seen.

"A cup of tea would be welcome, Mr. O'Malley. We could sit outside. It seems a shame to be inside when this sun is such a rare treat."

"We could of course." They sat with their tea on warm rocks at the edge of the clearing. Declan placed the teapot on a piece of driftwood pulled up from the shore and indicated branches carrying deep cerise flowers. "Now tell what are these flowers that the hummingbirds are fierce for?"

"We call them salmonberries, those bushes. The berries, when they come, are very flavourful and look a little like salmon roe, clusters of roe, I suppose. There's another one, too, with white blossoms, we call thimbleberry. You'll see those soon. I make jam with them when I can persuade the children to pick enough. A softer berry, too."

She paused, took a deep breath, and then continued. "Mr. O'Malley, I don't want to intrude on your privacy, but if there's anything I can do for you, will you let me know? In a small community like ours, we are used to troubles, our own and our neighbours', and it's no burden to help. You have only to say."

Declan looked at his feet, then turned his mug in his hands, peering inside as though the leaves might tell a fortune, a caution. "Mrs. Neil, you are very kind. I cannot speak of my own trouble, not yet, but I do thank ye from my heart for yer concern. I'd no thought or hope at all that I would find such kindness at the end of such a journey. I've no biscuit to offer ye with the tea, but perhaps ye'll take a bit of bread?"

Mrs. Neil looked at the piece of cedar shake he was holding in her direction. A round loaf with a slice or two taken from it: *Quite a coarse crumb, not a yeast bread,* she thought.

"However did you make bread, Mr. O'Malley? You have only that old stove the people before you rigged up from an oil barrel ..."

"I'm thinking ye have never heard of a bastable, Mrs. Neil. In Ireland the bread is often baked in the coals of an open fire in a little three-legged lad of cast iron. Well, to be sure I've nothing so formal as that, of course, but I found an old iron pot in the brush and scrubbed off the rust, oiled it up nicely as could be, and I've experimented with it, balanced on rocks in the coals of the stove, and this bread ye see is the result."

"But the bread itself, how did you know to bake it? Most men around here could make bannock, or fry bread, but it's hardly a bread at all, just flour and lard and leavening if they happen to have it, a mess they cook in a skillet and often as not is raw in the centre. Something to fill them up when they're in the bush."

"My mother taught me to bake when I was a boy as there were no sisters yet to learn, they came later, and me hanging around her, watching her work, she must've thought I might as well be useful. Buttermilk we used in Ireland, but sour milk, if it turns before I've used it in my tea, makes a good loaf with some bread soda. I'm sorry there's no butter to offer ye, but will ye have a bit of cheese?"

Mrs. Neil took the cheese he offered and broke a corner of bread off her slice. She tasted thoughtfully. "It's very good bread, Mr. O'Malley. How resourceful you've been! My husband is a great man for building and figuring out ways to preserve meat and fish, but I can't imagine him baking a loaf to save his life."

"To save his life, Mrs. Neil?"

His face, which had seemed to her to have relaxed with her praise of the bread, had suddenly become the saddest face she'd ever seen. Putting down her tea, she reached over to the rock where he sat and took his hand in her own, holding it briefly and then releasing it. "Just a saying, Mr. O'Malley, something we say without thinking. To indicate a thing is out of the realm of the possible, if you know what I mean."

"To save my life, Mrs. Neil, I am working on a project of translation. From Greek, which I learned as a lad from the priests at school, to English. My Greek is as rusty as the iron pot I found in the brush but looking at the letters — and they are not our alphabet, like Latin would be — is like looking at the tracks of a bird. If I take them into my mind, slowly, they make a sense after a bit. Once I could read them easily, and I'm hoping I will be able to again so." He had brightened in the telling of this, his blue eyes alight.

Mrs Neil remembered Greece from the globe in her own schoolroom all those years ago, in Glengarry County, but for the life of her she couldn't remember anything else about it, apart from its reputed heat, shepherds, and stories of gods and goddesses walking the earth, wreaths of laurel on their heads, and making trouble.

"And what are you turning into English?"

"Ah, Mrs. Neil, it's a great poem about the sea and a man who made his way from Troy, which as far as I can figure out is where Turkey is now, to a little island off the west coast of Greece. He was called Odysseus, and his story, the *Odyssey*, which means a wandering sort of adventure. And it is that, to be sure."

Mrs. Neil searched her memory for something, an echo, a name, and asked, "There was someone like that called Ulysses, wasn't there? I remember a poem, Tennyson, I think. My brother had a book, he'd read the poems aloud to us."

"Just so. He was called Ulysses by the Romans, later on. When I was a lad, I loved to imagine myself a wandering seafarer, though my father was a farmer. When the priests read to us of Odysseus, I'd put myself in his place, I loved every word, and it made me fierce to learn Greek as well as I could so I could read it for myself in the poet's own words. I wanted to go out in a boat and hear the siren's song and end up on an island like he did."

"Well, you've come to the right place, Mr. O'Malley. You can see for yourself how the bay is busy with islands. My husband is always heading to an island himself, in search of work — Nelson, Minstrel, wherever a gyppo operation might need a man for a week or a month. And boats, well, we'd all be lost here without a boat. But what you say about your lessons is interesting. My brother learned Latin, I remember, but not Greek. What did your family think about that?"

"It made me different, I'd say, and no one else, none of my classmates, seemed as smitten with the Greek as I did. We lived in a place in County Mayo called Delphi, and the priests told me it was also the name of a pagan temple in Greece. I could not help but want to know more. I made scribbles to myself, tried a line or two of the poem to see what I might make of it on my own. So that will be what I try to do for the next while, try to make an English story of Odysseus's long journey. There are English versions, I do know that, but they seem awkward to me, unsettling, as though the good parts had been taken out."

The woman could tell he was tiring, the day and night of trolling catching up with him. There was some warmth in the spring sun and a drone of bees in the salmonberry that might make anyone sleepy. She yawned herself. The warmth of the fire in the barrel stove made his small domain cosy, although she could smell the musty mattress and made a mental note to look out something more suitable in her attic. He rose with her as she said goodbye to him and asked did he need more milk that evening? He went to stand at the door as she walked away towards her own home and children. The tide was in, lapping at the edge of the clearing where his cabin stood, and a kingfisher screeched from a snag hanging over the creek. She smelled the smoke of his fire all the way back to her house, troubled by him but also intrigued. He was a man with mystery contained in his blue eyes, in the bag where he kept his papers. And some terrible tragedy, too, she thought, remembering an uncle who'd wept so often after the death of his wife that people avoided him and he turned to the bottle for company. No sign of the bottle at World's End, and it seemed it was the man himself who avoided company (he'd been invited to a gathering at the store, as well as a picnic, but never appeared), not the other way around.

> ὡς ὁ μέν ἔνθα καθεῦδε πολύτλας δῖος
>   Ὀδυσσεὺς
> ὕπνῳ καὶ καμάτῳ ἀρημένος`...

Weary beyond oblivion,
the noble man, Odysseus, slept on ...

You could never forget. Could you? And the memory was heavy baggage to be carried with you, slung over your shoulder like a hundredweight sack of potatoes, to be weighed and considered in every activity of your day. To be among the living when your loved ones were so brutally removed to the world of the dead ... And there could not be a God, no, never, to have let such a thing happen to innocent girls, to Eilis who never harmed a soul but who carried mugs of hot broth to the hungry stopping at houses to ask for a crust, a farthing. And his a modest salary, not overly much to carry them all, but with the potatoes they grew, and their chickens, and the butter Eilis made, sure there was food for the table, and to share, and the occasional penny for the girls to take to the shop for a sweet ...

Odysseus didn't know that the goddess Athene was plotting, as he slept, a plan to fill the head of a young girl with him, with the idea of him, as a way to get him a boat for the voyage home. Declan O'Malley pondered this for a minute or two and made some scratches on his paper. It was unsettling to think of dreams as something a goddess had planted in your head like seeds, with a particularly outcome in mind. When he dreamed of his family, when those images came with all their sorrow and pain, he tried to find a way to see the good in such dreaming. In one way, it made him less lonely because he could remember he had been Eilis's beloved, she had told him so in as many words, stroking his face with her long fingers in the early days of their courtship when he had walked out with her on balmy evenings where the boreen turned beyond her family's farm and kissed her in the lea of a hedge. He would remember with pleasure for a moment. But so soon, too soon, he would be aswim in the pain of it. No God, no, but goddesses at work on the sleeping? It was a thought.

> Ναυσικάα, τί νύ σ' ὧδε μεθήμονα γείνατο
>   μήτηρ;
> είματα μέν τοι κεῖται ἀκηδέα σιγαλόεντα,
> σοὶ δὲ γάμος σχεδόν ἐστιν, ἵνα χρὴ καλὰ μὲν
>   αὐτὴν
> ἔννυσθαι, τὰ δὲ τοῖσι παρασχεῖν, οἵ κέ σ'
>   ἄγωνται.
> ἐκ γάρ τοι τούτων φάτις ἀνθρώπους
>   ἀναβαίνει
> ἐσθλή, χηαίρουσιν δὲ πατὴρ καὶ πότνια
>   μήτηρ.

Nausikaa, how is it your mother has raised you to
    be careless?
Your clothing lies about uncared for
and yet soon you will marry
and will need stores of fine clothing
for yourself and those you love.

Beauty such as this will make your father and
    mother proud
and give those around you joy.
Let us go wash your linen in the clear air of
    morning!

The thing was to find the accurate way of saying it. Declan
was discovering that Greek was so much a language of its place
and time — not that he had ever seen the place, but one of the
priests at school had travelled there as a young man and had
been changed forever by the experience. He described the rocky
mountains, clothed in sharp-scented herbs, the stark white tem-
ples with columns lying across the ground like fallen gods.
Thorny bushes and lemon groves sloping down to a glittering
sea. There had been olive trees, he said, alive at the time of Jesus,
and their silvery leaves rustled in the wind like dry music. He
had never gotten over the warmth. And the storms, coming in
to wrap the bowl of the valley in mists like the smoke from
incense, and just as fragrant. Declan wondered if there were any
similarities between his own Delphi and the temple of the same
name. Both of them high in the mountains, tucked into clefts in
the rock. The weathers would be different, of course. Ireland's
rain, the intense sun of Greece. And no silvery olives, but the sallies by the river had their own soft leaves and music. And as for
being a language of its time, why, the problem Declan could
foresee was to find words to tell of honour, how a man would
lay down his life for something noble and larger than himself.
Where the actions of men reflected something foretold by gods.
To find equivalencies for olives, the magnanimity of kings.

There was a knock at the door. Opening it, he was surprised
to find a girl. He recognized her from the creek, one of the Neil
children at play in the reeds. She was fair, like the others, in a
skimpy dress of sprigged cotton, with a pullover knotted around

her waist. The girl was holding a small black puppy in her arms. It was struggling to get down, whimpering as it wriggled this way and that, a stream of urine falling to the threshold. The girl looked up and met Declan's eyes. Hers were a startling green, like new leaves, and there was a dusting of freckles across the ridge of her upper cheeks and nose.

"Please, sir, my mother thought you might want one of Queenie's pups. They're old enough to leave her now."

"Put the lad down so I can see what ye've brought me," Declan said, coming outside. He rubbed his eyes against the sunshine, which was heating the wet ground around the cabin. Steam rose and there was a smell of damp earth. Birds trilled in the thickets of salmonberry and gulls careened above the receding tide.

"Sir, it's a girl, not a lad. Will that matter to you? Queenie's boy pups have already been promised."

The puppy sat for moment on the step and then put its tiny nose in the air, sniffing for its bearings, and, finding something worth following, it moved in a clumsy way toward the creek.

"I've no preference, one way or the other. This little dog will suit me fine. I'll call her Argos and hope that she will be half as loyal to me as the original Argos was to his master, Odysseus," he told the girl, smiling.

"Sir, I don't know what you mean," she replied, looking puzzled.

"Ah, I'm rambling again. It's the book I'm looking at, ye see. It's like a world unto itself, and when I've been at it for a wee time, it surrounds me and I must work for a bit to leave it off. Have ye ever had a book take ye like that?"

The girl told him no, she couldn't read, and they had only a few books, but there were stories told by her mother that seemed so real she was sad to have them finished.

"Is it the same for all of ye, with the reading?"

The girl retrieved the puppy from its investigations of water and brought her back to where they stood. "Well, my oldest brother and my sister have gone to school more regular, like, but it's over around the point and there's only room in the skiff for Dad to take three, and Tom goes to keep David company. I stay home with my little brother Jack. There is a school boat, it comes to take children from all over the harbour, but my dad had an argument with the man who operates it and won't let it come for us. And anyway, Dad doesn't think we need the learning. He never went to school, and he says we're needed here. My mother went to school when she was a girl in Ontario, and she tried at first to make time for lessons, but it makes my father angry."

She stopped talking suddenly, afraid perhaps of giving a stranger too much of a family's secret drama. Then, in a rush: "I've got to get back now, if you're sure you want the pup?"

"I'm very grateful to ye for bringing her along. Thank yer mother for thinking of me."

He watched the girl walk back through the salal, nimble as a young deer. What age would she be? Twelve or so, most like. The age of Grainne, he supposed. And yet Grainne had been able to read in two languages, her own Gaelic and English, she could recite from memory whole passages of poetry, fragments in Latin of the *Aeneid*, a poem they read at home. She was hungry for learning and would take a book to the byre where they kept their chickens and the occasional pig; he'd find her reading as she stirred the mash or wiped the eggs. Maire, now, that was a different tale. She could read all right and had a good brain for sums, but she'd rather be exploring the bog, searching for the nests of corn crakes in the small barley field. Bird cries were like music to her, and she recognized in them particular voices or messages. Sometimes she'd bring back an egg that hadn't hatched and she'd carefully blow out the insides; she kept the fragile shells on the mantle. She would come to him and ...

Something licked at his ankle. He'd forgotten the little dog and broke from his remembering to pick it up.

"So, Argos, we'd best find ye a bed, eh, girleen? I've a dry sack somewhere and we'll put some of last year's bracken in it to make it soft for ye. And a meal ye'll be wanting, to be sure."

The pup licked his face with rapid warm strikes of her tiny tongue. He took her into the cabin and put her by the stove while he sought out the sack. Then he put a crust of soda bread into a battered dish, another relic of the bush, and poured a little milk over it. He warmed it for a few minutes on the stove and put it down for the pup. Argos had only ever fed from her mother's body and whimpered, not understanding that this was another way of being nourished.

"Ye'll learn to eat this or ye won't grow into anything worthy at all. Here, let's see what we can do with ye."

Declan crouched on the floor next to the puppy. He put his finger into the dish and then into the pup's mouth. She sucked at the milky finger eagerly. He moved her face down to the dish, keeping his finger in her mouth. Then he eased more of the milk into her mouth until she was taking it on her own. The bread was something again. She sucked at it, unable to get it into her mouth fast enough. So she stepped into the dish with her front feet and held one end of the crust with her paw while she sucked and gnawed at the softened bread. When she had finished, she collapsed into a small black heap and fell immediately into a deep sleep. Declan moved her onto the sack and sat at his table to puzzle over the poem again.

The tide was low. Lower than he'd ever seen it. From where his cabin stood, he could see no ocean at all, no bay, just a long expanse of mud. It reminded him of Killary Harbour, a narrow finger of water leading from the cold North Atlantic to Leenane, a village near Declan's home at Delphi. He couldn't remember tides such as this although there must've been because the fisherfolk would collect carragheen, or sea moss, at very low tide to dry on the shore above. It made a pudding that was good when you got the fever, he recalled. Cousins who lived near the water would give them a bag of the moss for winter. A handful of the crisp fronds, eggs, milk, some sugar, and Eilis would add a drop or two of vanilla essence. The girls called it fish-slime because it had a texture that slipped down the throat, all right, but he was fond of it.

Calling Argos from her bed by the stove, Declan took up a gunny sack and walked down the pebbly bank to the shore. The mud was very dark. It steamed in the sunshine. He walked out gingerly but found it quite firm to the boot. Gulls were swirling in the air and landing on the mud, taking up clams or stranded fish, he supposed. You could see where the creeks ran out into the bay, their waters sidling down into channels in the mud. He wanted to gather some oysters, the namesakes of the bay. Mrs. Neil had shown him how to shuck them with a sharp knife and had told them they made an excellent stew. With Argos at his feet, he strode out into the muddy estuary, following the course of the creek that ran by his cabin. Strands of kelp and other long seaweeds lay across the mud like ropes. A few geese picked at the eelgrass and gabbled nervously to see the dog, who ignored them completely, perhaps knowing instinctively that she would be no match yet for such birds.

Further down the bay, there were stakes showing in the mud. He'd never noticed them before, but he supposed he wouldn't see them at any time other than such a low tide. They looked like they were there to mark boundaries of some sort, and he made a mental note to ask Mrs. Neil about them. And yes, there were oysters, plenty of them. He gathered a few dozen of the biggest ones he could find. In Ireland, no one ate oysters that he knew of, though you could see them on the beaches, mussels, too. But for some reason, people believed shellfish to be an inferior kind of food altogether, despite the fact that there had been such a terrible hunger not so very long ago when people had eaten grass like cattle in the fields. In his own village, there were many abandoned cottages whose occupants had either died during the Famine or else fled to North America by the boatload. It had been an eerie thing to enter one of the ruined cabins and see the bits of crockery still about and the cold hearths that had once warmed generations of families who would have known each rock of the stony fields the way he had known the stones of his own small farm, the rocks on the shores of nearby Fin Lough. And there were Famine graves too when you knew what to look for — a single stone or cairn for entire communities buried together in a final intimacy, and some not buried at all but left in cabins with no one to offer the final ceremonies. On the roadside near Dhulough, there was a scattering of rock that his parents told him marked the grave of those who had died after being marched from Louisbourg to Delphi Lodge on orders by Captain Primrose for inspection to determine their status as paupers. Children with the thin legs of crows, women with no flesh left at all who carried infants light as fuchsia branches, men whose eyes were hollowed by hunger, all walking the rough track in the hope of food and instead falling by the wayside and lying unburied for days while crows and dogs fed on the scanty remains. The lucky ones had ridden the Famine boats and survived the dreadful outbreaks of disease that claimed so many even before they set foot on the soil of America. And was he much different from those other exiles? It wasn't hunger that had driven him to Canada, no, it was violence and loss; still, he imagined someone finding the ruin of his cabin and trying to piece together his own small story.

Argos was down on the mud, rubbing her shoulders against something, licking at it, then pressing her face into it. Declan hurried over to see what it could be. A fish — it looked like a small shark — was dead in the mud, its body decomposing. He didn't think it had ben stranded by this particular tide because it was missing its eyes and its side had been torn open by birds; oily fluid seeped out of the gash. There was a terrible smell, and Argos was rubbing her body with great joy against the rotting flesh.

"Leave off, girl," Declan shouted, and pushed her away with his foot. She yelped and ran ahead, shaking herself as she moved, her whole body wet with mud and stinking of fish. Declan's boots made sucking sounds as he walked, and everywhere he could smell the tang of seaweed and salt. There was a big rock with a flat top ahead, dry and warm from the sun. Brushing away barnacles, he made a place for himself and sat, looking down the bay towards the strait. It was easy in the salt air to be lulled into a kind of trance where you could hear the birds and the suck of water as the tide began to come in, drawn first into the channels and then the pools. It was almost peaceful.

He was thinking about Odysseus. Thinking of him lying under olive leaves waiting for the princess to find him. And then walking to meet her with only an olive bough to save him the shame of being seen naked. Still, the handmaidens fled at the sight of him, and the young princess must have been quite brave to have stood her ground. But her head had been turned by the goddess to thoughts of bridegrooms, and maybe she hoped he was a potential husband. So she encouraged her servants to bathe him and anoint him with sweet oil and clothe him in the few bits they'd conveniently brought to the river to wash out and dry on the banks. And then he followed her carriage into the city where he was welcomed to the palace in the way a stranger would always be welcomed. Food given, comforts, a bowl of water brought so that the stranger might wash. And you never knew, the stranger might be a god in disguise, testing your capacity for hospitality, kindness. In the case of Odysseus, it was the mother of the girl who recognized in the stranger a measure of nobility and worthiness. He'd been given a harp in the evening and, stringing it with authority and skill, he'd told them something of his wanderings.

There was loneliness and there was solitariness. What did he feel, himself, as he walked the long mud flats, searching for oysters and then sitting on the rock like a seal? He was not wanting human company this day. It was enough to be out with the young dog and her droll puppy behaviours, and anyway, if a man took a minute to take his bearings, if he looked around himself, it was evident he was not alone. There were the geese, yes, and some black fellas with yellow eyes and long red bills prying open oysters themselves, whistling a piercing *eep, eep* as they flew and then settling down to the business of shells. Gulls everywhere, some of them feeding on the purple starfish clinging to the undersides of exposed rocks. And when you moved aside a rock with your boot, small crabs scuttled off sideways, waving their pincers. Far, far out in the bay, almost where it met the strait, he could see a few boats, probably heading to the gathering of buildings in an adjacent bay with deep moorage. A store, a hospital, a hotel ... he collected his mail at the store, going by skiff once a fortnight. There was never much, but his sister wrote with news of Ireland, and occasionally a bank draft arrived, no return address or note, but the postmark was Galway, and so he imagined one of his cousins, involved with the Republicans, was sending him the kind of solace arranged for men such as himself. It paid for the use of the cabin, some provisions, paper and ink, an occasional bottle of the stuff they called whiskey but which was nothing at all like the bottles kept by Miceal Walsh in the Leenane pub; he'd pour you a drop of Connemara malt on market day and it was like swallowing sunshine, for the warmth of it spread through your body, tasting like the smoke of a turf fire captured in clear water off Ben Gorm. And the money paid for the odd book, too, ordered by letter from a bookseller in Vancouver.

He was dreaming in sunlight, wishing for Eilis. *Where are ye?* he thought. *When the tide moves in, I half-expect to see ye swimming strongly in its current though for the life of me I never saw ye swim, washing up on my bit of beach like Magdean Mara or a seal, the lovely grey seals of the Connemara coast. I am no one without ye, without yer hands bringing my face to yer breast, or holding my waist from behind me as we sleep. I remember each small place, each bone quietly covered with soft skin, the plump fullness of yer hips, the shallow bowl of yer neck which I filled with kisses, each a drop of tenderness coming from my deep heart. I am drenched with yer memory, drenched in each remembered gesture, the far grey of yer eyes and yer copper hair threaded with silver. I am a shipwrecked sailor washed up at the end of the world, no one to take me into the bed of a long marriage, held secret by the trunk of a living tree. Our oaken bed, brought from yer parents' house as a dowry, along with a grove of pines the age of yerself, planted by yer father at yer birth. When can ye be, my love, so long away that I am forgetting yer voice as it sang the old Irish songs to our lasses, keening low and rich so that each note held the sadness and pleasure of our kin, so our girls would know who they were in the world.*

The pup was licking his ankles, moaning. Looking around him, rubbing his eyes back to wakefulness, Declan saw that the tide had advanced almost to where he was sitting. He jumped down into the mud quickly and made his way to the shore. He would have to return to World's End by clambering along the rocks because he didn't think he could beat the tide as it eased over the mud flats. Slinging his bag of oysters over his back, he began to scramble towards his cabin.

He almost tripped over the girl who was crouched in the sand of a tiny cove. It was the girl who'd brought Argos to him, and she was scraping the sand with a claw of wood. The curled fingers of the claw brought up lumps that looked like stones, but he realized they were cockles, or clams they called them here. A bucket, sitting in the tide to keep cool, was nearly full. Argos ran to the girl and licked her face rapidly; the girl responded by kissing the pup's soft nose and trying to avoid the tongue which moved with surprising dexterity to find ears, nostrils, a salty mouth, for the girl had been eating sea lettuce, a tiny leaf of it stuck to her bottom lip. Bruises flowered on her upper arms, petals shaped like the ball of a thumb, her pullover on a nearby rock, taken off in the heat of digging.

"Do ye like the clams then?"

She thought for a moment. "Mum makes chowder, with potatoes and onions and milk, and I like that. I think it's my favourite supper because she always makes biscuits to go with it. But for themselves, I don't know as I could eat one on its own. I have lots. Would you like to take some back with you?"

"No need. Yer mother has me picking oysters, as ye can see. I'll make them for my own tea."

There was something familiar in her movements, a kind of grace balanced against the awkwardness of lengthening limbs. He'd seen it in his own girls and in the girls he'd taught over the twenty years he was master of the Bundorragha school. They'd come as infants, nearly, and leave in the fullness of young womanhood, and in between, they'd be both one and the other. Bent over their slates, their hair falling across the scarred wood of the desks, cheeks flushed with concentration, or laughing at the antics of one of the lads, he'd see in them such promise. Often as not, they'd marry as soon as they left the school and find themselves mothers of six or eight children before they were thirty. The boys would leave to work, either migrating to the cities or England or else making roads for the Congested Districts Board, but Ireland provided fewer choices for women;

he had been determined that his own daughters would have opportunities to further their education if they chose, or in the case of Grainne, perhaps music school. She'd been given a harp: one of the older families had no use for it, no one who wanted to learn, and they had passed it along. She'd found someone to teach her to play it, Bernadette Feeny from the mountains. Sheet music was hard to come by but through some miracle — it had seemed so to them — a whole pile of music had surfaced: sweet airs by the blind harper Carolan, planxties written in the great houses he'd visited. And loveliest of all, his "Farewell to Music," the last thing he'd played in the house of his patroness, Mrs. McDermot Roe. Declan loved to see his daughter's hands move across the strings of the harp, urging such beautiful harmonies from them. He imagined the bones of her hands growing strong with the secrets of the music within them. And now, her hands given to worms in the cursed soil of Ireland. He shook his head violently to rid it of her memory and left the girl in her tiny cove, pulling a claw of wood through the sand.

Back at World's End, he busied himself with shucking the oysters. There was a way of putting your knife between the lips of the shell and levering until the tight grip suddenly loosened and you could scoop out the meat of the oyster. It did not look appetizing at all, sitting wet in the frilly shell. But he'd been told to heat some milk in a saucepan with a piece of butter (Mrs. Neil had given him a pat) and some of the wild onions that grew in his field and then to add the oysters whole, just heating them through. Doing so, he understood what Mrs. Neil had meant when she told him the stew was for her the very essence of the ocean. You needed no salt, the oysters had a briny taste, like clean seaweed. And the milk provided a mild broth once flavoured with the oyster's own juice and the pleasant savouriness of the onions. He drank a bowl, and then another. It was like a tonic.

The tide was nearly to the shingle now and a steam was rising over the top of the water. It took Declan a few minutes to figure out why: the cool water moving over hot mud. Birds were everywhere, and on the far side of the bay he could see something black stirring by the shore. Argos, too, had got wind of whatever it was and began to bark excitedly. The black shape stopped and looked in their direction. Declan could see it was a bear. He was thrilled. He'd heard about bears, had been warned about leaving his food outside, particularly in the autumn when the creek was full of salmon, but he hadn't seen one until now. And yet it fulfilled every idea he had of bear. That rounded back, the broad shoulders, the way it swayed its head from side to side as it tried to figure them out on their bit of shore. After a few minutes of this, it turned and lumbered into the woods. Even from their distance across the bay, they could hear it moving in the dense brush.

"I'd better wash ye so, Argos, or it's bait ye'll be for that bear, smelling as ye do of rotten fish. Come on, lass, and we'll soon have ye fresh."

He took the pup and submerged her in the quick water of the creek. It was icy to his hands, and Argos yelped and squealed. He held her with one firm hand and quickly washed her fur with the other, taking care to ruffle the shoulders, which had taken most of the contact with the fish. Then he rubbed her down with a sack and poured a little of the oyster broth into her pan. She whimpered as she approached her meal, fearful of some other indignity, but soon was lapping up the good juice. When she had finished, she sighed deeply and curled up on her sack of bracken, falling into one of her immediate and profound sleeps.

The girl was at his door again in the same skimpy dress, telling him that her mother had located a better mattress for him and would he come to help them carry it over the marsh to his cabin?

He followed her lithe shape over the boardwalk and through the woods to the Neil farm. A dog, the mother of Argos he knew at a glance, came to greet them and sniffed suspiciously at her daughter, licking her face and then pushing her to the ground so she could sniff her underparts to determine where she'd been. It had not yet been long enough for her to forget her maternity although the pups had been given away. When she walked, her teats hung low still and occasional drops of milk fell from them to the ground.

Mrs. Neil was standing by the screen door, using a small broom to brush dust off a mattress leaning against her house. It was covered with blue and white ticking, faded and worn, but Declan could see that it promised far more comfort than the lumpy mattress he currently slept upon.

"I found a couple of sheets, too, in the attic that I'd put there for winter mending and then forgot about, Mr. O'Malley. I've got them airing over the line now. I made a few patches, rather quickly I'm afraid, and they aren't anything to look at, but you're welcome to them. Two of the boys and Rose, who came for you, can help carry it back for you." She stopped her vigorous brushing and put the broom down on a bench by the door. She called out towards the barn, and after a few moments two boys, an adolescent and one who looked a year or two younger than Rose, came running. She introduce them as David and Tom. Declan gravely shook hands with them.

"No school, then, boys?" he asked.

One of them, David, shuffled his feet and blushed. "Our dad's taken the boat and we've no way of getting over to the school."

Their mother smiled and admitted she was happy to have them home to help her sort out the attic. "Help me fold these sheets now, Rose, and the three of you can help Mr. O'Malley get his new bed home."

The woman and the girl held a sheet out and moved towards one another to bring the corners together. Declan had seen his own wife and daughters fold sheets that had wind-dried in the Irish morning. It was like a dance, each moving apart with an end of white cotton, then coming together to place palms against palms, a graceful smoothing of surfaces, stepping back to pull the length taut. He was moved to think that Mrs. Neil had sought out sheets for him when he had been prepared, even grateful, to sleep under coarse blankets for the rest of his days. He was taken back by the scene, somewhere, but where exactly he couldn't say. He noticed that the bruising on Rose's arms was fading, pale finished blossoms against the white of her skin.

He took one side of the mattress with Rose just behind him, the sheets carefully draped over her shoulders like a shawl, and the boys grasped the other side of the mattress. Over the marsh, along the trail of logs, the four of them quiet and careful as they moved up the hill where the arbutus trees hummed with their cargo of bees.

"Just so lads. We'll put her here by the door until I can ready the room for it. I can wrestle it through the door to be sure so I'll say thanks to ye for yer trouble. And thanks to ye, young Rose, for bringing the sheets so nicely folded. I'll sleep like a king tonight, I'm thinking."

He watched the children leaving his cabin, wishing he'd had a bar of chocolate to offer them, a few pennies even. They were as shy as fish, darting away through the dappled leaves. There had been children like them in his classroom; they'd come from hill farms and smelled of turf smoke, sheep. Yet he'd seen their eyes when he'd read to them of the Irish kings and knew there were dreams in them to take them through the days of sums, little food, moving sheep from one small stony field to another. He watched until the Neil childen had disappeared beyond the marsh, and then he busied himself with his bed.

Once it was arranged and organized, the old mattress put under the lean-to, Declan got out his books and puzzled over the Greek text. Some days he could make perfect sense of the words, their stern rhythms and harsh consonants. Other days he strained to remember, forgetting the tenses, the third declension. The passage he was working on concerned Nausikaa and her maidens. She had dreamed of her marriage linens and was moved to take her clothing to the river to be laundered. αὐτὰρ ἐπεὶ πλῦνάν τε κάθηράν τε ῥύπα πάντα. How the language moved along so rhythmically and how difficult to find the equivalent. *Now when they had cleaned all the stains ...* Something like that, or would you specify garments as the object? ἐξείης πέτασαν παρὰ θῖν' ἁλός, ἧχι μάλιστα became *They spread them out in an orderly way* (but was that felicitous enough? No, he would have to think about it some more) *on the stones of the shore.* And working over the text, he realized that he was smelling the fresh linen on his bed, having seen Mrs. Neil and young Rose taking the sheets from the line where the wind and sun had dried them clean. How lovely that a moment in a life could echo this richer poetry, he thought, and was taken back to Delphi where Eilis and the girls had carefully taken up the clean sheets from the gorse bushes that served as their drying rack, had moved in and out of the folding dance, fingers to fingers as they brought the edges together and smoothed the lengths of white linen.

And hearing the echo and its answer, the smell of clean linen, feminine arms holding cloth in Delphi, on the islands of ancient Greece, in the here and now on Oyster Bay, he knew for a moment a kind of joy in the remembering. Not this time the ache of all his previous memories of home, but a brief, piercing joy for the poetry of linen and women.

Chapter Two

The tide had come in and Declan was rowing his skiff over the moving water. It was early, the sky not fully lit, and quiet, with only the muttering of ducks in the reeds and the far-off moans of a cow waiting to be milked. Argos was standing in the prow of the skiff, her nose working the air.

He was rowing to the little community around the point to buy some provisions and to collect what mail might be waiting for him there. He had written away to a bookseller in Vancouver for an English translation of the *Odyssey* and a Greek grammar and lexicon, finding his project compelling enough that he wanted to make a good job of it. A student at the Bundorragha school had found his Greek text and a sheaf of papers containing his musings and attempts at versions of lines and had found a way to send them to Declan's sister. She in turn had sent them on to him. At first he had had no idea of what to do with them.

He supposed at one time he had hoped to use them as a teaching tool, having the occasional bright light who needed something beyond what the standard curricula could offer, supposed that there might have been idle moments in the classroom when he had puzzled over the poem, though he could not now remember. But it was something to keep his mind active now. His Greek was rusty, and he wanted to use the English translation as a rough guide for the passages with which he had difficulty. He had never liked the version the priests had made available to students all those years ago when he was himself a young scholar. Lang, it had been, and he remembered it as prose, not poetry at all, and the wanderer spoke as an English magistrate might, or a minister of God, not as a king of Ithaka. But still it would be fine to have it at hand for making sense of the story when he got lost in the syntax, the datives and the genitives.

A small holding came into view, tucked among apple trees. A couple sitting on the porch of the house waved to him and called out would he like a cup of coffee? He rowed in to shore and pulled his skiff up onto the shingle. The man came down to the shore to help him, introducing himself as MacIsaac. "And no need to tell me who you are, you're the Irishman settled into the Neils' cabin. O'Malley, isn't it?"

"Aye, and ye've a Scottish burr yerself. I'm very pleased to make the acquaintance of a fellow Gael."

MacIsaac told him, as they walked up to the house, that he'd come to the community twenty years earlier, having been left the little farm by an uncle who'd died a childless bachelor.

"It was an opportunity for us, Jeannie and I. We came out from Scotland as newlyweds. I worked on the docks in Vancouver but I missed a wee bit of land and this was a grand place to raise our boys."

Jeannie MacIsaac had a cup of coffee waiting on the porch where some wicker chairs were gathered in a comfortable grouping. She shook Declan's hand warmly and moved a cat from a rocking chair so he could sit down by a tray with a jug of cream and a small bowl of sugar. The cat sat a small distance away, looked balefully at them, and began washing itself although its tabby coat gleamed. Argos glanced briefly at the cat and realized it was lord of the demesne, or lady, and that a mere dog would be no match for such confidence. She curled at the foot of the steps leading up to the porch and settled into a deep sleep as though a short row had tired her out completely.

It was pleasant to sit in the early sun with the MacIsaacs and to hear them talk of their apples and lambs while the scent of blossoms wafted around them. They told Declan that their boys had gone off to work in Vancouver but that the youngest was hoping to return to the community to fish.

"He wanted the bright lights and nothing would keep him home but now he's yearning for the company of the lads he grew up with. He's got MacKay over at Whiskey Slough building him a small gill-netter and he's working around the clock in the city to pay for it. His mother will be happy to know he's close again."

Jeannie MacIsaac smiled and touched her husband's arm. "And you won't be, my dear?"

Declan asked them about the stakes he had seen in the mud at low tide, how firmly they had been planted, impossible to budge. MacIsaac knew their story.

"My uncle came here first in 1890, when the Indians still lived at your end of the bay. They fished here and those stakes were part of a system they used to trap salmon before they entered the creeks to spawn. Here, let me just show you the pile-driver my uncle found."

He reached down to a stone lying amongst others on the deck and lifted it up. It was wedge-shaped, with a face carved into one flat surface and two grooves worked into the underside.

Raising it up, he showed Declan how it would have been used to pound stakes into the mud bottom of the bay, or anywhere else for that matter; the user's thumbs fit neatly into the depressions created by the eyes, and the fingers used the grooves on the underside for gripping.

"My uncle was told it was a dogfish. I think it's ingenious myself and I've used it when fencing areas for my sheep. This rocky soil is murder for sinking fence posts!"

They discussed the fish-traps a little more, how effective they must have been in gathering the large numbers of salmon the Indians needed for winter use, MacIsaac saying that the bay fairly boiled with fish in the fall, returning to the various feeder creeks to spawn. Declan finished his coffee and went on his way, having assured the couple he'd bring back their mail. He felt calmed by his visit with them. Their affection for one another and their home was a balm, scented with apple blossom on a warm spring day.

Out onto the bay again, the skiff slicing through the water easily. Declan had never seen forests like these that grew right down to the sea's edge, although the old stories told of Irish forests full of elk and wolves. In the poems about the the wild man of the woods, Suibhne, the speaker sang of oaks and hazels, blackthorns, yews draped with ivy, and brown stags belling from the mountains. In his youth, Declan had walked in planted forests, and to be sure there were wooded glens, like those in the Erriff Valley, but he'd never seen trees like these. Sometimes, rowing past these wild headlands to the fishing grounds, he had seen deer walking across the sand. And the trees were extraordinary: cedars with their palmate fronds, the giant they called a Douglas fir, pines, prickly spruce. Often there'd be no trees at all near the shore but stumps so wide your mind had a hard time imagining the tree that had been taken down. Ledges were cut into the sides of the stumps, like stairs to the heavens, where springboards had rested so loggers could stand with their gut-fiddles, felling the trees to the ground like gods.

The store was perched on pilings that walked out into the bay like a long-legged shore bird, one of them bent at the elbow and braced with a splint of cedar. Men were always gathered on the verandah, smoking, their gear piled up around them, or boxes of eggs, or brown jugs that Declan knew held the local spirits. On a mail day, more than the usual number clustered here, waiting for the steamship to announce itself around the headland. When it appeared, most of the men descended to the wharf steps to help with the lines. Declan did not join them but entered the store. There was a smell, always, of wax used on the wide floor boards, strong cheese, smoked fish, blood (if it was a day the storekeeper hung a new side of beef on the hooks suspended from the ceiling joists), cabbages, and an acrid burnt odour that Declan eventually understood to be coffee in a scorched pot which steamed and frothed on the back of the woodstove. He could not imagine drinking it, but the storekeeper was never without a cup.

He had his list — a bucket of lard, a sack of onions, tea, hardtack for his fishing days (as he found his own soda bread did not travel well but grew mould in its wrapping before he could eat it), a few oranges, a bag of turnips.

"If you can wait awhile, O'Malley, I'll sort through the mail bag once it's come up from the boat and see what's there for you. Certainly you can take the MacIsaacs' mail too. And some beef for stew, you say? It won't be a minute." The storekeeper used a huge knife to hack off a chunk of meat, which he then diced, weighed, and wrapped in brown paper that he tied with cord hanging from a spool.

While his order was being filled, Declan wandered the aisles of the store, pausing to look at the tins of hair pomade, big bars of Sunlight soap, boxes of fishing tackle, bins of dusty vegetables, and the grey woolen overshirts the fishermen in the area all favoured. He settled with the storekeeper, packed his groceries and the packet of letters, and returned to his skiff, keeping wide of the steamship, which had docked with a host of volunteers securing its lines; they were now watching a horse, its eyes covered with a blindfold, being lowered to the wharf in a canvas sling.

Coming back with a good wind behind him, Declan eased on the rowing to watch a pair of geese guarding a nest on one of the rocky islets at the mouth of his bay. He had heard they mated for life, and there was a story told of a goose who followed his wounded mate, patient in the sky, while she walked with her broken wing. How did the story end? He couldn't remember. But these geese watched him, alert to his movements, ready to challenge him should he enter their nursery. He called to them that they had nothing to fear from him and chuckled as they hissed and gabbled back.

At the MacIsaac farm, he was offered a dram for his trouble. "It was no trouble at all, I assure ye," he told them, handing their letters over and accepting a glass with a generous measure of whiskey. The men raised their glasses to toast, in Gaelic, each to the other's surprise. Despite differences in accent and emphasis, they could understand each other, though MacIsaac confessed he had forgotten more of his parents' language than he'd retained.

"I have enough yet for toasts and cursing and the occasional song," he said cheerfully, downing his dram. It was redolent of peat and oak, a distillation of weather, sweet water, and barley malt. "I mind to share a whiskey now and then with someone who knows the old language. Come again!"

As they approached World's End, Argos began to whimper and moan. Her hackles rose, and Declan heard growls coming from her throat, not yet articulated in her mouth. He followed her looking as best he could and was startled to see a dark shape reaching for his herring rake. By now Argos was barking, her voice full and fearsome. The shape turned to see what made such a noise, and Declan recognized the bear. He used his oars to steady the boat, to push against the movement of the tide so that they remained the short distance from the shore. The bear abandoned its attentions to the rake, raising its head to the air, shaking it from side to side, sniffing for them on the wind. Argos barked and scrambled for a foothold on the gunwales in order to jump from the boat, but Declan ordered her to sit. He had never seen a bear so close. He wanted to look at it as long as possible, memorize the heavy head and small eyes, the glossy coat hanging from the body like a cloak several sizes too large. The bear made a noise, as though clacking its teeth together, then turned and ambled away, rake abandoned. Declan waited for it to disappear into the woods before bringing the boat into shore.

The rake still leaned against the cabin. What had been the attraction, he wondered. He brought the tines close to his face and sniffed them. Fish. Of course. Fish had brought the bear. Although he always cleaned his fishing gear when he returned from the water, the smell of the herring impaled on the rake for bait would remain. But surely a bear would not return for the smell if there was no actual fish for it eat? Judging from the scats he found near the creek, the bear was feeding on grasses anyway. Great dark piles of scat, threaded through with long strands of undigested grass, weighted with seedy heads. The Neils told him that there would be many bears on the estuary in the fall when the salmon were running. That made sense, an animal the size of the one he had just seen feeding on salmon. But he marvelled at the thought of such a large beast sustaining itself on grass. Idly he pulled on the ripe head of a tall stalk of grass growing near the rake. The stem came free from its sheath and he chewed on the tender end of it contemplatively. It tasted mild and sweet. He chewed a little further up. It was coarser, more fibrous. But the tender part? He could see making a simple meal of those, maybe finishing up with a handful or two of ripe berries. He laughed out loud to think he shared such a thing in common with a bear.

The girl was standing by his open door. He'd looked up from his books to ease out a kink in his neck and had seen her there, looking in. On her face was an expression of intense curiosity, a palpable yearning. He followed her eyes to the pile of books on his table.

"Rose! Have ye been there long? I'm sorry to have been so absorbed that I did not notice ye until now."

She told him not long, she'd not been there long, but had come to ask if the bedding had been enough. Her mother could provide more blankets if he needed them.

"Indeed what I have is grand. Yer mother has been very kind to think of my comfort as she has, with all her tasks for the doing. Now, can I give ye a cup of tea?"

She came in, moving in her shy way to one of the stumps which served as chairs. Declan found the extra mug and poured from the pot of tea stewing on the woodstove. At her nod, he poured in a little milk. He followed her eyes to the small stack of books on the table, his pen and bottle of ink to one side.

"It's the story again, Rose. I told ye the other time how it was a world unto itself and how true that is! I sent for a few books to make my work with it easier and I collected them off the steamship this morning. Would ye like to see them?"

He handed her the little volume he had ordered on a whim, *Tales of Ancient Greece*, by Sir George W. Cox. It was a pretty book, bound in blue cloth with gold stamping on the spine. Rose held it as though it were alive, carefully, and with great attention. She put it to her face and smelled the cloth, inhaling deeply, her eyes closed.

She opened the book to the title page and ran her index finger gently over the illustration bordering the text — cherubic faces and bunches of grapes and winged fairies.

"That's a 't'," she said reverently, touching the ornate initial beginning the quote, *This is fairy gold, boy; and twill prove so.*

"Aye, 'tis, Rose. And can ye read any more of it?" he asked quietly.

She shook her head and handed the book back. Taking up her mug, she sipped her tea, glancing at the papers on the table. It was very quiet in the cabin, only a droning of bees in the thimbleberry bushes outside the door to punctuate the still air. She had the look of one of his daughters when taking a pause between tasks, able to deeply relax at a moment's notice.

"Will I read one of the stories to ye, Rose?" Declan suggested, moved at the sight of her in his cabin, his books all around and her not being able to read them. Her reverence for the Cox made him want to give her something, and there was no point in sending her home with a book. Stories were all he could think to offer.

She smiled her assent. Almost at random, he chose "The Sorrow of Demeter," remembering incompletely the myth of the corn goddess and her young daughter.

> In the fields of Enna, in the happy island of Sicily, the beautiful Persephone was playing with the girls who lived there with her. She was the daughter of the Lady Demeter, and everyone loved them both, for Demeter was good and kind to all, and no one could be more gentle and merry than Persephone.

Rose sighed deeply and rested her cheek against her clasped hands. Declan would learn that she loved being read to; it was one of her favourite things. Mostly her mother was too busy, she told him, but sometimes, particularly if Rose was ill, she would sit on the bed with one of the mildewy books that she'd brought from her childhood home in Glengarry County and read a story while stroking Rose's hair.

> She and her companions were gathering flow-
> ers from the field to make crowns for their long
> flowing hair. They had picked many roses and
> lilies and hyacinths which grew in clusters
> around them ...

"We do that, Mr. O'Malley! My sister taught me how to make a chain of daisies by splitting their stems with my fingernail! I've never tried roses, although when we pick them for Mum, they fall apart in our hands. The wild ones, I mean. And there are lilies here, too, the orange ones. Those girls are like us!"

She was very animated, her hands touching her head as though placing a crown of wildflowers upon it, her face bright with excitement. Declan was moved to see what the telling of a story could do to a shy girl, a girl left on shore while her brothers and sister sailed off to school, a girl whose arms bloomed with someone's anger.

"To be sure, Rose. And isn't that the beauty of a story, that sometimes we feel as though it is our story that's being told? But listen, now, because what happens next is not what you'd know about, I'm thinking."

> ... the earth opened, and a chariot stood before
> her drawn by four coal black horses; and in the
> chariot there was a man with a dark and solemn
> face, which looked as though he could never
> smile, and as though he had never been happy.

In a moment he got out of his chariot, seized
Persephone around the waist, and put her on
the seat by his side. Then he touched the horses with his whip, and they drew the chariot
down into the great gulf, and the earth closed
over them again.

Rose's face was horror-struck. "Mr. O'Malley, what happens to her? Do you really mean to say that the horses take
them underground?"

"Ah, Rose, in these stories we are told many things. How
much of it is true, well, that's the thing we don't know. We are
told things to make us feel a certain way, to create a certain
mood, to explain things in a particular way. Do ye know the
meaning of the word *metaphor*?"

Rose shook her head.

"Well, it is when ye use words or phrases that everyone
understands to mean certain things, ye use them to make a thing
understood in a new or different way. If I told ye that sun was a
globe of golden glass, well, ye'd know I didn't really mean that it
was, in fact, but ye might take another look at the sun and see it
again, with fresh eyes. Do ye see what I mean?"

"I think so," she said, squinting her eyes and looking at the
sun, which was making its way towards the western sky.

"To continue with suns, the ancient Greeks, whom these stories are about, would talk of the sun as something alive that was
driven across the sky by a fella called Helios who had a chariot
and some special oxen. That little story is a metaphor, really, to
explain the passage of the sun from when it rises in the eastern
sky to where it sets in the west, where we can see it, each day."

Declan looked at Rose to see if she was ready to hear the
rest of the story. She was far away, gazing out the window. She
sighed, and then turned to face him. "Mr. O'Malley, I know a

story that's a bit like the one you've been reading me. Only it's true. All of it."

"Will ye tell it to me?"

She took a deep breath. "Where we live used to belong to the Indians. They still come up the bay in their canoes sometimes because they think this part here is special. One of them, a lady called Lucy, comes to have tea with my mum and she says her people began here, like we say that Adam and Eve began in a garden called Eden. But none of the Indians have lived here for quite a long time. My dad has pigs, you've seen them, and when he wants an area cleared, he lets the pigs run free. They are good at clearing land because they eat all the tough leaves and vines, and they dig stuff up, roots and such."

"Aye, their feet are like small spades so," said Declan, remembering his own pig.

"Well, one day a few years ago, in spring, the pigs dug up a canoe with a skeleton in it. My sister, Martha, saw it first and ran to the house to get my dad. He thought it was funny and let the pigs have the ribs to chew. He rolled the canoe over into the woods — I can show you what's left of it one day — and took the skeleton off; we didn't see where. Martha had nightmares about it."

"Aye, she would, she would." And then he wondered if he would also dream of the pigs at work on the long ribs of a man found dead in the earth.

"When Lucy came the next time, my mum asked her about it and she said it must've been a chief from a long time ago, because sometimes they were buried in their canoes with important stuff for them to use on the way to Heaven. It made it seem so wicked that the pigs would dig it up and eat the bones. My mum never told Lucy that part. Do you think it was wicked, Mr. O'Malley?" She seemed so concerned about this that Declan reassured her, saying that the dead man's soul would have long departed and that Lucy would have known this.

"Don't worry yerself so, Rose, but tell me more of the story."

She smiled at him, grateful for his understanding, and continued. "So then it was fall and my dad put our vegetables in the root cellar. Potatoes from the new area that the pigs had cleared and the other stuff we eat all winter. Turnips and beets that he buries in sand, and cabbages and onions. One dark night, well, it wouldn't have been night really but it gets dark early in winter, he told my sister and me to go to the root cellar under the back part of the house to bring up potatoes for the supper. We hate going in there because it's mostly underground and there are spiderwebs and even rats sometimes. But my sister took a candle and we kept together. We were leaning into the potato bin when we heard this awful sound, like sticks clattering, and my sister held up the candle. There was a skeleton waving its arms around! We screamed and dropped the potatoes and the candle, and we ran as fast as we could around to the kitchen door."

"Ah, ye poor lasses. Ye'd have been terrified, of course!" Closing his own eyes for moment, he saw the skeleton rise up, its bones clattering.

"My sister was screaming and crying — my mother says she's nervy — and I was afraid that the skeleton would follow us. But then my dad was standing in the doorway, laughing, and he almost never laughs. My mother calmed my sister down, and when my father stopped laughing he told us that he'd fastened strings to the canoe skeleton's arm bones and then ran the strings up into his bedroom, which is right above the root cellar. So he could jiggle the arms by pulling the strings. My sister had bad dreams for weeks — I know because we sleep in the same bed — and she wouldn't speak to my father, which made him really mad. My mother was mad at him too, but then he hit Martha and told her to snap out of it so we tried to forget."

What a brute the man was, thought Declan, to frighten his daughters so. He remembered the bruises on Rose's arms as he watched her digging for clams and folding the sheets. Aloud, he told her that the story was an interesting one and she'd told it well. He could see what she'd described, and he was sorry to hear that her sister had been so troubled by the event. His eyes must have revealed his distaste for a man who would strike a child because Rose quickly responded.

"She's fine now, sir, and my father didn't really hit her hard, and later he brought her a moonsnail shell for her collection, without a single chip off it, but don't you see that the stories are the same in a way?"

"Oh, aye. And in this story I'm working on, there's a woman, ye might call her a witch more rightly, who turns some men into pigs who then cry human tears. Our man Odysseus is saved from her magic by carrying a little sprig of wild onion within his clothing. So pigs, and the ground opening, and a king coming up from under the earth, from Greece to this Pacific. And indeed I'd like to see that canoe one day, if ye'd show me."

Rose nodded. "I'd better get back, Mr. O'Malley, or my mum will worry. Thank you for the tea and the story."

"They are a perfect pair, Rose, I'm thinking. Will ye come again?" He suddenly found himself hoping she would say yes.

"I'd love to. I'm sure my mum won't mind. Goodbye."

Declan watched Rose walk over the bluff with its crown of arbutus and disappear into a fringe of young cedars. He thought how nice it was to have a young girl to talk to, a girl the age his own had been, one foot in childhood and one in the rich sea of womanhood, uncertain of its tides and dangers. What was it that Nausikaa had been called in the poem? *Maiden of the white arms ...* Not an epithet for a child, exactly, and yet the princess cavorted with her maids at the river, throwing a ball in a carefree game until it landed in a stream, which woke the naked Odysseus. That was the part he would look at again.

Chapter Three

He had asked Rose to take him to see the canoe. The idea of it, buried with its chief, had been in his mind ever since he'd first heard the story.

They walked up past the farmstead to dense brush — salal, mostly, but trailing bramble and brittle huckleberry made the going difficult. Rose led the way and pushed through the brush until she was stopped short by the bulky shape of the canoe. Declan had never seen anything like it. It looked to have been carved from a single tree and had an elegant prow, shapely, but now rotting and split. When Declan reached to touch the side of the canoe, a little of the side came away like fragile paper. He wondered how long it had been buried in the earth. Even now the earth was doing its best to reclaim it, embracing it with sinuous vines of bramble and sending vigorous growth of salal up through holes in the bilge, displacing the thwarts.

"The skeleton was lying in it like this," Rose told him, indicating how the body had been positioned. "His hands were crossed over his chest and he had a basket at his feet and a big stone club with a fish carved into it. My father kept the club but the basket just crumbled away."

Remnants of red and black pigment showed that the canoe had been decorated inside as well as outside. Looking closely, Declan could see that the hull had been pierced with holes in a regular pattern, for drainage he supposed. There was a pungent smell of rotting cedar, and he could see that an animal, perhaps a field mouse, had constructed a small nest of dried grasses in a protected area under one of the thwarts.

Declan was moved to see the canoe at rest in the bush. He escorted Rose back to her home and then continued on to his own cabin, thinking about the vessel and its former occupant. It struck him as immeasurably lonely, the idea of being buried alone in a boat without the company of one's family around. There had been finds in his own country, mounds of earth or sometimes cists that contained tombs with single skeletons carried by wagons, some jewellery and jars of wine and tools arranged at their feet. Such belief in the afterlife, he marvelled, and yet what was found was cold bones, wooden wheels, a dagger, with no sign nor evidence of the soul's ascension. He remembered his rambles as a boy in the hills surrounding Delphi and coming across the Famine cabins with their communal graves nearby, subsequent generations taking the time, if money was available, to erect a stone to acknowledge who lay there. Some of the old townlands had completely disappeared, gone from the maps, having lost their entire populations to hunger, fever, or those dreadful ships. There had been families living in folds of the earth, tucked into ravines, who were gone with hardly a trace: a wisp in an aging memory, initials carved in the bark of a tree, a placement of stones to assist one's footing on a steep ridge. And yet what would become of him should he die here, so far from his own dead, or the living that had known him? He sighed deeply and went inside to work on his text.

The Greek alphabet reminded him of bird tracks. The sigma, Σ, for instance, and the gamma, Γ, particularly in its lower case, γ. He practised writing the alphabet, wanting the ease and speed of his youth. It was good to have the new texts to consult. The grammar, by Goodwin, was the one they had used at school. The introduction was opinionated but humane, containing moments of humour even, which Declan responded to by wanting to learn the language well. "My own efforts," declared Goodwin, in commenting on pronunciation, "have been exerted merely towards bringing some order out of this chaos." And was that not something of Declan's own intention? To have a project to take up the attentions of one's heart and mind? When he'd begun his scribbles all those months ago, years by now, in the Bundorragha schoolhouse, it had been a tentative way to take a long view of a life, to find correspondences outside the daily routines. A man's love for his wife, the complexities of homecoming, a lexicon for courage and honour, the importance of paternity: he hoped to find a way to share these with his students, or for the occasional student who shone with a fierce light and who needed something beyond the parsing of sentences and memorizing of Irish kings, a few equations to help a man account for corn.

He couldn't get the canoe out of his mind. How it lay at rest in the heavy growth of salal like a fallen idol, knitted into a shroud of vines. The smell of it, a faint resiny odour at the back of rot, a stronger reek that hit you like the back end of a skunk or the plants with the golden lanterns that smelled exactly the same. He went back to the bush again, but it was hard to get a sense of the canoe's proportions with the tangle of plants all around it. Going a little further to try to find a place from which he could see it entire, he came upon a hillock, covered with pale mosses and ringed with pines. It overlooked the bay, falling away from the clearing in a steep cliff, although the way up from the bush was gradual and clear. Wildflowers grew in a splendid profusion. It would not be difficult to drag the canoe up the hill if he had some help — and permission, of course. The Neil lads, for instance. He decided to ask their father if he might move the canoe, telling Neil he'd like to examine it and make some notes about its construction. He felt an explanation was necessary even though he didn't know himself why he wanted to move it.

Neil was repairing a piece of machinery outside his barn. He barely looked up. "Go ahead, I've no use for it. I'll get my boys to help you with it. It was a heavy bugger to drag there in the first place, and I'm thinking it'll be waterlogged for sure by now."

The boys accompanied Declan into the bush with several coils of rope. David, the older boy, looked to be about fifteen and was built sturdily. Tom, whom Declan had already surmised was younger than Rose by a year or two, was a slighter boy, thin legs coming out of wellingtons several sizes too large from the look of it. Dogs followed them, Argos dancing and skittering for the pleasure of being with others, and then Rose came running to the bush, wanting to see whatever it was they were going to do. Declan began to drag the vines away from the wood, pulling and loosening until the canoe was free. David wrapped a rope around the hull, knotting it securely, and then climbed the slope of the hill, stopping as he climbed to knot another length of rope to it to give him enough to take to the trunk of one of the sturdy pines. With Declan, Tom, and Rose pushing, it was a matter of winching the canoe up the slope, using the tree's strength to take the bulk of the weight. The boys were very strong, trading positions at one point so that Tom continued the work of winching that his brother had begun, his skinny arms straining as he pulled the rope. There was a natural space for the canoe between the pines, and with Declan's direction they managed to set it upright with the prow facing the bay. They sat on the dry moss and wiped their brows, puffing a little as the four of them looked out to Oyster Bay where a family of Canada geese swam in the eelgrass. One of the boys, David, threw a stone down, landing it in the water with a tiny splash. The geese barely paused in their feeding. Then Tom tried with a stone and missed. The dogs, who had collapsed in the moss after running up and down the slope as the canoe was winched up its face, looked up and whined a little.

"Ye've done a grand job, lads. Thanks very much."

The boys nodded shyly and ran down the easy slope in their great rubber boots, Tom tripping over his feet, then righting himself and catching up with his brother before they disappeared into the bush. Rose lingered a moment longer but then followed them, dogs behind her, while Argos stayed with Declan, watching with her ears alert and a tiny moan in her throat. Perhaps she had known after all that she had been among her tribe.

Well, now what? Declan thought to himself, and then aloud to Argos. The canoe looked expectant, powerful in its upright position, although it looked precarious, too. He found some branches of fallen pine and wedged them under the canoe to keep it stable; pushing against it, he was pleased it didn't budge. The sun was warm, and he could hear bees in the flowers that bloomed on the bluff. In his mind's eye, he was seeing the skeleton recumbant in the boat. Testing the stability of the canoe again, he found himself climbing into it and sitting on the one thwart that was still intact. It was slick with slime. He lay back against the damp wood and closed his eyes. It was as though he floated in calm waters, the sound of bees and water birds in the distance, a few lazy flies landing on his face.

Sound of bees, water birds, Argos snoring in the warm moss ... Declan hadn't realized he was asleep until he woke in a daze, wondering where he was. He had been dreaming of

Odysseus, washed up among the Phaiakians, telling his story to the assembled crowd. Harps, birdsong, the odour of roasting meat, honeyed wine ... he shook his head to clear it. His neck ached, but he felt surprisingly rested. Where was the company of kings and princesses to whom he could tell of his loss, his journey, his discovery of something like peace at the end of the world? Aye, that was the thing. You could not call Neil a king, although his wife had dignity in spades, and the girl, well, Rose was a natural princess, equal in her way to Nausikaa at the river with her handmaidens. He remembered the way she and her mother had lifted and folded the sheets they had laundered for his bed, the harmony of their arms, and the intensity of her listening as he told her the story of Persephone, a maiden of the white arms, and her bridegroom.

He left the canoe perched on its bluff, hoping it would dry out in the sunlight, and made his way through the brush to his cabin, his dog at his heels like a shadow. He could smell the rotting cedar on his hands and body, not an unpleasant odour but, like the forest, living and dead at the same time. There were logs he would come upon, big fellas like the one that had become the canoe, fallen in the dense woods. Sometimes he would see new sprouts coming from the roots, while in the length of decaying log small trees were growing, and ferns, salal, tall bushes of huckleberry, weird fungus. He remembered reading in the newspaper at home an account of men discovering a fifty-foot canoe at Lurgan, in County Galway — they'd been cutting turf and had come up against an enormous length of what they first thought was bog oak. The newspaper had a grainy photograph of the canoe being carried through the streets, a dozen men holding it upside down with their heads concealed in its ancient interior. That could happen here, he imagined, though not in a bog, but a man navigating these dense forests might come up against a canoe, partly hidden by ferns, and pass it by, thinking it a fallen tree.

A clipping arrived in the mail from Galway, sent by a cousin, the crisp black letters describing an attack in a village by a group of Black and Tans, the men brought from Britain as reinforcements for the Royal Irish Constabulary. They were a hard bunch, young men returned from four years of trench warfare who had not found a place for themselves in post-war Britain. So much of their work was conducted at night — their Crossley tenders roaring up to a house and men leaping off, hammering on doors with their weapons, searching rooms while a terrified family watched. Rumours of their activities had arrived even in Delphi, and then the men themselves, a sight in their khaki uniforms with the dark hats and belts of the constabulary. The clipping described a night of drinking at the village pub and then a devastating aftermath — a house burned, two men shot, others shackled and loaded into the armoured car to be taken to a barracks where one was hung and several mutilated. The cousin's letter asked Declan to take note of the name of the man hung — it was their own, O'Malley, Cathal O'Malley, another cousin, whom Declan remembered as a soft-eyed youth, a reader of sagas. The thought of young Cathal, grown to manhood but still a dreamer, strung from a barracks beam by rough rope, prodded by drunken thugs acting in the name of British law, made him weep with despair.

A broken man, he had walked away from his small holding with its blackened walls, its lonesome chimney, a scattering of rooks rising from the byre, the little hill of graves. He had not been able to enter the ruin, could not feel the presence of his women in the rubble and ash that was all that remained of their home. Alive, Eilis had coaxed such flowers from the soil of the yard — radiant hollyhocks, roses grown from slips given her by other women, delphiniums that drank the damp air and grew blue as the sky on a clear day. In the fullness of time, in a peaceful country, if

Eilis had died before him, Declan would have had her buried in the churchyard nearby and lived out his days in the cabin they had made into their home; but the thought of lingering a moment longer than he had to on such a violated ground made him ill. The parish priest had come to talk to him, a one-eyed man who it was rumoured communicated with birds, and spoke of forgiveness, the Black and Tans' foul hearts a result of their own time in France, their souls brutalized by the horrors of the Great War. But forgiveness was not possible, nor was revenge. The priest might have been talking to a bucket, hollow and empty.

The other house burned in the area, the big house owned by an old Anglo-Irish clan, well, that family had fled, too. The daughter and son of that household were enrolled in schools in London, their father not wanting anything to do with the country of his birth until the Troubles had been settled. He wrote angry letters to the newspapers, denouncing violence. Declan heard of these things in a haze of his own grief.

Money was pressed into his hands by well-wishers, and he was urged to make himself scarce. As if he was not scarce enough, a man alone after husbandhood and fatherhood, heart in tatters, eyes scoured by the salt of constant tears. He walked most of the way to Galway and found shelter among distant relations who gave him a bed and raised the money for a passage away. Papers were arranged. He was spirited to Cork, where he was cared for by kind strangers for more than six months until the day came when he was put on a boat and given a list of names of those who would help him on the other side. It was rumoured that Michael Collins himself had opened his pockets.

He had no recollection of the voyage, apart from sickness due to the turbulent waters, the sound of vomiting and the moans of those around him. He was met in New Jersey by a cousin of his mother's who took him to her daughter's home. He spent weeks not rising from the bed except to find his frail way to the toilet. He would not have the curtain drawn, would not leave the room to enter into the lively discourse of the family, his own kin. He kept a blanket pulled up to his shoulders and slept; when he woke, he would shake with despair until he tired himself enough to sleep. Broth was brought to him, little cakes, mugs of tea. The nightmares were dreadful. He imagined everything that must have happened while he lay in the farm yard, unconscious from the beating. His daughters screamed from windows, Eilis called for him until she was hoarse from the strain and the smoke. The pig ran from the yard, the bristles on its back carrying flames like the coming of angels.

One morning he woke and told the family that he wanted to go to the West Coast and what was the most economical way to get there? On a different ocean he wouldn't be kept awake by the distant crooning of water that knew everything that happened to him, the undertow muttering of murder, of grief, a sky that had watched impassively, pierced by late stars, while his daughters burned. A train, long passages of darkness, pauses in dirty cities, mornings crossing plains that stretched out from the tracks like golden water, then arrival in a jaunty town on the coast. In a library, he'd studied a globe, running his finger up the line that was the Pacific coast, and closed his eyes. When he opened them, his blind finger had found the Sechelt Peninsula, north of Vancouver. Checking maps, he discovered a tiny community nestled in one of the bays. He'd travelled up on a boat with crates of seed oysters that rested in the cool darkness of the boat's hold; they were attended by a boy who kept lowering a bucket into the ocean to dampen the sacking that covered the wooden boxes. No one asked questions when Declan arrived at the store on the long-legged pilings but directed him to the Neils, who had an empty cabin. When he said he had no means to get there, he was given a skiff that had belonged to a man lost on the fields of France and told he could pay a few dollars for it later if he was able.

"What is that white flower, like wild garlic, or maybe a lily, that grows on the dry bluff?" Declan asked Mrs. Neil. He had been working on a passage from the poem and had come to the lines where Odysseus meets Achilles in Hades. He puzzled over the lines, wondering how to find words for the sadness and anger in Achilles.

> βουλοίμην κ' ἐπάρουρος ἐὼν θητευέμεν ἄλλῳ,
> I wish I was at labour as a farmhand,
> ἤ πᾶσιν νεκύεσσι καταφθιμένοισιν ἀνάσσειν,
> than lord of all the exhausted dead.

And reading ahead, he had come to the lines where Achilles strides off across the fields of asphodel. He remembered the priest, the one who had been to Greece, telling the class that asphodel was known as the food of the dead. It was a lily, and bulbs of it would be planted near tombs. A white flower, as befits the pale skin of the dead.

She was peeling potatoes on a bench by her door, her apron covered with curls of brown skin, which she then flung to the hens. Eilis had done this, too, on days when the sun would lure a woman from her kitchen to the outdoors. Declan was holding the milk jug but wanted to prolong the moment, to watch a handsome woman's hands deftly scrape a knife across the surface of a potato without having to look. A tendril of brown hair had loosened itself from her bun and graced the side of her face.

"Was it growing among other plants? Blue-flowered ones I'm thinking of in particular."

He remembered that it had been. And she told him it was the death camas, to be avoided. The blue ones, she said, were also camas and the Native people ate the bulbs that produced them, drying huge quantities of them. But the white ones were poisonous, sheep each year were lost to them.

"Two small bulbs of it, Mr. O'Malley, contain enough of the poison to kill a person. As for the sheep, I've no idea of how many it would take. Their stomachs are certainly more resilient than our own!"

So not unlike asphodel then, he thought — a plant echoing the pallor of Achilles. He couldn't remember poisonous plants in his own childhood or with Eilis raising their girls. Mushrooms, certainly. There were some they collected for the table — the mushroom called St. George and field mushrooms which they had with their breakfast sometimes when the person up early to milk the cow found scatterings of them in the pasture — but mostly they were to be avoided: the red ones with white warty blotches that could be used to kill flies, tiny parasols that grew in the fields among the tasty ones and which paralyzed at a touch to the tongue, or so it was rumoured. He didn't remember flowers, though, had no memory of those that might have killed a person or animal.

Back from the Neils' with a pan of potatoes to use for seed, he mused about what he had learned. *I have put the canoe in a field of deadly flowers*, he thought. Then, moving the poem aside, he took out his fishing gear to polish his spoons.

Chapter Four

Rose was at the door. It was late May, and the sun was very warm. Leaves were every shade of green on the trees overhanging the creek, thimbleberries were nearing the end of their blossoming, and the bay was filled with water birds and their young — mergansers, geese, a single loon, golden-eye. There was a hum of industry in the air, of birds at the work of feeding, boats in the far water, a man shouting at the team of horses pulling a plough through the fields of a farm nearly half a mile away.

"Rose, come in. I've just made bread and am about to cut it. Would ye like to try a wedge?"

She smiled and nodded, putting the milk down on the table. She took the bread he offered, dotted with currants and spread liberally with her mother's butter. Declan watched her take small bites, a few crumbs lingering on her mouth. She pronounced it delicious.

"Have ye come for a story?" Declan asked. Rose had begun to visit him often, bringing the milk or messages from her mother, the occasional letter after a trip had been made to the store. He liked her obvious pleasure when he opened *Tales of Ancient Greece* or else recounted the part of the *Odyssey* he was working on when she arrived. Stories made her eyes glow, made her talkative, responding with an account of a boat trip to Nelson Island in a storm or the time her father came home from a logging camp up past Minstel Island with wolf cubs in his skiff, one of them going on to become the mother of the mother of Argos. Declan noted how she liked to hold the books, too, and how she would examine the pages. Sometimes she would announce she had found a certain letter and once her name tucked into a paragraph about flowers, but mostly Declan thought the markings must look the castings of lugworms on the sand looked to him; he knew what they were but not the why and the how of them. Whether they were marks simply of passing or a trail to discover and follow.

"Mr. O'Malley, would you tell something about Ireland, where you come from?"

The simplicity of her request pierced his heart like a flint. He felt the pain of it, couldn't breathe for a moment. Ireland. He could smell the Irish earth he had shovelled over the pine boxes with his potato spade, rich and boggy. Sprays of cowslips, wood sorrel and gorse, carefully arranged on the mound. He closed his eyes to take his bearings, his head spinning with memories like a compass in the presence of a disconcerting metal. When he opened them, Rose was sitting at the table still, eating her soda bread and butter, waiting for him to begin. So he did.

He told her about the area where he'd been born, Delphi, and how there was a temple in Greece with the same name; his Delphi had been named so by the Marquess of Sligo, who had travelled to Greece with a famous English poet, Lord Byron, and had seen the ancient temple in the bowl of mountain, which reminded him of the area where he'd built a hunting lodge. The Irish Delphi was actually not even a village at all but a townland, a collection of farms where the same families had lived for centuries. Rocky soil, stone walls defining fields, the boreens leading from one small holding to the next, from Tullaglas to Ardmor, winding along the shores of Dhulough, Fin Lough, and the Glenummera River and back into ravines pleated with rock and the odd surprising house built into the side of the hill. As a child, Declan had explored the country surrounding his family's farm with an enthralled curiosity, returning to his hearth with questions. His parents, born Gaelic speakers who acquired English as a slightly unsavoury but necessary second language, were full of the stories of the townland and its families. Their English used a Gaelic syntax, the past being spoken of in the present, and for years he was puzzled as to whether Padraig Og was an uncle or the brother of a great-great-grandparent, whether the landlord of the area, the Marquess, whose hunting lodge provided work for some local families, was given land directly by Cromwell or was a descendant of your man. Old grudges, old loyalties — they were one and the same. If his family had had reason to shun the Joyces three generations earlier, there was no reason for the present family to speak to a contemporary Joyce.

"What's Gaelic, Mr. O'Malley?"

"Ah, Rose, the loveliest language that ever was created, the language of the ancient Celtic people who lived in Ireland, Scotland, Wales, and some in France and Cornwall, too. Let me think what I can say to you in it so ye'll get an idea of its music. Well, yes, here's a bit of poetry.

A bennáin, a búiredáin,
a béicedáin binn,
is binn linn in cúicherán

do-ní tú 'sin glinn.
Éolchaire mo mennatáin
do-rala ar mo chéill —
na lois isin machaire,
na h-ois isin t-sléib …"

He paused. "Do you ye like the sound of it then?"

"Oh, it's lovely! Like music, or water. What does it mean?" Rose's face was radiant, and she clasped her hands in front of her in delight. A girl in a shabby dress, her hair braided in two untidy ropes, green eyes alive with the poetry.

Declan thought for a minute, wanting to give her equal joy in an English version. "It means something like this, Rose. I will try to make it poetry as well. It's from a long poem about a sort of hermit, living on his own after being a prince of Ulster and going mad in battle:

Little antlered one, little belling one,
melodious little bleater,
sweet I think the lowing
that you make in the glen."

He stopped. "So that's the first bit, Rose, about a deer or a young stag, I guess. And this is what follows:

Homesickness for my little dwelling
has come upon my mind,
the calves in the plain,
the deer on the moor …"

Rose exclaimed again and clapped her hands. Declan had seen this in the past, when a girl from a mountain farm, with knowledge of sheep and turf cutting, would hear, in poetry, a chord that struck deep within her heart. He wished it could become more for them than a momentary fragment of joy in the classroom. The future held little poetry for these girls. Marriages would be arranged for some, others would enter service in a country house, some would work in the wool industry in Leenane, carding or spinning or weaving, and most would lose their bloom early with the harsh conditions that awaited them. One young woman in the nearby village had disgraced herself and her family by consorting with an English soldier and had been publicly stripped, her hair shorn, tar roughly painted onto her young body, and the feathers of geese and ducks shaken over her. Declan had known her father and knew the shame that he felt when the young woman left for England and word came back that she was carrying the child of the soldier. He hadn't heard whether the man took her in or not. He felt such pity for the girl and wished there had been something he could have done besides making his opinion known, in the quiet way he was known for, as he had always done. Sometimes love did not strike in a seemly or proper way — having taught school for years made him alert to the sighs of a boy yearning for a strapping lass twice his size or to the sight of a shadow against a stone wall splitting in two as his presence parted an embrace between a mountain girl, shoeless and clad in homespun, and a lad from a village family.

"Have ye heard of the Famine, Rose, the potato famine in Ireland? My parents called it the Black Hunger." Declan led the way back to the cabin, carrying a covered dish holding cheese.

She hadn't, and so he told something of it, how a terrible blight had killed the potato plants overnight, and overnight, seventy-five years ago, life had changed for the Irish forever. Most people depended utterly upon the potato for daily life; a few, like his father's family, also grew modest crops and animals for market and didn't fare quite so badly, but they, with their small amount of cash, were the exception. The populations of entire townlands disappeared, villages emptied of their occupants. Those who could fled for America, assisted in some cases by the Crown or by landlords who wanted them off the land, their rents so far in arrears that the landlords pleaded insolvency but still ate regularly, kept good horses who ate precious grains, and sent their children to fine schools. Human dignity was reduced to the lowest possible denominator as cows were bled for the sustenance their blood provided, people fed on grass and the herbs of the fields, fevers raged through the shelters constructed over ditches after the cabins had been tumbled by bailiffs and soldiers, and entire families died with no one to bury or mourn them or keep the dogs from their bodies. Afterwards, people carried the Famine with them like a sacred object, a prayer to protect them against such tragedy again. Declan told Rose what a sad thing it was to come upon the remains of the cabins, roofless, surrounded by thistles, cleansed by decades of wind. Sorrow attached itself to the stones, to the abandoned thresholds, made a syllabary of the grass stalks. Wind said the names quietly — O'Leary, Mannion, Murphy, Cronin. Sometimes a noise would issue from one of the ruined cabins and the young Declan would wait, trembling, until a black-faced mountain sheep trotted out, as startled as he was by the encounter.

Rose was quiet at first, knowing nothing of hunger and perhaps trying to imagine a table without bread or fish or over-wintered potatoes. And all she had known of death was a baby born too early and buried on their property, a jam jar of wild-flowers kept by the small stone, and the kittens her father drowned in a bucket thrown to the shore for eagles.

"Did you have brothers and sisters?" she asked, finally. She silently accepted another slice of currant bread, this time with some cheese, and ate it almost without noticing.

"I had four brothers and three sisters. I was in the middle, a dreamy boy whom they could not keep from books. I am grateful to my parents for not attempting to do so. The Irish have a great respect for learning; before my time, some schoolmasters even set up classes in the shelters of hedges, before the National Schools were built and schooling was made possible for most children, Catholics and Protestants. A way was found to send me from Tullaglas to the priests for further education."

"How did you get there?" she wondered.

"By donkey-cart, Rose. I'd never been away from home and pined for the first few weeks. We slept in long rooms, fifty boys to a room, and I could not wander the hills as I had in Delphi. I pined for the dog, the ravine behind our cabin, the sound of wind in our fuchsia bushes — as well as my mother's barmbrack ..."

"What's barmbrack, Mr. O'Malley?"

"A bread like the soda bread, Rose, but with some peel in it, sultanas, a bit of spice. But there were books at the school, and men who would understood what they meant."

Rose nodded. Declan intuited that she was beginning to understand what a gift an education might be. She picked up the *Odyssey* that Declan used as a reference for his translation. She was interested to see that he had made marks in it with a pen, little scribbly marks, and had written words of his own alongside the printed words.

"I can read this word, Mr. O'Malley." She pointed to the third word in from the beginning of the story, *Muse*, and said it aloud. "Muse. Muse. It's close to Rose, and I know *M* from Mother. My sister told me how the vowels sound so I know this letter is *u* and sounds like 'you.'"

"What a clever girl you are, Rose! And you are absolutely right. *Muse* is just what it is. Do you know what it means?"

She shook her head.

"The Muse is a source of inspiration for poets, a goddess who helps them to sing. This is maybe like the idea of metaphor that I explained to you. There are nine Muses, actually, and each of them is responsible for a particular kind of singing. The poet here is asking Calliope, the one who helps poets writing very long heroic poems, to help him tell the story of Odysseus. 'Tell me, Muse, of that man, so ready at need, who wandered far and wide, after he had sacked the sacred citadel of Troy; and many were the men whose towns he saw and whose mind he learnt, yea, and many the woes he suffered in his heart upon the deep, striving to win his own life and the return of his company.' And throughout the poem, he asks her again and again to help him with his poem."

He handed her the book and watched as she peered into the text, looking for more words. Loose hair swung over her cheeks, dark gold, and her brow was very serious. The schoolmaster in him determined his plan.

His farm in Delphi had been very small, the grass of two cows as they said in that area, and they had a pig, too. Chickens who roamed the haggard and ate the cabbage stalks boiled with potatoes. A rooster to strut and crow at dawn and impregnate the hens on a regular basis so there were always a few extra chickens for the pot. A dog with brown intelligent eyes and a good sense for sheep. There had once been more land available to the O'Malley family, partly through leases and partly according to the ancient rundale system which allocated tillage and forage in a fair way to those in the townland. The Famine changed the system and changed the availability of land, both to lease and to own, as the local landlords either went bankrupt or increased their holdings.

The house had been inherited from Declan's parents, the usual pattern of succession of eldest son interrupted as two brothers had gone to Australia and two to the Western Front, dying on the fields of Ypres. (One sister married and two went to the nuns at Montrath.) It was a typical cabin of the country style — a kitchen, small scullery in the south porch, and two large fireplaces, one in the kitchen with a settle bed alongside and one in the west room where the elder O'Malleys had lived after Eilis and Declan married. The girls slept in a loft while their grandparents were alive, and after their passing Declan and Eilis moved into the vacated west room for its privacy, the girls moving down to the small back bedroom. A pig shed and cow byre were off the gable end. The turf shed was opposite the door, and there was a shed for tools and small pieces of equipment necessary to the keeping of a farm. The farm's work seldom varied. For Eilis, it was washing on Mondays, ironing on Tuesdays, making butter on Thursdays, a trip to the village market on Fridays with that butter imprinted with her mark — a stalk of wheat — and wrapped in greaseproof paper, along with extra eggs. Bread was baked daily, using the soured milk or else buttermilk on butter days, with soda to make a light crumb. Declan had the care of the beasts, apart from milking, which the girls took turns doing; he cut the meagre hay of the meadow and prepared the ground for potatoes, although the entire family planted them and harvested them. The family also helped to cut turf, foot it, and stack it. They were busy and worked hard, but they did not want for anything. Grainne had her harp, which sweetened the long winter evenings. There was a deal table that held the lamp for the kitchen, and on winter nights Declan would sit up late, reading, while the women of the house slept under quilts Eilis had pieced together. Chores were always there for the doing in seasons with light after the tea, but in winter he tried to renew his Latin and read again of the doings of Aeneas, the strange wonders of Pliny.

It was a breezy morning, and Declan called Argos, walked through the bush to the canoe. It was drying out on the rocky bluff, helped by wind and open sky. Gulls wheeled in the air and dropped to pluck stranded fish, for the tide was out, leaving an expanse of mud, and rivulets of fresh water from the feeder creeks trickled out to meet the sea. Steam was rising as the sun warmed the mud flats and the atmosphere was otherworldly, huge trees dark in the background and the white birds swooping and calling. Declan examined the canoe, brushing off dried moss and lichen, and ran his fingers along the decoration at the prow. He could see how traces of the pigment he'd first noticed when the boys had helped him move the canoe remained in lines that had been incised. There was an eye, a ball surrounded by an ovoid socket. Black pigment had coloured the ball. He bent to smell it but could only detect the spongy smell of decaying cedar. There was a face of some sort, a beak. He thought it must be a bird, but it was not any bird he was familiar with. He knelt in the bow of the canoe and looked out to the bay. A figure at the far side caught his eye. It was Rose, her skirts tied behind her to avoid the mud, carrying a bucket. Clams again, he supposed. Her hair was blowing in the wind. The gulls were undeterred by her presence and continued to take up fish and whatever else they found to eat in the mud. The steam blurred her image a little, softened the lines of her limbs. She must have thought she was completely alone, unobserved, because she put her bucket down on a rock and began to dance, her arms slowly swaying and her face upturned to the wind. Declan could see she was barefoot. She looked like a seaborn nymph there on the steaming mud, her long hair unbound, bending and turning to an inner music. He remembered watching his daughter Grainne bringing back the milk cow from a tiny meadow high beyond the house; she had been unaware of anyone watching and had pirouetted with her willow switch above her head like a dancer, an image he recognized from a book on the school's small library shelf. She was lovely in the moist air, curls escaping from her plaits, a woman shadowing the girl, and remembering brought tears of such deep sadness that he covered his face with his hands.

Rose was dancing in the muddy bay like a strand of delicate seaweed, swaying and bending low. She stopped suddenly at the sound of her name being shouted from the direction of her house. It was her father's voice, harsh and angry. Hurriedly she picked up her bucket, unknotting her skirt as she ran towards home. The slow suck of the tide coming in erased her footprints in the mud.

Declan had been wondering how to approach Mrs. Neil for permission to give Rose some lessons. When she brought the milk one morning, he invited her in for a cup of tea.

"Mrs. Neil, I am thinking it would not be a difficult thing to teach young Rose to read so. She is always looking at these books ye see around ye and I would like to do something to repay yer family for its many kindnesses. As I have told ye, I taught school in Ireland and would consider it an honour to help Rose."

The woman regarded him gently. "There is no need to think you must repay us at all, Mr. O'Malley, but I know Rose has so enjoyed talking to you about your paperwork, and if you could spare her the time, I'll try to make sure she comes to you. My husband ... well, he has old-fashioned ideas about girls and education. He has allowed Martha to go to school because I really did insist but somehow Rose ... oh, there's not enough room in the boat or he wants her to help me with the laundry or some such notion. I've tried a little to help her, but the days are not long enough, it seems, for the work that needs doing. I would like to keep it from my husband, though. He is a good man but strong in his opinions and it's not always worth arguing with him or challenging him."

"Mrs. Neil, it would give me great pleasure to teach Rose. And I will say nothing to Mr. Neil. Shall I wet the tea again?"

It was three days before Rose appeared in the door of the cabin. She carried four eggs wrapped in newspaper and the jug of milk. Declan carefully took the eggs from her and put them in a small pudding basin, noticing as he did so the bracelet of bruising around Rose's wrists, as though she had been grabbed and held in anger. He carried the bowl and jug to the creek where he had a little cuddy made of stones and moss, a square of sheet metal level against the creek bed. A slab of cheese in a lard pail was there already, keeping cool. He wondered whether he ought to comment on the marks.

"Mr. O'Malley, have you ever seen a baby caddis fly in its nest?" Rose asked, leaning over the creek and carefully removing a clump of twigs and fir needles. She took a grass stalk and gently prodded one end of the clump. Antennae shot out with a tiny insect behind. She put it into Declan's hand so he could see it close up.

"Rose, it is truly an interesting little construction. How did ye know where to find it?"

She brushed her hair away from her eyes and confessed to spending hours looking into creeks. She'd find as many living things as she could and collect them in a bucket. Her father's friend, a devotee of fly-fishing, identified some of them for her — the larvae of stone flies and May flies, leeches, caddis flies in every sort of casing ... "You'd never know they were there, Mr. O'Malley, unless you looked really closely."

"In a way, Rose, that is true of stories, too. Here they are in books, in black and white, looking for all the world like hen tracks. But ye saw what happened when ye looked at a word for a time, how it told ye its name. *Muse*, it was, and near to yer name, ye thought. In a way ye were reading the creek when ye found the little lads that were part of what it was. Can water on its own be a creek or is a creek really a collection of things, like words, that make it real?"

Rose thought about that for a moment. "Well, creeks change, Mr. O'Malley. This creek is full of spring things. In summer it's different, and in fall, different again because of the salmon who lay their eggs in it. And winter, that's the best time to see the bugs and other creatures. Creeks change course, too, when the snow on the mountain melts quickly and makes them too full to stay within the banks. So if a creek is a story, it's never quite the same one."

"That is such a good way to think of a creek, Rose. I hadn't thought of them ever as stories, and changing ones at that. I think that's true of stories in general, too, would ye not agree? A story my mother told me was always a little different from one my father told. She remembered details he didn't. She would describe meals, who was sitting next to someone at the table, who the grandmother was, and where the grandmother's people came from originally. My father liked the physical details, whether there was a fight or an injury or even an insult. And in his stories, these things became bigger with each telling. And of course in families, each generation has something new to add. The stories we tell about the Great Hunger in Ireland are different, I'm thinking, from the ones that my grandparents might have told, with the sight of the starving still in their minds."

While they talked, the day became warm although it had not started off that way. Gulls called out on the tide flats and shore birds hunted in the stones for food. Vines of smoke climbed out of Declan's chimney to the blue sky, blossoming into high cloud, and at the mouth of the creek, salmon fry flipped for joy as they left the fresh water finally for salt. Declan brought some paper outside, and ink, and two pens; he began the task of teaching Rose the alphabet.

Rose was a quick learner. Her mother had spent some time with her, going over her letters, but it had not been a sustained learning, and she had not had the opportunity to apply the letters to actual words. With the *Odyssey* at hand, Declan would find a word using little clusters of letters.

Tell me, Muse, of that man, so ready at need, who wandered far and wide, after he had sacked the sacred citadel of Troy, and many were the men whose towns he saw ...

"This one, Rose, the *m*, then the *a*, then the *n*. Can you try to sound it out?"

And she would make the clear sound of each letter on its own, then shape them together, worrying the three until a word emerged from the soundings. "Man!" she said triumphantly, "Man!" Taking the pen and dipping it into ink, she would form the letters on a piece of paper, copying it several times over. Her list of words grew: *man, need, wide, towns, mind*.

"I've a mind to tell ye a story, Rose, which this talking of muses and towns has prompted, though I am still not certain of its meaning. When I was riding the train across America from my cousins in New Jersey to, well, what became this although I didn't know it at the time, the train made a stop in a town on the great plains. What state it was in, I have no idea. We had a few hours while the train took on freight of some sort. It was a cold day but clear, and I thought I'd walk to loosen up my joints, all cramped they were from the days and nights I'd spent already on the seat. It didn't take long for me to leave the little town completely behind and before I knew it I was standing by a field, watching a woman feed her pigs. They were big ones, black and white, a few tawny, and she was putting out some grain for them. They were polite animals, or so it seemed to me, and the woman spoke gently to them as she fed them, assuring them that there would be enough for all of them. When she saw me, she beckoned to me to come to where she was. I told her I was off the train and what fine animals she had. 'Ah,' she said, 'they are better than humans for company most of the time for a woman on her own.' She explained that the farm was hers, she worked hard, but with her horses and her goats and especially her pigs, she wanted for nothing."

Rose murmured that her father's pigs were too fierce to talk to, always wanting to root around and find more to eat, but maybe these ones never had to work for their food.

"These pigs were almost courtly, Rose, the way they waited for her, one of them sniffing her wrists. When I said I was thirsty and might she have a glass of water, she took me to her pump and drew off a jug of the most beautiful water and poured some into a tin cup. I have never tasted any like it. We talked and there was sun and the sound of her pigs eating their fill of dinner. When at last I thought to check my watch, Rose, the old pocket watch I have here, I saw I would be pressed to be back at the train on time. The woman suggested I might not want to leave, that there was work for a man like me on her farm, and for a moment I was tempted to stay. It was like a spell had been cast over me for that moment, Rose. It was all I could do to say my farewells and run along that country road to the town where the train was building up steam for its leave-taking. I have occasionally wondered what my life would be like if I'd stayed. She struck me as something of a muse, that woman, a lass to inspire a man to do something fine, there with her pigs and her fields. But I never found out what I might have done. That's it, Rose, my little tale, and in telling it, I see that it still mystifies me now as it did then. Let's look at the poem again and see what you can make of these lines."

They worked at the task until Rose said she must go, her mother would need her help with dinner as a chicken had been killed and must be plucked. Declan watched her disappear beyond the bluff, then set about making a simple meal for himself. He felt he had been a coward for his inability to mention the bruises to Rose but was also reluctant to enter into another family's troubles. *Sure each has its own difficult times*, he thought, *and who is a stranger to judge another man's actions?* He sat on a rock by the shore, eating his cheese and the end of a loaf of his brown bread. A line came to him, from the poem he had recited to Rose. *Homesickness for my little dwelling has come upon my mind.* Was it the mind where homesickness struck, he wondered, or the heart? He felt it in his heart, of a sudden, like a grey bruise, but the heart surely could not summon up the image of home? The two must work together then, the one passing the memory along to the other to be yearned for and hungered for. What the mind offered, in clarity and purpose, the heart turned to grief. Looking out at the water, he could see a boat far away in the strait. His heart felt like that boat, alone on the ocean, buoyed up by salty water, a bottomless pool of tears.

Chapter Five

Four days of rain when he didn't want to get out of his bed and couldn't remember where he was, Delphi or New Jersey or Oyster Bay. Four days when he called to whichever Neil brought the milk to just leave it by the door, thanks, and he would bring it in later. Four days of daylight dreaming and weeping. "Cold icy wind, faint shadow of a feeble sun, the shelter of a single tree: Suibhne indeed," he wept.

On the fifth day, he rose, dressed, called Argos, and walked to the canoe.

The deadly flowers were finished now, drying seed pods opened on the stalks, rustling as the breeze rubbed them together. You could not tell which had been the white camas and which the blue. Tiny pink blooms covered the bluff. The moss was spongy underfoot, and the canoe was wet again, a puddle collecting where part of the wood had warped and created a depression. The drain holes took the rest of the rain away. Declan touched the beak at the prow. It reminded him a little of a rook's beak. Those birds had haunted every farm he'd ever known, waiting to eat afterbirth, scattered grain, their nests in a grove of high trees nearby, untidy formations of sticks and broken vines. His daughters had loved a rhyme about crows in a collection of nursery poems, *One is for bad news, two is for mirth.* A note on the text told them that the rhyme often used magpies instead and that there were variants: *One is for sorrow, two for joy* was one they liked, too. As Declan was examining the carved beak, he heard a strange noise from the sky. *Klook, klook, klook.* Looking up, he saw two black birds floating above him. *Klook, klook,* and then a run of notes like gurgling water. Ah, ravens. He'd seen these birds before, sitting in trees near the creek or tumbling down the sky like groups of boys doing acrobatics. One of the Neil boys had told him what they were and that they were cousins to the crow, which he could understand; they did look like the Irish rooks, only bigger, heavier. One of them flew to the bluff and settled in one of the pines, looking down at him curiously. A sound came from it like knuckles on hollow wood. It tilted its head and made the sound again. Declan found he could make the same sound in his own mouth by clicking his tongue hard against the back of his palate. *Tok, tok.* The bird answered. It was perched so he could see its profile, a smooth head with the beak extending, extending … quickly he looked to make certain, yes, extending just like the one he was seeing on the prow of the canoe.

"So ye are the lad I see here," he called up to the raven. "Mirth, to be sure!" The bird preened itself, adjusting its wings, and looked away. The other raven had settled in a tree further down the bay. Declan took advantage of the bird's presence to compare its profile with the carved bird. There were differences, of course. The real raven's eye was round and alive, not ovoid and bald. The shape of the beak was very similar, but the carved beak was open, holding a tiny disc. The real raven uttered another of the watery cries and flew up, circling the bluff lazily before flying to meet its mate down the bay. "Thank you," Declan called to it, "thank you for letting me know who this is."

Speaking to Mrs. Neil later that day, Declan mentioned the carving on the canoe, explaining he had been looking at it when a raven landed nearby, as if to solve the little riddle of identity. She was amused.

"Mr. O'Malley, the ravens are very clever birds. I wouldn't put it past one to decide to help you out. The Indians hold them in very high esteem, you know. In fact, they believe that the raven brought light to man by stealing the disc of sun from Heaven and that the birds have the power to command the tides. Sometimes when I'm working in the garden or hanging out the wash, one will sit in a tree nearby and talk to me. If I close my eyes, I can almost hear the words, although of course they aren't words exactly."

One for sorrow, two for joy ... Declan found himself noticing the birds as never before. Had they always loitered in the tall cedars around the creek or was this new? The sound of them threaded through the branches, drawing his attention upward. He found them oddly congenial. Going out in his skiff one morning to catch a salmon for his dinner, he saw them tumbling in the sky the way he'd seen boys tumbling in the schoolyard in spring, full of high spirits and energy. Coming back with his salmon and a few herring to fry for Argos, he could see a pair of ravens in a fir near his cabin, looking for all the world like sentinels. One of them croaked as he pulled the skiff up onto the shore. Declan tried to find the sound in his own throat and offered something resembling a *croanq*.

The raven tilted its head and looked him in the eye. *Tok, tok.* Declan made the sound back. The raven answered. Then, as he began unloading his fishing gear, the raven floated down from the tree to the beach and began foraging among the stones. Declan watched as it selected a large mussel and flew up with the shell in its beak. When it was about fifteen feet above the beach, it dropped the mussel over the rocks below and immediately flew down to scoop out the meat from the broken shell. It returned to its perch and looked at Declan.

He was amazed. "What a clever lad ye are!" he called up to the bird.

The raven ruffled its feathers a little and then flew away, followed by the second one, which had not uttered a sound but sat on its branch watching the activity of its partner. Declan saw them rise and drift westward on the May wind. He tucked his salmon in a piece of clean burlap and laid it in the cuddy to keep cool, then took his herrings inside to cook for Argos.

The Black and Tans had come to Tullaglas in the night. He'd awoken from sleep with the sense that something was not right. It was too quiet. That was because they'd slit the throat of the family dog, who might have whined a warning. They'd taken Declan outside in his nightshirt and told him they'd heard of his teaching. The one that seemed to be in charge hit him with the butt of a rifle and asked him if he knew what the penalty was for sedition.

"I am aware of your laws, to be sure, but it is no crime to teach my students what it is to be Irish and to teach them in their own language. Our Gaelic League has made this possible and lawful. We mean no disrespect to your king but one day we will be a republic, that is certain, and my students will know who they are as citizens of a free Ireland."

"You are mistaken there, schoolmaster. This lot of pigs and fools could never govern themselves. They can't even keep themselves clean."

There was more hard talk and more beatings with the rifle butt. He fell to the ground at one point and tried to protect his face. Heavy boots kicked him in the small of the back until he blacked out.

Waking, he smelled the smoke and tried to clear his head. Every part of him hurt and he could taste blood in his mouth and throat. It took him a minute or two to focus his eyes, but then he was fully awake. His house was burning. Fiercely. The thatch acted as a tinder and smoke was pouring from the windows, which had blasted out their glass from the heat. Scrambling to his feet, he called to Eilis, thinking that she must be near, with the girls, perhaps moving the hens or the pig to a safer place. After a few moments of calling, a terrible feeling filled him that she, that they, might still be inside. The door had been braced closed with a fence post, and Declan beat it aside with a spade. The scullery, the main room — both seethed with smoke. Using the spade to push aside burning stools and fallen timbers, he made his way to the west room, where he saw them in the far corner. It did not take a minute to realize he was too late. Their bodies were like candles, intense light flaring fom the wicks of their hair, their cotton nightdresses. Eilis must have told the girls to put on their shoes to escape to the predawn fields, and the shoes hadn't burned. What was the body but tallow and wax, oil for the lamps of British hatred. There was an old poem about burned children, by Aodhagán O Rathaille, he'd recited it in Irish over to his classes over the years, in part because it gave rise to discussion about metaphor, and he'd wanted them to hear the sombre tone of the language; he'd stop to make the lines into English, too.

They were ears of corn!
They were apples!
They were three harpstrings!
And now their bodies lie underground ...

And that was the grief of it, in either language, that the living flesh of children could be so quickly consumed. Rather that
they *were* corn, rippling in a calm field, green and gold in sunlight, or apples, veined with pink through the pale flesh. Perhaps
he would think of them that way when he had got far away
from the fire, in memory and in years, his house a cold and
empty hearth, the stools all burned. He might forget the smell,
like meat roasting, the hideous stench of feathers and hair.

The lines were difficult to wrap his mind around. Some days the
Greek revealed itself to him so clearly that he might have been
reading his own name. Other days he could not for the life of
him figure out the meaning; the entries in the lexicon moved in
and out of his consciousness without leaving a trace. It had to do
with clarity, he knew, in his own mind, with what he brought to
the poetry. He closed his eyes and tried to clear out whatever it
was that kept him from reading properly. Deep breath. *Just get the
meaning for now,* he thought, *and shape it to poetry later. Begin again.*

ἦμος δ᾽ ἠριγένεια φάνη ῥοδοδάκτυλος Ἠώς.
(Yes, now he could understand it.)
As soon as the dawn with her rosy fingers
    made the morning light,
φιτροὺς δ᾽ αἶψα ταμόντες, ὅθ᾽ ἀκροτάτη
    πρόεχ᾽ ἀκτή,

I sent my shipmates to the house of Circe,
οἰσέμεναι νεκρόν, Ἐλπήνορα τεθνηῶτα,
To bring the corpse of Elpenor.
Πηιτρουσ δᾶ αιπσα ταμοντεσ, ηοτηᾶ
 ακροτατε προεψηᾶ ακτε,
Quickly we cut logs of wood and gave him
 burial on the final headland,
θάπτομεν ἀχνύμενοι θαλερὸν κατὰ δάκρυ
 χέοντες,
Far out to sea, grieving, tears pouring down
 our faces,
αὐτὰρ ἐπεὶ νεκρός τ' ἐκάη καὶ τεύχεα νεκροῦ,
But when the corpse was burned, and all the
 dead man's fittings,
τύμβον Χεύαντες καὶ ἐπὶ στήλην ἐρύσαντες
We built up a barrow, dragged to it a pillar,
πήξαμεν ἀκροτάτῳ τύμβῳ ἐυῆρες ἐρετμόν.
We erected his perfect oar against the sky.

He was weeping, like Odysseus's men wept as they gave a fitting burial for Elpenor. Not a hero, Elpenor, but a young man who tumbled in drunkenness off the roof of Circe's house and who broke his neck in the fall and died. Encountering him in Hades, Odysseus listened to Elpenor's tale of falling and losing his spirit to the dark and promised his friend that amends would be made for leaving him unceremoniously on the island of the witch.

 σῆμά τέ μοι χεῦαι πολιῆς ἐπὶ θινὶ θαλάσσης,
 Commemorate me by the grey sea,
 ἀνδρὸς δυστήνοιο καὶ ἐσσομένοισι πυθέσθαι,
 A wretched man that others, yet unknown, may
  learn from.

The imagery of that passage pierced Declan to his very heart. What had been left of him on the Irish hill where his wife and daughters had been burned and buried, commemorated by pink Connemara granite? He had fled into nothingness, it seemed, spirited away to Cork and then America, a story emptied of its narrator, its action, its consequence. And now, on his own small promontory, he was a cairn of living grief, grey as water.

He put the poem aside and walked out to the shore. He never tired of the bay, stretching out to open sea. Today the tide was coming in over the exposed mud flats, threaded with silvery runs of fresh water. There were birds everywhere — sandpipers on the shore where he supposed their nests must be, ducks coming in with the tide, a solitary loon, silent in daylight, geese gathered by the small rocky islands where some of them nested. He loved the smell when the tide came in, the rich fecund mud, warmed by the sun, meeting the sharp iodine of the sea. He supposed men had always stood by water, admiring the liveliness of its movement, loving the sight of birds feeding on its shores, fishing its depths with their strong bills.

There were days when he felt close to Odysseus, when working on parts of the poem that were Odysseus's story he would stop and think of it as his own story. But truth be told, he had never done anything bold in his life. He'd left his parents' house to be educated, returned to that very house with a wife, fathered two daughters, taught children the basics of reading and writing and simple geometry at the Bundorragha school, as well as the Irish history and grammar that had been his ruin, taking them on walks by the river below the school to see the trout, the yellow flags of iris. Odysseus journeyed home over a period of years, stopping here and there to prove his worth to gods who had no use for him, but then he was protected by the grey-eyed Athena and managed to survive — although he had lost his men, not least among them young Elpenor. He was not only brave but also clever and could outwit the obstacles in his way. Declan had journeyed a long way by sea but alone. And the biggest difference between them? Odysseus was struggling homeward to a wife and son. Declan had no one. Home was a far country that he wanted no part of.

He left off his musings and gathered some wood to make a little beach fire to cook his salmon. Mrs. Neil had shown him a way to roast the fish, in turn shown her by Lucy, the Indian woman who had known this bay as a child. He made a fire, using alder sticks from a stash he had cut from branches found on the ground. First he cut off the head of the fish, saving it to roast for Argos. Opening the salmon, he flattened it as well as he could by splitting the backbone. Sharpening a long green stick, he threaded the salmon lengthwise, using slits he'd cut into the tail end, the middle, and the top. Two thin sticks were woven horizontally through slits along the edges of the fish to keep it open and flat. Another long stick was lashed to both ends of the first stick to offer it some support and strength. Once the fire had burned down to hot coals, he staked his salmon on one side of the fire, angled so it leaned into the smoke and heat, then added more alder.

They had wanted Grainne to have music lessons. She'd been taught rudimentary fingering for the harp by an old woman in Leenane who had played the harp in her youth. Another local woman, though from farther afield, would stop in to offer Grainne assistance from time to time, but she was the mother of a large family living in an isolated area so her visits were regrettably few and far between. At first Grainne's fingers bled — the wire strings were like nothing her hands had encountered and her fingernails were not long enough to allow her to pluck in the traditional manner — but eventually calluses formed, her nails grew, and she coaxed song after song from the plangent strings. She learned to read music, a language in itself, and studied the sheets for hours, humming bars and tapping out sections to learn the timing. She would listen to a tune at a ceilidh, say a fiddle piece, and Declan could see her lips move, her fingers pluck the air as she transposed the song in her mind. A daughter from one of the wealthier families, Maeve Fitzgerald, had studied harp for a time at the Royal Irish Academy of Music in Dublin, and she passed along her workbooks to Grainne. It was the latter's hope to sit for the Local Centre Examinations and perhaps go on to the RIAM herself. She became very proficient, playing whenever she could, and the music eased them through the dark winter afternoons.

Legend told of the wife of Dagda, a faery king, who had given birth to three strong sons. During her confinements, Dagda's harpist played to make the pains of the labours pass more easily. As the first son was being born, the harp moaned sadly, as if in pain. During the second labour, the harp's music was merry and light. And as the third son was being born, the harper played a mysterious air, soft and sweet. Each son was named for the music that accompanied his birth, and Irish music ever after contained those three strands: the notes of pain, joy, and enchantment. Grainne loved the planxties of Carolan, with their animated melodies, a series of triplets that she played quickly, hearing harmonies in the strings to accompany the melody line. Declan's favourites were the laments; he heard in them the yearnings of his boyhood when he roamed the fields and famine cabins, feeling the ache of loss, although he didn't have a specific occasion to which he could attach the feeling. Not then, when his girls grew like healthy corn and his wife welcomed them to the table with floury potatoes splitting their jackets and cabbage cooked with the

bacon of their own pig. Now he could not bear to hear a lament
with its inconsolable phrasing.

There was keening enough in the wind and the strange cries
of the loons piercing the night and his sleep that he would rise
and go to the door, wondering at the loneliness of the birds who
made such sounds. And where was Grainne's harp now, with its
elegant curves of bog oak and its strings of brass that rang under
her fingers like bells? Gone up in smoke, as transitory as weather.
The house of the family that had given her the sheet music had
been burned before his own, the wolfhounds shot by Paddy the
shop to keep them quiet (or so it was rumoured), the family given
a moment's notice to leave in the darkness in their nightclothes,
and it was said that the burning of Declan's home was a retaliation by the Black and Tans for that atrocity. And yet, despite their
class and religious differences, the two families had been friendly.
The woman of the demesne had consulted Eilis about her arthri-
tis, sharing the aches and pains of aging over a cup of tea in sunlight by the cabin door, roses wreathed above the entrance, while
the woman's horse waited, tethered to a bit of gate. The mister
brought cartons of children's books to the school for the young
scholars, and their daughters, Grainne and Maeve, loved the same
music, played the same instrument. It made no sense.

The salmon was ready, he thought, and carefully removed the
stake from the proximity of the fire, planting the fish closer to
water to cool it a little so he could eat it. He'd roasted the head
in the embers and scooped it out with a stick so Argos could eat
the meaty bits. The ravens were back, drawn by the smell of
cooking fish. When the salmon was cool enough, Declan laid it
across a rock washed clean by the tide and pulled morsels away

from the skin. Chewing slowly, he knew it was possible he had never tasted anything so delicious in his life. Slightly oily, slightly sweet, the salmon flesh, muscular and firm, tasted of the sea, of tides, of journeys through wild waters. He paused in his eating and went to the cabin to bring out his tin mug filled with creek water from the jug. There was sacrament in consuming the flesh of this fish, in drinking water of the creek that fed into the bay, nurturing a season's worth of infant salmon and gently releasing them to the ocean. He ate until he could not eat another mouthful, then walked over to the creek to pull up a handful of the peppery cress growing there; chewing it took away the slightly greasy glaze against his tongue. He scooped up another mug of water, straight from the creek this time, and returned to the edge of the bay. There was sun and the wash of waves against the rocky shore and the mutter of water birds over the tide. Declan tidied up the remains of his fire on the beach, scattering the ash, throwing he fish bones as far out to sea as he could. For a moment, the skeleton skimmed the current, light as air, the spirit of the fish lit by the falling light before sinking under a wave.

Looking up into the trees, he made the *tok, tok* against his palate. The ravens tilted their heads and looked down at him. "Here, lads," he called, and tossed shreds of salmon skin down the shore. The birds kept looking at him, a steady gaze from each pair of eyes. He moved down the shore with his mug of water and busied himself washing his hands in the sea. When he looked up, one of the ravens was tugging at the skin he'd thrown. It would stop, tilt its head back to swallow, and then, holding the skin in place against the pebbles, it would tear off another morsel. After a few minutes of this, it hopped along the beach a little and the second raven glided down from the tree and took its turn to tug and tear at the skin. Their feathers in sunlight were blue-black and shining. Declan watched them for a time and then returned to his cabin to continue his work.

The days passed, whole weeks passed, with ravens visiting, the tides going out and coming in, the occasional fish leaping right outside his cabin. There was not a pattern to the days, exactly, but Declan tried to make sure that work was done on the poem and that Rose got as much help with her reading as he was able to give. She began to blossom as a reader, needing help less and less as they worked through the passages. It was as though a framework had been in place, provided by her mother's scanty lessons and Rose's natural intelligence, and the framework was strong enough, and true, for what it was to hold. He could not rid himself of a small sour anger, though, when he'd see the boat leaving in the morning to take the other Neil children to school, the father grimly rowing them around to the other side of the harbour, Tom in the bow with the lines. Declan determined to make Rose's lessons as useful as he could, thinking of questions about geography and mathematics to fit into their reading. Sketch-maps of the Mediterranean on paper or in the sand, simple scales to work out relative distances, even a chart to plot the family connections of the House of Atreus to make the war that Odysseus was returning from something of a reality across the centuries. Rose was hungry for all of it.

On his next visit to the canoe, Declan took his copy of the *Odyssey* to read. He was working on the passages where Odysseus's men had angered the gods by feasting on the cattle of Hyperion; Zeus sent a storm to destroy them all. Only Odysseus survived, riding the spar of his ship to the island of Calypso where he was cared for and loved by the goddess. So many storms in the poem! He imagined waters around Greece to be constantly turbulent, various forces at work to make life difficult for sailors: Sirens luring boats to grief on the rocks; the dangerous passage between Scylla and Charybdis, the one a monster with many arms and the other a whirlpool that sucked boats down to a watery grave. Homer was a poet who had paid attention to what men told him of their sea adventures, thought Declan, and his poem made particularly vivid the storms at sea. Odysseus had clung to a fig tree overhanging Charybdis, waiting for parts of his ruined ship to appear in the spume; he used a spar as a canoe, his arms as oars, to take him to Ogygia and Calypso.

> ἦκα δ' ἐγὼ καθύπερθε πόδας καὶ χεῖρε
>   φέρεσθαι,
> I let go with my feet and my hands,
> μέσσῳ δ' ἐνδούπησα παρὲξ περιμήκεα δοῦρα,
> And plunge into waters beyond the tall spars,
> ἑζόμενος δ' ἐπὶ τοῖσι διήρεσα χερσὶν ἐμῇσι,
> And seated upon them I row onward with
>   my hand.

Idly, Declan dangled his own arms outside the canoe. They would make terrible oars, he decided, barely reaching into what would be water. Grasses tickled his forearms. In Ireland, oars on boats were very long, their long blades reaching deep to propel the currach forward. They were fitted over thole-pins on the gunwales of the craft, and the pins were kept damp so that the oars didn't squeak. He had brass oarlocks on his own skiff, little windows on the marine world. Declan would use them to sight a headland or the bobbing heads of kelp where fish might be found. Leaning back, he lowered himself down into the canoe, one hand clutching a tuft of ripe grass. No oarlock to view the view, just the tiny holes drilled in the bottom to drain away rain. Down he slid, and farther down to the bilge where the damp wood smelled of old earth and rot, where he had to brace his arms against the sides to keep himself from sinking lower to where the drain holes pierced the hull. Where was he bound for in this broken canoe, marooned on a bluff of poisonous flowers gone to seed? Who waited to dry him and offer wine and fresh linens, the use of a harp so he could sing his story? No goddess emerged from the trees in a shaft of golden light, no fire burned in readiness for meat.

Σκύλλην δ' οὐκέτ ἔασε πατὴρ ἀνδρῶν τε θεῶν τε. εἰσιδέειν· οὐ γάρ κεν ὑπέκφυγον αἰπὺν ὄλεθρον.

I could not have passed Scylla without the father
of gods and men. I was kept from her sight and
saved from utter destruction.

He was falling, down into the opened earth. He saw nothing but fields covered with fog, the same fog that swept across Oyster Bay like cold smoke. Coming across the fields was his mother, dressed in her burial smock. It was Tullaglas and it wasn't, some of the trees at the edge of the view were the tall firs beyond World's End. "Is this a dream, Mother?" he called to her, and the answer she spoke made Declan's blood run cold.

O my son, alas,
most sorely tried of men, the god's daughter,
Persephone, knits no illusion for you.
All mortals meet this judgement when they die.
No flesh and bone are here, none bound by sinew,
since the bright-hearted pyre consumed them
        down —
the white bones long exanimate — to ash;
dreamlike the soul flies, insubstantial.

"Are you my mother?" he called, surprised at such language coming from the throat of the Gaelic-speaking, rough-dressed woman of the house of his memory. In answer, she turned from him while shadows crowded around them. He reached out, but she had disappeared into the fog. He had no lambs to offer, no blood to pour into a trench for her sustenance. Would he see Eilis and Grainne and Maire, and what he would say to them, how he could ever explain that he would have saved them from the fire had he not been knocked out by a rifle butt? He had not heard their screams in time, had woken to smoke, the house in flames, their bodies ignited like torches. What would they want of him? Would they blame him for surviving, for fleeing the earth that held their sorry remains? Half-fearful, yes, and yet he yearned for them, watched for the sight of their familiar faces, their shoulders, the heartbreaking turn of their ankles. To encounter them in this swirl, their strong bodies fog-hidden in the fields of shadows — he would give his own life for such a meeting. There were shapes in the fog, but try as he might, he could not discern his own lost women. In panic he strode across the fields, trying to see the faces of the shades.

Here was great loveliness of ghosts.

Is that what he was seeing then? The words came to him from the book, he was gasping for air, surrounded by the wraiths and fog, he was trying to climb back the great height from which he had fallen ...

"Mr. O'Malley, are you all right, sir?" He opened his eyes, blinked, looked around to see where he was. Rose was standing by the canoe where Declan had fallen into a deep sleep, his open book across his chest.

Ah, the canoe. Grabbing the gunwales, he pulled himself up, wincing a little as his muscles announced their displeasure at having been cramped against damp wood for such a time. "I was reading the poem, Rose, and must've fallen asleep. For a minute there, I couldn't place myself at all."

(But my heart
longed, after this, to see the dead elsewhere.)

"My mother said I could come for a lesson and I didn't see you there. Your boat was ashore, and your oars leaning on the cabin, so I knew you wouldn't be far. I called for you and Argos came running from this direction so I thought you might be up here doing something with the canoe." She didn't tell him how she had been startled to find him stretched out in the canoe and had thought him dead for a minute, the length of him in his shabby trousers and faded shirt absolutely still. She had watched for a few minutes before trying to wake him and realized how sad she would be if he was indeed dead. His soft voice was something she tried to conjure up sometimes before sleep, his patience a gift she was only beginning to appreciate, having thought that adults were mostly like her father — quick to anger, dismissive of a child's feelings, impatient with clumsiness, but also capable of a brief tender word.

He brushed his hand across his hair and closed the book. "Certainly ye may have a lesson, Rose. We'll just walk back to the cabin so."

Rose ran ahead with Argos, her sandaled feet sure on the grassy slope down from the bluff. She wore a faded blue dress, lines around the bottom where the hem had been let down twice. Seeing her reminded Declan of how he had longed to meet Grainne and Eilis and Maire in his dream. For months he had tried to keep their images from forming in his mind, fearing the grief that accompanied the memories. How he missed them! He would hear a phrase of harp in the wind, a laugh coming over the water from the Neils' farm, and he would sink to his knees in sorrow. Yet, waking from the dream, he felt curiously close to them. Rose, running ahead in her faded frock, was a thin but tangible thread leading him to ... something, he wasn't

sure what. Through the bush, across the corduroy path over the
marsh, and back to World's End where Declan busied himself for
a few minutes gathering together the papers they'd been using,
and the books.

Rose knew the alphabet well now and could write simple
words. What she liked best was tracing her finger across the lines
of the Lang translation of the *Odyssey* and figuring out each word
in turn. Her memory was good, and she had memorized many
of the lines by heart; she loved the names, too, and never forgot
their pronunciation after Declan had taken her through it once:
Calypso, Telemachus, Menelaus, Laertes, the faithful Penelope.

"How old are you, Rose? I'm thinking about twelve?"

"Yes, Mr. O'Malley. I was twelve just after Christmas. My
mum cooked roast chicken and made me a coconut cake."

"About the age of my Grainne, then. She was the elder of
our daughters. Maire was nearly two years younger."

"Your daughters in Ireland, Mr. O'Malley? Did they come
to Canada, too?"

"They died in an accident, Rose. The two of them both, and
their mother. I buried them and then couldn't stay there anymore. The life had gone out of the place, you see." For some reason, he found it easier to talk to her than anyone else thus far.

"I'm so sorry, Mr. O'Malley. We knew something had happened but not that you'd lost your whole family." Her face
looked so sad that Declan stroked her cheek with his finger. Her
skin was damp. He was moved that she would shed a tear for
girls she'd never known.

"Ah, Rose, it is not something I have wanted to think much
about, let alone speak of. For months I could only weep at the
memories of them, living and dead, and everything reminded
me — from birds to the moon to poetry. I could not have spoken of them to anyone without my heart breaking again. But
these days I want to remember them more, not just grieve them.

I have done plenty of that, and it has not brought them back to be sure. I want to know them from this distance we have found for ourselves, them in graves I dug by myself, me on the other side of the earth. My older daughter, Grainne — we named her for the Irish pirate queen, Grainne O'Maille, who was the namesake of my family. Grainne is the Irish for Grace. And Maire is the Irish for Mary. It has been lonesome without them, but thinking of them, remembering Maire's laugh and the music Grainne could create from the strings of her harp, well, it is a comfort sometimes. Is it enough? No. But in a strange country, even the memories of a family are better than nothing, or so I am thinking."

(... my heart longed ...)

Declan tried to continue this thread, of memory, the way a heart could conjure up wrists and ankles out of thin air, the deep dreaming in the old canoe. But he felt each word stiffen before it left his lips, awkward as speech might be under water.

So they continued with the lesson, Rose working her way through a passage, stopping to ask about a word, wondering aloud at meaning. The language of the translation was stilted, somewhat, and Declan paraphrased lines so that Rose could understand them in an idiom closer to the one she was familiar with. The haths and didsts, the spakes and needests were replaced with the simpler language of everyday speech. Still, she heard the poem in its beauty hidden in the awkward phrasings, the archaic usages.

While Rose finished the last few lines he had set her as a brief assignment, Declan made tea and cut them each a piece of soda bread with a slice of cheese. Taking their mugs outside, they chose rocks near the water and sat there, balancing their bread and tea on smaller rocks nearby. Argos, who'd been sleeping in the warm grass behind them, suddenly leapt to her feet and charged off towards the woods. There was something crashing through the bush on the southern side of the bay, something large. Rose and Declan stood up to see whether they could determine what it was while Argos bellowed from within the trees. A deer jumped out of the salal, a stag, and dashed down to the water, its head turning rapidly from side to side. On its head, it wore its rack of antlers like a crown. Behind it, in pursuit, a tawny animal paused at the sight of the pair on the beach. No such caution for the stag, who entered the tide and began to swim strongly out to sea.

"A cougar, Mr. O'Malley! That's a cougar chasing the deer!"

Declan had never seen such an animal before. It was big, much bigger than the big dogs people favoured in this area. It looked like a lion but without the heavy mane he'd seen in pictures. Powerful legs, a heavy body, a long tail behind it, and Argos barking for all she was worth fifty feet away. Seeing the cougar was like looking at a painting, its tawny colour set against the tapestry of greens in the background. The cat looked at the stag swimming, the dog howling, and the people watching from not far enough away, quite, for its comfort, and then it turned, loping back into the woods. Argos pursued it for a minute or two but then ran to join Declan and Rose on the beach, panting and trembling.

"What a brave girl ye are, Argos," Declan told the dog, rubbing her head. "But I'm thinking ye'd be no match for a cat like that if it decided to turn on ye."

Rose was watching the stag. He was beyond the first small island and hadn't looked back. She wondered aloud if he knew the cougar had given up on the chase. The sun was over the western sky and for a moment, it hung between the stag's antlers like a burnished lamp. It was like poetry, she said, like the poem Declan had told her in Gaelic, and she turned to ask him to recite it for her.

"Little antlered one,

little belling one,

melodious little bleater
sweet I think the lowing
that you make in the glen."

"Is there poetry for everything, Mr. O'Malley?"

"Rose, there is a poem for any moment, any feeling. And sometimes one poem might say it all. That poem ye like, about the deer, has very sorrowful passages, too, because although the poet finds so many things in nature to give him joy, he has also given up another life. *Dismal is this life*, he says, *to be without a soft bed; a cold frosty swelling, harshness of snowy wind.* But he wouldn't give up his life as wild man of the woods, I don't think, because he keeps telling us how much he likes cress and cold water from the clean brook. He's a bit like myself, Rose, I'm thinking. I've had salmon today, and mugs of the cleanest water I've ever tasted, and a handful of cress! *Though you like the fat and meat,* the poet says, *which are eaten in the drinking halls, I like better to eat clean watercress in a place without sorrow."*

When Rose left, Declan put away the books, emptied the teapot into the bushes, banked his fire for the evening. *Well, I have buried Elpenor, burned his corpse and his weapons,* he thought. *And in a way, I have saved Odysseus today,* he mused, *helped him with the words to climb on a spar and row himself to shore. I have slept in the canoe of a dead man myself while waiting for a girl to wake me, in fields of dying asphodel. Did I know I was waiting? And I have thought of Grainne playing her harp, remembering her hands without weeping. Eaten a fish which was the best I've ever tasted. Ah, maybe yet there is hope for a fellow like me, a drinker of creek water, an eater of cress.*

Sorrows could visit a place, come unbidden through the windows and doors, hover in the trees like birds, and they could leave, too, taken by tides, or cracked open and eaten like a night-coloured mussel by a bird half-capable of speech.

Chapter Six

What was that smell? Waking, Declan inhaled deeply, the cabin filled with a scent so sweet and wild he imagined he might be in Paradise. Flinging back his bedclothes, he went to the open window and leaned out. Ahhh ... The shrubby bushes around his cabin were roses, he could see that now, and the morning sun had caused hundreds of buds to open. Pale pink, deeper pink, some half-opened, some fully, the roses scented his cabin like a rare perfume. He could hear the hum of bees among the blossoms, and looking closely he saw them stagger from flower to flower with their pollen sacs laden. Each bloom had a wreath of gold in its centre that dusted the legs of the bees as they extracted nectar from the flower.

He built a fire, filled with kettle from the bucket by the door, and put it on the stove to boil for tea. Then he went outside to bury his face in roses, ignoring the prickles and the bees.

It was a smell that went directly to the heart, reminding one of all the times the scent of roses had been inhaled. This plant was different from the roses that grew near Declan's place of birth in Ireland. These flowers were large, some of them three inches across, in varying shades of pink, from light to deep. Declan remembered smaller flowers in Ireland but sweetly scented, blooming in a tangle amongst the hedgerows of fuchsia, elder-berry, and haw, and then the red hips alight in the dark canes of winter. And always birdsong coming from within the depths of the vegetation. What birds sang in those hedges, he wondered, as he listened to the robin whistle in the wild roses at World's End. Thrushes, he supposed, and then he remembered chaffinches feeding on the berries in autumn, hedge-sparrows pecking for worms, small birds plucking the seed heads of old man's beard for lining nests tucked inconspicuously into the branches.

The hedges fenced off the small holdings, kept the cattle and sheep from the boreens. Some of them were very old, surrounding ancient hill-forts and barrows, following the demarcations of stone walls down hillside paths to the roads. Once, at dusk, coming from the schoolhouse, Declan had seen a badger coming out from its sett within the hedge, peering at him before retreating. He had listened to the scuttle of the animal among the trunks of haw, thinking how there must be a whole maze of tunnels through the hedges and how safe it must feel tucked with its mate and their offspring in amongst the roots of the sleeping vegetation. His father had told him, in boyhood, that badger setts were often hundreds of years old, each generation adding its adjustment or extension. Another time, walking down to the village of Leenane in early evening, he had observed two badgers on the grass beyond the hedgerow by the Erriff River, and when he'd stopped to watch, he could see that they were playing with their cubs; he had entered Leenane dazzled with the mystery of it. On a spring day he had come upon the soiled bracken and hay of their winter sett, taken up through the roots of the hawthorns. As with the stag and cougar, he'd had the sense that he was looking into a picture of ancient meaning, an embellishment of the Gospels, the text of his days surrounded by images of beasts and plants.

No such hedges here that he'd seen but such rampant growth of ferns, salal, berry bushes, and trees of every description. This was a wilder landscape than Ireland's, not having such an obvious long history of settlement and industry. The Native people had lived on the coast forever, and Declan was often able to identify where their campgrounds had been, the places where they had gathered clams or prepared their fish. He'd see the heaps of broken shell that indicated their clamming areas, and once, having stopped in a small bay on his way back from the store, he sat back against warm rock, stretching out his arms on either side to ease the ache of rowing, and found himself clutching a perfect blade of slate. It had been resting on the little shelf of rock his hand had homed to, and when he examined the area around where he sat, he found mounds of chipped slate where someone had prepared fish knives, sitting right where he sat. He had seen such knives at the Neils' house, unearthed in areas they had turned to garden, along with a stone pestle, a rock pierced through to be used as an anchor, and a disc of stone, carved with serpents, which Mrs. Neil told him was spindle whorl.

There were forests tumbling down to the water's edge that held in them some of the secrets of the universe, Declan increasingly thought. What had happened with the stag and cougar was part of it. How one of them, stately and antlered like a beast out of the Book of Durrow, could come leaping out of the dense thickets, a lean tawny cat in pursuit, how one would enter the water and swim towards the western lands, Tir Na Nog in Irish lore, the land of eternal youth, while the other watched from the shore, uneasy about following. Such things seldom happened in that life in Ireland, although the mountain sheep stepping out of the famine cabins were nearly as unsettling, bringing with them stories of the dead tangled in their fleeces with bramble and the seed heads of nettles. And the badgers, moving through the grass like small bears, noses to the wind, as they had done for centuries, the *broc* of their Irish name attached to the place like a burr.

Perhaps that is what I find so satisfying in this poem I am contemplating, he thought. *That mine is not the first loss, that I am not the only man to find himself on a beach in a far country, alone in the world, and that there are possibilities. But are there? I cannot think what, at this moment. I do not wish to be Achilles in Hades, grieving his separation from Peleus:*

I cannot help him
under the sun's rays, cannot be that man
I was on Troy's wide seaboard, in those days
when I made bastion for the Argives
and put an army's best men in the dust.

And yet I am surrounded by the death camas myself, cousin to pale asphodel, and I put in the dust the burned bodies of my own dear love, our daughters. My own possibilities are unimaginable to me. No bed awaits, strung with ox-hide, and rooted in the earth, a gnarled trunk of olive.

With the tide agreeable, Declan decided to go out in the skiff to make an exploration of the bay. Argos wriggled with pleasure when she saw him taking the oars down to the shore and was ready to leap into the craft as soon as it had been pushed down into the water. She loved to sit in the prow of the boat like a figurehead, her nose working the air. So many odours, such potent breezes that swept over her, carrying news of the intimate lives of seals, egg-rich fish, an abundance of ducks, drifts of kelp clotted with herring spawn. She liked it when they stopped in shallow bays where she could jump from the boat and investigate each rock, each dimpling in the sand indicating clams or, when really lucky, the siphons of geoduck. Sometimes an exquisitely rotted carcass of a fish or bird would beg to be examined for edible morsels and rolled over while Declan shouted at her to leave off, then forced her into water to rinse away the smell, never completely successfully. At night, when the oil-drum stove heated the cabin past warm, Argos would steam like a fishy broth until finally Declan was forced to put her bed outside the door. She would whimper, but he found the smell unbearable, and he'd cover his head with the blanket to drown out her cries.

Past the watery thickets of eel-grass streaming over the surface of the bay, past the reeds where nests were concealed, past the tiny cove where Declan had stumbled upon Rose digging for clams with a stick shaped like a bird's claw. There were sandy areas punctuated with oysters, the small Olympics that tasted sweet when you pried their shells open and drank them back like nectar, and there were rocks encrusted with the bigger Pacifics brought from Japan. The man who'd given Declan passage up the coast had told him that he was growing the big oysters on the beach in front of his homestead, hoping to market them to the steamships; he brought boxes of seed by boat from Vancouver, his young son responsible for keeping the boxes damp. "If it's a high sea," the man had said, "I tie a rope around his middle so he doesn't wash overboard." Declan imagined them coming up from the strait in wild seas on their boat with the boxes of oyster seed, the child tethered to the wheelhouse while the father steered a straight course for home. He heard the echoes of Odysseus resisting the song of the Sirens, lashed to the mast, while his men rowed past the pretty music. What song might lure a child from the deck of a small boat heading north to Pender Harbour into the dark waters of Georgia Strait? His own children had loved the story of the seals of Lir and listened to their grandmother tell them that humans had followed seals into the ocean and had lived underwater perfectly happily. The stories involved enchanted bridegrooms and trust. On visits to the shore, Maire and Grainne would scan the water and wonder which of the bobbing heads of curious seals might be the one that they would follow, knowingly, to an underwater home. This they could imagine, yet the thought of a marriage to a Mannion or a King from the hilly farms north of Leenane would cause them to shriek with dismay.

Argos sniffed the wind happily as they wound in and out of rocky covers. They were paused by an outcropping of granite, watching a seal surface among the kelp, when they saw the canoes. There were five of them, the big canoes of the Sechelt people, each carrying ten or more passengers. Declan steadied his skiff by holding a straggle of fir branch growing out of a crevasse of the rock and watched the progress of the canoes. He could hear chanting and weeping, the sound of a drum, and wondered if he ought to call out that he would come with them if necessary and help with whatever they were doing. The canoes glided in to the shore of a small rocky island near the mouth of the bay, not very far from Declan, and the occupants disembarked, some of them remaining by the canoes while others climbed to the high point of the island, a bluff crowned with a grove of pines. Four men bent over the biggest craft and lifted out a wooden box, its painted surface visible to Declan. They carried the box up to the grove, assisted in the task by those already there; two people reached down to steady the box from above as the carriers secured footholds on the rocks. Several of the men stood by the trees, bent to each other in discussion. Then one of them began to fit some pieces of wood between the trees. Declan could see he used a knife to make the slats fit securely. After some of the others examined the arrangement, the box was lifted up and set on the wood. The group of onlookers chanted while this was happening, and after the box was settled into place, the lifters joined the chant. Declan saw similar arrangements in the other trees, some of them trailing lengths of cloth that he had first thought to be

the pale moss that hung from trees in this part of the world.
After a short time, the entire group went back to the canoes
and, without a glance at Declan, headed south, paddles moving
in unison.

What have I seen? he wondered. It had been very beautiful,
the stately procession of canoes, the painted box, the strange
music that sounded like wind or the hollow bonging of logs
knocking together in water. He had thought, earlier in the outing with Argos, of exploring the group of islands at the mouth
of the bay, but now he was reluctant to go near them. They contained mysteries in their rocks, those stunted trees embracing the
wooden boxes, draped in veils.

At Tullaglas, he had dug graves with his potato spade, knocked
boxes together of rough pine, lifted each charred body into its
final cradle, and wrestled the boxes into the earth. Offers of
help had been rejected. No one would do this but himself, his
hands blistered and raw. There had not been music, nor a wind
to cool the sweat on his neck. The priest came, his cloak billowing behind him in rain like a gloomy shadow, and tried to
insist that the coffins be taken to the churchyard for a proper
Christian burial. He peered out of the cave of his hood at
Declan, his single eye fierce, his hand ready with the rosary.
Declan shouted at him to leave his land, that no God on earth
nor in heaven would have his prayers forever after, that he
considered God to have abandoned him and wanted no part
of His terrible mercy.

"Think of His wrath at such words, O'Malley, think of
damnation!" the priest reminded him, but Declan shouted back,
"And what of my wrath, man? Do ye think I have not been

damned by this burning? If this is not hell, then I don't know what could be. I want no part of yer God, not now and not ever. Ye know nothing of a husband's pain, a father's. Nothing. Do not speak to me again of God."

When he got back to World's End, Mrs. Neil and Rose were sitting on the beach in front of the cabin. He realized he had never seen the former so still. Always she was hanging out laundry or coming in from the barn with the cans of milk or a bowl of eggs. He had seen her hoeing the garden, running after the dog who had dug in the tomato beds that she had fertilized with living starfish. Once, she had sat in his cabin to drink a cup of tea, but he had been so distressed that he had not been mindful of her comfort. How alike they were, she and Rose, their hair scattered a little by wind. Each had strong shoulders and hands that knew work. Mrs. Neil inclined her head towards her daughter, and Declan thought what a womanly gesture it was, one he had seen Eilis effect towards their daughters; it was a way to give complete attention, of making a private world where the words spoken were between two people, their hair framing them in softness.

"We have brought you your milk, Mr. O'Malley. Rose showed me where you keep it in the creek and I've put the jug there. A clever idea!"

"Thank you, Mrs. Neil. I am just back from a turn around the bay with Argos here, and we saw the strangest thing. Perhaps you can explain it for me." And he told them of seeing the canoes, hearing the chanting, then watching as the box was taken up the rocky incline to the grove of pines.

"That would be one of their burials, Mr. O'Malley. The islands you speak of are where they bury their dead. Well, they don't really bury them but put the bodies in those cedar boxes and place them in trees. Sometimes, depending on whether the deceased is of lower rank, the body is wrapped in cloth and placed on the wooden platforms they make, not even in a box. One of my sons brought home some bones once, having found them lying loose on the island, taken down by birds, I suppose, or animals. Of course I made him go back with them and forbade the children to go on the islands at all after that, but it will give you some idea of what happens. This is all changing now with so many of the Indians becoming Christians, but many of the older people still prefer the old way of burial. I saw the canoes once and thought it a beautiful sight, although my husband would not agree, I'm afraid."

Mrs. Neil declined tea but allowed that Rose might stay for a cup and a lesson. Declan got the paper and books and made a study place on a flat chunk of granite; driftwood logs made convenient benches.

"Because I have just seen the canoes, Rose, and because it was so strange and beautiful, I'd like us to read a passage in the poem about ships visiting the underworld. Our religion calls it Hell, but in the *Odyssey*, it is something else, a place where people talk and wander and eat the asphodel flower. Let me find it now."

Declan quickly turned the pages of the *Odyssey* until he found Book XI. He passed the volume to Rose and asked her to read aloud.

> Now when we had gone down to the ship and
> to the sea, first of all we drew the ship unto the
> fair salt water, and placed the mast and sails in the
> black ship, and took those sheep and put them
> therein, and ourselves too climbed on board, sor-
> rowing, and shedding big tears. And in the wake
> of our dark-prowed ship she sent a favouring

wind that filled the sails, a kindly escort — even
Circe of the braided tresses, a dread goddess of
human speech. And we set in order all the fear
throughout the ship and sat down; and the wind
and helmsman guided our barque. And all day
long her sails were stretched in her seafaring; and
the sun sank and all the ways were darkened.

Rose's reading skills had improved markedly. She read the
passage well, only stumbling over the unfamiliar words — Circe,
goddess, helmsman, barque. When she finished reading, Declan
explained what the words meant.

"What think ye, Rose? Is it as vivid for you as it is for me?"

Rose thought for a moment. "I'm not sure I understand what's
happening, but the words are so interesting that it makes me want
to know more. When he says, 'The sun sank and all the ways were
darkened,' it makes me think something bad is going to happen."

"Just so. We cannot imagine entering Hell as though a place,
yet here's our man planning to go there. The sheep are for a sacrifice. Odysseus wants to find out whether he can ever get himself home to Ithaka and he goes to the underworld to talk to a
fellow called Teiresias, a blind man who knows everything. He is
even able to talk to his own mother. Imagine such a thing, Rose
— to be able to talk to the dead!"

And then Declan was silent, thinking that he'd had that
experience in a dream and maybe Odysseus's trip to the underworld was in the manner of a dream. It was time for Rose to
return to help with the evening milking and have her supper, so
he sent her along, then took out his Greek text to ponder over
the poem in its ancient original language.

He was reading, thinking, pausing now and then to look out
on the bay where the tide followed its own journey, in to the
shore, then out again, constantly moving, searching, bringing in

gifts of silvered wood and bark to the littoral zone, once a green glass globe that Neil told him was a fishing float from faraway Japan, retreating to take to the deeper waters the bodies of seals, herons with eyes plucked neatly out, a strand of rope, the broken boxes that once held oyster spat, and returning to the poem in its beautiful alphabet. And reading, he arrived at Odysseus's encounter with his mother in Hades, he read of her sorrowful face and he began to weep.

Τέκνον ἐμόν, πῶς ἦλθες ὑπὸ ζόφον ἠερόεντα,
Child of mine, how is it you've arrived to this
    gloom at world's end,
ζωὸς ἐών; χαλεπὸν δὲ τάδε ζωοῖσιν ὁρᾶσθαι.
You, who are alive; this sight is hard to bear for
    the living.
μέσσῳ γὰρ μεγάλοι ποταμοὶ καὶ δεινὰ
    ῥέεθρα.
Between us there are great streams that flow.
Ὠκεανὸς μὲν πρῶτα, τὸν οὔ πως ἔστι
    περῆσαι.
First is Oceanus, which no one can cross on foot.
πεζόν ἐόντ', ἢν μή τις ἔχῃ εὐεργέα νῆα.
Only a well-made ship can do it.
ἢ νῦν δὴ Τροίηθεν ἀλώμενος ἐνθάδ' ἱκάνεις.
Have you come here from Troy?
νηί τε καὶ ἑτάροισι πολὺν χρόνον; οὐδέ πω
    ἦλθες
With your ship and your companions, after all
    these years?
εἰς Ἰθάκην, οὐδ' εἶδες ἐνὶ μεγάροισι γυναῖκα
Have you not reached Ithaka yet, nor seen your
    lady in its chambers?

The passage was a message directed to Declan's heart. He had not expected his mother to speak to him from the pages of a Greek poem, she who had never left the southern hills of County Mayo, and yet he had yearned for the dead to make contact, somehow; longed, as the poem had said, to see the dead elsewhere. "It was no Troy, Mother," he wept, "but a burning house, the house you and Da left for Eilis and me, Tullaglas, on the slope beyond Delphi, the walls of our ancestors a foot deep and hewn from the stony face of the hill. I have no companions and my ship is small, a skiff only, too timid to navigate the waters of Hades' dark streams. Eilis is no longer in the chamber but buried in the ground above where our vegetables grew. I would not allow a priest near to bless it. The stone walls we built and repaired each year to keep the pig from the cabbages, those surround her chamber now." And putting his books aside, he made his way, by shore so he wouldn't have to cross the Neils' farmyard, to the canoe on its bluff.

The canoe was drying out in the run of fine weather. It smelled less of rot now. Declan climbed in and made himself small against the flaring sides. A green frog sprang from the thwart, jumping clear of the craft. If he closed his eyes, he could almost imagine the waves beneath him, around him, ahead like white horses racing the wind. And with his eyes closed, he could almost imagine himself a man untouched by sorrow.

Again he slept. The canoe was where the deep dreams came, their imagery summoned from the cedar, traces of pigment, the carved beak of the raven at the prow. Right now he wanted to dream of Eilis and the girls; in the first stages of sleep he urged them into the dream. Wherever they were, in the shadows, on the other side of the streams of the underworld, in the fields of asphodel, they did not come. He slept heavily and woke to Argos whining in the moss beside the canoe.

She was looking out at the bay and then at him. He followed her gaze and saw the big canoe heading towards the

Neils' farm. He didn't know if it was one of those he'd seen earlier that day. There were four people in it, all paddling with easy, rhythmic strokes. They were not speaking. He wondered if they'd notice the canoe he'd dragged to the bluff, perched like a bird on the crest. There was no sign they'd seen him.

He spoke gently to Argos, wondering if she sensed, as he did, that something out of place had happened, now and earlier, as though the planet tipped and history shifted. The birds were still, the tide high and quiet, and although the canoe had disappeared around the curve of the bay, he thought he could still hear the strokes of the paddles as they entered the water, *whisk, whisk, whisk.* He remembered that some of the Indians visited Mrs. Neil upon occasion and he decided to walk back through the Neils' yard in the hope of seeing them.

"Mr. O'Malley, come and meet our visitors!" Mrs. Neil was waving to him from the porch. He walked over, seeing three men and a woman sitting with her, drinking tea. "Lucy and Simon grew up with this as one of their village sites, Mr. O'Malley. In those days, the Indians had many villages spread out all over our area, and they moved to them seasonally. Isn't that right, Lucy?"

Lucy was a very old woman, Declan saw. Her face was as wrinkled as a winter apple, and when she smiled, he could see no teeth in her mouth at all. Her voice was low, and he had to move closer to hear her.

"Kalpalin, the big one, was over near the store. This was Smisalin. We spent time here every year. Calm waters and lots of geese! Pink salmon, too."

The ancient man with her was her husband, Simon, and the two men that Declan would have called elderly were their sons, Jimmy and Alex. They were heavily built men, the sons, with broad shoulders and hands which made the teacups look like thimbles. They were taking their parents around to Jervis Inlet to visit relatives. They came into Oyster Bay to visit Mrs. Neil and to bring her cured skins. She explained that she sent down deer-skins from the animals her husband shot and Lucy and her sister tanned them in exchange for part of the finished hides. There was an elaborate way of tanning them by burying them in the ground with a special fungus called Turkey Tails. Mrs. Neil had tried it herself, but the dogs kept digging up the skins and drag-ging them off to roll on. The two women laughed at the mem-ory. "Better this way," said Lucy, smiling. "I get some skins and you get them tanned right."

Declan watched the old people drinking their tea. He thought he must seem rude, not talking at all but watching, yet he could not help himself. These were the people of the canoe, the canoe he had placed on the bluff — perhaps the skeleton was their ancestor — and the canoes he had seen approaching the small island where the ceremony he had witnessed from his skiff was conducted. The things he wanted to know from them had no words, yet. He finished his tea and took his leave, hold-ing out his hand to each of the guests; the men gravely shook it, and Lucy held it between both her hands, saying, "I saw you in the old canoe, eh, and hope you are lucky on your journey." Before he could reply, Rose was pouring out more tea for the assembled group and they were laughing at the antics of kittens in a basket near the door.

His hands smelled of them. It was not an offensive smell, but it was odd, earthy. Dried fish and some bitter plant and the wood of paddles cured in the salt of perspiration and the sea. He held his hands down to Argos and she sniffed them for a moment before licking rapidly.

"Argos, I'm afraid ye have the breeding in ye to do terrible things, hearing of yer mother and the deerskins. We will have to watch you so."

Chapter Seven

Mrs. Neil had sent her older boy, David, to the cabin. He stood by the door in his rubber boots, uncertain of himself, a forelock of sunbleached hair falling across his brow.

"Please, sir, my mum needs some help. My father has gone on a job and my brother needs to see the doctor. Could she use your boat?"

"Of course. I will take her where she needs to go. But now, tell me — is there a doctor in the area?"

David explained that his brother had injured his arm yesterday and overnight it had swollen up and his mother feared it was broken. As luck would have it, this was a day when the mission boat would be at the village dock and there would be a doctor available.

"You run on to yer mother, lad, and tell her I'm just going to row around to where ye keep yer own boat."

Declan quickly damped down his fire and told Argos to stay put. He took his oars to his skiff and eased the craft out into the bay. It was a short row to the Neil farm where Mrs. Neil waited on the planked dock with her son cradling his arm like an injured animal.

He helped them into the boat as the other Neil children watched silently from the porch of their home, the oldest girl, Martha, holding the youngest boy, Jack, to her side as though to keep him from a similar harm.

"Tom is in some pain, I think, but he is very brave. I am grateful to know that a doctor is available at the Landing today as we so easily could have had no one to see him. I have set a lamb's leg in the past when the silly thing got too close to a skittish horse, but I did not want to use my limited skills on my own son."

Declan did not ask how the arm had been broken in the first place. Mrs. Neil was talking quickly, out of nervousness, he thought, and he remembered the silent children watching them leave. Tom's face was pale, his cheek bruised, and Declan also remembered the dark blotches on Rose's arms. He talked gently to the boy about fishing and canoes.

The mission boat *Columbia* was tied to the dock at the Landing, a busy hum of comings and goings on the plank leading to its deck. Declan tied up near it and helped Mrs. Neil and Tom out of the skiff; Tom was still cradling his arm and wincing as he tried to steady himself while the dock swayed a little in the wash of boats entering the little harbour and departing again. Mrs. Neil went ahead to make certain Tom could be seen by the doctor. Declan took the boy up in his arms and walked briskly to the boat where Tom's mother was speaking to a kind-faced man.

"Ah, here is Tom," the man said, "and come right on board. We will have a look at your arm, young man, and see what can be done."

There was a surgery with an examining table in it and, as indicated, Declan sat Tom upon it. Putting a hand on the boy's good shoulder, he told them he would just go to the store for a few provisions and collect them when he returned.

As they were rowing back later, Tom fell asleep against his mother's shoulder. His arm had been set and splinted, a sling of clean cotton supporting it. He was young, and his mother had been told it was clean break; it would no doubt heal quickly and well. Mrs. Neil's eyes forbade Declan to bring up the subject of how the arm had been injured and how the boy's cheek had received its angry bruise. He had already deduced that her husband was a man with a quick temper and brutish behaviour, as evidenced by the story of the skeleton and his daughters. But he was also hard-working, taking the supporting of his family seriously. For instance, he had taken himself off in his boat to make three days' wages in a gyppo logging camp on Nelson Island. He had rowed as his Easthope was not functioning properly and he was waiting for a part, a piston-connecting rod, to arrive. Nothing would keep the man from meeting his obligations to his home and family — or what he perceived as his obligations, thought Declan, remembering Rose's absence from the boat as the children were taken to school and she was left at home to help with laundry and canning.

Mrs. Neil talked instead of the mission boat and how it brought medical care to these small communities, particularly the logging camps of the remote inlets, where previously a man would have to be taken great distances when injured on the job. Many of them had died. Many still did, but there was hope for others. There was also hope offered in the form of religious service, which took people's minds off their difficult lives for a time.

"Reverend Greene is a wonderful man. He'll bring out a portable organ, called 'Little Jimmy,' and ask for a table to use as the altar, and that will be the chapel, right on the beach. He'll baptize babies and marry couples; he'll bury anyone who needs a proper burial, too. He has said that the doctor will save our bodies and he will save our souls, those of us whose souls need saving. He's rescued many a fellow from the drink, I have heard tell." She brushed the hair of her slumbering boy with her worn hand and hummed a little of a hymn to soothe his sleep.

When he eased the skiff up to the planked dock at their home, Declan asked if there was anything else that he could do to help. Mrs. Neil told him that Lucy had left some liniment made from willow bark which she would use to wash Tom's arm and that Lucy herself would be coming by in the next few days to collect more skins for curing (a deer hanging around the garden had finally been shot).

"She has fine knowledge of plants and medicines," Mrs. Neil said, "and I know she will give Tom something to drink which will help to ease his pain, too. If he is too bad tonight, I will do as I did last night and give him a measure of rum in a cup of warm milk. That will have to do. Come and join us for a cup of tea before you continue on to your own bay, Mr. O'Malley. Martha will have seen us and will have the kettle boiling for it now."

There was tea waiting and four children quiet at the sight of their brother's arm in its sling of clean cotton. Declan carried Tom to his bed and returned to the kitchen while Mrs. Neil removed the boy's shoes and settled him under his blankets. He was surprised to see there was a violin on the table, a bow resting against it.

"Who is the musician?" he asked, and was told it was Martha. The violin had been sent by her uncle as a gift, and an elderly man at Irvines Landing had given her some lessons.

"He's blind, Mr. O'Malley, but he plays any tune you could care to hum," Rose said. "He taught Martha to play quite a few songs and sometimes the two of them play at dances. When my father lets Martha go."

"Could ye favour us with a tune yerself, Martha?" Declan wanted the tense atmosphere in the kitchen to relax a little. Clearly the children were unnerved by their brother's injury, by Rose's mention of their father.

Martha smiled and lifted the violin to position. She drew the bow across the strings, playing scales. Then she thought for a moment and began to coax a melody from the violin. Declan listened carefully, realizing it was a song he knew. He hummed along, and then quietly began to sing, finding in his own voice the tempo of Martha's playing.

> Red is the rose that in yonder garden grows,
> And fair is the lily of the valley;
> Clear is the water that flows from the Boyne
> But my love is fairer than any.

He stopped as Mrs. Neil entered the room. Martha stopped too. "Oh, don't stop," the woman asked. "It was so lovely to hear you sing. Martha learned that melody but we never knew there were words for it. Continue, please?"

The girl's eyes met his own, and he nodded. She drew out the first notes, waiting as he found his place in them, and they resumed the song.

> Come over the hills, my bonny Irish lass,
> Come over the hills to your darling;
> You choose the rose, love, and I'll make the vow
> And I'll be your true love forever.

It was a song that contained Declan's own longing for Eilis, his loneliness, the yearning he had for the days of marriage and husbandhood. The great tender plea of the lover to the beloved, the summoning of garden flowers and love, the sorrow of family members ... "It's not for the parting that my sister pains, / It's not for the grief of my mother." He sang for their potatoes, the green of their corn on early summer mornings, the sweetness of her kisses. Each time Martha thought the song had ended, he found another verse until finally he had run out of lines to express the fierce pain of loss.

He took up his cup and drank his tea, glad for a moment not to have to talk. There was murmuring in the room and Mrs. Neil clapped her hands, telling him what a treat it was to hear such a song in her kitchen. Rose's face glowed the way it did when she heard the verses of Suibhne. And both the woman and the girl knew something of what the man had been given and lost, something of the bleakness of his solitary life at the edge of the water, the woman knowing his grief and the girl having knowledge of the poetry in his soul without understanding the price that had been paid. Martha played a short dance tune which the boys danced to like dervishes in the darkening room.

"Will you sing again, Mr. O'Malley," and he sang to them of Ireland's lamentation, "The Wild Geese" — "How still the field of battle lies! / No shouts upon the breezes blown! / We heard our dying country's cries ..." — and then the most ancient of airs, "The Hawk of Ballyshannon." In each song, there was something of his own life: the rocky pleated earth of County Mayo, the long stretch of Killary Harbour heading to the Atlantic, seabirds' plaintive cries over the foggy water. And after he finished, he accepted more tea, and then, looking at the climb of the moon over Oyster Bay, he begged his leave, thinking of Argos and his cold fire.

Leaving the Neils, Declan tried to suppress his anger at Tom's injury. A song, however deeply felt and offered, seemed little comfort to children who'd witnessed the violence of one parent, the helplessness of another. He brought to his mind the memory of the canoes approaching the rocky island. What he had liked best was the way the canoes moved in the water, not in it but of it. He remembered the currachs in his part of Ireland and thought there was a similarity. But the canoes were more stately — this would be due to the weight, he supposed, thinking of the cedar trees that grew around World's End; even hollowed out and shaped, they would be extremely heavy. But buoyant, like the currachs in Killary Harbour, on their way to take up lobster pots. And the canoes had vision as well, one raven eye on each side of the prow. They would know where they were, in time and space, and where they were bound for.

Work on the poem was going well, and fishing had been good, too. One day he had gone out early and caught enough young coho to pay a month's rent. It was lonely work and frightening when the weather changed, but each time Declan's line pulled at his hand to tell him a salmon had reached for a spoon was as exciting as the first time. Such beautiful fish, those bluebacks; even their fight had grace. He learned to kill them quickly and then lay them in the fish box, covered with a damp sack. If he caught a number of them, he'd layer seaweed in between to keep them fresh. He'd pull up kelp from the area where he fished and cut off the long tails of weed from the bulb. He loved the clean smell of the seaweed, the way it kept the fish cool.

One morning he was coming back from a new fishing spot, kelp beds north of where he'd fished in the past, when he noticed activity in a clearing close to the water's edge. A couple of men were standing next to something big, a log Declan thought, and one of them waved to him. He could see it was Alex, the son of Lucy and Simon whom he'd met briefly at the Neils. He decided to see what they were up to and nosed his skiff to the shore.

It was not a log, he could tell that now. Or it had been, but was now on its way to becoming a canoe. Rough bow and stern, the inner log hollowed out and contoured. The men helped Declan secure his skiff, and Alex told them something in their own language. They said a few words in reply and, turning, smiled at Declan and shook his hand.

"I've explained to them where you live," Alex told Declan. "Charles is my son and Albert is my sister's son. They are fine carvers. This canoe is for them, but I'm here to help. We are from a carving family. My father comes with us when he feels strong enough."

They all turned to the canoe. Declan asked Alex how long they had been working on it and was told all winter.

"Winter is the best time because the wood stays damp. If it dries out, it can split. We've got the shape now. See the adze — that's the tool we're using right now. We each have a couple because you need different ones for different tasks."

The area where the men worked was near the water, with logs set up to support the emerging canoe. Light filtered through the high branches of neighbouring cedars and the air was fragrant with their resins. Curls of wood scattered about the ground, and a small circle of stones contained a fire. This was where the men took their breaks: a lard pail steamed on a flat rock to the side and some clamshells had been discarded below it. The men worked quietly, companionably, each stroking the wood with an adze in long, smooth movements. The craft was not as big as the canoes Declan had seen approach the burial island. He guessed it to be twenty feet in length, with a generous prow extending from the bow; he could see that it was carved as a separate piece and fitted on with pegs. But essentially it was a log, the width of a big cedar. It seemed narrower even than the canoe he had placed on the bluff. As if reading his mind, Alex told him that in the next few days they would be steaming the vessel, filling it with water and putting in heated stones to create steam which would expand the gunwales, helped by sticks and canvas; this would prevent waves from splashing in and give the boat ballast and stability.

Declan was amazed. How had they figured out to do that?

"We've always known," replied Alex. "Our people have been building these canoes since the beginning of time. We have different tools now, don't need to use bone and slate the way the old ones did, but the way to build canoes hasn't really changed. My father showed me, his father showed him. That's how we know, eh."

In the forest behind the work site, a raven klooked. Another answered, and then another. *One for sorrow, two for mirth, three a message, four is a birth.* The men said something in their language and laughed. One of them made the sound of the raven in his own throat, very skillfully, and then an unseen raven called back, a note of inquiry in its reply. Charles turned to include Declan in the joke, touching his arm and laughing. Back and forth between birds and men, *klook, klook.* One man made a *tok* sound by moving his tongue against his palate. A shadow of wings brought three ravens to the trees right beside the canoe. *How many generations of men have built canoes on these shores,* Declan thought, *and how many generations have kept them company?*

Five is for riches, six is a thief, seven a journey, eight is for grief. After the birds departed, the men assured him that he would be welcome when they steamed open the canoe. They were set up a camp fairly near his place, around the point; it was a fish camp and they'd be spending several weeks there. When the right day came to steam, they told him, they'd stop at his cabin and bring him to the work site with them. Waving goodbye, he returned to his skiff and the journey home.

They came so quietly up the bay that he wasn't aware of their arrival until Argos whined by his side as he sat in the doorway of his cabin writing a letter to his brother in Sydney. Alex stayed in the canoe as Charles came to see if Declan was able to accompany them to their work site for the steaming of the canoe. He quickly damped down the fire in his stove and made sure there was food in Argos's bowl. Taking his waterproof jacket and a few provisions, he went with Charles to the canoe.

Alex smiled in greeting and indicated where he should sit. He was handed a paddle, an elegant piece once painted, the design faded now but faintly showing the ovoid eyes and a claw. Without further ado, they headed to open water, the three men paddling in a relaxed way which Declan observed for a few minutes and then tried to fit into. He felt wonderful, paddling in a canoe so like the one he had placed on the bluff and dreamed within. It was as though his time in the old canoe had prepared him for this, the feel of the waves through cedar, the worn thwart beneath him. The men were silent, stroking the water with their paddles. Occasionally one would point with the tip of his paddle and the others would follow with their eyes, seeing an eagle on a snag or an otter at the mouth of a small creek. There was a fine mist, not rain exactly, but soft on the face and hair, and it carried the salt of the spray. At one point, Declan laughed out loud for the pleasure of the experience. Alex reached across and touched his arm, saying, "You never thought you'd paddle an Indian canoe, eh?" Declan was warmed by the observation.

They reached the work site and beached the canoe. Albert lifted out a large basket and took it to a level area under a tree. He then set about making the fire. Alex and Charles gathered driftwood and began stacking it on the beach for another fire, which they started with dry cedar sticks they took from a cache in amongst the trees. The cedar burned hot, snapping quickly, and soon the driftwood blazed. Declan joined them in selecting rounded rocks which they placed carefully in the fire, many rocks, and then the men returned to work on the canoe. Declan took the lard pail to a nearby creek and filled it with fresh water to boil on the campfire for tea. The men were easy to be around. They talked a little in quiet voices and their silences were comfortable. They drank tea, resting their tin mugs on their knees, and warmed their hands over the low flames.

When the beach fire had burned down and the rocks were red hot, the men stopped work. One of them made several trips to the creek with a bucket and tipped water into the canoe until there was six or eight inches of it. Using a shovel, Charles lifted hot rocks, one at a time, and placed them into the water, standing back as the rocks sizzled. He kept adding rocks until steam was billowing out of the canoe. Albert brought a sheet of canvas from the basket and draped it over the canoe to contain the steam. The men waited for a while and then prodded the side of the canoe gently. Alex nodded to Albert, and the latter brought sticks from the edge of the work site. Alex selected a couple and placed them across the width of the canoe, just moving the canvas aside in those areas to keep the steam inside.

About midday, Charles went to the basket and took out another lard pail and a skillet. He put the skillet on a flat stone within the circle of stones to warm it and scooped water from the creek into the pail. Mixing something inside with a clean stick, he then put a lump of lard into the skillet, and when it had melted, he poured in batter from the pail. It spread, like a pancake, and then began to puff up. The most delicious smell filled the air. "Bannocks are ready," he called to the others, and they came to stand by the fire and eat the pan-bread, moving it quickly from hand to hand because of the heat. Declan had brought a round of his soda bread. He cut it up and handed slices to the men, then offered around chunks of cheese as well. The four of them chewed by the fire, pausing to drink tea. From time to time, one of them would make a comment or an observation, but the silence, too, was comfortable.

They continued to work on the canoe, urging the sides of the craft to spread with sticks while splashing hot water against the gunwales with a branch of cedar. Wider sticks were cut and used to spring the sides until they eased out. The cedar was very flexible, responding to the sticks, flaring out at the bow and stern. Declan was amazed at the change in the wood, the way it responded to the work of the men, and at their skill in shaping it.

"Why did you choose this place for the carving?" Declan asked.

"Good trees," was Alex's answer. "Good old cedars, them's the ones. You want them close to water so you don't have to sweat too hard to get them to the shore when you've finished working. A group of them, that's best, so you can pick one. You chisel out a little core to see if there's rot but some of the old ones can tell without that. Branches healthy, eh, and straight growth."

Declan looked at the trees beyond the work site. He could tell the cedars from the firs but wouldn't know a healthy one for the life of him.

"You bring the log to water and let it float. The side that goes to the bottom, that's your bottom, your keel. It's the north side of the tree, less branches, better grain. Then you haul it back and try to see the canoe."

"Can you do that, Alex? See the canoe in the raw log?"

Alex smiled. "Not right away, not me anyhow. I walk around it, touch it, get a feel for its shape. You look at lots of canoes to see how the wood helps the carver to decide the shape. It's there all right. Sometimes you dream it. That's best. Then we take wedges of cherry wood or yew, yew is best, to split the log down the centre. It comes open with a loud crack when you do it right."

Declan tried to imagine the process. Looking at the big living trees and then the unfinished canoe, he could almost see what Alex meant. But then seeing the tools — the adzes, the axe, and the hand-plane — he knew it was something beyond his own abilities. He would not know where to begin.

What happened when the steaming was finished was that the canoe now possessed elegant lines, flaring in the middle parts and pushed up slightly at the bow and stern. And yet the log was there, as ghost and pattern, the shadow behind the shape. "Could you see that shape beforehand?" Declan asked Alex, thinking about how thick the original sides would have been, newly liberated from the circumference of log. Now he thought they were probably an inch thick, maybe two at the bottom, near the keel. Three men working together, with chisels, wedges, mauls and adzes, had accomplished this in a quiet way on an isolated shore with ravens for company (*nine is a secret*). Perhaps boats passed and their occupants never noticed, the pattern of shadows concealing the raw canoe and the fire in its circle of stones hidden in fog. Declan looked at the canoe again while he waited for Alex to answer.

"Yes, it was there. We just had to give the canoe a chance to become. It will be so much stronger now, too. The steaming makes the wood strong."

When the men gathered around the fire for their final mug of tea, Declan wanted to ask them about the canoe he had moved to the rocky bluff. He hesitated, wondering if they would think it wrong for him to move something associated with death, but decided he needed to know. He told them how Rose had related the story of the pig digging up the canoe and how he had been so moved to see it there on the forest floor, knitted into its shroud of vines. How he had wanted it out in the light and how the Neil boys had helped him to elevate it to the bluff. There was silence when he finished his story, the men looking into the fire and drinking the last of their tea.

Alex spoke first. "My mother knew the canoe when we passed the place on our way to see Mrs. Neil. She said you must have needed it. My father said the canoe had done its work already, it had taken its owner from this world to the next, and if it could be of some use again, then that was good."

"Why would the man have been buried there and not on the islands?" Declan asked.

Charles waited to see if Alex would answer and then he replied, "Different families would treat the dead in different ways. Put them in trees, in canoes, bury them wrapped in special blankets. Now that the priests are here, they say we must bury our dead in their graveyards. Some families do, some don't. Some families went to the islands and took the bones of their people home for church burials."

Alex added, "My father's father told us that the reason for so many different burial areas was to confuse the souls that were restless and wanted to come back. So maybe that was the reason for the canoe to be where it was. My mother was not happy about the bones when Mrs. Neil told her what her husband done so she went to the place on her own, burned some yarrow and other plants to cleanse the area. It's not that the soul was still there but that proper respect had not been shown."

Declan thanked them and then they began to gather up their belongings. Alex told Declan that the men would be returning in the next few days to take the new canoe back to the reservation in order to finish it. They'd use sandstone to abrade the surface, then dogfish oil to preserve it. They'd paint a design on each side of the bow. He used his foot to scatter the ashes of the beach fire.

The trip back was quick as the wind was behind them. Declan felt in unison with the three men as they paddled down the coast, coming into his bay with the tide. Argos barked from the shore, excited to see him. He climbed out of the canoe and turned to thank the men for taking him with them but they were already on their way. Charles raised a paddle in farewell.

Declan watched them until they'd disappeared with the sun, the falling notes of a loon bringing the day to a close.

Rose appeared the next morning, clutching a book which had been sent to her by a far-off uncle. "Mr. O'Malley, only look! A book of my own!"

She held out a book, *Tales From Shakespeare*, to show him. Her mother's brother, in Montreal, had sent it to her as a late birthday gift. Her mother told her that she might bring it to show Declan but then she must come quickly back as there was washing to fold from the line.

"Ah, Rose, those are wonderful stories. I had that book in my little school in Ireland and I'm thinking ye will like them as much as the scholars in Bundorragha did. Have ye read any at all then?"

"My mother told me I would like one about an island and a shipwreck. We started that as soon as the parcel arrived but haven't finished it yet. But just look at the pictures, Mr. O'Malley!" She held out the book to Declan and pointed to a picture of Ariel pinching Caliban; Declan recognized the style of Arthur Rackham. He noted that there were a number of colour plates in the book and knew each one would delight Rose, helping to form her understanding of the old stories within. He handed the book back to her.

"How is Tom's arm, Rose? Has it healed at all?"

"My father was angry at my mother for taking him to the doctor. He said she was making a sissy of him. But then he saw the splint, and the special sling the doctor gave Tom. He said Tom could have some time away from chores but that only meant the rest of us had to do more. But then I saw him with Tom in his lap, helping him to flex his fingers as the doctor told Mum he must do, and he didn't say anything else about sissies."

She was holding her book as though it was a small living animal, stroking the binding of blue-green cloth, and tracing her finger over the gold titles, the border surrounding the cover. It occurred to Declan that it was her only book. A world had opened for her with reading, he thought as he watched her run back to her home across the marsh. He had seen this in other children, of course, but this girl, in this place, seemed to be opening a door of the world for him, too. Her joy in the stories, her curiosity, the transparency of her emotional responses — these were serving to coax his heart back to life. At times it was unbearably painful to be in the company of a girl similar in age to his own daughters. What might they have become, in the fullness of time, with their love of music, birds, their patriotism forming against the backdrop of violence? He and Eilis had wanted them to be bold, to know their hearts, their own place in the family, the community, their country as it emerged, as it must do, from behind the shadow of British oppression. Each recollection carried with it the fierce pain of loss and the bottomless depth of his love for them. He hummed a little of an air Grainne had loved, a planxty for Mrs. Judge, and felt awash on the shore of a foreign land. Which he was, to be sure. Even the Scottish fishermen over near Whiskey Slough, who sometimes spoke a Gaelic not too far removed from what he knew, belonged to this place because of the boats they'd built and skippered and the children they'd sired; strong boats and sons alike a rugged connective tissue. Whereas he might be a name in a story, a momentary pause while the teller explained what was known of him, where he had lived, the cut of his boat. He thought of the pieces that Grainne played, composed to remember the harpist's sojourns in houses around Ireland, for the wives of prosperous men, and the men themselves — George Barbazon, O'Reilly, Doctor John Stafford, immortalized for prescribing a cure for depression which included whiskey. Grainne went through a phase of just playing the melody, the single lines of music, which was how the score was printed. But as she became more proficient, she could not help but double some notes, simply at first, then embellished, decorated counterpoint, arpeggios which improvised upon the melody. The ringing of the strings was encouraged and damped. He could not get Mrs. Judge out of his mind, humming the opening; its sweetness brought him briefly home.

A few notes only. That's all it took. He followed the planxty air, its sweet, plangent notes, back to the house on the stony hill near Delphi. A cabin only, but four-square and tidy. The west room with its fireplace and marriage bed. The scullery where the hens hurried when the door was open to peck at the clean-swept floor until Eilis noticed them and scurried them out with the goose-wing she used as a duster. The weather outside with all its humours: soft rain and strong winds, hail, clear blue skies with a few white clouds scudding across as if in a hurry, mists that enveloped the entire mountain and all its valleys and slopes, rubbing out the grazing sheep and moorcocks. The beloved hills were quilted with stone walls, coarse durable stitches anchoring forage to the rocks beneath. A heart could be lodged in a cleft of rock among the gorse and tough grasses and never know itself to be lost, gazing to the purple of wild rhododendron denoting streams, bog earth. A boreen tramped over by generations of O'Malleys would be imprinted with the shape of their boots like an inky thumb pressed onto paper. Here, the smoke from the chimney at World's End was indistinguishable from the smoke of the Neils, the MacIsaacs. What lasted were the cedar stakes in the mud, a blade of worked slate.

A month earlier, Declan had fished for a day near Moore Point and he had gone into shore for a look-see. Once he'd got his bearings, he found he had pulled his boat up onto a rocky peninsula sheltering a small bay white with clamshells. The tide was low, and he walked over to the other side of the bay where he saw orange flowers in bloom. Looking at what remained as the tide receded, he could see a pattern of stones on the bottom of the bay. Half-circles, layered upon one another, making bowls that he could see held water as the tide moved out. When he had looked long enough, he became convinced it was a way of trapping fish, and a clever way at that. The tide might wash in feed and, with it, hungry fish; drifting out, it would leave the fish trapped in the half-circles of stones where they could easily be scooped out. The middens of shells told him this was a beach used for a long time. Clams, obviously, fish, oysters nestled against the rocky peninsula. Looking up, he'd seen the platforms of sticks created by eagles for nesting their young, and turning he saw the remains of fire-circles, little piles of slate chips. He began to understand that the landscape could be read like a book, if you knew the alphabet. No gammas or epsilons, no deltas or omegas, but stones ingeniously placed to create bowls on the ocean floor, stakes pounded into estuary bottoms to hold lattices made of sticks and cordage, graceful hammer stones, and knives for slicing open the belly of a fish. Picking one of the orange flowers, a lily it looked like, he'd tucked it into a pocket for Mrs. Neil to identify.

A Columbia lily, she'd told him, a plant with bulbous roots which the Indians had eaten, along with another plant often growing nearby, a nodding brown-stippled flower called a chocolate lily, or rice-root, for the numerous bulbils producing the flowers. The Indians would dry them, steam them in pits like potatoes, and eat them with fish grease. She'd said her children always thought the flowers smelled of Christmas oranges, and putting his nose to the flower, he had thought it must be so, remembering the rare occasion such a fruit had come to Delphi. He'd asked Mrs. Neil about the bay at Moore Point and she'd said it was a campsite used annually by the Indians, although she supposed that would change with the number of settlers moving to that part of the coast.

She was a woman who would be remembered in the stories
of this area, he thought. Kind, resourceful, a mother of children
who had never known another place and who had eaten food
grown from its soil. She had lost one child shortly after its birth
and had buried it beyond her house in a little enclosure of pick-
ets, wild roses growing around the grave. That was a thing to
anchor a woman to a place, he supposed. A woman would want
to nurture a child, even after its death, remember its birthday,
croon a lullaby to the seeding grasses. He'd read of tribes who
buried dead children around their cooking fires so they would-
n't get cold. A woman would understand that, he thought, even
if she might not do it herself.

One morning when he woke, he was startled to hear voices
right outside the cabin. He peered out the window and saw
Alex, Charles, and Albert sitting on the stones with a newly
painted canoe drawn up onto the beach. He quickly pulled on
a shirt and went out to greet them.

The canoe was beautiful. They had fashioned thwarts of
clean, new cedar boards, and painted the prow with a stylized
serpent, its tail curving elegantly down towards the keel. Declan
marvelled again that this vessel had been contained within one
of the big trees growing near the work site and that these men
had purposefully and expertly brought it to life.

Charles came forward with a paddle. "We made you this, for
your help, and for you to use when you come out with us." He
handed the paddle to Declan.

It was cedar, nicely shaped and finished, and it had the
same raven painted on its surface as the burial canoe had on
its prow.

"They are clever fellows, the ravens, and we noticed you liked it when we spoke to them."

Declan didn't know what to say. He thanked them with a catch in his throat. He could smell the canoe, the spiciness of cedar and salt and smoke. They invited him to go with them for the day, out to one of the village sites. He couldn't think of any reason not to go when his heart longed to be in the big canoe, his arms pulling in unison with theirs.

There was a brisk wind and some scattered rain clouds, although the sun came out between them with a welcome warmth. Declan sat on the middle thwart, finding the right position for his paddle. Out to open water, then north, past the canoe's work site, past the mouth of Sakinaw Creek and its ancient middens, past the logging camp on Nelson Island with its congregation of ravens watching (*for sorrow, for joy, how many for belonging?*), and then they were gliding into the shallow waters surrounding a small, grassy island.

"My mother has asked for some kinnikinick," said Alex, "and this has always been a good place for it."

Declan wondered what kinnikinick was.

"Look all around you," was Alex's reply.

The island was covered in a low-growing plant, like heather, with flowers like small pink urns. It resembled a plant that grew in Ireland, he thought, a plant that produced berries and brilliant red leaves in the fall.

"Shhh ..." whispered Charles, and listening, they could hear the low hum of bees foraging in the little flowers.

Moving carefully among the bees, the Indian men cut lengths of leafy stems, trying to leave the flowers for the bees, and so that they could turn to berries, once pollinated. When Declan asked what Lucy wanted the plant for, the men laughed. "Tobacco, eh," said Alex. "She thinks the store stuff is too expensive so she mixes it with this. She says it was good for her mother and it will be just as good for her. Later she'll pick the berries and dry them for winter."

Leaving the island, Declan could see that they were entering an inlet with a tall mountain to one side and rocky headlands on the other. But tucked in a bay on their starboard side was a tiny village. A dock, some cabins clustered close to the shore, smoke blooming from the chimneys. "Whites call it Egmont, but our name is Sq'elawt'x. Means 'sword fern,'" said Alex. "We're going over to the reserve on the other side of the inlet. Name of that place is Cetx'anax, or 'bear's bum.' We want to show my old uncle the canoe."

Some small children were gathered on the beach as the canoe glided to the shore. It was quiet in the village. A couple of dogs play-fought on the boardwalk, and it sounded like someone was splitting firewood, a crisp chop, then a rattle as the logs broke apart. Alex had said only a few families continued to live there, most of them caring for elderly relatives who wouldn't move. A very old man sat in front of one of the log cabins. As he got up and slowly walked towards them, Declan could see that his back was bent and his head twisted to one side. But as he got closer, Declan noticed how bright and alive his eyes were. They took in the canoe first, a smile forming on his mouth, then glanced at Declan. He nodded a time or two and quietly said some words in another language.

"My uncle speaks no English," explained Alex, "but he is telling you that you're welcome here. He thinks the canoe is very fine and wonders if you helped with it. He sees you have a paddle of your own."

"Thank him for welcoming me but tell him that the canoe is all your own work."

The men conducted a conversation in their own tongue, softly, looking towards Declan occasionally and gesturing towards the canoe. The uncle, helped by two children, crossed the pebbly beach to examine the craft. He asked a few questions which Declan thought must have had to do with the steaming because he held his hands across the widest part of the canoe, murmuring and nodding at the responses from his nephew and great-nephews. After a few minutes, the uncle turned and led the men to his cabin where an ancient woman came out with mugs of tea. She smiled profusely and indicated dry stumps where they should seat themselves.

There had been rain clouds with watery sun, but now the sun shone full. There was a smell of fish, not unpleasant, but as though drying or smoking. Gazing around the village, Declan decided that the small sheds with smoke filtering out between the siding boards must be smokehouses. Further down the shore, a woman was raking for clams, putting them into an open-work basket beside her on the stones. There were no gardens, but bushes growing around the cabins were laden with blossoms that would soon become berries, given the fervent activity of hummingbirds in sunshine. He heard ravens chuckling unseen in the stands of big trees, their throaty voices adding to the mild din of dogs wrestling and a few children throwing pebbles to the water. The low voices and the rhythmic chopping conspired to make him sleepy. Putting his emptied mug on the ground beside his stump, he leaned back against the warm logs of the cabin and closed his eyes.

He was walking the boreen from Delphi, down through Tawnyinlough and Lettereeragh where the track accompanied the Bundorragha River to its marriage with Killary Harbour. Birdsong was sweet in the hedges, and off to the west, the Mweel Rea Mountains still had a crown of snow on their peaks. Shadows made the mountainsides a velvet of purple and dun. Willows along the riverside rippled silver in the breeze and trout rose to the surface of the water for the long-legged flies. A magpie was squawking in a hazel, *one for sorrow, two for joy.* He thought he could hear the second one but woke with a start, realizing it was a raven.

The men were indicating it was time to leave. Alex carried a basket of smoked fish down to the canoe and placed it carefully under his thwart. They eased the canoe through the shallows and stroked out of the bay, lifting their paddles in farewell.

Declan thought they'd head back, but the men guided the canoe in the direction of a group of islands emerging out of spray. The current beneath the keel was strong and paddling was easier.

"Skookumchuck," called Charles from the front thwart. "Tides meeting from Hunechin side and Jervis side. We won't go through. Just wanted to show you."

It was quite a sight, the convergence of two powerful tides, the force of their meeting creating spreading whirlpools. Albert told Declan a canoe had been taken by one of the whirlpools, sucked under, and its passengers, two young men, never seen again, although the canoe eventually found its way to shore a mile or two down the inlet. Charles pointed out the rising heads of sea lions in the tumult of water, saying they fed there regularly, pursuing schools of eulachon or herring through the rapids. Two of the animals came close to the canoe so that Declan could see that their faces were dog-like, smooth. Their bodies were massive, joyous, as they plunged into the quick-moving water, their tails coming as something of a surprise after their faces. You expected legs, not flippers and a fishy tail. Declan said this to the men and they laughed.

"Our people hunted them with harpoons and cedar floats, each family with its own special type. The chiefs would wear their bristles in their headdresses. Not much of that anymore, though," explained Alex.

They were quiet on their way back to Oyster Bay. The sun had been covered again by cloud and big, cold raindrops fell.

Alex reached into the basket and handed each man a piece of smoked fish. They slowed the canoe and took a moment to eat what seemed to Declan like the very essence of the place in which he had found himself — the fish tasted of woodsmoke and salt and itself, of course, the flank of a salmon caught in one of the Indian gillnets or weirs, and carefully prepared to provide nourishment and solace in the dark months. Passing the island where they'd gathered the kinnikinick, he could see the mountains of the mainland, wreathed in cloud and crowned, like Mweel Rea in his brief dream, with snow. He felt desperately homesick, of a sudden, but he didn't know which home he was missing: the cabin at World's End where his loyal dog waited or the burned husk in the shadows of the Sheefry Hills where no one kept a fire going or a bit of dinner warm for his return.

Chapter Eight

The poem was leading him on a merry dance. So many false
starts for the homecoming, so many obstacles. There was abundant
weather in the poem, elemental forces that affected the sea, and
affected also the characters. He was not pursuing it from beginning to end but entering parts almost at random and hoping for
the poetry to speak to him. Sometimes it took him by the coat-
tails, as when he read of Elpenor's burial, shook him like a cloud
of rain until all the tears inside him had been released and he
was cleansed by the accompanying wind. Other parts, as when
Odysseus encountered his mother in Hades' kingdom, were deep
wells of sorrow that swallowed him up. His translations showed
him the poem from the inside out, how words connected to other
words made a framework, a structure, how each image provided a
layer or element to the structure, how it echoed and rang as
images reappeared, changed slightly by weather or circumstance.

Some days he would sit on the table and brood on what the poetry told him about living. It was as though life was a long series of obstacles in which a man's own nature was put in opposition to something he could not see — the fickle bickering of the gods and goddesses, the capricious whims of a witch.

In early July, he had begun to bathe in the sea. The days were often hot and his cabin was stuffy. During the cooler months, he had heated water from the creek on his stove and washed himself by lamplight; now he chose early morning to enter the sea, if the tide was right, and plunge himself down into its chilly depths. He could not swim. As a boy growing up near Fin Lough and Dhulough, he had heard of people who could swim, but his parents shared the fatalism of most of the country people in the area, particularly those who fished for a living: if the sea wanted you, it would have you, and there was no point in resisting. But as children would, he paddled his feet in the lough and loved the freedom of following the course of a creek down from the side of a mountain, bare-footed and stepping from stone to stone when the creek ran too deep or cold for comfort.

The sea was something again all right. Bone-chilling at first, but gradually the body appreciated its coolness, its brine and soft currents. The mud under his feet felt luxurious. Some days, when the tide was far out when he rose from his bed, he would wait until it had sidled in to shore; he would enter the water over the rocks, warmed by the sun, and sit in a shallow depression in a large boulder. Steam would rise where the cold water met the warm rock. Leaving the water, he felt like a new man, his pale limbs tingling and his eyes stinging a little from the salt. A month passed and his skin softened with its acquaintance with the sea.

Once, after his bath, he climbed to the canoe, leaving his clothing to drop to the ground beside him. The grasses on the bluff were dry and crisp underfoot and the flower pods had withered away. The air was warm, bees at work in yellow flowers tumbling down the rock face, and the water was calm. In the distance he could hear the Neils' cow mooing for her calf, which had recently been weaned. Looking into the canoe, he saw a lattice of spiderweb woven from gunwale to gunwale. Off to the sides of the construction, spiders rested. There was peace in the sight, peace even in the sight of the tiny wrapped corpses of flies who had been unlucky enough to drift into the webs. Nature in all its cycles went on as it should. He brushed away spider silk and reclined in the warm canoe. For a brief moment, he felt utterly content, a naked man in the vessel of the dead, accompanied by the ancient pharaohs in their spidery winding cloths.

He heard splashing, and the sound of laughter. Startled, he walked to the edge of the bluff and looked down. Nothing. But then the sound again, and he followed it with his ear to its source. He was startled to see Rose, naked and poised on the edge of the shore. Her dog was trying to chase a goose and she was laughing. She tossed her hair back and plunged into the tide, swimming strongly against it towards the mouth of the bay. She would stroke forward, then flip to her back and kick her legs in a scissor movement, her hair drifting behind her like kelp. Her dog swam with her, paddling determinedly to keep up. After a few minutes, Rose turned and swam back to shore, walking up from the shallow water carefully to avoid the sharp stones and shells littering the tide line. Water dripped from her torso and limbs like liquid silver and the weeds of her hair hung down her back and shoulders. Declan realized he had stopped breathing.

(*Oh, maiden of the white arms ...*)

Rose was a girl, yet her body was becoming womanly. Her hips gently flared out from her waist, and her breasts were swelling like small apples. He imagined Nausikaa, at play with her maidens at the river of Skheria. She was preoccupied, having dreamed of her bridegroom; Rose seemed as open as the sky.

Declan averted his face, feeling as though he had come upon one of his daughters naked, but then returned to the sight of her. He could not keep his eyes off her and was filled with something exquisite, not desire exactly, but tenderness: for her innocence, her beauty, the way she moved in the water as easily as a fish, her laughter. He did not want her to know he was there and slowly backed up the bluff until he was beyond her sight.

> ὁ δὲ μερμήριξεν Ὀδυσσεύς.
> Odysseus came then, full of anxiety.
> ἦ γούνων λίσσοιτο λαβὼν ἐυῶπιδα κούρην;
> Should he embrace the beautiful maiden's knees
>   in prayer?
> ἦ αὔτως - ἐπέεσσιν ἀποσταδά μειλιχίοισι,
> Or should he keep a distance, as he had, and
>   speak in soothing words,
> λίσσοιτ', εἰ δείξειε πόλιν καὶ εἵματα δοίη;
> And ask for directions to the town and a gar-
>   ment to cover him?

Declan put his clothing on quickly. He took care to return to his cabin by the long road way rather than circling around the Neils' homestead. He was certain they would know from his face, the tremble in his hands, that he had seen their daughter bathing. In ancient Greece, perhaps he would have been set upon by hounds, having glimpsed the virgin goddess. And yet he had not sought the sight of her. But he had not turned away. He sat on the rocks in front of his cabin and thought about that.

He had been the father of two daughters. When they were infants, he had loved to see Eilis bathe them in a basin by the fire. He had delighted in the folds of their plump arms, their stomachs, the softness of their buttocks. After they learned to walk, Eilis began to bathe them in private. He felt sadness that the tableaux had ended — him in his chair with a mug of tea, Eilis laughing and gently splashing an infant girl, then wrapping her in a linen towel and handing the child to him to dandle on his lap. He would count their toes in Irish, nuzzle their clean necks, kiss their plump shoulders, and sing them lullabies half-remembered from his own infancy.

But Rose was not his daughter and she was not an infant. He was troubled that he had seen her in the tide like a young Artemis, troubled and ashamed. He kicked a stone out to sea and watched some tiny mottled crabs scuttle sideways from the shadow of one rock to another. Argos whimpered at his feet, wanting to be fed. He went to the creek and took some fried herring, wrapped in old newspaper, out of his cuddy and put some in the dog's dish. It was too hot to cook and he was glad he'd made the effort to prepare things in the cool of the morning. A bit of bread, some meat in a tin, a handful of berries — that was a midday meal for August. He had planted a small bed of potatoes and looked forward to digging the first hills. He was restless, wanting new potatoes boiled in their jackets and something else, something he had no words for. He had been immersed in the sorrow of the fire and the deaths of his women, everything coloured by it, and now he felt ready for, well, what? It was as though bathing in the sea had washed off the stale skin of grief and made him new. In the canoe, he had been aware of his body, the feel of worn cedar against his buttocks and warm wood behind his bare shoulders. Soft air had moved through his chest hairs, the nest of his groin, arousing him slightly. He had not felt that way in more than a year. Two, and more. He was not surprised that he dreamed of making love to Eilis, their naked bodies meeting under the weight of blankets, creating a heat which he still felt upon waking.

And not surprised, a morning or two later, to see the Indian canoe nosing into his shore. He went out to meet the men and was told they were going up the coast for a few days and did he want to accompany them? When he mentioned his dog, they told him to bring her. Without another thought, he went in to the cabin, made sure the stove fire was out, rolled up his blanket, took a mug and a tin plate, and put the remains of a loaf of bread into a sack. He lifted his paddle from its position against the cabin and went down to the canoe.

He stashed his sack above the bilge and positioned himself on his thwart, Argos between his legs. They were heading into the breeze that was bringing the tide in and it felt good against his face. Once out of the bay, they headed north, keeping to the west of Nelson Island, and rounding the northwestern tip of Hardy Island. A pod of killer whales passed them as they paddled into the passage between Hardy Island and what the men told Declan was mostly Sliammon territory. It was frightening to see the dorsals, maybe twenty of them slicing through the water like an image out of a nightmare, but the whales went on their way without bothering the canoe. Mountains rose high on the eastern mainland, their shape mimicking the dorsal fins, white still with snow in the middle of summer. The sound of water was everywhere, splashing off the paddles when they were lifted as the men paused, unseen water falling with great force from the rocky cliffs, swift streams tumbling down from the slopes and entering the sea, losing their clean, clear silver to the green salt of the ocean.

Declan lost track of direction. A stop had been made on a deserted shore to show him a carving of a fish on a rounded boulder and a bowl, scooped out of a slab of sandstone above the high tide line, filled with rainwater. Looking into it, Declan saw himself more clearly than in any mirror. Alex told him the bowl had probably been carved out for mixing ochre and other pig-

ments to colour the fish when it needed to call its brothers to
the mouth of the creek. There were such streams and such
images all around the territory, Alex said. "More power back
then than now but still something there, I think. Probably a
painting where you live if you look. Sometimes they are covered
in seaweed but it doesn't matter. They know their job."

They had followed the wind and been followed by it. Gulls
plunged in their wake and once, looking behind them, Declan
saw the small head of a seal, then another. He had to urinate and
hoped that a stop would be made before too long. Just as he was
thinking he would have to ask that they make land, the canoe
was nosing into a tiny bay overhung with arbutus trees. A slope
of golden grass rose gently from a sandy shore, strewn with boul-
ders, and a stream fell to the ocean down a series of steps of
mossy rocks. Declan headed into the bushes, quickly relieved
himself, then joined the men on the shore.

"We'll camp here," Alex told him. "This is a good beach for
clams and there's fresh water. Charles wants to fish for halibut with
the new canoe and there's deep water out there where we've
caught halibut before. We thought you'd like to try fishing, too."

The site reminded Declan of a trip he had made with his
mother's cousin who lived on an island beyond the mouth of
Killary Harbour, an island called Inishdegil Mor, to distinguish
it from the smaller Inishdegil Beg. He had collected Declan at
Clogh, where the boreen leading down from Delphi met the
Leenane Road. His boat was one of the Galway hookers, a craft
called a gleoiteog, which sported three sails made of dark brown
calico, the jib extended beyond the bow on a bowsprit. Declan
had never been on a boat, apart from a few brief pulls on Fin
Lough in a currach, and this was a big boat compared to that.
Twenty-six feet, his mother's cousin told him, and he remembered the hull was decked, although apart from the decking
there was barely a flat timber used in the construction. They'd

kept close to the coastline, the boat low with its load of turf. The
cousin brought the hooker into a small bay where he'd set some
lobster pots a day earlier and put down an anchor while he
pulled up the pots and showed Declan how to remove the lob-
sters, grabbing them by the back legs to avoid the claws. They
put them in a box, baited the pots again with chunks of dogfish,
and let them down again into green water. A few of the pots
accompanied them to Inishdegil Mor to be mended, the willow
broken in places and affording a clever lobster exit room. Seeing
the land slope up from the water, covered with flowering gorse,
Declan had felt strangely restless — so much of his own country he would never see or know! A track led down to the bay,
and what would be encountered if one followed the track to its
place of origin? The mountains on that side of Killary Harbour
were wild and wind-swept, but he knew flocks of sheep wandered the hillsides, and tracks like the one they saw threaded the
grassy hills, leading to small holdings, hidden lakes, even a few
isolated townlands. Doovilra, for instance, where his cousin said
fine horses could be found, and long tawny beaches at
Carrickwee. Island life was much the same as in his own small
village, apart from the proximity of the sea. Stories filled the
evenings, and music, and a few beautiful women step-dancing to
fiddle tunes while the bachelors looked on hopelessly; this could
have been Delphi, with the men from the hill cabins coming
down for the craic. But the trip by boat had made him aware of
all he didn't know, from the names of sails and rigging, species
of seabirds and fish, the pattern of human travel over the Mweel
Rea Mountains. When he had returned home from that time,
he'd felt the world was a different place, larger and more various.

Seeing the men steam the canoe caused him to feel that old
way. Here was a world of skills and knowledge, of form and utility, but it was not his. He helped to bring gear from the canoe
to a place above the high-tide line, under a tangle formed by

two close-growing arbutus trees; each man laid out his bedroll on soft moss.

Charles used his knife to cut a branch with a claw at its tip and began to dig for clams. He put them into an open-work basket of withes, and then, when he had enough, he rinsed them by dipping the basket in the tide. Meanwhile Albert had made a fire and heated rounded stones. He brought fresh water from the creek in a lard pail.

"We want to show you how our people cooked food before lard pails and cooking pots," Alex told Declan. He brought two wooden boxes from the canoe, tipping some fresh water into each of them. Using a pair of tongs, which he also took from the canoe, he plucked stones from the fire, rinsed them of ashes in the smaller box, then put them into the bigger box. Steam began to billow out. Charles brought the basket of clams and set it into the bigger box and then covered the box with a cedar mat.

"In a few minutes, the clams will be done!" said Alex happily. "Nothing tastes better than clams steamed in a cedar cooking box."

Charles used a big spoon made of horn to ladle clams onto each man's plate, and Declan sliced his soda loaf, handing each man a thick round of it. He watched how the other men removed the meat from its shell and did as they did. Some shells contained enough of the clam's juices to sip as broth. It tasted of the ocean and seaweed. There was tea made in a lard pail. Albert disappeared for half an hour and reappeared with a basket filled with red berries.

"Now for a treat," he said. "Soopolallie, we call it. Indian ice cream!"

Declan watched as he washed out the smaller of the cedar boxes. Albert put in a few handfuls of the berries and then tipped in the same amount of fresh water. Using his hands, he whipped up the berries and water to a froth, adding a little sugar towards the end. Each man held out his drinking mug and Albert scooped some of the froth into the mugs. Declan tasted it. Despite the sugar it was bitter but not unpleasant, and he was not surprised to see the other men hold out their mugs for more. He held out his own, smiling: "The first time I had ice cream was when I went away to school. We had it the first night and I thought it was not such a scary place so. It never appeared on the table again!"

"The priests brought it to our people, too, for special days. It would arrive on the steamship at the dock in Sechelt and whoever had gone to bring back the provisions would have a little group of children following. I ate it so fast once I got a headache but that didn't stop me from wanting more. Careful how fast you eat the soopolallie, though. You won't get a headache but maybe a bellyache."

They talked quietly after rinsing out their dishes in the creek. The fire was low and warm and the sun was falling behind a big hump to the west, which the men told Declan was called Texada. A few mosquitoes whined but not many — bats kept swooping down out of the trees to make a meal of them. Argos was curled up near the fire and the men laughed as her feet began to move in her sleep.

"Dreaming she is chasing a cougar maybe," said Albert, chuckling.

"Or running from one anyhow," added Charles.

Declan told them of seeing the cougar coming out of the bush in pursuit of a deer and how Argos had chased it back into the woods. He remembered how lovely the deer had looked, swimming out to sea with the sun between its antlers, and wondered if it had drowned or found safe landing. It mattered, suddenly, in the soft air, that a wild thing had not come to harm. As darkness fell, the men found their bedrolls and wrapped themselves up for the night.

At first, Declan could not remember where he was. It was very dark and he was outside. In panic, he moved his hands around his body and found Argos alert at his side. There was snoring coming from quite nearby. Ah, yes, he was camping with the Indian men somewhere on the edge of the world. Why had he woken? And then he heard the sound, the sound that had Argos tensed and ready beside him. Wolves, it must be, and near, too, from the sound of them. What an unearthly noise, lonely and cold. He could see one of the men, Charles, he thought, sitting up, too. Declan called to him softly.

"Is it wolves?"

"Yes, but nothing to worry about. There are lots of them around here. Your dog probably comes from them, with a head like that. I like to hear them at night. It reminds me of being a boy, heading out to the summer village, and stopping for the night in places like this."

Declan remembered the story of Queenie's dame coming down from a logging camp in Neil's small boat, one of a litter of wolf pups. It was as though Argos's relatives were calling for her and she was alert to it, listening to each voice. But she had forgotten their language, lost her deep bond with the wild night.

"It's all right, girl. Ye've another place now, not with them. Go back to sleep so."

Argos moaned and whimpered, but once the howling had moved farther away, perhaps in pursuit of deer, she sighed heavily and went back to sleep.

Declan was wide awake now, and listening to the wolves made him feel lonesome. It was that kind of sound; it entered your ears and made its way to your heart, awakening the ache of your loss and your homelessness. How far away he was, held only by the frailest of threads to their memories. In his mind, he heard the shivery strings of a harp, felt the strong arms of Eilis surround his shoulders, touching him there and there, smelled sweet turf burning hot in the grate. How far away, and how long it had been. Even now, called to them in this way, he had no way of knowing if anything might be found, or where. And he felt far from World's End, its temporary protection. These men he was with seemed so self-contained, carrying their boxes to cook in, their lengths of fishing cord, in a craft they had taken from standing tree to completion. Yet this was, or had been, their home — this entire length of coast with its seasonal villages, its campsites, the slopes of kinnikinick ready for gathering. It was all familiar and known, as a small plot of potato soil had been known to Declan. And, he supposed, as the western slope of Ben Creggan and Ben Gorm, the streams running down from the mountain loughs, the billowy clouds announcing rain, had all been known to the generations of his family in their shadows. How a stone from the Sheefry Hills might find its way into a sheep fence or a house wall, an anchor against rootlessness, and how a man idly thumbing a worn flint or stumbling upon an ancient cooking ring would know himself to be hinged to the place by such fittings. The hinge both a part of the structure and the door, as well as the means of its opening.

When he slept finally, he dreamed of Rose. Not as a young goddess rising from the waves, her body fair as any man might want, but as the girl he had taught to read, a girl who reminded him of his daughters, the pupils who arrived each morning at the Bundorragha school house in patched frocks, eager for books. He was ashamed to think that he had seen Rose naked, and yet in the dream she was utterly recovered to him in her innocence and youth.

In the morning, the men made the fire, brewed the strong tea they favoured, and ate the remainder of Declan's loaf. Then

Alex announced it was time to go fishing. He reached into one of the storage boxes in the canoe and brought out a coil of line. It was made of the inner bark of cedar, Declan was told, and it was very strong. It needed to be strong for halibut; they were big fish and put up a fight. Fishing line could also be made of kelp, knotted together, and nettles. Lucy made the cedar line after cutting and preparing the bark, and it was agreed that her fishing lines were best.

Out of the storage box came hooks, elegant devices made of bent yew wood with a barb of sharpened bone. Albert lashed strips of octopus, kept cool in a vessel made from the bulb-end of bull kelp, onto the hooks below the barb with fine twine, also made of cedar bark. The sinkers were round stones pierced through with holes, fastened to lengths of the cedar line.

Once the gear was prepared, the men pushed the canoe out into the surf and paddled strongly out to sea. The area where they stopped to drop the lines was a halibut bank, well known to the Indian people, Alex explained.

They didn't have to wait long. Albert's line pulled taut and he began to ease it in. "No hurry," said Charles, "it's best to be patient."

Declan was unprepared for the fish that fought its way to the surface. It was big, perhaps three feet in length, and flat. One side of it was brown with blotches of white, and one side was ghostly white. It thrashed and flailed, turning its body this way and that. Albert brought it to the side of the canoe and caught its tail with one hand. Charles held the line above the hook and Albert quickly killed the fish, using a polished wooden club to do so. He laid the fish on the bottom of the canoe and carefully removed the hook, cutting it from the fish's mouth where it had lodged itself. Declan was startled to see that the halibut's eyes were on the same side of its head, the brown side. It was eerie.

Alex noticed him examining the eyes and told him that the halibut was a very odd fish, beginning its life by swimming upright in shallower water but gradually sinking down into deep water and lying on its side with its eyes moving to its topside.

The men caught two more of the fish, bigger than the first one and each putting up a noble fight before being dispatched quickly with the polished club. Examining the hooks after they'd been removed from the halibut mouths, Declan was surprised to see pitting and teeth marks where the fish had attempted to free themselves by biting through the hooks.

It was late afternoon when they returned to the camp, the three fish covered in seaweed, and Argos waiting for them on the shore. Albert and Charles took the fish aside and cleaned them, disposing of the entrails by throwing them back to the sea, followed by two mewing gulls. They cut generous chunks of the meat, and once the fire had settled, they steamed it in one of the wooden boxes with hot stones and some sliced onions. When the fish was ready, a small jar was set by the box and the Indian men spooned some of its contents over their portion of fish. They told Declan it was grease, made from eulachon, and that he was welcome to try it but in their experience most white people found it too strong. It was indeed strongly flavoured and deeply salty, but Declan thought it very palatable. The halibut was mildly fishy and the grease was a good condiment. He told the Indian men of having to take fish oil, cod he thought it had been, at his school during the winter season, and how many of the boys hated it but he it found it rich and comforting. They nodded, having had a similar experience at the school in Sechelt, but for them the taste reminded them of grease, and for the children who were far from their homes, it was a poor reminder. Charles had made bannock, too, and the men used it to soak up every last drop of the cooking juices on their plates. There was sweet tea to drink and Declan looked into his cup to see a calm face regarding him. It took him a moment to realize it was himself, on a western beach, his clothing alive with woodsmoke.

No wolves broke the silence of the night, and Declan slept, lulled by waves and a mild wind. Morning came with a fine drizzle of rain and the group broke up camp quickly, after a meal of tea and last night's bannock spread with eulachon grease. A brief look for a fish carved into a rock but nothing. Charles thought the creek was perhaps too small to sustain a run of salmon. The wind was behind them on the journey back.

As the canoe glided into Oyster Bay, Declan tried to find a way to thank the men for including him in their days. He looked at each one of them, their strong shoulders and weathered faces, and he wanted to embrace them. Instead, he began to say thank you and Alex touched his arm, held his elbow gently, and said, "It is good for us to know you and let you see something of how we used to live. You are a man who has lost something too."

They raised the paddles as they left the bay.

Mist enveloped the shore when Declan woke the next morning. He could see no farther than the back of his hand, held at arm's length. Ravens muttered in the trees but he couldn't see whether there were two or seven (*for joy, for a journey*). He had dreamed he was home, and this time it was his farm at Delphi, it was Tullaglas, where animals waited to be fed but the house still smouldered. There was no sign of Eilis or the girls so he knew they were dead. In the dream, he fed the animals and began to gather stones to rebuild the house. A cairn of them grew, before long, as he brought offerings from old field walls and famine cabins, using his donkey and cart to carry them back. Potato plants were blooming in the lazy beds and mint was riotous in the damp corner of the garden. *My life is in this soil*, he said as he gathered stones, his shoulders tight with the work of it, *my garden must be tended, my potatoes dug for the winter.* Declan woke with the clear image on the stones in his eyes, the smell of boggy soil in his nostrils. When he walked out into the fog, he might have been anywhere, Oyster Bay, Delphi, even the cove on Ithaka where Odysseus was left by the sailors of Skheria to make his own way home.

Chapter Nine

Declan had a mind to fish for lingcod. The Indian men told him it was a prized fish, with firm white flesh or, in the case of young lingcod, vivid green, a colour that would disappear upon cooking. They gave him a special hook to jig with, carved of yew, with a lure of abalone shell tied above the shank. He loaded his gear into his skiff, along with a small loaf and a chunk of cheese; he expected to be gone for the day and knew he would be hungry. For this trip, he left Argos behind.

Out past the settlement, past the rocky headlands with their peeling arbutus, to the kelp beds where he'd been told it was not uncommon to catch a fish of forty pounds or more. He baited his hook with a piece of herring and lowered his line, easing it down with a long pole. Then, keeping his boat steady with his oars, he waited.

Within ten minutes, Declan was hauling in something that looked more like a serpent than a fish, its body thrashing to break away from the hook. It was dark blue, with tracings of orange, and its mouth showed large teeth. Its fight shocked him, and he realized he was not expecting anything like it. He wrestled with it, losing line at one point but then recovering it, wrapping it around his hands and pulling until they bled. He decided he was willing to lose both the fish and his hook when suddenly the fish gave in, and he saw that its stomach had emerged through its mouth as it decompressed, following the herring up from the kelp bottom. It was still alive but had no fight left in it. Its eyes met his, the fish's shadowed with a fleshy plume. Declan apologized to it for causing it pain and, mindful of the spines on its cheeks, he quickly killed it with his club and opened it to clean it.

He had not noticed the weather turning, the wind rising, so absorbed had he been in the business of the lingcod. Washing his bloody hands over the side of his skiff and wincing at the resulting sting, he realized that a chop had come up and it had begun to rain, huge drops quickly forming puddles in the bilge. He had to think quickly. Two small islands lay off the headlands, closer to him by far than the shore, and he decided he had better make for them as directly as he could, as he did not feel he could safely make it to the beach below the rocks north of the settlement. It was a hard row, pushing against the current and the wind, and he wondered if it might not be best to make for the shore, but could not imagine controlling his skiff in the turbulent sea. Finally he dragged his skiff up onto the smaller island's shingle, soaked through to the skin. His bag of bread and cheese was mush.

There were some pines in a grove up a long slope of scorched grass, now slippery with rain. He dragged himself up to the small shelter they provided and sat to wait out the storm.

His hands ached with the burns they'd sustained from his fight with the lingcod. He leaned against a tree, felt it moving in the wind, and something fell to the ground beside him. It looked like the bone of an animal. Idly Declan touched it, then recoiled as he remembered the burial he had witnessed, when the canoes had brought their sad cargo to the islands at the head of Oyster Bay. *Dear Lord*, he thought in panic, *I am stranded on a burial island.* He closed his eyes and tried to calm himself.

He opened his eyes. The wind was very wild and branches whipped around, seed heads cast their fine litter to the air, long strands of moss flew from the trees. The bone was very smooth. It would have belonged to someone like Alex or Charles, he told himself, someone familiar with these waters. Someone who knew winds like these and who might have fished for lingcod in those very kelp beds. Or a woman who had cooked what was brought back from such expeditions, who might have dug for camas on slopes of golden grass, or taken clams from the sand, or softened sinew for stitching skin clothing by chewing on it. Someone who heard the wolves and watched seals, who knew the healing powers of nettles, the pain of devils club.

Looking up, he could see a platform fastened to a natural gap between three pines. The trees were alive in the wind, and the platform creaked as the trees pulled it this way and that. Shreds of cloth blew off what he supposed must be a skeleton. There was a clatter and then another bone fell to the ground beside him. Taking a deep breath, he rose and carefully replaced the bone — what was it, the long bone of an arm? — on the platform, which he could just reach. The ends of his fingers felt cloth, felt bones, felt wood that must have been part of a box to hold the corpse. He was no longer afraid but bent to pick up the other bone to replace it, bracing the platform as best he could by securing branches of pine beneath it and around it to cradle it against the storm. Other storms had raged around this island, and when he looked, he could see that other remains had fallen from trees not this time but in storms past. Trees too had fallen and lay upon the ground with their mortuary boxes in fragments around them. Birds had scoured the bones, had taken thread of the fibres for their nests. *How could it be otherwise*, he thought. *The dead must be honoured but they have left their bodies and, like the trees returning to earth, the dead leaves turning to soil, their remains will enrich the earth, a compensation for what the living are given in the way of berries, of timber, of slate for tools and the roots of cedar for fishing line.* Declan settled himself back down in his shelter and waited out the storm, feeling himself to be a small peaceful nest of calm as the weather raged and the white horses of waves broke themselves upon the shore.

When the storm had exhausted itself, he made his way back to his cabin where Argos waited and where he cooked his ling-cod over a beach fire, washing it down with strong tea. That night he slept the long sleep of a man who had known storms and death but who was nourished by the sweet flesh of a fish brought up from the kelp, lured by the glitter of abalone shell and the smell of herring.

> ὅς τοι ὑῶν ἐπίουρος, ὁμῶς δέ τοι ἤπια οἶδε,
> Find first the swineherd who cares for your flock.
> πὰρ Κόρακος πέτρῃ ἐπί τε κρήνῃ ᾽Αρεθούσῃ,
> This will be done when you look near Raven
>   Rock and the well of Arethousa.
> ἔσθουσαι βάλανον μενοεικέα καί μέλαν ὕδωρ
>   πίνουσαι.
> There eating acorns and the black water drinking,
> τά θ᾽ ὕεσσι τρέφει τεθαλυῖαν ἀλοιφήν,
> The wild swine gather, their rich fat blooming.

This passage was giving him some trouble. What man, once returned to his home after an absence of nearly twenty years, would want to stay still, talking to a swineherd and watching the pigs fatten? Yet Athene counselled just that.

> ἔνθα μένειν καὶ πάντα παρήμενος ἐξερέεσθαι.
> Be seated on the shelf of rock and speak
>   with him.

And what man would not want to see his wife and son immediately? Yet for that, too, Athene had her explanation — he would visit his palace in disguise once his son arrived back from the home of Menelaos and that beauty, Helen — and her comment:

> ἤ μέν μιν λοχόωσι νέοι συν νηί μελαίνη,
> ἱέμενοι κτεῖναι, πρὶν πατρίδα γαῖαν ἱκέσθαι·
> ἀλλὰ τά γ᾽ οὐκ ὀίω, πρὶν καί τινα γαῖα καθέξει
> ἀνδρῶν μνηστήρων, οἵ τοι βίοτον κατέδουσιν.

> Young men lie in wait in their black ship
> ready to kill him before he comes to his
>   father's land
> but I do not see that happening. The earth shall
>   hold fast the suitors
> who ate what is the life-gift of your son.

Declan shivered to think of such treachery. He thought of that Greek word for homecoming, νόστος, nostos, and how it was something a traveller carried inside him as a kind of expectation, a certainty. Throughout the poem, Homer would say that a homecoming was assured if the sacred cattle were avoided, if the proper measures were taken towards the gods. Within this notion was the deep knowledge of home, the way it shaped a man and all he did. A man might meet any number of obstacles with this in his heart. And looking up, he saw young Rose before him in her

faded blue dress. It was the first time he'd seen her since he'd witnessed her swimming naked in the tide. She looked a girl this
time, any womanly development hidden by her dress and her old
shoes, the girl he had dreamed of on the northern shore after
waking to wolves. He was relieved.

"Ah, Rose, I am after reading of our man's homecoming. It
is not happening as he hoped — no grand scene of reunion with
Penelope and Telemachus, no moment of glory. The goddess
Athene has dressed him in rags and is up to her old tricks, I'm
thinking. Have ye time for a lesson?"

"I'm not allowed to come anymore." Her face was very serious. "Only now, to tell you. Dad found out I've been learning to
read, he heard me reading the book my uncle sent, and he got
into a rage. He said it was up to him to send me to school or not.
He was so angry at Mum for sending me behind his back that he
hit her and now she's got a black eye. Oh, Mr. O'Malley, I'm so
sorry, I loved learning about Odysseus and Suibhne and your little school in Ireland. He can't take knowing how to read away
from me, though, and I need to thank you for giving me that."

What kind of man would rage against a child's education or
hit a woman, the mother of his children? Declan was so upset
he was shaking. Rose noticed and came to him to put her arms
around him. He entered her embrace, smelling the laundry soap
her mother used and a slightly sour odour of perspiration.

"Rose, I never meant for harm to come to ye or yer mother. I'll talk to yer father and explain the way of it." He held her
at arm's length and looked tenderly into her eyes.

"It's no use, Mr. O'Malley. He never changes his mind. And
anyway, he's gone for a month to work on Texada Island for the
logging company. He wants you gone when he gets back
because he says you can't be trusted to know your place."

The bully, thought Declan. For a moment, anger flared in
his heart, then subsided. A small voice inside him told him he

was guilty, not of what Neil believed him to be, but of being a man who had looked upon his daughter naked. It was an act the priests at home would have an opinion on, he was certain. If he was to be entirely honest with himself, he would have to admit that the sight of her had been what had led to his arousal later. He had told himself then that he was thinking of Eilis and in fact had dreamed of her, of making love to her in the old sweet way they had had with each other. But the image in his mind had been Rose. He imagined himself in the dusty confessional and the silence on the other side as the priest listened, the click of the rosary beads after as he went through the process of penance. He could not confront Neil with anything approaching innocence, he decided. He would take the man at his word as he had proved no match for ruffians with a case against him in the past.

"Come, Rose, I'll walk ye back. I'd like to speak to yer mother, apologize for her troubles."

Mrs. Neil was feeding her chickens when Declan and Rose entered the yard. She turned to them, her face puffy and one eye badly bruised. She showed no signs of embarrassment, though, asking Rose to put a kettle on the stove and extending her hand to Declan. "I am very sorry, Mr. O'Malley, that you will have to leave. My husband is not a bad man, but he has his own ideas and one of them is that he makes the decisions about his family. I knew that, of course, and should not have involved you in Rose's education."

"Mrs. Neil, the apology is mine to make, not yours. For the life of me, I cannot see how Rose learning to read should result in your husband striking ye as he has." He could not tell her about watching Rose bathe. His hands, clasping one another, read the knots of each knuckle in an act of contrition.

"It is not the reading in itself but that I did it without consulting him. He has a temper and I ought not to have crossed him. Now we will have a cup of tea and you will tell me what you plan to do next."

Rose brought out a tray of tea things, asked her mother for permission to swim, and left the two adults to sit under an apple tree. Tea was poured into pretty cups, one handed to him, but Declan could not find his face in its depths, just milky liquid. A few of the braver chickens clustered around them and clucked insistently until Queenie appeared to chase them away. It was very peaceful in the yard. The Neil boys could be heard splashing in the bay in front of the house and there was the sound, far away, of a boat engine kicking along. Seeing Mrs. Neil's eye, the stray wisps of hair escaping from the neat knot she wore at the base of her neck, the rough skin of her hands which he had seen in laundry suds, wiping milk cans, working the tools of her garden, shucking oysters with a blunt knife, folding the sheets she had found for his bed, and stroking her daughter's face, made him want suddenly to tell her about Eilis. She listened without saying anything, was quiet when he stopped to swallow the lump in his throat when he came to the part about the fire, refilled his teacup when his voice became strained as he recounted the burials.

"I had no idea you'd suffered such a loss," she said finally. "We knew you were here to escape something, but then that is the case with so many men. Even now, these years since the end of the War, a man might come and want only a bolt-hole and a tin to boil water. My husband says that there are shacks up and down the coast, on the islands and up the inlets, where such men live. Mr. O'Malley, I am truly sorry for what has happened. I wish I could continue to offer you a home, modest as it is, but you see for yourself that I don't make the decisions in my family."

"It has been a balm, in many ways, living at World's End and helping Rose. But I think I was beginning to understand something about what I'd left, too, before this business with your husband. I have yearned for Eilis and our girls, kept finding them in my dreams, kept hearing Grainne's fingers plucking the strings of her harp. And working on the poem, I couldn't see what was in front of my eyes all along."

"And what was that, Mr. O'Malley?" She was leaning forward in her chair, as though wanting something of great importance to be his answer.

"That I was like yer man Odysseus. Oh, not in courage or cunning, but in the way I was trying to find my way home and fearful of what I might find there. I have the knowledge that he hadn't, I know my family won't be waiting for me as his most certainly will be, although he does not yet ken that. But I am thinking, Mrs. Neil, that a home is something more, is it not, than simply the walls of a house?"

She looked at him with tenderness. "Does this mean you will return to Ireland, Mr. O'Malley?"

He didn't answer immediately, but fingered the delicate handle on the teacup, the worn gilding of its rim. "It is like this. Things have changed now that the Irish Free State has come to be."

He told her something of what had happened in Ireland over the past year, the Treaty signed which gave Ireland a constitutional status like Canada's, but not yet a completely independent nation. After centuries of oppression under British rule, it was a chance for Ireland to take control of her own destiny. There were those who felt that change could be brought about little by little, with the Treaty as a beginning; and there were those, the Republicans, who wanted all or nothing, who wanted no part of a Treaty that allowed Northern Ireland to opt out and remain with Britain.

"My sister writes to tell of these things so. In many ways, it is not the place that I swore I'd never return to, if that is to matter anymore. And yet I don't know what I'd be returning to. I have my bit of land, still, and the means to buy a few beasts, a pig and a cow, some hens. There is still not peace but at least that sad yoke of British control is gone. And I might be able to be of some use, though I couldn't say how as of this minute. I am of two minds, if truth be told."

"In what way do you mean?" She passed the plate of sugar cookies to Declan, who took one, breaking it in two without looking at it, then in two again.

"Could I find work in Vancouver, I wonder, or should I be going back to Delphi? I am thinking I might be best off trying to find any small piece of what we had as a family there. I have even dreamed of me own mother, Mrs. Neil, and her giving out in speech I'd never heard from her lips. A ghost she was, and yet it was her, I'd know her anywhere, though I mind her best in our own west room, in a chair by the fire, with a basket of Eilis's darning at her feet. It is a lonely business, meeting the dead in a strange land." His hands worried the handle of his cup as he talked. It was like a knuckle, the curve of a finger. He stroked it, remembering the small hands of the children he'd taught clutching at him, wanting him to see a drawing, to approve their arithmetic, and he also remembered the wishbone of the Christmas goose, cleaned and dried to the texture of this china, breaking apart as he wished for the good health of Grainne, the happiness of Maire.

They spent the next half-hour finishing their tea and working out the details of Declan's departure from Oyster Bay. The steamship schedule was known to everyone who lived on the bay; they'd see it round the rocky point on its way up to the small ports of call on the islands and up the lonely inlets where logging camps and canneries depended on its service for supplies and the transportation of everything from cooks to schoolteachers to sewing machines to horses arriving to plough the forest floor on remote homesteads. Everyone knew when to expect the sound of a whistle piercing the quiet of the small communities and word could go out ahead to alert the captain to a passenger. Taking his leave of the Neil garden table and his hostess with her one blackened eye, he realized he had never known her Christian name.

There would not be much to pack. The sheets would be shaken, folded and returned to the Neils. The books and papers he would take, of course, apart from *Tales of Ancient Greece*; Mrs. Neil agreed it might be left for the children.

(*"My husband has no objection in principle to them reading, Mr. O'Malley. It is my underhandedness that angered him."*

"But why should Rose be the child to remain uneducated?"

"I'm not saying it makes sense, Mr. O'Malley, I'm just presenting his side."

"Will she ever go to school so?"

"That I cannot say.")

His few clothes, one or two personal effects. After a great deal of thought, he decided to take his paddle with him. It would be awkward to carry, but he wanted a solid reminder of his travels with Alex, Charles, and Albert, a talisman created out of one of the trees he had come to know like the sallies of Ireland. Any of the minor improvements he had made to the cabin, its stove and rudimentary furnishings, those would benefit the next poor soul who might find within its walls the slow and imperfect peace he had begun to find.

And what about Argos? he asked himself, looking at the young dog lying faithfully at his feet. *What can I do about her?* It hurt to know he couldn't take her, particularly as he had no real idea of how his days would proceed after leaving Oyster Bay. He decided to ask to the MacIsaacs about her.

MacIsaac helped him to secure his skiff and they walked up to the house, Argos following. On the porch, his host poured Declan a measure of the golden whiskey and they touched glasses with a few words of their mutual language.

"Sir, I have a problem. Neil wants me away from the place as he has discovered I was teaching young Rose to read. I am minded in a way to have it out with him but he has not been kind to his wife over this and I would not like her to suffer more for it. So I will be leaving in a few days' time and I am thinking to go back to Ireland. The problem is the wee doggie ye see at my feet. I cannot take her with me with my plans so unsettled like. I am wondering if ye need a dog or might know of someone who does. She is a good lass, no trouble really, apart from her liking of old fish for rolling in."

MacIsaac laughed, a big loud guffaw. "O'Malley, I have never known a dog to avoid dead fish, or anything dead for that matter. We'll take Argos, to be sure. Our old Nellie is a little too stiff now to keep the deer from the orchard and could use some help in keeping the lambs safe from cougars. Think no more of it. She's a fine dog. Neil has his weaknesses, all right, but he has always had good dogs."

They enjoyed their whiskey and then Declan took his leave, saying he would drop Argos off with them on his way to board the steamship when it made its call at the store en route to Vancouver. "*Saol fada chugat* to the both of you," Declan told them as he left.

Declan made his arrangements — the forwarding of his mail, for instance, and reserving passage on the steamship south to Vancouver by asking the postmaster to pass the word — and was preparing for departure. One morning he was surprised to see Rose and her sister, Martha, running to his cabin from the arbutus bluff. Their feet turned up dry leaves and scattered a grouse feeding on salal berries. With the fluttering of the grouse's wings, Declan could also hear that the girls were crying. He opened the door to them and waited while they caught their breath.

"Mr. O'Malley, oh, a terrible thing has happened." Rose was crying as she tried to talk.

"Rose, try to calm yourself. I am putting the kettle on the stove for tea," he said, drawing the girls inside and then going out to fill his kettle from the bucket by the door. Rose and Martha were sobbing, gasping, as they filled the small space with their distress.

"It's our father. He's ... he's been killed!" Rose cried out the words and then covered her face with her hands.

Declan reached out to her, his arms enfolding her, her hair damp with tears and sweat. Martha crouched on the floor beside them, her shoulders shuddering as she wept.

"What has happened to him?" Declan asked as he patted Rose's back and knelt down to Martha. It was a shock, so soon after Neil's censure of his teaching Rose her letters. A foul man, in his opinion, but the father of five children, a husband, a man who tended his fields diligently and well, bringing cleared forests to life with apple trees, hay, animals with their young: some sympathy was due his family.

The story came out gradually, between bouts of anguished weeping. Their father had been working on Texada Island, for a small gyppo company. Around noon, two days previous, he and the fellow he was working with heard the lunch whistle sound and began to climb down the wooded side hill to the place where their lunch buckets were kept. Neil went a little further into the bush — to relieve himself, the other man thought — below the area where the fallers were working, and was decapitated by a dropping tree. The rest of the crew was stunned. The donkey puncher swore up and down that he had not sounded the whistle, but Neil's partner insisted he'd heard it too. The only explanation anyone could come up with was that the ravens who haunted every work site, particularly the areas where food might be given them, and who were superb mimics, had imitated the whistle. Men told of accidents in other camps, of ravens creating havoc with bells and with whistles, two sounds they could simulate with ease. Neil's body was not being returned, given its grisly condition, but had been buried in the woods; a limestone slab was to be brought in from the quarry and his name chiselled in by a fellow who made stone carvings as a pastime. Once that had been done, the family would go to Texada for a ceremony. His boots had been brought back, caulks which were still in good condition and which someone, maybe even one of his sons, could use.

What words could Declan tell them that would help? He could think of none but tried his best, offering tea and a little piece of candied ginger from a pot his sister had sent. He took a piece of clean flannel and wet it in the cool water of the creek, giving it to each girl in turn to wipe her face. And when they had stopped crying, he walked with them back to their home where their mother, ashen-faced, was tidying her kitchen after serving tea to the bearers of the terrible news; two women had stayed to help her, one of them scrubbing potatoes and the other taking a basket out to the clothesline to bring in the laundry. Declan could see the departing boat, carrying their husbands, from the kitchen window. He could also see the boots, well-greased and the laces knotted together, on the floor by the stove.

"I am sorry for yer troubles," he told Mrs. Neil quietly. "You must just say if there's anything I can do for ye."

She smiled at him and wiped at her eyes with her apron. She led him to the parlour, a room he had never been in. "I thank you, Mr. O'Malley. It seems like a bad dream still and yet here we are awake, the day going on as though it had not happened. The men who came were very kind and said a collection is being taken up in the area so we will have no immediate worries about money, I suppose. I've sent David to the post office to send a telegram to my family in Ontario. And for now we must just go on." Before sitting on a deep red sofa, she called out to her daughters: "Martha, you must bring in the cow and milk her, please. Rose, the hens haven't been fed. There's a bucket by the door with some scraps for the pig. Put that over the fence on your way."

Declan marvelled at her gentle and capable way with her children in such a difficult time. Her eye was still bruised, though fading. He felt he must say something, anything, that might be of practical use to her.

"I have booked passage on the *Cassiar* for Tuesday week but I would be honoured to stay on to help ye. Ye have only to say."

"I am so grateful for your offer, Mr. O'Malley, but the men who came to tell me of Harry's accident have already made arrangements for us. Someone is coming in the morning to draw up a list of what will need doing. Although I haven't really had a chance to even think about it, I think that the sensible thing will be for the children and I to go to my family in Ontario."

"I thought yer brother was in Montreal so? Did he not send Rose the book?"

"Ah, yes, my brother is there. But my sister and her husband farm our old family place near Dunvegan, in Glengarry County, and there is plenty of room. They weren't able to have children, and Martha — our Martha is named for her — has often written to invite us for an extended visit. She knew that things were difficult for us …"

She stopped for a minute and put a finger to her lips as though to tell him, *shush*.

"I am not speaking of my husband's temper though I knew you were upset by his reaction to Rose's reading …"

"I do not want to speak ill of the dead so but the man hit ye. Ye've the bruising still."

She continued as though she had not heard him. "… but of our hardships earlier in our lives when a child died and there was a problem about Harry's enlisting in the army. He had done it without my knowledge, on a trip to Vancouver for machine parts, and could see no other way to feed us. But he was refused because of his health — he was consumptive for a time in the early years of our marriage though working this place made all the difference — and then things improved with fishing and our pigs have done so well so we were able to make some improvements on our place here. He was not a bad man, Mr. O'Malley, although that was how many saw him, I know. He did love us and do his best for us."

She began to cry. Thinking that tea might help, Declan went to the kitchen where he exchanged a few words with the women there. They poured a cup for her as well as one for himself and put the cups on a tin tray printed with faded roses, one arranging the cups while the other took down a tin for biscuits. While he waited for the tray, he looked around him. A small parade of wooden animals, some native to the area and some fanciful — a giraffe, an elephant — stood on the dresser with the plates and bowls. He touched one, a little bear. It was very nicely made. One of the women told him that Harry had carved the animals and put them in the children's Christmas stockings each year. Declan stroked the smooth wood of the bear's back and thought how very unsettling it was to think of a man who would strike his wife, break his son's arm in anger, carving tiny animals to wait in the toe of a Christmas stocking. He felt that he ought to try harder to convince Mrs. Neil to allow him to help her with the small holding, but hadn't he sat with her only a short time earlier and listened to her offer him solace, suggesting that his place was in Ireland, putting his own ghosts to rest? She was a determined woman in some ways, he felt that, and he was certain that she would know what was best for her children and herself in the face of such tragedy. From his location on the sofa facing the open door to the kitchen, he could see the boots sitting by the stove as if waiting for someone to fill them — and he knew somehow that he was not the man to do so. He finished his tea and rose to take his leave, offering again any assistance he might be able to provide.

Rose returned from her chores and asked her mother if she might walk back partway with Declan. Mrs. Neil nodded her assent. The two walked slowly over the fields to where the trail led to Declan's bay; Argos was quiet at their heels. Rose said nothing for a few minutes but sniffed, wiping her eyes with the heel of her hand. Declan handed her his handkerchief. Then she turned to him, clasping his arm between her two hands.

"Who will take my brothers and sister to school now? Mr. O'Malley, please don't leave. You could stay now and even move to our farm. Argos would love to be near Queenie and you could teach all of us about Odysseus. How will any of them get to school? I know how much the others would love to hear your stories. You could teach us sums and even geometry — David has been showing me how to measure the sides of a triangle and I just know there's so much more to learn. Please don't leave me here now that you've become my only friend."

Declan was stricken by her plea. He had shifted his heart towards home and had begun to dream of Dhulough, its dark waters. He could smell the peaty earth of his garden, the rich clotted blossoms of gorse; he could not wait to fill his mouth with rain, the western rain of Ireland which had its own flavour, wild with hawthorn and flint. He told Rose that he knew her mother had plans that would be best for all of them and if it was any consolation, he would write to her from Ireland, even send her books from time to time. He would leave her his marked copy of the Lang *Odyssey*, the pretty edition of *Tales of Ancient Greece* where she had traced the ornate "t" with her finger in what now seemed another life. She wept at his refusal to stay on Oyster Bay and turned from him, running back to her mother without a word. The word νάστος sat in his chest like a stone, but one whose weight he was becoming accustomed to carrying.

The morning of departure was misty and grey. Declan rose early and went outside with his mug of tea, wanting a final imprint of the place. The roses had long finished and their seed pods had formed, turning scarlet as the nights cooled. He could smell clover, reminding him of the scent of it on the breath of the family cow, and how rich the milk was when she'd been feeding on new clover. He could smell the sea, too, and knew he would miss its familiar sound and iodine sting as he lowered his body into it on August mornings. A scattering of ducks swam by the perimeter of the bay, feeding in the wash of the creek. Rose had told him it was a favourite feeding place for mergansers when the salmon were spawning; they waited for the stray eggs to float out on the freshets, gorging them-selves on the rich morsels. It would be insects now the ducks were eating, he supposed, and was stung for a moment by the thought that he would not see the salmon runs he had spent the last months hearing about. The bay boiled with them, MacIsaac had said, and the Indian men told him that the creek by World's End was known far and wide for its *yah'no-kwuh*, or chum salmon, which they smoke-dried in great numbers. There had been no tide low enough during waking hours for Declan to search for a rock with the calling fish, no chance to look for a bowl on the shore nearby still carrying traces of its pigments, red ochre and soot.

Argos whined for her breakfast, and Declan cleared out his cuddy of a few pieces of cold rock cod, a lump of cheese, and an inch or two of milk in the jug. Putting the remains in the dog's dish, he crumbled a wedge of soda bread over it and set the bowl by the door for her. He had taken such delight in her over the months as she chased her tail and bumblebees in sun-light, swam like a seal, went deeply into sleep seconds after throwing herself down at his feet, trusting as any lover. He would miss her company.

He hummed a little, and then realized it was Carolan's "Farewell to Music" that he had in his mind and would not leave him alone. How many times had he heard Grainne struggle to get the harmonies right, her fingernails plucking the metal strings, a bell-like note ringing out and stopping as she paused to think it through again, listening to something only she could hear. For himself, it held the beauty and sadness of a life — the beginning, slow footfalls of the harper's horse as he headed for one house or another, the lonely wind, silvery water from creeks coming down from the high hills as he rode from Roscommon to Athenry, the startled cry of a moorcock as it rose from the side of the wild boreen, a bit of revelry and quick dance, a last mournful plea for remembrance. A farewell, written in old age and illness by a quiet window in a room near Ballaghadereen, before the harpist died in the home of his patron, before the wake which lasted four days and which would certainly have provided a drop of whiskey to the mourners, and perhaps a few renditions of the planxties performed by travelling harpers in honour of his passing.

Time to set out, time to look once more at the worn door whose hinges he had rubbed with lard, the stove he had coaxed to bake bread, the windows that let in mosquitoes, tree frogs which would cling to the glass with their tiny hands, peering out in surprise, stray birds, moths, but also the scent of wildflowers and sea-spray and which looked due east and due west, both to the rising and setting of this Pacific sun. He had said his good-bye to Mrs. Neil, though Rose had hidden away and could not be found. He made a small packet of the books as well as a letter for her, his Irish address printed out with the hope she would write to him.

Time to gather Argos's bowl and her burlap bed — the MacIsaacs might have other plans for her but these would comfort her once the skiff had rounded the point, gone from her forever. He would not look back, once Argos had been left off with the Scottish couple and the obligatory measure of whiskey had been downed with a *Slainte, sonas agus beartas* and a quick firm handshake. He had the lines in his mind, lines he had only just translated, before the trouble with Rose and the wrath of her father.

Αργος, 'Οδυσσῆος ταλασίφρονος, ὅν ῥά ποτ' αὐτὸς
θρέψε μέν, οὐδ' ἀπόνητο, πάρος δ' εἰς 'Ίλιον ἱρὴν

Argos, the brave-hearted dog of Odysseus, trained by himself, but no joy of him once he'd gone to sacred Troy.

Were they tears in his eyes or mist off the water as he rowed to the settlement? Whatever, he brushed the moisture away with his hand.

Part Two

Delphi,
County Mayo, Ireland,
Fall 1922 to Spring 1923

Chapter Ten

He had managed a ride as far as Leenane with a man driving home to Crossmolina from a job in Galway Town. A pleasant chap who had driven quietly, commenting now and then on current events and the dreadful state of the road, murmuring at one point that the barracks they passed had been a target of one of the flying squads. A small photograph of Michael Collins hung on a hook above the windshield. The man asked no questions, not even why a fellow would want to be let off in Leenane, not why a man carried a paddle painted with the image of a bird, fantastic as St. John's eagle from the Book of Kells. A dog in the back of the automobile sniffed Declan's arm briefly, then curled up in a neat ball on a piece of old rug.

"Can I give ye a pint for yer trouble?" Declan asked as the man stopped on the main street.

"Sure it was no trouble to give a traveller a lift. Thanks all the same but I am expected home," the man answered. "Good luck to ye then."

Declan stopped in the shop to buy a loaf, some matches, and a few other provisions. He didn't recognize the woman at the counter. She commented on the weather and asked did he have far to go. He replied he was not certain how far and left before she could pursue it. It was a day of soft weather, fine mist that dampened the hair and skin but did not soak the clothing. Not so different from days at Oyster Bay, thought Declan, as he followed the road north of Leenane to where the main route followed under the shadow of Croagh Patrick to Westport and the sub-road left to meander along the northern finger of Killary Harbour where the Erriff River drained into it. He could hear the Aasleagh Falls pouring down, sounding for all the world like the waterfalls he'd heard while travelling in the Indian canoes, overhung with bushes — rhododendron and sloes and the mountain rowans — as dense as the salal and devil's club, hardhack and vine maple of the Pacific. Yet this land smelled different, in part from the turf smoke held close to the earth by cloud as it left the chimneys of the isolated houses. He felt he could follow his nose right up into the Dhulough Valley, nestled between the Mweel Rea Mountains and the Sheefry Hills, the green fields watered by rain and the clean rivers running down into Glencullin Lough, Dhulough, and Fin Lough, which his own small holding overlooked.

A farmer walking beside a horse and cart loaded with turf passed him on the road, and the man lifted his cap. It was Eamon O'Toole, but he walked by without recognition. *Am I so changed,* thought Declan, *an Odysseus riding the stream back to Ocean, paddling as fierce as ever he could until the wind helped him out? And it's true: I am not the man who left, carrying his grief like a broken bowl, fearful that the last few drops might spill out onto the road. All the same,*

I ought to have taken a moment to speak to Eamon. It's his children I'm after teaching, and him helping to cut the pig.

It did not occur to him that he may have been disguised, as was Odysseus for the long walk home, Athene saying to him,

> ... not a soul will know you,
> the clear skin of your arms and legs shrivelled,
> the chestnut hair all gone, your body dressed
> in sacking ...

His sacking, a coat bought on Hastings Street in Vancouver, made of oilcloth, his burden a rucksack and a cedar paddle. The mists of Ithaka, the mists of the rising track into Delphi.

The track took its familiar climb up from Tully and Lettereeragh, past a couple of isolated farms where the dogs barked but no one came to see the stranger passing by. A curtain might have twitched, a figure in a garden might have straightened, but it was though the man was smoke on the holy trail, and the days so unsettled with civil unrest that breathing inside might stop until the smoke disappeared up the track, a puff from a rifle or a torch made of rushes. The school on his left at Bundorragha, windows closed against the rain and a wisp undulating from the chimney with a chorus of the times tables carried to heaven from the mouths of young scholars. The beautiful creeks flowed down from Ben Gorm, and Declan paused to drink the water, blessing himself by instinct without thinking until the words *Holy Spirit* faded from his lips. And then it was Tullaglas, where his old life had ended.

First he stood by the track and simply looked. Two walls of the house had collapsed or been tumbled, two remained but were scorched black, a window blown open like an egg. A ten-dril of burned curtain hung on one side. The chimney stood like one of the cairns you could find in isolated areas, erected in the deep past by the ancient tribes of Ireland. Someone had tidied the ruin, raked out the rubble, and stacked the useful rocks in a heap.

The haggard walls still stood, though plants grew in untended proliferation — gooseberry canes, a mallow, some leeks gone unpulled and sprouting seed heads as big as a fist. Declan forced himself to look towards the small hill where the graves were. The grass was long, ungrazed by geese or the cow, and Michaelmas daisies rose on leggy stems beyond. He walked over. Someone had kept the area tidy; a jam jar held the remnants of a fall bouquet: a branch of red haws, some daisies, roses that Declan recognized as those Eilis had trained around the front door, slips of which had been rooted and given to anyone who asked. The plant had not survived the fire, he could see that, but someone had brought a cluster of roses for the graves of his women. Aodhagán O Rathaille's poem came to him then: *They were ears of corn! / They were apples! / They were three harp-strings!* He felt tears come to his eyes, but he quickly wiped them away. Despite the charred stone and the rubble of the walls, it was peaceful here.

What was left? He looked around. The byre stood, supported by the gable end; the pig shed too. The shed where they'd stored turf was untouched by fire. He looked down the slope of hill to where Fin Lough slept under the rain like a seal. Smoke rose from the two chimneys he could see, Mannions and O'Learys. Farms he had known all his life, families he had known, too, and generations before that had helped his ancestors as his helped theirs. Their cabins were tucked into the hills to protect them from weather, as his house had been, hedges of fuchsia planted for windbreak and beauty, and blackthorn for strength. One of the women from the cabins had probably tidied the graves, kept a few blooms there to grace the final ground of his wife and daughters. He would visit soon to thank them. He remembered the women in the Neil kitchen, how they took over the work of the place without a second thought, folding the family's laundry, peeling their potatoes, their kindness a halo of light.

He would sleep in the turf shed, he decided, knowing it would at least be dry, and the smell of bog earth would be preferable to generations of cows and pigs. He took his rucksack and walked to the door, a few slats of wood he had nailed together with a bridge of broken chair rung, hung to the frame with hinges of thick leather. The turf bucket stood outside, full of rainwater. He opened the door, then clasped his hands in shock. In the darkness of the shed he could see the outline of a harp. Grainne's harp, in front of a pile of crumbling turf.

Pushing the door open as wide as he could, Declan stood his rucksack against it to keep it from closing. Light entered the shed. He could smell burned wood, and his heart turned in the cage of his chest. The frame of the harp was dusty, and when he brushed it, soot came away on his fingers. He brushed a little more and saw that it was really just the surface that was charred. The soundboard seemed intact and undamaged by heat, but most of the strings were broken, a few of them melted to lumps of dull brass. Carefully he lifted it outside where he could look at it in full light. A little rain couldn't hurt a harp that had come through a fire.

Grainne had loved this harp. Made of bog oak, it was heavy and dark, not like some of the harps she had seen made of walnut or lighter woods. This oak had depth and burnish, which had something to do with the change wrought by the action of the bog. The wood had long been used for furniture, torches, even fuel; a few famous harps had been made of it — and Grainne's, not famous but certainly beloved. A harp might emerge from the earth as one did, in Limerick, still carrying its strings. Once, while cutting turf, Declan had seen an ancient oak stump unearthed by a group of men, and they'd managed to pull it up to the uncut area of the bog with the help of two donkeys. The lines of it were beautiful, and if you squinted and looked, you could see the lyrical shape of a harp there. The men were cross that the neat and straight face of their bank was ruined by the stump — "A feckin' disaster my working has become," one man muttered as he surveyed the gaping hole, a man who'd taken pride in his clean cuts — but someone was pleased to take it home for fuel. It puzzled Declan that Grainne's harp had escaped relatively unscathed and everything else had been immolated almost beyond recognition. He had only identified his daughters by their shoes. Yet a harp was wood, *this* harp crafted from a wood given all the qualities of fine fuel from its long residency in the earth, as plants and roots and whatever growth that had been taken over by the bog had turned to such a usable heat source.

Using a sally branch, he swept out the turf shed so he could put down his blanket from the rucksack, a rolled gansey for his head. Then he hunted around the site until he found a rag. Dipping it in the turf bucket, he carefully washed the harp. The soot came away easily, flakes blowing off when rubbed a little with the damp cloth. He thought about unstringing the harp but had neither the tools nor the expertise to remove ruined strings, some of which might still be made usable. He ran his thumb across the few intact strings and winced at the sound. There were no words. Nothing like the tale sung by Demodokus with his gut-strung lyre, a tale of Troy and the departure of the twelve ships, the battle with the Cyclops and the prison of love on the island of Aeaea. This harp guttered of fire and sorrow, ugly sounds, a last string shuddering as he took his hand away. He wondered who had put it under shelter after he'd fled, not knowing anything had survived. Perhaps the same person who tended the small garden of graves, kept flowers in the jar. He cried a little for the kindness of these acts.

Declan ate his bread and cheese on a stone by the garden which had always been used as a bench. Sitting there, he could see for miles. In the morning, he would talk to neighbours, find out about turf. If he were to stay, he would need fuel. Just before the fire, he had spent a week on the bog with his daughters, cutting their turf for the next winter's fires. They'd cut and footed but never had the chance to bring the bricks home to stack against the wall, with a good lot filling the turf shed as well. Maire especially loved being on the bog. She'd carry the sleáns, and Grainne the sack with their meal and a jar of cold tea. Depending on the climb of the year — sometimes they began to cut soon after St. Patrick's Day, some years they had to wait until the spring winds had dried the bog out and that wouldn't be until May — there were wildflowers and interesting plants to be seen and collected to bring back for Eilis: butterwort, the spotted orchids, sweet gale, gilly flowers, marsh marigolds. There was a purple moor grass that looked splendid rippling over the surface of the unstripped bog, and when the marsh marigolds were in bloom, the sight of them, brilliant yellow against the dark earth, was a picture to gladden the most winter-weary heart.

That was a happy memory, and Declan was startled at how it arose without the accompanying stab of pain. It made him want to remember more. Maire running down from the bit of pasture beyond with the cow at her heels, or calling owls at twilight and having them call back, so convincing were her imitations. Grainne conjugating Latin verbs as she wrung the milk from the cow's teats, Eilis beating the hearth mat with a stick in a brisk spring wind, the dog herding a wayward chick back to the haggard as seriously as it would herd a flock of sheep.

He made a small fire just outside the door of the turf shed, using dried stalks from the garden to ignite the broken sods. How good it was to smell the smoke! He held his face very near, breathing it in like medicine. The evening was cold, and he put his hands very near to the smoldering sods. He sat there for a long time before curling up on his blanket in all his clothes, that familiar smoke the last thing he knew before sleep.

Waking, it took Declan a minute to orient himself. No sound of water lapping at the shingle just there, no muttering of ducks at the mouth of the creek over there, no soughing of wind in the wild roses that tangled themselves by the window. No excited whimper by the door as Argos heard him rise, wanting her pan of food. He rubbed his eyes, massaged the crick in his neck from the lumpy pillow the gansey made, and climbed to his feet. *Imagine*, he thought. *I am in my turf shed where I've no doubt I'll be spending the winter, God willing.* The turf smoke had woven itself into his clothing, soft against the sharper smell of cedar kindling, which he carried from Oyster Bay like incense.

Someone was walking up the boreen, carrying a basket. As she came closer, Declan could tell it was Bride Mannion. He went out to meet her. She put her basket down and took him in her arms, crying, both of them were crying. She murmured a welcome, a blessing, then held him at arm's length.

"It's too thin ye are, Declan, but never mind, we saw the fire last evening and I told Fergus I'd take ye a bite in the morning. We've been expecting ye somehow. Fergus drove off the gentlemen who came to ask about rates, saying he'd a mind to put his foot to their backsides, did they not have an ounce of sympathy in them at all. I said I knew ye'd come, ye'd never leave them alone on that little green hill forever, and yer potatoes still in the earth."

They seated themselves on available stones and she passed him barmbrack, thick with currants, and spread with the butter she made from the family's cow. Cold salted potatoes, a slab of bacon, and a jar of tea, still warm.

"Was it ye, Bride, who cared for the graves and put the harp to shelter?"

She told him it was. The graves looked so forlorn on their slope and sure it was no trouble at all to tidy them up a bit and keep flowers there. Eilis would have done the same, she said. Grainne's harp surprised them all, coming out of the fire with only the wee bit of damage, but hadn't enough sorrow come to them?

"And Declan, ye'll be wondering about the beasts so. We put the cow to our grass and killed the pig with our own last fall. Her hair never came back quite right and she was always nervous after she'd been singed, but what animal wouldn't so? The cow can come up any time ye're ready for her, and I'll have young Seamus bring a side of bacon once ye've a place for cooking. When our pig farrows, we'll give ye two of the wee ones. I can give ye a few chicks once we've let the rooster at the hens, too, and maybe a hen or two until then. I've no idea where yer hens went but foxes would know they'd nothing to fear of course with the dog gone. Those lads can sniff out a misfortune from the other side of Ben Gorm."

Her practical kindness made Declan think he had indeed done the right thing, coming back to Delphi, although there were moments, awake in the turf shed in the night, when he had wondered how he could possibly build a life out of such debris — a pile of stones, daisies gone to seed, a scorched harp with melted strings. He still wondered. Yet this piece of land was once as unpromising, before his family had poured their love and labour into its rocky terrain; a forefather had seen the possibility of making a home of the raw stone, of raising a few animals to feed a family, of creating lazy beds for potatoes wherever a little bit of soil might exist to be planted and improved, had named it Tullaglas, the little green hill. This was where his ghosts might greet him daily when he fed the chickens or milked the cow, a few notes from an air for Bridget Cruise hanging in the grey air.

"I stopped in Leenane to buy a loaf and didn't recognize the woman in the shop. Have there been many changes, Bride?"

"Well, Paddy the shop was accused of burning out the Fitzgeralds at Aasleagh and made himself scarce. An aunt came from Roscommon to take over the shop. That'll be her ye saw. Nice enough. Fitzgeralds moved away, although there's someone there now, a cousin, in the old cabin the gardener used, him up and gone after the fire. Mostly it's us as it's always been, but I mind that the Troubles have us more careful now and ye don't know quite how it sits. Some of the younger lads ye taught only a year or two past have taken up guns, Declan, and there's the damage, I'm thinking. Men like my Fergus refuse to carry arms even though he believes the Free State is not enough and that more must come. Sometimes I am so sick of the names, De Valera, Griffith, poor Michael Collins, rest his soul, that I could spit, if ye'll forgive the expression. And to see the lads heading into the gap of trees towards Tawnynoran, where ye know they've guns and are practising shooting at old sacks filled with straw — well, our old parents would turn over in their graves."

He did not know yet how he thought about it all. He would need to listen and pay attention to his neighbours. He knew one thing, and that was that the old order was in upheaval. On the boat coming back to Ireland, Declan had met a young student carrying the poems of William Butler Yeats. The two had spoken much over the duration of the crossing, and the student had recited poems in great excitement. One of them had been particularly powerful. Declan had borrowed the book to copy the poem into his journal. The lines shimmered as he recorded them:

> Things fall apart; the centre cannot hold
> Mere anarchy is loosed upon the world,
> The blood-dimmed tide is loosed, and every-
> where
> The ceremony of innocence is drowned;
> The best lack all conviction, while the worst
> Are full of passionate intensity.

He had a minor quibble with the student about those lines, saying that he felt himself that it wasn't that the best lacked conviction but perhaps had a sense of what was at stake in a way that the worst mightn't have. Anyway, conviction was the wrong word for what the poet meant, he believed. Conviction was what kept him giving the scholars at the Bundorragha school their lessons in Gaelic and simple history that did not glorify England but told the long, sad tale of hunger and poverty. He remembered the big talk of the small men who drank for hours in the public house in Leenane and years ago he had marked Paddy the shop as one of them. A man willing to shoot dogs, all right, and to kindle house-burnings under the anonymity of night, but not to face his actions or act over the long term to change things. And the young boys carrying guns into the trees when they should be ... well, what? Could he say that sums were worth more than a free Ireland? There was a question.

He asked about his turf and was told it was still on the bog. When he wanted to collect it, the Mannions would lend him their donkey and panniers and a couple of boys to help.

"My mam always said that field had a way of producing strays," Bride mused, looking toward the grassy enclosure sloping down the long hill. "There was an uncle, Declan, was there not, who went astray, disappeared into thin air and returned after a time with no memory of being away? I have thought of your going as that, going astray altogether. One day, I told Fergus, he will find the gap in the wall and come home. Well, 'tis a butter day, Declan, so I'll leave ye now so. But ye've only to come to the door and there's lads to help with whatever ye need, and the mister himself could be persuaded as well."

She walked back down the hill towards her own farm. The way she bent to the slope of ground was as familiar as the sight of Fin Lough below; all his life, Declan had seen women move between the farms, help with the animals, trudge the boreens with baskets containing the butter they produced for sale and the extra eggs from their hens. Their voices had something of the weather in them, a low murmur like wind, and when they sang, it would break your heart, for all the sorrow of the old songs was also part of their daily lives: children leaving for America, the memory of starvation never far from the mind, the deliberations of love, washing a dish of earth-crusted potatoes and realizing that youth had gone forever. He minded a time when Bride Mannion was Bride King, a girl with a copper-coloured plait down her back and a quick laugh that drew people to her, including Fergus Mannion, who won her with his fiddle playing and the promise of a new churn.

He'd forgotten the uncle who'd gone astray. Fechin, it had been, a brother of his grandmother. It had been a story told on winter evenings, with other stories of changelings and faery brides. A gap in the wall and a return — ah, if only that had been his own story. A life interrupted but then continuing in the way it had been begun with no memory of hardship or grief.

He surveyed his yard. What first? An oar must be planted for those who would never again see the ocean.

> οὐδ' ἄρα τοί γ' ἴσασι νέας φοινικοπαρήους,
> knowing nothing of ships with painted prows,
> οὐδ' εὑῆρε' ἐρετμά, τά τε πτερὰ νηυσὶ
> πέλονται.
> knowing nothing of well-fitted ships that
> could fly.

Declan put his raven paddle in the soil near the graves, thinking of the cedar canoe and how much Maire in particular would have loved its speed, and said the words of the ancient poem. Then he walked over the threshold of his front door into the open, derelict space that had been his kitchen. Remnants of a swallow's nest rested on a shelf in the standing wall, a few shards of eggshell on the ground beneath. He studied what was left, a smear of yolk against the fragile shell, and began to formulate a plan in his head.

Chapter Eleven

ὥς οἱ μεὺ τοιαῦτα πρὸς ἀλλήλους ἀγόρευον,
This was what they spoke of to one another,
ἑσταότ᾽ εἰν Ἀίδαο δόμοις, ὑπὸ κεύθεσι γαίης.
under the depths of earth in the house of Hades.

Declan was sitting by the graves, reading the *Odyssey* aloud.
The girls had loved the evenings when he read to them in firelight, saying that shadows and darkness made their imaginations
work harder. "Aye, and my eyes, too," was his reply. The day had
dawned grey but was not raining, and Declan put in some few
hours bracing the walls that still stood with whatever timber he
could find, including fence posts; he stacked rocks where he
thought they might best fit, and in the shelter of the byre he made
a cooking area with stones already blackened with soot. In doing
so, he remembered walking the surrounding hills as a boy and

finding the strange standing stones, some with whorls of carving, and the ancient, lichened fire-circles at Cartrún An Phúna, indicating a kind of occupancy over thousands of years. Sometimes he would encounter an official-looking fellow in plus-fours sketching the sites; the men would ask if he knew other such places, and one of them told him stories of the old tribes that had lived in Ireland, when there were wolves and the elk whose antlers would rise out of the bogs, wide as any tree branch. He showed one man the place on the hill where he had looked down to see stone rubble in the shape of a circle. That man was very excited, and for some time after, Declan would see groups working in the area with shovels and brushes. On Inishdegil, there had been middens, he remembered, full of shells, limpets' and mussels', as well as flakes of tools, and it was there he'd been shown the site of a tomb — a wedge of rocks looking out to sea, the entrance so low that a man would have to bend to enter. As in the poem, it would be like entering a passage into the depths of the earth. Would a man emerge as he had gone in? Or was it only in poetry and the Bible that men walked out of the underworld changed but alive?

He boiled a kettle of water on an old grate balanced on his ring of stones, the fire licking the bottom of the vessel. He wished he had a cedar box for cooking, remembering the clean flavour of clams steamed with the hot rocks. What an experience that had been, sitting with his friends on a beach far from any lights or settlement, eating clams, and later listening to wolves. He was suddenly very lonely. He imagined Alex, Charles, and Albert even now paddling over to Cetx'anax, watched by sea lions, the sky hung with eagles. If he remained very still, he could hear them talking, or was it the wind coming down off Oughty Craggy?

The harp rested in its corner of the shed. Declan polished it again to remove every bit of soot, the dark oak gleaming, and as much for the sense that it was something he had seen Grainne do again and again. She had discovered that it was not common for a harp to be made of bog oak. Mostly they were ash, or walnut, or willow. There was one, called the Downhill harp for the place of its making two hundred years earlier; it was bog oak, she learned, and played by an Ulster harpist named Denis O'Hampsey. Grainne had read about him and knew the harp still existed in someone's collection. She had hoped to see the famous harps if she managed to find a way to attend the Royal Irish Academy of Music in Dublin; the Brian Boru harp was kept at Trinity College, and there were others she knew of. Declan determined, as he rubbed at the soot, to see them for her one day. He would rebuild the house and try to see the world as his daughters had dreamed to, the way his wife, lingering by the doorstep with her broom, had foreseen the passage of the girls to Dublin or Cork or beyond.

He would go to the bog for his turf, he decided. He might be able to salvage bits and scraws from the corners of the shed, enough for a week or two, but that would not do to offer comfort when the winter promised to be hard enough: no house proper, no potatoes but what might be left in the lazy beds, no prospect of music of an evening when the chores were done and the kettle filled for the morning.

Fergus Mannion was happy to lend his donkey and the hazel creels for bringing back the turf. He'd be happy to come himself, he said, but was after hurting his back digging the spuds. Young Mannions were produced and offered, but Declan said he'd be fine on his own with the donkey. The tea Bride produced went down nicely, along with a piece of her bread spread with thick butter and crabapple jelly. They shared some talk of the area — who had married, who had died, God rest their souls — and then there was a silence. Fergus Mannion cleared his throat.

"Just so it's said, Declan. The men, the Black and Tans, who burned ye out were taken by a few of the lads and shot in the backs as they were being marched towards Westport where the Republicans were conducting trials. That's the way of it. We need not speak of it again. But ye will find, being back, that opinions differ as to the direction the country should be moving towards, with Ulster or without. I mind that we are all Irish, have our families to provide for, and each other, and the sun is still setting across the Mweel Rea Mountains, same as it always has, for my parents, and theirs before. And my family still needs potatoes, Treaty or not. There has been too much bloodshed for family to be against family so. And neighbours, for that matter."

Declan thanked him for the information. To be sure, he had had moments when he thought he must do something other than weep — file a report, find the men; there was no telling what might be done. As he walked up onto the bog with the placid donkey, he mused about what he had been told. He was not a vengeful man, or had not yet known himself to be so. When he had been teaching the local children, there had been a father, now and then, who would make life difficult for him, who would not want his child to learn about evolution, or who would grudge the time a daughter spent in the classroom when she might be scrubbing floors in one of the big houses in the area or else carding wool at Leenane. Declan would speak to the man as reasonably as he could, keeping in mind that most wanted the best for their children and felt helpless at their own lack of learning when they believed their wishes were being ignored. Sometimes the child would carry the father's hostility, and Declan would remind himself that hard lives awaited many of these young people and he would strive to make his school harmonious. What times they were passing through. A Civil War they called it, with Sinn Fein and those supporting the Treaty struggling against one another. There was insurrection and violence. How ironic, Declan thought, that *civil* and *civility* had the same root.

His was the only turf still on the bog, the rickles standing like cairns on the dark earth, visible for miles. The girls had helped with the footing, and Declan touched a few of the turfs for the comfort of their footprints, the passage of ghosts over the surface of the rickle. Then he began to load the creels. At one point, he noticed some turfs dislodged at the side of a rickle and poked with his toe to see if an animal might emerge from what looked like a tunnel. His toe came up against something that was not turf and was not an animal seeking shelter in the drying earth. He reached into the tunnel and touched cloth of some kind. He pulled. Something heavy, something wrapped in oilcloth. He pulled it all the way out to discover it was a bundle of rifles, Enfields, all oiled and gleaming.

For a moment, Declan could not think straight, could only feel sick and bruised. He looked around, half-expecting to see someone watching him. It was an ugly find, rifles in his winter fuel. Who had placed the bundle here, taking advantage of the fact that no one would touch the turf of a man who had lost a family, who might never return? And what could be done with the rifles? He wanted them to disappear into thin air but supposed that would not happen, so he pushed the bundle back into its burrow like a reluctant weasel. At least it did not snap at his ankle. He finished filling the creels and walked beside the donkey down from the bog towards his home. He passed a few men working on a length of wall. They waved and said 'twas a good day for bringing home the turf. Stopping at Mannions, he told Fergus what he'd found in the turf pile.

Fergus was quiet. For a moment Declan wondered if he'd made a terrible mistake telling anyone about the rifles. He had been away, he didn't know who might be drilling the lads in the gap by Tawnynoran. But he quickly remembered that Fergus had lent his donkey, that Bride had been upset about the boys and their drills; they wouldn't send him to his own turf if they knew it held a cache of rifles.

"Declan, I am of two minds about the guns. This is not an unused road and I know Bride has told you of doings in the gap so I'm thinking they're put there by local men. I'd like to take the bundle out to the middle of Fin Lough and hurl it into the deep water so, for all the good it would do. I know I don't want them here and I'd say ye've the same aversion to them yerself. I'd not tell the Garda. With feelings as they are, I'm thinking that it would not go right with some. It's possible they've been left and forgotten. And just as possible they've not been forgotten. We'll take a cup of Bride's tea and then we'll go and see so."

One of the Mannion boys was dispatched to take the donkey to Declan's farm and unload the turf, his father asking him to stack it neatly along the wall of the shed. The two men walked back to the bog, carrying some creels, both of them a little uneasy on the road they had known all their lives. From the position of the rickle, they could see the bundle had been removed; the side of the stack had collapsed a little.

"I was that uneasy, Fergus, as though I was being watched, and this a bog I've worked since childhood. That's the way of it, I'm thinking. There are eyes in the country that were not there before."

Each man filled a creel from the violated rickle, Fergus wincing as the weight nagged his cricked back, carrying it back down the road in order that the trip not be without consequence. They stacked the dry bricks in the pig byre as there was no eastern wall remaining to protect the fuel from the damp winds blowing in from the west and Declan did not want to share the entire of his own shelter with turf, there being scarcely enough room for his bedroll and few belongings.

Fergus Mannion encouraged him to keep the donkey until all his turf was home. Declan hobbled the animal and took the scythe from behind the shed to cut some grass for its dinner. Then he made a fire with the remains of the old turf and sat in the doorway of the shed, warming his hands over the low, smouldering mound. He would not let the memory of the rifles alter what was in his heart: a gladness for the fire and the stores of fuel, the temporary gift of a donkey to assist with his burden and to offer a kind of company as it munched the grass he had cut for it. Yet he thought of Odysseus, returned to wife and son, revealed to father by his knowledge of the trees, and he could not help but feel alone. There were no photographs, even, although a tinker had sketched Maire at a cattle fair once and Eilis had framed the bit of yellowed paper. That would be gone, too, sent up to the heavens in ash, like the clothing that might still contain a daughter's odour, like the bits of furniture polished clean by their hands. He walked to the graves and sat by them. *They were harpstrings!* He must learn to hear this new music, coming deeply from their earth and the recesses of memory, must learn how to talk to them in the queer language of Hades. It would not happen all at once. How could it? Yet he remembered how comforted he had been to find Bride's jar of flowers and how he had known there was meaning in the act. Wind rustled in the stalks of wild-growing barley, seeded from an unharvested crop, and he leaned into the sound of it, listening. Once he had imagined the voices of those who died near Dhulough, thin cries of hunger as the bodies of the dead were tumbled into bog workings. Listening was a way of keeping something alive, if only names, dates held in a parenthesis of longing.

He had in his mind a letter. He wanted Rose to know he had arrived safely and that Grainne's harp had survived the fire. He wanted her to know about the bog, how his turf was neatly stacked (he would not mention the rifles), still as they'd left it, branded with the prints of his daughters' boots, and how the marsh marigolds had thrown their seed pods to the wind. He wanted to tell her he had smelled home as soon as he'd been left off in Leenane, the blue smoke leading him to Delphi as surely as any map, while the hedges on the roadsides glowed with the last fuchsias. *Rose,* he would say, *I'm sorry to have missed the salmon but these creeks are running down from Ben Gorm like music and I am after feeding Fergus Mannion's donkey to ready him for a good morning's work. I have put aside the poem for now, Rose, but intend to work on it again once I have more than the turf shed over my head at night. I want to send you the lines where Odysseus visits his father and remembers aloud the trees the two planted, ready to be kissed alive by the god of summer days.*

So a letter would be written and sent off from the post office in Leenane to travel, like the wanderer himself, over two oceans to arrive at Oyster Bay, and then forwarded to Dunvegan, Glengarry County. And a girl, wearing the new knowledge of reading as carefully as one might wear jewels, would sit under an autumn apple tree to read of figs and harps and might, if she closed her eyes, smell the roasting pig, taste the amber wine from vines planted in Odysseus's youth.

He brought a pan of water down from the creek and put it on a flat stone by his shed. It was an old pan, an enamelled one they had used to boil up the hens' mash, flakes of the paint broken off and rust showing through. He wanted to wash away the work of the bog and began by pulling off his shirt. Leaning over the water, he caught sight of himself and startled again to find himself so unchanged. At World's End, he had imagined himself old, at the very end of his days on earth, a man washed up on the furthest shore from home, the man discovered by Nausikaa who hid himself with a fringe of leaves. But this reflective man, he might still be the lad who courted Eilis, hair a little thinner but still dark, eyes blue as a summer sky — he had been told this once and never forgot it — and shoulders as suited for labour as teaching the young their letters. He could use a shave, he supposed, and would heat water the next day for that purpose, once he'd looked out his gear in his rucksack. For now he dipped a handkerchief in water from a stream whose route he had followed as a boy to its rocky birthplace high on Ben Creggan. A marvel how water emerged from the earth, clean and cold, its entrance heralded by cress and a few reeds. And a marvel to feel it on his chest and arms, drops of it wrung from the square of worn linen and entering the pores of his skin.

On the fence by his path, where his land met the road, he found a note weighted down with a stone. *Sir*, it read, *sorry for your troubles. You were not meant to see what you saw. Don't worry as we never meant you harm. If you think back to your lessons, you will know why we are doing this. Erin go bragh, and God bless you Mr. O'Malley.* He was moved by the note, that fierce young men with dreams of Irish freedom would take the time to apologize to a schoolmaster. He remembered those lessons to be sure but was ashamed to think how sickened he'd felt at the sight of rifles in his turf. What had he imagined would bring his country its independence from British rule? Poetry, or the old tunes of a blind harper? In all his dreams, he had not imagined bloodshed, or rifles as heraldic emblems of boys coming into manhood.

Word had gone out to say he was back. A passing farmer would stop and offer him a spade, a cabbage, a few hours labour for the rebuilding of his house. A young lad, wearing the gleaming ring of new marriage, stopped to say that his missus had said Declan could be sure of a welcoming meal if ever he would honour them by knocking on their door. It took Declan a few minutes to realize that the young man was Padraig Breen, a boy he had taught and given up after realizing that the lad wanted only to court Pegeen Devaney, daughter of the horse-dealing tinker from beyond Tawnyard Lough. And she would be the missus, Declan decided, as he shook young Breen's hand and told him he was surely grateful for the invitation.

O'Learys below brought up a few hens, one of which Miceal admitted would be as good in the pot as out, she was that stringy and no great layer. But Declan thought the occasional egg would prove more useful than one meal of tough chicken and let the bird peck for bugs in the haggard. Mrs. O'Leary, whose family had owned the farm for as many generations as Declan's had owned theirs, an unusual length of ownership for lands so close to those held by the Marquess of Sligo, came up the hill with a much-mended blanket and a small stool. After surveying the turf shed, she returned with a ticking made of faded flour sacks stuffed with feathers. She told him she would not hear of the schoolmaster sleeping direct on the bare ground and if there was anything else he could think of, he was to let her know and she would find a way to help him.

People appeared with tools and the means for making mortar and slowly the walls of the house were constructed. The gamekeeper at the nearby hunting lodge came with a window, someone else had enough boards for a door. The tinkers from beyond Tawnyard Lough made hinges and hasps and provided a kettle, Devaney remembering how patient Declan had been with his children who came to school so sporadically that they forgot more about sums than they remembered although there were no children like them for their knowledge of animals and the river. They could catch trout with their bare hands, and one of the girls could summon otters with a curious call that was almost the only sound she made.

At night Declan would sit in the doorway of the turf shed with his small fire sizzling in rain and listen to his hens fuss in their makeshift coop. Foxes lurked in his fields, and he knew he would have to get a dog before the winter was through. Some mornings he would see the vixen in her pretty coat and she would meet his eye for a moment or two before vanishing into the side of the hill. He salvaged potatoes from forgotten beds, scrubbing them in creek water, and once marvelling at one, perfectly round, on which the markings of earth outlined the continents of the world as exact as a globe. He remembered jabbing his finger at random on the library globe in Seattle that day when he'd been directed by fate to Oyster Bay. He turned the potato in his hands, brushing at the soil until the world disappeared.

He was waiting for something, he couldn't have said what, but one morning he looked up from fitting a window into the eastern wall of the house and saw a woman framed within it, standing at the top of the boreen leading up from the Delphi road. He thought at first it was a warping of the glass, a flaw, so that looking through it a man would be dizzy, disoriented, and he rubbed at the window. She was still there, hatless, with dark hair in a plait reaching down below her shoulder, and she was carrying a basket. He put down his tools and walked around to the other side of the house, his hand extended in welcome.

Chapter Twelve

She was the cousin of the man from the big house near Aasleagh Falls, the house that had been burnt, the one with the wolfhounds and the harp-playing daughter. Una Fitzgerald, she was called, and he remembered that Eilis had met her when the cousin had been staying at the big house. Eilis had been invited to make some tinctures with Elizabeth Fitzgerald and came home to tell of a young woman of uncommon intelligence, who argued with her cousin in a spirited way about politics and religion. Hugh and Elizabeth had moved to London, unable to reconcile themselves to living in the area after the fire, and Una had joined them for a time, her own parents having removed themselves to France, but she missed Ireland, "even though many don't consider me Irish at all!" After returning to live for a time in a flat overlooking Stephen's Green in Dublin, she had come to Marshlands to live in the groundskeeper's cabin, which had not been burned; and certainly a groundskeeper was no longer needed for a garden gone wild, haunted by peacocks and pheasants left to fend for themselves.

"It was our grandfather's house," Una told him, "and there were so many happy summers, wading in the river and rowing in Killary Harbour. I do understand why Hugh couldn't stay. Being burned out by people you've known for years, well, how could you want to go on living there, as though nothing had happened, always wondering who had given the order? No one was willing to *do* anything about it afterwards. Yet I do believe that it wasn't directed at Hugh and Elizabeth personally, if I may say that, but at what they represented. And Elizabeth was so distressed by your tragedy that I think it was part of what made them certain they couldn't live here any longer."

Declan thought about this for a moment. "Aye, the problem was never between our families so. Eilis's first thought at hearing about Marshlands was to offer whatever she could. But as ye know, the retaliation was swift and terrible. I mind that your cousin made such generous gifts to the school, and of course there was the sheet music your younger cousin gave to Grainne. Ah, the whole thing was so sad, it drove me to Canada, a little cabin by the ocean."

The two of them talked carefully. Una Fitzgerald was surprised to see that Declan had embarked upon rebuilding his house and he was surprised to learn that she would not be doing the same at Marshlands. She explained that she did not want to live in a house of ghosts; everything had been lost, and she felt that it would be too much like trying to recover childhood with its odours and feelings, the wolfhounds waiting by the door for a walk up to the bog or along the shore.

"I'm content enough with the cabin," Una said. "It's bigger than the flat I'd been living in and it has its garden, a little shed for hens if I decide to keep some. I'm going to have some work done inside, making two little rooms into a studio, but apart from that, it suits me perfectly well."

A studio? Declan noted she had a drawing block in her basket and a bundle of pencils and asked was she an artist?

She laughed and confessed that she was only now thinking of herself as one. "It was put aside for years, Mr. O'Malley. I did train as a botanical artist at the Dublin School of Art and Design and did some illustration work for the National Botanic Gardens, assisting with a flora they were producing." And then her face went sad. She sorted her pencils into a row according to length, her long fingers busy with nothing. "I was to marry, you see. A botanist I met while at school. We hoped to collaborate on a book of the wildflowers of the West — I grew up in Donegal and of course spent summers here, and David's grandparents live down near Clifden so while he grew up in Dublin, he knew the West quite well from visits to them. I think our happiest days were spent walking the Sky Road near Clifden and taking samples of bog cotton and primroses."

"Aye, they are a pretty sight, the primroses. Eilis used to dig up bunches of the earliest ones and bring them into the house in an old teacup so she could look at them while she washed the dishes."

"I'd never seen such beautiful drifts of primroses as the ones growing in a stretch of hedge near Streamstown," the woman continued, her eyes shining with the memory. "David carried his vasculum everywhere, kept damp with his grandmother's tea towels, and was always looking for the perfect specimen. And I made notes about colour and skies and how the late-afternoon light changed the yellow of the primrose from butter to gold."

"It sounds grand, I'd say. Will he join ye at Marshlands so?"

Tears came to Una Fitzgerald's eyes. "David joined the army and was killed at Suvla Bay."

"Oh, Miss Fitzgerald, I am so sorry. I didn't mean to …"

She interjected quickly, brushing her eyes impatiently, a single tear lingering. "You weren't to know. How could you? But I mourned for too long, I think, giving up all the things I did regularly, and I spent days in my bed, weeping. I couldn't bear to think about painting for years. I'd hear his voice telling me to notice how the bees plunged into the spur of the toadflax to get at the nectar and I'd lose myself to days of weeping. And yet he would have wanted me to keep on with my work, especially wildflowers. It was what drew us to one another, after all."

Declan was quiet, listening to her. It was a story so unlike his own and yet its theme was loss; there was a similarity in the days of weeping. Her fingers did not stop arranging the pencils while she spoke, a nervousness not apparent in her voice. "What have ye been sketching on a day like this one then? I'm thinking there's not much in bloom to catch yer eye so."

She showed him a drawing of dog rose, bare of leaves, and told him it was just as important to record the seeds nestled in the soft lining of the hips as it was to match the various pinks of the blooms. Blackberry, with its little fringe of flower remains clinging to the frostbitten fruit, a canister of seeds that followed the silken poppies. A palette changed from season to season like a wardrobe — the fresh greens of spring through the brilliant yellows and oranges and pinks of summer, the russets and reds of autumn hedges, the duns and dull ochres of winter. *Well, thought Declan, a wardrobe did not change for those of us in these cabins*, but he did not say it aloud. Una told him it reminded her of life again, observing the plants in their seasons. She was not sure she could continue with the book — she was not a writer by nature — but she would make a record of the plants in their seasons, working from the checklist they had compiled, as well as David's life list.

It was a window opening, thought Declan, into a life, a partnership, so different from his own. He could not imagine such travels with Eilis. For one, they hadn't enough money; for another, her parents would not have allowed her to go off with Declan unchaperoned, beyond a walk or perhaps to a ceilidh in a neighbouring house. After another word or two about the sketches, she abruptly said goodbye and disappeared down the road, telling him she hoped they'd meet again, her basket swinging from her arm, shawl enveloping her like the mists of Athene.

Thinking about the visit, Declan was undecided how he felt about Una Fitzgerald. She had the mannerisms of her class, a regal air that came with generations of deference from men such as himself. But he could not deny she was friendly and that her company was not unwelcome. Did he hope they would meet again? He decided he did. And what a sad story about her fiancé getting himself killed overseas. It was a war which had caused any amount of argument in Leenane, and other parts, he was thinking. There were those who felt the Irish lads should support the English effort and those who believed a more important war was taking place on their own soil, perhaps not so dramatically, but Irishmen were needed to further the cause of Republicanism at home. Yet there was the opportunity, in remote County Mayo, to remain silent in such discussions. From what Una had said, he realized how the issue was not simply relevant to one religion and class. He wondered how she felt about her David enlisting, and when they met again, near the river where he'd come upon her sketching on a folding easel, he tried to ask as gently as he could.

It took her a long time to answer. At first her mouth struggled for words. Then she began to sing softly, and it was a song Declan knew.

> Right proudly high over Dublin town
> They hung out a flag of war.
> 'Twas better to die 'neath an Irish sky

Than at Suvla or Sudel Bay.
And from the plains of Royal Meath
Strong men came hurrying through;
While Britannia's sons with their long-range guns
Sailed in from the foggy dew.
'Twas England bade our wild geese go
That small nations might be free.
Their lonely graves are by Suvla's waves
On the fringe of the grey North Sea.

Declan found he was singing the last phrase with her and realized he had never once thought where exactly Suvla might be.

"The Gallipoli Peninsula," answered Una. "So far away for an Irishman to be buried. I never wanted him to go. Britain had such a nerve, Redmond such a colossal nerve to ask, given our history. And yet David felt it was his duty. There were sermons preached which told young men it was their duty. So he joined, with a number of his former classmates from Trinity College, and they left in April of 1915 for training in England. I was relieved that a colleague from the Royal Botanic Gardens was also in his regiment for at least they could do a little botanizing. At first I think he saw it as an adventure ..."

"Aye, others have said the same," concurred Declan.

"... and he wrote the most brilliant letters home, always including a wildflower so I could imagine the surroundings. I'd check them against the map — the Dardanelles, Cape Helles, Achi Baba ... I imagined wild tulips and the sorts of things we knew only as rare plants grown under glass although I suppose there would have been plenty of grey prickly things as well. Thistles, thorn trees ..."

She was quiet, remembering his letters, gay at first and full of the humour of finding himself on a ship heady with grease and the fumes of fuel. He had loved Alexandria, where the regiment had stopped and been marched through the streets, where a carpet on the ground indicated a shop, a tumble of amphora, baskets of figs and dates, where fruit sellers beckoned with slices of melon held on the tip of a knife, where everyone was robed and veiled, and where they were finally given a meal of salty cheese and tomatoes and cups of coffee thick as syrup. He wrote wonderfully, bringing the same attention to his descriptions of what waited on the Gallipoli Peninsula — the flowers, certainly, but also the squalor of the trenches, the endless digging both to try to drain the flooding water and to provide more safety, a visit from Lord Kitchener, the men instructed to shave as best they could and to polish their buttons, where daily a man would rush to the latrines and not return, victim of a sudden, deadly dysentery. He described the smell of decay overlaid with sage and other strong herbs, wild rosemary bushes displaced by graves, and the horrifying sight of the carcasses of mules, ribs exposed like ships' timbers, half in the tide, their eye sockets filled with tiny crabs.

"When the beautiful *Pancratium maritimum* arrived, wrapped in David's monogrammed handkerchief, still damp, I couldn't have been more surprised, particularly as he'd added the note that it grew profusely among the sand dunes. I forgot for a moment that he was not on a plant-collecting trip but at war. When we were notified of his death and given a date, I realized from his note that the plant must've been collected and put into the mailbag that same day. I kept going to the Botanic Gardens to see the living plant, thinking how dreadful it was to have your life bracketed in such a way: October 20, 1890 to August 28, 1915. To be contained within such an artificial frame when we always expected our three score and ten, and how like the brief lives of things grown under glass. David ought to have grown old gathering plants on the Sky Road with the wind and ocean and rainstorms. I am not putting this very well, but I feel you must know what I mean."

Declan could not think of anything to say to her at that moment, hearing the catch in her voice and seeing moistness in her eyes. He reached for her hand and patted it gently. When she had cried a little and dried her eyes with a handkerchief, he told her that he had gone to Canada so that he would not have to think of Eilis and his girls contained within the mound of earth marked by granite. "It seemed to me then to have nothing to do with who they were, and I could not bear it. Yet now, strangely, I am comforted by the sight of the stone. They have become something else to me, I am thinking. A source, maybe. And I don't feel them confined anymore. I have planted my oar for them, as Odysseus did in his poem, so they will know where I've been and that I mean to farm our land again."

"Is that what you'll do, Mr. O'Malley? Farm this land?"

"Aye, I suppose I will. There have been O'Malleys at Tullaglas for centuries, with lives harder than mine, and losses aplenty. But please, call me Declan. Our families have been neighbours for nearly as long!"

Tears dried, she smiled at him. "And will you call me Una? In Leenane, it's Miss Fitzgerald this and Miss Fitzgerald that and sometimes I forget who I am with no one to call me by my name. Miss Fitzgerald is so obviously a spinster, and when I'm at Marshlands, I always feel like a girl of thirteen. So it would be so generous of you if you'd indulge me and let me be her!"

"Una it is. A fine Irish name to be sure. If ye would not take offense, I could make ye a cup of tea if ye came back to the farm, but it's only an old pan I have for the making and cups ye won't have seen the likes of. It's our own water, though, and sweet as ever there was."

"I would be honoured to have a cup of tea with you. It's the tea I'm thirsty for, not a fine china cup."

They walked back in mist. Declan busied himself with the fire and kettle and produced two mugs of strong tea, offering milk from the Mannion's cow. They drank their tea and then Una took her leave, asking Declan to visit her when he came down into Leenane.

"Either I'll be in and happy to give you tea or I'll be sketching, in which case you can come in and make a cup for yourself if you like. If I knew ahead, I'd make sure to be there but this isn't Dublin with regular post and even telephones now. Perhaps we could get messenger pigeons, Declan, to take notes over the mountain! That would be something, would it not?"

He had not seen a woman like her for some time. She was handsome rather than pretty, an angular face with strong cheekbones and grey eyes, a confident way of talking, as though she expected to be taken seriously, and she was not worn in her person as were the women he was accustomed to speaking with. Hard work had not lined her face and chapped her hands, poor diet had not taken her teeth, and her clothing was not pieced together from whatever might be at hand. Briefly he put his hand to his hair, smoothed it a little, wondered if she had noticed that his shirt was missing three of its buttons and could certainly use a washing in creek water with good lye soap.

The next time Declan walked down to Leenane to order some materials for his building project, he found himself noting plants as he passed the fields. Many of them he knew, of course, and he had always listened to Maire when she described a flower she had seen or an unusual tree. There had been a few books with plates in the school's modest collection, and Maire was not shy about asking people who might know — an old woman famous for her simples, the dyers in Leenane who collected plants and barks for the vats of colour that the wool would be immersed in before weaving. Harder work to know a plant without its flower, he thought, bending down to examine some sticky leaves that he thought must be corn spurry. And the fleshy leaves growing out of a length of old wall would be house-leek. Down by the river the tall straps of iris were browning and the nests they concealed, in amongst themselves and the bulrushes, looked forlorn without the hovering blackbirds. Kingfishers nested along this river, too, but built tunnels in the steeper banks to conceal their young.

He could not simply walk past the school as he had on the way home to Delphi. Voices buzzed from within the walls like bees in an industrious hive. He walked to the door and knocked tentatively. A young man in shirtsleeves, tie askew, opened the door and looked relieved. "I ought to be wearing my jacket of course, but the fire is fierce today and I was drilling them in the times table and got a bit excited. I am so pleased you are not the Inspector. Will you come in?"

Declan began to introduce himself, but a chorus of children called his name as he entered the familiar classroom.

"Ah, Mr. O'Malley, is it? I am so pleased to make your acquaintance, sir. The scholars are full of your lessons, the ones you taught. There is no end of reminders to me that you would have asked this of them, or would have expected them to know their sums before handing out a storybook. I am grateful for your mentorship, even if it has come to me second-hand, so to speak."

The children were delighted to see him. Mr. Kenny, the present master, allowed them to gather around him, leaving their slates on their desks, and stood back smiling. Declan was shown neat papers of handwriting, sketches of the classroom with its rows of long desks and rough benches, poems copied from books and surrounded with borders of pansies and traveller's joy. He took his leave, wishing the present master well. Mr. Kenny followed him to the door.

"I am so pleased to have met you, sir, and invite you to visit us at any time. There is a point I would like to discuss with you, it would be improper for me to say more just at present, and I wonder if I might come to you one evening? I am boarding with the Byrnes who are just by the Skeery bridge."

"Mr. Kenny, I can promise you a measure of whiskey, if not a sitting room in which to drink it. And a willing ear, to be sure. It is warming to see the children so settled and content, given the state of our country. I'll say goodbye now, and bless ye."

He continued down the road to where it met Killary Harbour, the Bundorragha River having gathered into itself the waters of seven or eight smaller streams idling down Ben Gorm. A few boats were on the water, coming in from fishing. He watched a heron rise from the muddy shore and head towards the tall evergreens by Clogh where brown fields stood stripped of their forage by sheep down for the winter. It was landscape plainer in its bones than the one surrounding Oyster Bay but he saw it with his heart as well as his eyes. It was as though it took the fuss of those coastal rainforests, the lush growth of the estuary, to make this one clear to him. Now there was a reference point, a transparency to hold to the land of his birth, to make its contrasts evident, shaped by stone and a history of hardship.

He noted, when passing, that Una's fire was burning behind the shrubbery that kept her cabin hidden from the road. In Leenane, he went about his errands, calling into the shop for provisions, only what he could carry, and he ordered some windows from the builder, as well as other materials he would need before spring. It was arranged that the builder's helper would bring the supplies by cart once they'd arrived from Galway and Cong. At the publican's, he bought a bottle of whiskey; he'd found that a small measure of it before he slept helped his body to adjust more easily to the ground, lumpy even with Mrs.

O'Leary's ticking, and the chilly air of the turf shed now that the dark season had arrived.

He turned into the lane that led to the Fitzgerald demesne. He could see the ruin of the big house, the walls with their pretty wash of pink lime scorched and destroyed. Even the stable yard, where Una's cousin had kept a pair of carriage horses as well as a hunter for himself and ponies for his children, had been ruined. Ivy was creeping up the side of the chimney, which still stood, as his own did; nettles flourished in the rose garden, though brown with frost. Before he could knock on the door of the groundskeeper's cabin, Una was standing there on the threshold, smiling.

"I saw you pass earlier and thought you might stop in on your way back to Delphi. It gave me time to bake some scones to offer you with a cup of tea!"

Declan looked around the cabin. It was like many of the others of its sort in the area — a large room which was the sitting room with kitchen facilities at one end, doors leading off either side of this, and a narrow staircase rising to a second floor. But it was bigger than his own house had been and spoke of something more than hard country lives. It was furnished simply but comfortably: two chairs, covered in a faded rose-patterned chintz, faced each other and the fire with a low table in between them, a long pine table under one window with an assortment of chairs around it, some grander than others, a proper cooker with a hot-water reservoir to one side, wide sinks, cheerful braided rugs on the slate floors. Paintings hung on the walls and pots of bright leaves and late flowers graced almost every surface. A piano against a wall with photographs on its polished top. On the low table by the fire, a cloth had been laid with a napkin-covered plate, some cups, a jug of milk, a small dish with a square of butter, and a jar of jam. Declan realized he was very hungry, having done the walk to Leenane and this far back with only his morning porridge.

"These are fine scones, Una!" he declared, buttering his fourth. "It's been a long time since the morning porridge, and me with the walk to Leenane under my belt."

She smiled and took the plate away to replenish its contents, wetting the tea again from the kettle suspended on a hook above the fire. After she had given him more scones, Una went to a dresser on the other side of the room and removed a folder from a drawer. She returned to her chair by the fire and handed the folder to Declan.

"These are some of the drawings I did of plants on Ben Gorm. You saw the rose, of course, when we first met, but I thought you might be interested in the others. I've added some wash to a few."

Declan opened the folder and carefully lifted the first sheet. The drawing was done in pencil but he recognized immediately the furze of the open fields. The detail was impressive, from the spines to the veining on the flowers. Such shading and delicacy of line! He could almost smell that odour that Eilis remarked was near the almond essence she put into the cakes at Christmas. The next drawing was a clump of marsh marigolds and again there was the fine detail, even to a bit of a withered leaf. Inset showed an open blossom with a small fly entering to drink, while the anther waited, heavy with pollen. Each drawing had tiny notes alongside, describing light, colour, time of day, surrounding landscape.

"These are truly fine, Una!" He looked through the folder at what remained: bell heather and bilberry, willow herb, pellitory-of-the-wall, and hemp agrimony. "Did ye mean to paint them as well? I see that ye have these notes with them so, and these little patches of colour."

"Ah, well, yes. I have painted some, in watercolour, but have meant to do more, and will, once I've my studio set up. It's not easy to cart my painting supplies to the sites where the plants are, although I do take a small box of paints to make those small palettes to remember, and notes of course, though even with notes, it's difficult to paint from memory. I intend to do more of them, of course. Some artists are now taking photographs, and there is even some thought that the photographs might well take the place of drawings and so forth, but I have yet to see a photograph that manages to get the plant in all its dimensions. I never use one single plant for a model, you see, but study many of them to get a sense of the possibilities of variance in form. Soils and weathers can affect the depth of colour, the habit of the plant. Looking at many will allow me to develop a prototype, you might call it, or the ideal plant, perhaps."

Declan enjoyed hearing her speak of her work. She obviously knew a lot about the wild plants and loved them; listening to her, it was like hearing a version of a story, one he hadn't heard yet but which made the story he did know larger and more various. There was a priest when he'd been away at school who believed that no one could know Ireland who didn't know Gaelic, that it was a way to understand the country in all its complexity. Declan had been interested in this, knowing that the ancient methods of land use in his own area made sense when you knew the Gaelic names for the fields themselves and the common pastures, and that a place itself echoed its history in its name: *Baile*, which had come to mean town but previously indicated both settlement and the landhold together, *Dun*, where a fort had been, *Doolough* or *Dhulough,* the dark lake, even Leenane, its Gaelic name *Lionan Cinn Mhara*, which meant something like "a place filled by tides at the head of the bay."

She showed him where she worked at present, a table pushed up against the window in one of the two small rooms on the second floor. A microscope, partly covered with a tea towel, stood close to the window. Una described her plan to have the interior wall knocked out and skylights installed to let in more light. Shelves held paper and tubes of pigment, as well as books, jars of liquids, and powders. There were jam pots filled with brown stems hung with seed pods, branches of hawthorn and rowan with bunches of berries beginning to dry out and wrinkle, clumps of grasses, a collections of nests, the fragile skull of a bird. A few framed paintings of flowers hung on the walls, and a deep cabinet took up half the length of the room: it was her herbarium, she explained, where she kept her dried plants, pressed and mounted. A tray with several cups, a teapot, some dry crusts of bread: it was evident Una spent a good deal of time in this room, and Declan could see how a larger space would make it easier to spread her work out, how more light would make the new room congenial and bright. He wanted to see everything, to understand about everything, but he realized he was getting tired and thought of the long walk ahead of him.

When he took his leave, he asked her to stop for him the next time she was sketching in his area. He wanted to know more about the plants on the mountain he had known all his life. She stood in the doorway and waved until he was beyond the Aasleagh Falls, the smoke from her fire visible above the wych-elms and sycamores by the river.

When he returned to his shed, he found himself seeking his *Odyssey*. Because of weather and the lack of a good place to spread out his papers, he had not been working on his translation for some time, although sometimes he would take the Greek text out to puzzle through a passage he was reminded of. This day it was Penelope's dream he had thought about as he'd walked the last mile or so. He found the lines and read them over and over, wondering for the life of him why the images kept appearing before his inner eye.

ἀλλ' ἄγε μοι τὸν ὄνειρον ὑπόκριναι καὶ ἄκουσον,
χῆνές μοι κατὰ οἶκον ἐείκοσι πυρὸν ἔδουσιν
ἐξ ὕδατος, καί τέ σφιν ἰαίνομαι εἰσορόωσα;
ἐλθὼν δ' ἐξ ὄρεος μέγας αἰετὸς ἀγκυλοχέιλης
πᾶσι κατ' αὐχένας ἧξε καὶ ἔκτανεν· οἱ δ' ἐκέχυντο
ἀθρόοι ἐν μεγάροις, ὁ δ' ἐς αἰθέρα δῖαν ἀέρθη.
αὐτὰρ ἐγὼ κλαῖον καὶ ἐκώκυον ἔν περ ὀνείρῳ,
ἀμφὶ δ' ἔμ' ἠγερέθοντο ἐυπλοκαμῖδες Ἀχαιαί,
οἴκτρ' ὀλοφυρομένην ὅ μοι αἰετὸς ἔκτανε χῆνας.

Listen to my dream and help me interpret it.
Twenty tame geese have come from the water
to eat wheat by my house. I am so happy to
    view them.
A great mountain eagle comes with a crooked
    beak
and kills them by breaking their necks, scattering
    their bodies.
He soars up and away and I shriek aloud,
this is in my dream, and around me gather
the Achaian women, all mourning
because the tame geese are dead.

A message was contained there, about husbands and mourning, but he didn't know how to take it into his life. Take what was blessed and good, and expect the worst? Zeus would appear in the form of an eagle and take the soft geese away?

Around his walls, tall grasses rustled in the wind off Fin Lough, where the wild ducks swam in the reeds, fat with stolen grain. One of these days, Miceal O'Leary would appear on his threshold with a string of them, tied by their wings, offering one for his fire.

True to his word, Liam Kenny came by an evening later. Over whiskey, he told Declan something of his background. A Galway man, he had been raised in a Republican household and his father had been a member of one of the Flying Columns near Oughterard. His education had been interrupted at times by his father's imprisonment, but he had completed his teacher training and Bundorragha was his first school. He told Declan he had been approached, shortly after he'd arrived, by some men, Irregulars, who knew his father; it was assumed he'd assist with Connemara Division ambushes.

"I am not saying of course what my reply to them was. They are an active lot. Mostly they've been trenching roads, which the Nationals repair soon enough though the Republicans have had the benefit of the Galway County Surveyor among their supporters, which has helped a great deal with technical knowledge. There has also, I understand, been the occasional bridge. But the lads have made the hills their territory, sir, and like you, they know every wrinkle, every bush of gorse. No one would hurt you, I am thinking, but I want to tell you that it's not altogether a safe thing to walk at night as you evidently have always done."

Declan could not respond. The hills had always held their secrets — a still where poteen was made by moonlight; an outlaw; the remnants of a fire ring or field boundary pre-dating the Famine. He had walked at night because it was peaceful, because the work of a schoolmaster required long hours, because he might have needed assistance with a difficult calving, or simply because the long-eared owls were to be heard in the conifers near Tully on March evenings and he would accompany Maire to listen to them. And more recently he walked at night because the dark came so soon and daylight could not contain all the tasks to be done — he might walk to O'Learys to borrow a tool or to the shores of Dhulough where he knew a certain shape of rock might be found, moonlight a frequent companion.

"Mr. Kenny, are ye drilling the lads? They have been seen entering the gap near Tawnynoran with rifles. And I suppose it is no secret that rifles were hidden in my turf, with it known I was abroad and no one to take the fuel of a family burned out in such a way."

"Mr. O'Malley, I was raised to believe in a free Ireland. There are differences of opinion as to how this will come. I mind that the Treaty has not done away with Partition and I hope that negotiation will bring us a sovereign Republic, one that includes Ulster. In the meantime, work must be done — even here, in these lonely mountains."

Declan spoke quietly about the boys who had done sums at the desks in his classroom, who had learned the genitives and subjunctives of their grandparents' language, how he had hoped that they might have opportunities not available for him and his own brothers, particularly the ones at rest in France. He told Liam Kenny that he was opposed to guns and violence, that any loss of life was a tragedy that cast a long shadow over fields that had seen too much bloodshed and sadness already. Yet he too believed in a free Ireland and knew that it would not come without a cost. He did not want his scholars to pay the ultimate price, though, when hardship was what had defined their family histories for too long and the loss of a son was terrible fodder to gain a country.

"I am thinking we are not at odds in our ideas, Mr. O'Malley. I have not come to argue with you but to ask that you be careful. Or perhaps mindful is what I am hopeful you will be."

A week later, while he was working on the house, he was startled to hear a car horn on the road below his farm. So few cars travelled the Delphi road! He was more startled to see it stop on the side of the road by his gate and to see Una emerge from it, laughing. She was wearing trousers and stout leather boots and a cloche pulled down over her hair. The fog-coloured shawl was flung over her shoulders.

"Declan, look what I have!"

"How on earth did ye get a car, Una?"

"Apparently Hugh decided I could not live at Marshlands without one and he arranged for the estate to buy it. Fintan Walsh came by the other morning in a great excitement because a call had come for me to the Post Office, saying I was to take the bus to Galway to collect my automobile. Fintan would not let me wait …"

"Aye, he wouldn't, that one!"

"No, he had the bus schedule worked out then and there and nothing would do but that I got my old bicycle and rode behind him to Leenane to catch the bus, the one that lugs itself up over the Maam road to Oughterard and then Galway. The Clifden bus would of course been an easier trip but it wasn't scheduled for another three days and Fintan could never have waited!"

Declan smiled. Fintan Walsh was a busybody if ever there was one and Una's description was exactly right. He could see the man racing over the Leenane road on his elderly bicycle to get Una on the bus on time, and no doubt he would have accompanied her to Galway too, given any encouragement.

"Sure enough, Hugh's solicitor was waiting at Eyre Station with this little car, having been telegraphed by the Post Office to say I was on my way. I know how to drive a little, David taught me, although it took me ages to figure out these gears."

"Did you make the trip in one day so?" Declan asked.

"No, I stayed overnight in Galway, waking up through the night with the most excited feeling, like Christmas morning, and then remembering that I now owned a car, or at least Marshlands owns a car. I was able to shop for some supplies in Galway, and didn't I feel proud to tuck them into the boot and then, making sure I had enough petrol, to drive home in this wonderful car. I stalled many times and almost hit a sheep near Ballynahinch, but I got back safe and sound, stopped once by Nationals near Recess who cautioned me about blood-thirsty Republicans near Clifden and once by Republicans near Kylemore who cautioned against trigger-happy Nationals. I gave Fintan first ride as a point of gratitude, and now I've come to collect you for a sketching trip!"

"Were ye not frightened, Una, to be stopped by soldiers?" It unnerved Declan to hear her speak to flippantly of soldiers stopping her on the road, their guns at the ready.

"I remembered reading something in the *Connaght Tribune* a year or two ago, when the Republicans held Clifden. They expected everyone to carry a permit and Monsignor McAlpine was quoted as saying he absolutely refused to do so. When he was stopped from visiting a house without permission, he declared he would rather die by the roadside than ask for a permit from boys he had baptised. I feel a little that way myself."

"But surely it could be dangerous?"

"Oh, what could men who have burned my family home possibly do to me now, apart from shoot me? All the memories of my childhood, the happy rooms — poof, they're ash. And I will not live my life in fear. My elderly aunt in Donegal had her car taken from her by the IRA, and her a supporter! They needed it for some reason, and when it hadn't reappeared in her courtyard several days later, she marched down to the Barracks — this was after the Republicans had taken the town — and demanded it back. She reminded the captain she had known him since he was a mewling infant in nappies and that she expected him to behave in a more civilized fashion. All this she told me in a letter as well as the fact that she had received a profuse written apology!"

Declan simply looked at her. Her lightness, her laughter, made him think of her in one way, and this was a different woman, fierce, refusing to be intimidated. He followed her to the car, an Austin Seven painted dark blue, and let her show him each feature, each wiper, each wheel, as well as the spare tyre in the boot and special tool for jacking up the car if there should be a need to change that tyre. ("Hugh's solicitor had a man show me how to change a tyre in the parking area for the Great Southern Hotel.") Una had packed a basket of food along with a flask of tea so all that remained for Declan to do was to gather his waterproof jacket and open the passenger door.

"I'm going to drive up to Cregganbaun, Declan, as there are some small lakes just west of there with plants I'm hoping to collect. Are we forgetting anything?"

He didn't think so. It was a little unsettling to feel the car shake and judder as they left the farm, but Una assured him she was still getting used to the clutch and hoped he would bear with her because it couldn't take forever, could it? Bride Mannion was bringing in wash as they passed the Mannion farm and Una waved gaily to her, calling out that she'd take Bride for a run to Leenane one of these days if she liked. Bride looked as startled as Declan had been to see a car on the Delphi road, one that didn't belong to the marquess's estate, and when he waved to her, when she recognized who Una's passenger actually was, her amazement showed.

"Oh, Declan, I'm afraid they'll have us married off by the end of the day, sure as anything." Una was laughing, but Declan knew there was an element of truth to her words. Men and women did not spend time together unless they were married or promised. But the Fitzgeralds were a family planted in the area nearly as long as his own, and he felt the differences of their upbringing — the Fitzgeralds were Ascendancy stock, supporters of the Church of Ireland, while he'd had the teachings of Rome inculcated from the cradle — could be put aside for the sake of a friendship. And he knew the Fitzgeralds had entertained proponents of the Gaelic League in their home (in a small community, everything was known; it was not that the walls had ears, exactly, but that the serving people and grooms were from local families), had supported the notion of national pride of language and literature, and surely these were in accordance with his own family's hopes and dreams, though expressed in the different terms of class and privilege. And both families had lost homes to the Troubles, had lost, temporarily or permanently, their sense of security and belonging. So now he would drive with Una Fitzgerald up the winding road past Dhulough and Glencullin Lough to look for marsh plants on a chilly day in early December and would pinch himself under the guise of adjusting his weight in the passenger seat to make sure he was not dreaming.

Una had David's vasculum in the back seat. Declan had never seen such a thing before, a metal box with a domed lid, and many place names and dates engraved on its sides.

"David used to engrave the place and date of each trip onto the vasculum, a trick he'd learned from a professor at Trinity College. He kept lists of plants, of course, like birders do — he and his friends called them life lists. But he liked to see at a glance where his passion had led him, and when. An uncle who was a jeweller gave him a small engraving tool which he kept fastened to the underside of the cover. In his journals, he'd make detailed notes about the trips, like a mariner exploring foreign seas. Compass bearings, weather notations ... This one, well, this was heaven."

Declan looked closely and saw "Dingle Peninsula May 1914" engraved into one side of the vasculum. It was the most recent date he could see. He asked Una how that trip had come about, to County Kerry, a place he'd only heard about.

"David's grandfather knew a priest in Dunquin who invited us to visit — he loved botanizing and wanted the opportunity to show his favourite places to us. We went down by train and then bus, over wild country. It was so beautiful. I remember the bus winding up the Conor Pass and seeing the fields and bogs laid out below like swatches of velvet. The priest met us in Dingle and drove us in a battered old car to his home in Dunquin. He lived beside the old graveyard, which seemed to exist over a community of beehive huts, quite wonderful. You'd be walking along, looking at graves, and suddenly you'd realize that you were standing on a mound from which poked the capstone of a clochan. And the wildflowers, oh, they were exquisite, Declan, particularly the saxifrages."

"And were ye long in Kerry?"

"We spent the whole of a week there, almost entirely outside, even when it rained the way it can only rain in the West of Ireland. We would get soaked to the skin without even noticing, and David would spend his evenings with the priest, preparing his specimen for his herbarium, while I read books I'd only ever heard of before, never seen, because Father Mulcahy had the most eccentric library, with our wet clothing sizzling by the fender. And we'd be served huge dinners by a housekeeper who plainly disapproved of Protestants sleeping under the same roof as her employer. She was grim, but the food was delicious."

The road was rough and the car rattled as Una navigated the potholes and rubble. Damage had been done during the time of the Black and Tans and repairs had yet to be executed; if Liam Kenny was to be believed, there was every chance that the roads would remain dreadful for some time yet. Hills on either side of the road were dressed in the russets and browns of winter with the occasional vivid red as a tree still clung to its last leaves. A standing stone stood impassive on one shoulder as they approached the little hamlet of Cregganbaun, watching for the side road to the lakes Una wanted to visit. It was more a sheep track than a road when they found it, deeply rutted and overhung with trees. It threaded its way over tussocks and gravel, over the rushing water of the Carrownisky River, and sidled up to Lough Mahaltora after passing an ancient tomb standing on the road like a patriarch. This was where the car stopped and Una began to unload her equipment, pulling on wellingtons as she talked.

"I am looking for a few good characters, Declan, a few things my herbarium is without. One is the bog asphodel ..."

Declan interrupted. "Do ye mean to say that asphodel grows here?" His voice was so tremulous that Una was suddenly a little concerned.

"Well, yes ...," she began.

"The same asphodel that grows in Hades, that Homer calls the food of the dead? Do ye remember Achilles, striding off across the fields of asphodel?"

Una was surprised to hear him refer to Homer, and with such familiarity, as though he was talking of a family member or character in the community. She had not thought of him as a scholar, particularly, although he was known in the area as an excellent teacher. She thought for a moment and then said, "I think the asphodel in Homer must be the white asphodel, or Royal Staff. *Asphedelus Ramosus*, that's the one that would occur in the Mediterranean. So, no, not the same plant, Declan, although I suppose they'd both belong to the same family, *Liliaceae*. This one is *Narthecium ossifragum* and it grows in boggy areas here and in England. The *ossifragum* part is interesting because it means "bone breaking" and refers to the belief that people had, still have, that it causes that disease called cruppary in sheep, where the bones break easily. The thing is, it doesn't cause cruppary at all but sheep eating in areas where it grows are feeding on fairly un-nutritious fodder so their bones might well break easily because of deficiencies in their diet, not the bog asphodel. But how odd that you would mention it. Have you read Homer then?"

He told her about his project, before the fire and in Canada, of translating parts of the *Odyssey*, how it had worked nicely into Rose's education, how it began to echo his life without Eilis and the girls. He told her about the canoe and how he would lie in it on its bluff and dream of home or Elpenor and would wake, disoriented, and how he had noticed the flowers which Mrs. Neil told him were the death camas growing all around the canoe, his initial dread, and then how it seemed to him a mirror of the pale fields that Achilles strode through, mourning his afterlife. It was all so unexpected to her, and to him, after so much time, this story of a life two entire oceans away. She had in her a tremendous capacity to talk and did not always stop to listen carefully to what was said in reply. She wondered if she'd heard him tell any of this earlier but decided she would have remembered, although there *had* been a reference made to planting Odysseus's oar, perhaps. Or had she imagined that? And as was her way, she determined to try a little harder to listen.

"This is terribly interesting, Declan. In a funny way, I have felt certain plants to be companions of mine, the pancratium for

instance, after David's death, and the delphiniums my grandfather grew, of which I found survivors in the long stretch near
the stable wall and have saved seed from for my own border, and
the foxgloves that grew at Dunquin. I hope we'll find some of
the asphodel so you can see what our own looks like, although
it does seem prosaic, doesn't it, after thinking of its reputation
in Homer, to be looking for a plant thought to cause broken
bones in sheep!"

"I haven't seen the asphodel in Homer, though, Una; I just
know how it is described — the fields of it, pale as ghosts. So ye
see, it will be a new thing for me. Although I am thinking it will
not look like much this time of year so."

"I have done some drawings of the flowering plant, in July,
when it is very pretty, with its yellow flowers, and the fruiting
plant later on, in September, when areas of the bogs can appear
to be cloaked in orange. Now I want just the plain plant with its
withered leaves but the stand I had used, near Marshlands, has
been eaten by sheep, more's the pity for them, poor sods.
However, Ciaran O'Murchu told me that he had seen it up this
way, in abundance, when he came to see a man about a horse a
couple of months ago. Luckily Ciaran hates it with a vengeance
as he has had trouble with his own sheep, so he remembered the
orange coverage."

They left the car and walked down towards the shore of the
lake where rushes were fluttering a little in the wind. Declan
stopped and pointed to the far shore where a small herd of red
deer grazed on the rough grasses. One animal lifted her head
and stared at them, then returned to feeding. Moving carefully
through the boggy ground, Una paused to examine a clump of
something Declan didn't recognize.

"Remind me to come back here late in the spring, Declan.
Well, I'll make a note of this exact place, if you don't mind waiting a minute while I draw a little map." She extracted a notebook

from her haversack and made a quick sketch with a pencil, arrows and approximate distances noted. "There! I can see that at least three kinds of orchid are growing here. Nothing much to see now, of course, but this one here is the marsh orchid, unless I'm very much mistaken, and this one just here is the fly orchid. They're both somewhat rare and I'd like to draw them in situ once they're blooming. This other one — and I'm not entirely certain about this, as it's so discoloured — is the common spotted orchid. Oh, and the devil's bit scabious, another good find! I'll just lift one of each for the dormant portrait, but only after we've found the asphodel as that's really what I've come for."

She kept taking out a small notebook and making quick notations, looking to the road and obviously estimating distance and scale. And then she found what she was looking for, some wintry plants of bog asphodel, which Declan had expected to look somehow monumental and which were instead brown leaves with stalks holding hollow pods, nothing he would have stopped for, unknowing. But he remembered the death camas stems, dry on their bluff of tawny grass, papery seed pods broken open by wind, and watched while Una took a trowel from her bag and carefully dug up a single plant, brushing the soil away from the root system. Making sure she had the plant entire, she opened the vasculum and laid the plant inside on a damp cloth, covering it with a second square of cloth. She made more notes, asking him at one point what he thought the temperature might be, crumbling a bit of the surrounding earth with her fingers to get an idea of its composition, squinting into the sky for a reading of the light. Then, after lifting a plant each of the orchids and scabious, and placing them carefully into the vasculum, she announced she was perishing with hunger and needed to eat. They returned to the car, stowed away the gear, and took out the basket of food and the flask of tea. There was cold pheasant—a casualty from Una's first attempt to park the car under a rhododendron hedge at Marshlands; the hen had been frightened to death by the sight of the vehicle approaching its roosting branch — and wholemeal bread with wrinkled apples from surviving Marshland trees.

They ate their lunch in the shadow of the tomb, its lichened rocks providing support for their backs.

"What a place to be buried!" exclaimed Una. "The mountains to the south, these lakes, the glorious bog ... It is humbling, don't you believe, to imagine people living here thousands of years ago and commemorating their dead with such a handsome dolmen?"

Declan agreed. He told her about what he'd seen as a boy and how the archaeologists had come to study the cathair he had told them about. "I never felt alone when I explored the land as a boy," he explained. "Always there were the shadows of people who had hunted and farmed, and the sad ruins of the houses tumbled into nothing during the Famine. I think it was what I yearned for most in Canada, though it took me a fair few months to determine that. I knew some Indian men who travelled by canoe and knew every rock, knew where there was water deep enough for halibut fishing, and knew where the summer camps of their old people had been, even though no one had lived that way for at least a generation. It was wonderful but lonely-making, too. Even though I haven't much here, not even a house really, and me sleeping in the turf shed, it's right to have come back, to be among my own people, even the dead ones. Even Eilis and the girls, planted in my land same as potatoes or corn. There is more company to the dead than most living people think."

Una could think of no response to such eloquent words and quietly began to gather up the remains of their lunch. Listening was proving surprising. On the way back, Declan asked if they might stop by the Famine grave on the shore of Dhulough, where those who had been ordered to present themselves for inspection at Delphi Lodge and whose famished bodies did not survive the sixteen-mile march from Westport through mountain passes and over this same rough road as they now travelled were buried. It was only a pile of stones but memory preserved the knowledge that those stones marked a mass grave. For years Declan's mother had told them of this site, cousins of her mother's having been among the unfortunate dead. A relation had sent her mother a clipping about the event from the Mayo Constitution, dated April 10, 1849, and it was kept within the pages of the family bible, which had been reduced to ash with everything else but the harp, it seemed, when the house had been torched.

The place was very silent, just the mountain coming down to the shore of Dhulough and the road cut through, a low mound of broken stone to indicate a grave, and grass eaten to the quick by sheep. Wind punctuated the quiet, rustled the reeds, but did not interfere with the peace of the place; it was as though the stones issued forth a low keening to keep one mindful of sorrow and loss. Over the far hill, light filtered through dark cloud, you could not call it sun exactly, but a brightness that gave the moment of their stopping a brief clarity.

After Una had dropped him off, refusing tea in her eagerness to take her plants back to press and catalogue, Declan surveyed his work thus far. The house was coming along, slowly but surely. On his last trip to Leenane, he'd ordered slates for the roof and hoped to have the structure ready for them in the early part of the new year. He made a fire and sat by it, thinking of the day he had spent, unexpected, and how his life and Una's were so different, yet overlapped in ways he was only beginning to understand. She had left him with one of her plant books after he had asked her how he might become better acquainted with wildflowers. "You are already acquainted with them, Declan. On intimate terms, one might say. You just don't know their proper

names. Read the little introduction to this book. It explains taxonomy and such. You'll find out that the main things you'll need
to know are family, genus, and species. Once you've figured that
out, it's really a lot easier. And knowing those things makes the
plants so interesting. I'm very fond of genus — you'll figure out
such a lot about the history of botany by knowing that. A bit like
how our surnames reflect our history: Miller, Baker, etc. Now,
what would be the Irish equivalent? Oh, I don't have time to
work it now but next time we meet?"

Declan opened the book and began to look for things he
recognized. Ah, there was the yellow iris, well known to him
from the banks of the Bundorragha River, golden with it in
May. Family: *Iridacae*. Yes, fine. Then: *Iris pseudacorus*. He knew
from his days with the priests that "pseuda" meant false. Reading
a little of the text, he could see that it came from the plant's
resemblance to *Acorus calamus*, or sweet flag, and that similarity
related to the shape of the leaves. That would be why it was so
often called the flag iris, he thought. And iris itself, now there
was a tale. From the Greek, referring to a messenger of the gods
who was also a goddess, Iris, her name also meaning rainbow,
touching heaven and earth, linking the two realms. He was
beginning to see that this could be an engrossing pastime. And
then he was looking at a plant so familiar to him, a plant Eilis
had used to make a simple salve to encourage the healing of
wounds, a plant he had drunk as a tea to ward off the onset of a
cold. Yarrow. But here he learned its noble origins. *Achillea millefolium*, named for the great Achilles, who had been held by the
heels and dipped in the River Styx to make him immortal, yet
was vulnerable in the one area untouched by the powerful
waters and who used the plant to heal his men wounded at Troy.
And "millefolium" for its multitude of leaves.

Declan was so surprised to learn that a plant as common as
yarrow had its provenance in the world of his beloved poem.

While he had been thinking of its landscape as remote and exotic, grey-green with olives and strong herbs, it had been populated with the plants of his own Delphi. And with a plant Lucy had used to cleanse the violated ground where the canoe and its occupant had been dug up by pigs. He put the book down and went to the rise beyond the turf shed where he found some yarrow, brown now in winter but still releasing its pungent oils to his hand as he gently crushed the leaves. He inhaled deeply. Looking at it in his hands, he thought he would try the trick of making himself invulnerable. The next time he filled his basin with water heated over his turf fire, he would sweep his body with branches of yarrow, taking care not to miss his heels or any part that might prove his downfall if unprotected. Wrapping some stalks of yarrow with a length of supple grass, he hung the clump over the doorway of his shed. It brushed his head as he entered and departed, reminding him of Achilles, and the herb they kept in common.

Everything traced a path to the poem, he sometimes thought. A plant, weather, the look of the mountains. He took out his copy of the *Odyssey* and opened it at random. Book 11, the journey to the underworld. He mused that of course this was where the book would open as he had spent so much time with these lines of intense encounters. It was Odysseus's mother again, telling him news of home. His son, she tells him, holds the household together. But Laertes, his father, has taken to the farmed area, sleeping among his slaves in winter on the floor by the fire's ashes, his body wrapped in old skins. And in summer — and here Declan paused to think deeply about the lines:

> αὐτὰρ ἐπὴν ἔλθῃσι θέρος τεθαλυῖά τ᾽ ὀπώρη,
> yet at the height of summer's luxury *(and this*
> *seemed to mean the end of summer, with a hint*
> *of what stars might be evident),*
> πάντῃ οἱ κατὰ γουνὸν ἀλωῆς οἰνοπέδοιο,

all around the vineyard, down its slopes,
φύλλων κεκλιμένων χθαμαλαὶ βεβλήαται
  εὐναί,
he bends to make his bed of fallen leaves,
ἔνθ' ὅ γε κεῖτ' ἀχέων, μέγα δὲ φρεσὶ πένθος ἀέξει
there he lies, great grief in his heart, sorrowing,
σὸν νόστον ποθέων, χαλεπὸν δ' ἐπὶ γῆρας
  ἱκάνει,
growing older and older while he yearns for
  your return.

He closed the book and clasped his hands together. *I have
become my father, he thought, or has he always been in me all along?
No slaves, of course, but the foolish hens who must be kept safe from
foxes, no vineyard but these hills of potatoes and the sloes which make
a drink they say to keep away the winter chill. And although it's cold
today, soon the blackthorns will be blooming and soon they'll be dan-
dling those mealy bitter sloes. And I am hoping that I will not be sleeping by the ashes of my fire for evermore.*

A letter came from Rose, written with the careful handwriting of one new to the craft. *Dear Mr. O'Malley,* she wrote.

Just after the salmon finished in Anderson Creek,
we left for Ontario. It was sad to leave. I said
goodbye to your little house and to Argos. The
MacIsaacs are good to her and she loves Mrs.
MacIsaac but when I went to say goodbye, she
followed me back to my boat and howled as I
rowed back to our house. Dunvegan is lovely. My
aunt Martha has made things so nice for us and
Mum has stopped crying so much. We're going
to school in the same schoolhouse where our

mother and aunt and uncles went. At first I was put with the smaller children because I am a late starter, the master calls me, but thanks to you I am now with those my own age and the teacher says I am his top scholar for my years. Our readers are nothing like the *Odyssey* and when I told the master this, he went very quiet and then came to me later with a book he said I could use instead. It is about a girl called Jane Eyre who loses her parents and lives with mean relations, nothing at all like Aunt Martha and Uncle Oscar, but then she becomes something called a governess. Some of the words are hard but the master showed me how to use a dictionary and oh, that has helped such a lot. I am so glad the harp has survived. Your friend, Rose Neil.

He would not think of Rose, dancing in the tide, her white arms raised like wings. He would not remember those arms dark with bruises, would not think of Argos. Not now. But the harp … Ah, yes, it had survived, but Declan would look at it with its broken strings and wonder what might be done with it. He worried that the frame might warp in an unheated turf shed, or worse, that the moisture in the wood might freeze and expand, causing cracking, and it would be impossible to repair. He felt responsible for making sure it continued to produce music although the why and how of it was beyond him. When he next saw Una, he asked her for advice.

"Well, I'll write to Maeve, of course, and ask her what to do. I know she has found a teacher in London and has continued her studies. She will know, if anyone does."

And a letter came back from London as part of a package containing a book that demonstrated the stringing of harps and a number of lengths of harp-string and a tool for affixing the brass wires. Maeve was very excited to know that the harp had come through the fire intact, but for strings, and wrote that the stringing was not too difficult. The book she was sending had a clear chart, and Bernadette Feeny, near Glenummera, would be able to help them with the tuning as the strings would have to be tuned to pitch morning and evening, for five days ideally, or at least over the period of a week. "What a fine way to honour Grainne, Mr. O'Malley!" she wrote. "I hope to visit Una next summer and will of course help you then if you find this too daunting."

It would in a way be the measure of him, he thought, the stringing of the harp. To make true peace with Eilis, Maire, and his beloved Grainne, to take the only thing to survive the fire almost whole, apart from himself, and make it usable again. He had left Delphi in pieces and returned patched and mended as an old shoe, wearable — but for what? He was building a house from salvaged walls, stones that might have come from more ancient structures and which contained within them the silences of history. If he could restore to the harp its old utility and power to make music, he might find in the task a way forward for himself, too. Once the house was finished, was he to milk a cow daily for himself only, was he to grow potatoes to fill his own belly? Would he end up like one of the isolated hill bachelors, coming down once a year to buy some tobacco or to sell a pig, the jackets falling off their backs for want of a stitch, their skins tanned by turf smoke and tea? Or would he learn to pluck the strings of a harp and sing for his supper as some of the composers loved by Grainne had done, would he put on his wedding shirt and ask some apple-cheeked maiden to become mistress of his hearth? The thought of any of it made him want to curl up in his bedroll like old Laertes and sleep among the ashes.

Chapter Thirteen

One morning, walking along the fenceline to check for gaps — he was going to take a calf from Mannions to his grass — Declan saw movement across the water at Tawnynoran. Light figures moving among the trees, one here, one there, perhaps a dozen altogether. It was a Sunday, and he was not surprised to recognize, even from that distance, the tall profile of Liam Kenny among them. Where the trees grew thicker by the damp banks of Sruhaughboy where it washed down from Oughty Craggy, the figures disappeared.

It was like seeing ghosts, Declan thought, an army of boys, lost into fretful history. Republicans again had taken Clifden to the south and the mood was uneasy, for it was felt violence was to come. There was a line running down the length of Connemara, with the west being Republican-held and the territory east of the mountains contained by Nationals. Padraic O'Maille, Deputy

Speaker of the Dail and a Kilmilkin man himself from the Leenane Road west of Maam Cross, had been shot in Dublin, had taken ten bullets, including one lodged near his spine, though he was expected to recover. Boats ran men up and down the coast, Lewis guns were hidden away in old pig sheds, and the stories circulated about explosions and wild fist fights in local pubs as friends and neighbours fought at the slightest provocation. Declan found this desperately sad, that those who had faced the enemy together both on native soil and in France and elsewhere now could not agree to disagree about whether or not Collins and the others ought to have settled for the Articles of Agreement for a Treaty which gave Ireland dominion status. The names were flung about with astonishing familiarity that was Irish to the core: de Valera, Brugha, Collins, Griffith. Boys whom he knew could never keep the Irish kings straight for more than a minute were suddenly experts on constitutional matters and willing to shoot their brothers. It was all too much, and yet he had returned to be Irish on his own soil.

He met three boys on the boreen, with a look in their eyes of heroes and rebellion.

"Lads, ye are not long out of school. Are ye in work yet?"

"No, Mr. O'Malley. But we ... oww!" and the one that had been about to say something of their activities was kicked sharply in the leg by the boy beside him.

"I have me own idea, boys, of what ye are up to, in the gap near Tawnynoran. Didn't I plant the seeds meself, with our readings of Oisin and the high kings. But I mind ye have families, have something in front of ye that is precious, though ye might not ken that yet. Ireland needs brave men, to be sure, but wise men are needed too, and I am asking ye to think hard before ye act."

The boys murmured that they would keep his words in mind before they ran down the road towards their homes, the weight of the guns left behind in a secret cache a thrill that their shoulders remembered while they fed the pigs, repaired walls with silent fathers, joined their families in the rosary before bed. When they slipped out of those beds, over the sleeping bodies of their brothers, to take up arms in Tawnynoran, their mothers would weep beside the still shapes of husbands, a cow would stop in its chewing to watch them disappear down the slope of a field to where others waited for them in the dull light of a tallow candle filched from a dresser drawer. What did they tell their priest at confession, Declan wondered, and did they take the communion with the rest of their families? The one-eyed priest had gone to Limerick and another had come in his place, a young fellow with a voice like a choirboy; it was said that he was altogether more human than his predecessor. Who knew, perhaps he even counselled the lads to take up arms for Ireland, whatever that meant.

The harp had been moved to Una's cabin after Declan had read Maeve's book and learned that a harp needed a stable environment, neither too damp nor too warm and dry. He wondered if it might even now be too late. But examining the instrument carefully, he could find so sign of cracks or twisting. Perhaps it had been a blessing that the strings had broken and melted as they might otherwise have caused the harp to pull itself apart from the tension.

Una collected the harp in her car, wrapped in an old blanket. When she and Declan lifted it out at Marshlands, it was like carrying a child, one of them at each end, supporting the harp's weight with their arms.

"Let's hope no one is watching," Una laughed, as they struggled through the doorway with their cargo. "I wouldn't want it talked around that we are smuggling guns or invalids into my house. It might get back to Hugh and he would decide there was nothing for it but to confiscate my car."

It was natural to want to place the harp near the fire, but Una wisely asked that it be set in the little room off the main room; she thought the heat from the fire and sunlight streaming in the southern window might dry out the wood and damage the finish. *Well,* Declan thought to himself, *any finish it had was lost to the fire.* When he ran his thumb along the grain, small blisters could be felt on the surface of the wood. He remembered Grainne smoothing mineral oil into the wood periodically and then buffing it with a clean soft cloth until it shone with the deep glow that bog oak could attain, if cared for. The heat would certainly have caused the oil to blister, and he would find a way to restore the patina.

Una was making a meal for them before Declan walked back home. A chicken was roasting in the oven and potatoes were being scrubbed in the deep sink. He asked could he do anything, and she had him scraping carrots over a basin. She hummed while she worked, as Eilis had done, and it was pleasant in her warm room with the smell of cooking and some books on the table to look at once the carrots were scraped and rinsed.

"Declan, I brought down some floras and such from David's collection. I thought you might enjoy seeing the real masters of the work I'm trying to do. I'll pour you a glass of sherry and you can look through them while I finish making our dinner. I've also brought this, which had been an inspiration to David; it's the results of the Clare Island Survey, done around 1910, I believe, by experts in every field — botany, zoology, geology, archaeology, family and place names, even the native names for flowers and things — and then published in these three rather large volumes. It was meant to echo work done on an island off Dublin, Lambay, but in fact the proportions of the Clare Island survey grew beyond anyone's expectations. Anyway, look at them all if you like."

Declan carefully lifted one of the books, *Flora Londinensis*, and opened it. He recognized many of the plants — a primrose, a clump of the stinky plant that often tangled itself in amongst the potatoes and which he learned was *Geranium robertianum*, or Herb Robert. The plates were nicely done, delicately coloured. "Una, what is the meaning of the bits the fella has drawn on either side of the plant?"

She came and looked over his shoulder. "Oh, yes, well, those are called dissections. The idea is not just to portray the plant itself but also its function, its anatomy, how it reproduces itself. That all began, really, with the artists who illustrated Linnaeus."

"Linnaeus? Should I know the name?"

"Oh, I'm sorry," Una laughed. "I am so immersed in this that I imagine everyone must know exactly what I know. Which isn't much, mind you. Well, Linnaeus. He was a Swede, born in the eighteenth century, and he spent his life working as a botanist. He was a bit odd, but I think his brilliance lay mostly in his efforts to simplify the way plants were classified. Remember I told you a little about taxonomy when I lent you that book? He came up with the binomial system, really, the one I explained to you — the genus and then the specific name. The first designates and the second sort of describes. It's a bit more complicated than that when you get into things like classes dependent on sexual parts or lack of them, but the basics of it are brilliant."

"Well, Una, I can't say that such things were covered by the priests who taught me. Latin, aye, but many of them would not let the name of Darwin cross their lips and perhaps this Linnaeus fella was thought of in the same way."

"It wouldn't surprise me," she replied. "Now, if you open that folder there, you'll find some loose plates of things David was able to find in London. My favourite is that one there, yes, the one you've got in your hand, the saffron crocus. That artist, John Miller, published something called *An Illustration of the*

Sexual System of Linnaeus, and I think his work is wonderful. Some of the illustrators would clutter the page with too much detail and there wouldn't really be any system to it. But Miller's eye was very good. There is something so clean and fine about this plate, and it's quite accurate too, considering it was done about a hundred and fifty years ago. And see what he's shown — a couple of views of the plant at different stages in the life cycle, details of the corm, the roots, seed pod, leaf. It's what I aspire to, but I'd like to be able to also develop a logical way of showing the plant in all its seasons, even dormant, without the page getting too busy. Who knows, it might be possible."

"Ye explain things very well. Have ye thought of teaching so?"

She smiled and replied, "I haven't had a plan at all, really, and have just gone from one thing to the next, particularly since David died. I have a small trust fund and haven't needed to think about work in order to eat, which is lucky, I suppose, although it's allowed me to lose any focus I might have developed. But I feel too old to drift now and want to apply myself to the illustrations and see if I am able to produce something good. And speaking of producing, I think the food is probably ready for us to eat."

The table by the window had been laid with two places, two blue willow-ware plates and two settings of heavy silver, two shining wine glasses, damask napkins, and a loaf of grainy bread on a wooden board with a border of carved wheat. It was a welcome meal to Declan, who had not eaten anything but food fried over his fire, or pans of stew kindly brought to him by Bride Mannion, and once, the promised meal of mutton cooked by Pegeen Devaney, or Breen as she was now, a strapping young woman hugely with child and settled into a cabin at Clogh with her Padraig and a brace of sheep dogs. To be a guest at a table, a meal prepared for him as for a guest, a glass polished with a tea towel before placing it just so at the tip of the knife — this moved him, made a lump form in his throat. He had felt solitary and lonely for so long that he had almost forgotten how people spoke to one another at a meal, how they acted the courtesies of host and guest, passing a bowl of potatoes, the dish of sweet butter. For the care shown him, he might have a travelling god, disguised in homespun, testing the hospitality of a chosen household.

After dinner, Una told him she had been approached by two women in the village and asked if she might like to join Cumann na mBán, the women's organization within the Republican movement. As it turned out, she had acquaintanceship with some of the organizers throughout Ireland — Countess Markievicz and Mary MacSwiney — through her family's involvement in the Gaelic League, and word had filtered down to women at the local level that she was reliable and sympathetic to the Fenian cause.

"I'll attend meetings, Declan, having now begun, to see what might be done but I suppose I am in part being asked because I might be able to contribute money. It is very difficult to completely embrace the Republican position, though, because I had such admiration for Michael Collins and sympathy for how his days ended, shot down in his own west Cork. However, these are nice women and I have been hungry for conversation. No doubt you have wondered how one woman can talk as much as me!"

It would not have occurred to him that she might be herself lonely, but of course she would have been accustomed to the company of women and men in Dublin and London. Watching her draw in firelight, he realized that she was finding ways to claim a place for herself, both in the context of Marshlands and the larger community, that was hers alone. Not rebuilding her grandfather's house, driving a car, making friendships, such as their own, taking up the sketching again — these things were hinges to a life that would be hers, self-forged.

"The first meeting I was able to attend was fascinating. Breda O'Toole's friend was visiting from Dublin and her experiences with the 1916 uprising were so inspiring. She told us about the little summer house in Stephen's Green which they used as a first aid station, putting people in the potting shed when they needed more light to treat wounds or extract bullets. After the surrender, she spent time in Kilmainham Gaol where she could hear the pistol shots as the leaders of the uprising were executed."

Declan listened in wonder. "It seemed so far away to us, here in the West, although there were men of course who made the journey across the country to join the Citizen Army. And there'd be rallies in Leenane, too, which we'd go to and get fired up — though there didn't seem to be roles for many of us then. I mind that many of the same fellas that came out to those rallies were also there when the King and Queen came to Leenane, oh, it must be twenty years gone now, the big yacht I'm thinking they called it, a big boat at any rate, coming down Killary as proud as you please. The same fellas waving flags and helping to put up the buntings and waving pleased as punch as the two and their entourage motored through the village and down towards Kylemore. Anyway I thought teaching was the best contribution I could make to Ireland, to make sure her citizens would know their own history and language."

Una said she agreed with him, that it was important. "I did nothing, really. Con Gore-Booth, well, Markievicz now, is even a distant relation and we all thought she was wonderful — though rash. She is afraid of nothing and never cared a whit for what people thought. When I mentioned her the other day at the meeting, people acted like I was talking of a personal encounter with God himself. When I confessed that she was a distant cousin, that I'd picnicked with her as a child at Lisadell, well, then there were the questions. Was she as beautiful as everyone said, was it true she could shoot like a champion? All true, I told them, and fired up with courage as well. Look, here is a sketch I did at our meeting. They seemed such a comely collection of women and as interesting to draw as flowers."

She showed Declan a pencil drawing of nine women in a parlour he recognized, tea tray at hand, and papers on the low table. And the women he recognized, too, mothers, some of them, of children he'd taught, parishioners he knew from church, a publican's wife, a doctor's wife. Una had captured their variety and purposefulness, he saw, and the differences in their economic stature could be seen by the costume they had worn to this event. The doctor's wife wore a loosely fitted suit with a lace-collared blouse draped over the jacket, a hat resplendent with feathers, a long knot of beads. The mother of one of his students, a farmer's wife who sold eggs for extra money, wore a plain skirt and what was probably her one good blouse, high-necked, with a cameo at her throat, and her hair escaping from its pins, no hat to contain it. A young woman, a cousin of the barrister, whom he'd met once at a ceilidh, wore one of the new dresses which showed the leg, her pretty shoes drawn with great detail. Her hair was bobbed in the new way, too, making her look exotic in that group of women in their middle years.

"I have seen more than one son of these women on the road recently, Una, travelling to or from exercises in the area near Delphi, and I am rather relieved that in those families at least, there is agreement between mother and son on their politics. I have heard of dreadful cases where the fathers are staunch Republicans and the sons support the Treaty, or vice versa."

"Oh, I agree, Declan, it is a terrible thing. And I sense that the women agree, too, although we rolled bandages and made certain that disinfectants were on hand in case of emergencies, as though that was all we had to think about. So much is unsaid but communicated nonetheless in stray comments or opinions on local businesses. I have learned that the other publican might well be an informant and is being watched. This was not said outright but it was certainly implied and agreed upon by hums and sighs."

They returned to the floras and Una showed Declan some examples of pressed flowers she hoped to draw, quickly sketching one so that he could see how she would try to reanimate the flat specimen, bringing its dry stems to fullness again, its opaque petals. There was the asphodel, a sample gathered the previous summer, just one stalk — before Una's discovery of the excess at Cregganbaun — laden with bright yellow blossoms; to Declan's eye, it so resembled the death camas tossing in the wind around the canoe and for a moment he was back on that bluff, the stinging sea below him and the talkative birds telling him to look at the prow to see how their brother still carried the craft forward, if only in dreams.

When Declan walked to Tullaglas later than night, carrying a candle in a tin with holes pierced to make light and a wire fastened to the opening for a handle, his mind was filled with the memory of flowers. The books had been a revelation, a new way of seeing, of understanding how a single plant might fit into the great pattern of nature with its stamen and stigma, the small dignified ovaries, the glow of pollen, hum of insects, and then the fruiting phase. As he walked, he could hear a fox yipping beyond the river. Badgers would be out from the setts, he imagined, rustling in the darkness, thinking his candle lantern a small constellation moving through the night. He passed a cabin with a lamp lit in the window, perhaps for a man returning from the shore with a few salmon, caught by torchlight, and a dog ran to see who was passing so late, hackles raised: Declan spoke quietly to it and gave it a crust he carried for just such an occasion. There was the smell of fires damped for the night and the deep reek of soil turned for potatoes. He thought of Rose's letter and was glad that such a thoughtful girl now had the opportunity to attend school. He gave himself a brief moment to remember Argos, a pang of sadness rising in his throat and suffusing his shoulders and face with regret. It all seemed so far away now and he could scarcely believe he had been that man in the cedar canoe, paddling in Jervis Inlet with the sea lions swimming nearby and the whirling rapids of the Skookumchuck, which Alex had told him meant "strong waters," calling to them like a siren.

And close to his home, he could see the far-off smudge of light at Tawnynoran, heard the crack as a rifle fired. Ghosts were abroad in the night, a few phrases of "The Lowlands of Holland" floating across the lake like a whistling of blackbirds. The voice of a young woman singing, as it had always been, he supposed, making music out of the sorrow of losing men to guns and war. And yet there were the battles countesses had gone to prison for participating in, and where women had nursed the dying in potting sheds for the light the small windows provided, carrying iodine and gauze bandages rather than trugs and secateurs.

κλίμακα δ' ὑψηλὴν προσεβήσετο οἷο δόμοιο,
εἵλετο δὲ κληῖδ' εὐκαμπέα χειρὶ παχείη
καλὴν χαλκείην· κώπη δ' ἐλέφαντος ἐπῆεν.
βῆ δ' ἴμεναι θάλαμόνδε σὺν ἀμφιπόλοισι
    γυναιξὶν
ἔσχατον· ἔνθα δέ οἱ κειμήλια κεῖτο ἄνακτος,
χαλκός τε χρυσός τε πολύκμητός τε σίδηρος
ἔνθα δὲ τόξον κεῖτο παλίντονον ἠδὲ φαρέτρη
ἰοδόκος, πολλοὶ δ' ἔνεσαν στονόεντες ὀιστοί

Climbing the high stair, leading to her room
she grasped in her strong hand the hooked key,
a key of fine bronze, with a handle of elephant-
    ivory,

She took her maids to an outermost chamber
where her lord's stored treasures were kept:
copper and gold and hard iron, all wrought
    with effort,
and the back-bent bow and a multitude of arrows,
groaning in their quiver.

Una had suggested Declan bring his books and pages of translations to her cabin where he could have a table near the fire for working on them. It had not seemed right at first — he had begun the task in isolation, first at the school, then at World's End, as a way to stave off grief, then loneliness — but he came to think that his version of the poem ought to reflect the ongoing changes in his life, as the original poem reflected the rhythms of Odysseus's: companionship, survival, *amours*, friendship, reunion ... He could tell how much better his later lines were than the earlier ones; he had learned to hear the poetry and find approximations not just in his own language but in his own experience. So he accepted Una's generosity and put his books on the little shelf she provided and set out his ink, his pens. He would come every few days and spend several hours at the table. Una was generally at work in the upstairs room although she would come periodically to show him things: a slice of stem or section of leaf mounted to view under the microscope, a pressed flower she was rehydrating in order to examine its structure and then draw as though fresh, the notes kept by David from their trip to Dingle before the War.

And waiting all the while, in the storage room, was the harp. Declan had cleaned it as thoroughly as he was able, had rubbed mineral oil into the thirsty wood. It drank it in. More would be applied, left briefly, and then rubbed and buffed until something like its original patina began to develop. The smell brought back the image of Grainne working on her instrument with a small tin of oil and a rag, her hands stroking the harp's lines and learning its contours as a lover would study the body of the beloved. She had entered the earth without having been held by a man, save the embraces of a father, had not been kissed in the drenched air of an Irish evening with the fuchsias blazing in the hedges and the perfume of primroses making a person dizzy with joy. She would never hand Declan a wrapped bundle of child, a granddaughter for him to cradle and adore. Her life was an instrument without music, gone beyond his love. He kept studying the diagram for stringing the harp, trying to make sense of each new term, seeing in them a language as foreign as Greek: tuning peg, pitch, the tension of the frame, not foreign in themselves, as words, but their meaning, relative to the harp, was a puzzle. He wanted to know more before he asked Bernadette Feeny for her assistance. He wanted the strings to be loosely strung, ready for tuning, he wanted to understand the importance of tension and the trick of the knot.

A tussle occurred on the road south of Leenane, not long after the National army converged on Clifden and arrested a number of Republicans; when the dust had cleared, it was discovered that Liam Kenny had disappeared. Where had he gone? His name was not on the lists of prisoners taken to Galway Gaol, unlike a handful of local lads who were taken away by armoured car to Galway; they were released to their families after they signed an undertaking that they would not take up arms against the Irish government, although arguments raged as to what was legitimate government and what wasn't. But Liam Kenny: was he among those who had escaped to the Partry mountains or among those who had spirited away by boat? No one could say. But the school had no master. A contingent came to ask Declan if he would teach. He did not want to do so until his house was finished, and perhaps not then, but was moved to be asked.

"Can you recommend anyone, sir?" he was asked, "And could you keep the idea of it in yer head for the future?"

He considered both things. The first was not difficult. A Conneely from down towards Renvyle had finished his university degree and was willing to come. The second request proved more of a conundrum. He assured the men he would think on it, and think on it he did.

He had never been idle, had never been offered any opportunity to be so. His small holding could certainly fill his time, but it would not allow him to engage young scholars, to offer them the benefit of his knowledge and experience. Seldom had he risen from his bed in the days before the fire and not looked forward to the trek down the Delphi road to the Bundorragha school, often joined by his students for a portion of the walk or the way entire. His daughters had always walked with him and that had been one of the pleasures of his life. As had been the returns, the homecomings, to a warm fire and a loving wife.

So now, he thought, it would be different. But perhaps that was not entirely a bad thing. He would see with his own eyes what Maire had directed him to see — blackbirds gathering nesting material, stitchwort and shepherd's purse coming into bloom, a pine marten disappearing into hazel scrub. And Grainne's great gift of music might find its way into his teaching, somehow.

There was time to think on it, anyhow. Cathal Conneely arrived, and was suitable, if dull. The work on the house was slow, but Declan was nothing if not patient. Some days, on his walks, he would notice a particularly fine stone and would borrow Fergus Mannion's donkey and cart to bring it to his farm where he would find a way to work it into the structure. Down by the lake, where the river emptied into it near the lodge, he found a millstone and mortared it above the entrance lintel. A flat slab of limestone made a splendid step by the door, and a tall pillar of basalt stood by his gate like a totem from one of the western islands, marking a burial or a death. Or, he fancied, a Janus head, to look out at the world and inward, as well.

Una had gone to London to spend Christmas with her cousin and his family; her parents were joining them from their home in France. Before she left, she handed him a package, wrapped in green tissue, and tied with silver ribbon. "Don't open it until Christmas, Declan. And make no decisions until you've seen it."

Her cryptic comment puzzled him. But he tucked the parcel away in a corner of his turf shed, wrapped in a clean shirt to protect it against the smoke and dust, and thought no more about it. The Mannions stopped by to ask did he want to go to Mass with them, and he realized it was actually Christmas Day. He declined, politely, still at odds in himself with the notion of God and not wanting to have to explain himself to his good neighbours.

He had a rabbit, skinned and cleaned, to cook in a pot over his fire, he had a few measures of Connemara malt left with which to honour the day, and, he remembered, he had a gift. He removed it from its covering of shirt and untied the ribbons carefully. Inside was a book. It was not a new book but one with a well-worn cover, dog-eared around the corners. The pages were thick paper, very dry to the touch, with a heavy impression of ink. It was a herbal, a book about plant remedies for various illnesses, and each plant entry was illustrated with a woodcut in black and white. Declan opened to the plant he felt he shared with the great Achilles. The woodcut did not give a detailed view of the plant but simply an impression. Declan read the litany of the plant's names through history — staunchweed, sanguinary, Knight's milfoil, soldiers' woundwort — and how it was one of the herbs dedicated to the Evil one and had been used for divination purposes. Tisanes were prepared against the ague and cramps and it was useful to stop headaches by its ability to cause nosebleeds, thus drawing the old blood out. How fascinating, he thought, that a plant might have such a history!

And with the book there was a card, hand-drawn by Una, showing a pretty stand of pines. Her note read, "Happy Christmas to you, Declan. I am so grateful to have found you as a friend! And I am hopeful that you might consider working with me on a project, for which this little volume might serve us as one model. A few sleepless nights led me to an idea: I have in mind a book about the plants of our area but not a flora such as David and I might have produced. I have been talking to some of the older women in Leenane about the dyeing process for wool and realize there is a huge repository of plant knowledge here, not just the medicinal or decorative or food use, but their place in the economy, in folklore, agriculture, and so forth. We would include the Gaelic names and some of the lore surrounding the native taxonomy. If you go back to the school, and I am so hopeful that you will, perhaps the children might be included in gathering information for such a book by talking to their families and observing the plants around them. Think how exciting it could be, Declan! I do look forward to seeing you in the New Year. With my very warm wishes, Una."

He didn't know what to think for a moment. He couldn't help her with a book; what on earth could he possibly do? She had the skill and knowledge to do such a thing, not him. Sure he was only just learning the proper way to classify, and him a middle-aged man. He wondered if it might be too late for him to learn something so complicated and new, although he suspected Una would tell him there was nothing new about it at all and it was the stuff of life and he was already familiar with so much about it that it was only a matter of learning its vocabulary. ("All your life," he could hear her voice telling him, "you have watched bees enter the flowers, transferring the pollen from the stamen to the stigma, you've told me Eilis collected seed of her favourite annuals, and you've kept seed of necessity from the cabbages and onions. So that *was* botany, Declan, although you didn't call it that.")

Weather that Christmas was mild and he worked hard on his house, borrowing a crude ladder from the O'Learys to place the ridge beam from gable end to gable end; he nailed on the rafters and prepared strapping for the slates, then applied them, working up from the eaves to the ridge beam. It made all the difference. The interior dried out, and Declan began to think about plastering the walls and washing them with lime. It was beginning to look like a house that might be lived in, although there was still a deceptive amount of work to be done. He noticed how the rain sounded on the slates, more noticeable than on thatch, sharper, pointed. Fergus Mannion told him that some in the area thought him foolish for using slates instead of barley straw, but Declan remembered how his house had burned, the thatch acting as a wick for the fierce flames, and how he kept to himself the smell of smoky thatch in his nostrils for months after, like a harsh and caustic punishment. Fergus helped him fit the windows in their frames.

And he walked as he always had, sometimes uneasy although the young men had been captured, although Liam Kenny had disappeared like smoke. There would be a sound, a fox yipping, a cry, something almost like a phrase of music — and he would start. Yet there had always been ghosts abroad in these hills. Once, walking near one of the lakes beyond Tullaglas as a boy, Declan had found a number of small, uninscribed stones in loose rows; his father had told him it was a cillín, a children's burial ground, that if he looked closely he would see the diminutive head and foot stones to indicate a child lay under the earth. A place of early grief, huddled in a corner of an old enclosure where dug-away bog revealed drystone walls, the remains of a shelter. When he asked his father how he knew it was children buried there, his father told him it had always been known.

Una returned from her holiday and surprised him with an embrace as she came through the gate.

"How was your time in London?" he asked, the weight of her arms around his shoulders an unsettling sensation long after she'd released him.

She told him about the concerts she'd attended with her cousin's family and the pleasure of seeing her parents. She had visited Kew and described the abundance of rare tropical plants kept under glass, a grove of evergreens she had enjoyed for their resemblance to the plantation of pines near the Aasleagh Falls. But she'd begun to long for the West of Ireland not three days into the holiday.

"Everyone advised against me coming back, of course. Lloyd George has them thinking that the Irish are all bloodthirsty. I had to remind those in the company that I *am* Irish and that I want a free Ireland, too. My parents agreed with me on that point but were unhappy I was coming back to uncertainty. I had to tell them that we never see any sign of the Troubles around here and then was promptly stopped on the way back and asked to account for myself, a woman driving alone on the Maam Road. 'If you are worried that I am carrying gelignite,' I told them, 'then by all means search the boot.' They let me go on."

Looking down at her hands, she confessed that attempts had been made to encourage a courtship, a lanky Englishman who owned a castle and a title. He was a fervent collector of rare lilies, climbing mountain ranges to bring back the seeds of beauties from China and Turkey.

"He spoke as though his mouth was filled with marbles," she laughed, "and owned that a woman just might be able to classify as well as a man but could they sleep in tents, could they boil a kettle on a spirit stove? My mother thought I was mad to spurn what I suppose amounted to advances, although made in such an odd and chilly way that I could be forgiven for having imagined him to be indifferent."

Declan felt a little stab of something, a sour sting of ... well, what would he call it? And then thought: that's it, *envy*. And then he looked at Una again, the rich weight of her embrace still warm upon his shoulders. He wondered if she'd given the collector of lilies a book with a note that she hoped to work with him on a project. It surprised him to find he hoped desperately that she hadn't.

She had also located and purchased a copy of a book Maeve had recommended to help Declan with the harp. It was *The Ancient Music of Ireland*, a collection of airs for harp collected by Edward Bunting at the great gathering of harp players in Belfast in 1792. Bunting had not only notated the performances of the harpers, among them Denis O'Hampsey, but he had talked to them, gathered information on their playing, on the harps themselves, and put together the book, prefacing it with an excellent and useful dissertation. Declan recognized the name from some sheet music Grainne had been given. Bunting was a great man for the harp. The airs were arranged for piano, and Una, insisting she was no musician, very ably played a selection of them.

"I'll try this one, Declan, Scott's lamentation for the Baron of Loughmoe, composed in 1599," she announced, reading aloud from the notes. "Imagine! It's one of the pieces that O'Hampsey played, presumably on the bog oak harp."

Declan noticed, in leafing through the book, that Bunting was not particularly keen on Carolan, calling him a genius to be sure, but also calling into question his delight in the Italian and German schools of composition, feeling that the delight translated into something less than a total commitment to the ancient music of his own country. "Like me and the poem," wondered Declan to himself, "an Irishman hungry for the lines of Greek …?" And yet, though totally unschooled in music and only a little more in poetry, Declan had always felt a deep Irish current in the Carolan compositions so beloved by Grainne. There were threads of melody you could hear in the fiddle playing at the Leenane pub or in the room at any ceilidh, even in the tune hummed by a farmer as he brought home the sheep. *Irish is as Irish does*, he thought.

And then Una was asking, "Have you heard this piece?" and she was playing something so achingly lovely that he felt tears come to his eyes. It entered his heart, played the strings of memory and yearning, and when she finished playing, she told him it was a lament for Grainne Mhael. He did not know it from his own Grainne but it felt like a piece of music that might have been fitting to accompany her into the earth, had he known or been willing for anything like a ceremony.

And lines came to him, lines he had in the recent past laboured over, never sensing in them a message but hearing now the act of persuasion.

> ὣς ἄρ ἔφαν μνηστῆρες· ἀτὰρ πολύμητις
> 'Οδυσσεύς,
> the suitors made their declarations but Odysseus
> the wise,
> αὐτίκ' ἐπεὶ μέγα τόξον ἐβάστασε καὶ ἴδε
> πάντῃ,

straight away took up the great bow and looked
    to all directions,
ὡς ὅτ' ἀνὴρ φόρμιγγος ἐπιστάμενος καὶ
    ἀοιδῆς,
like a singer, a player of the lyre,
ῥηιδίως ἐτάνυσσε νέῳ περὶ κόλλοπι χορδήν,
easily stretches a new string on the peg,
ἄψας ἀμφοτέρωθεν ἐυστρεφὲς ἔντερον οἰός,
fastens to both sides the twisted length of
    sheep-gut,
ὣς ἄρ' ἄτερ σπουδῆς τάνυσεν μέγα τόξον
    Ὀδυσσεύς.
so effortlessly did Odysseus string the great bow.

"Una, I think I will try those strings now."

They brought the harp into the big room and lit all the lamps. Each string was wrapped in a bit of paper with its note written on it. There was a chart as well, which gave him the Irish names for the strings, or combination of strings, and a pattern for the stringing itself.

First, the Sisters, two strings in unison, which would be the first to be tuned to the proper pitch. They divided the instrument into bass and treble and answered to tenor G on the violin. There were holes in the sound box of the harp, through which one pushed one's hand in order to thread the string through the tiny string hole. The ends were taken up to the tuning pegs and put through the holes in the pegs and wound on. It took ages to do this; Declan found his hands were too big, his concentration not right. The first time he did it, he neglected to tie off the string he was threading through and the whole length of it slid out as he was trying to wind it on the tuning peg. He stabbed his finger with a sharp end of wire and it bled more than he would have imagined possible.

The clean cotton that Una wrapped around it made everything more difficult.

Several of the strings went through more easily. A was called Servant to the Sisters, and B, Second String Over the Sisters. Then there were the Sinews, the half-tone F, and G was Answering. It was a curious language of relationships, one he felt he might be on the verge of understanding. Of course he had no idea of the tuning but that would be Bernadette Feeny's province. Grainne had used a tuning fork, he thought, and sometimes asked Maire to sound a note on the tin whistle. He wished he had paid more attention. The book cautioned against tightening the strings too excessively. It would be asking a frame to take hundreds of pounds of tension right from the start, and the wood needed time to adjust to, or in this case remember, the tension. Tighten the strings just enough to keep them from sagging, the book suggested. The wrench Maeve had sent was used for this purpose. He thought to himself, *What is a schoolmaster and erstwhile fisherman doing stringing a harp?* And then he remembered Grainne, her deep and abiding hope for herself as a musician, the way her eyes shone when Maeve Fitzgerald told her about the courses that the latter had taken at the Royal Irish Academy of Music, and how Eilis would tell her that they would have to see what happened, she had years yet to practise and play, but that God worked in miraculous ways, and he read the instructions again, made his fingers seek out the tiny string holes again. The book also recommended a particular knot for tying off the strings and advised slipping a thin length of stick through the loop to anchor the knot. The first few strings Declan tied off began to slip, and he followed the book's advice on the sticks.

Finally he had completed the stringing and he returned to the instructions, studying them again to make certain he had followed them correctly. Running his thumb across the strings, he was satisfied that they were all fastened securely to their tuning pegs. From what he could understand, the range of tension between untuned and tuned was narrow. Too little tension, and the sound was twangy. Too much could damage the soundboard. Now he could only send a message to Bernadette Feeny and wait.

A week later, she arrived in a donkey cart with her shawl and her tuning key. Through a complicated set of transmissions, she had let Declan know when she needed to go to Leenane on errands and he arranged to be at Una's cabin to assist her. She greeted them both and then conveyed her sorrow at hearing of the fires. The Feeny farm was beyond Delphi, at Glenummera, nestled in a hollow of the Sheefry Hills. It was very isolated. Declan had not seen a Feeny since before his house had burned. The Feeny children had only attended school when they could arrange to stay with cousins for a week or so as the distance was too far for them to travel on a daily basis. But Bernadette and her husband, Joseph, had assisted them with their lessons at home and one of them, Tomás, had gone on to the college in Galway and was on his way to becoming a doctor. Bernadette was a fine harp player herself and was in as much demand as one could be, living so far from the centres of population. She played at weddings and funerals whenever possible, and at ceilidhs, too, alongside silent, toothless men on fiddles who could pull reels or slow airs out of their instruments like lengths of many-coloured yarn.

Una gave Bernadette a cup of tea and hung her shawl by the fire. They chatted for a few minutes as they both sipped their tea. Then Bernadette turned to the harp, which had been moved to an area near a window. She praised the job Declan had done of stringing it and then showed him a few tricks that would have simplified the job. She told him she would tune it to the natural key, in Irish called Leath Gleas. She affixed the small wrench to a tuning peg and turned it slightly. She listened, then pushed the string a little with her finger.

"I am only to take the slack out of them this first day so," she told them. "Ye cannot expect the poor harp to take any more strain. But I will stay with my sister in Leenane and come back for the next few days and we will get it to pitch over time."

Declan told her how grateful he was and how he hoped he was not giving her too much trouble.

"Ah, sir," she laughed. "I will have a good visit with my sister and she will do some spinning for me, I've that much wool from our sheep this year! So she'll spin for me and I'll tune for ye and God willing ye'll teach our children again so. And I won't say no to another cup of tea."

Declan was surprised to hear her mention the teaching but then reflected that word must've got around about him being asked and not saying no, and it was ever so: there were seldom secrets even though the distances between houses were great and there was scarcely a telephone in the area. News travelled like wild seeds or magpies, settling wherever a little area of welcome might exist. Indeed, he learned the comings and goings, births and deaths, of all the families in Glenummera and beyond simply by sharing a cup of tea with Bernadette Feeny. And as good as her word, Bernadette returned almost daily, working in the warm room with her wrench and tuning fork, sometimes asking Una to give her a particular note on the piano. From full notes to semitones, she adjusted and listened, until the harp sounded true. She cautioned that the tuning might just slip and new strings were notorious for losing their pitch until they had wrestled with the wood of the frame enough to find a way of holding their own against its greater strength. It was as though they were speaking of an animal, a spirited horse being gentled to the plough, learning to harness its strength to a practical task. Bernadette stroked the harp, praising its comely waist, the deep glow of its wood.

"Do ye have someone in mind to play it?"

"I haven't. But it seemed a terrible thing to leave it unstrung."

"Aye, just so. Someone will come along who will know its beauty and whose fingers will long to bring out its airs."

Bernadette had been playing short passages of music, long silvery argeggios, in order to complete the tuning, and now Declan asked her if she would favour them with a song. When she asked did he have a particular piece in mind, he nodded, his throat already filling.

"'The Farewell to Music,' Bernadette. Can ye play that one?"

"I can."

It was as he remembered, the slow beginning, the musical images of a life lived, roads travelled, the sound of a passing horse, birdsong, the revelry at the end of a dark road, and then the sweet, sad notes of a man anticipating the end of his days. He did not wipe the tears from his eyes but let them spring forth, a weeping for all that he had lost, each specific thing given a note, a rising scale, a specific relationship between fingers and strings, ringing and dampening, melody suggesting harmony, and the dignified conclusion.

Bernadette said, as she rose from her seat, "Declan, we call an air like that a tiompán. I am thinking one was never played for the women of the house so."

None had. He had left without arranging the proper rites. And would still have done the same, knowing what he knew. Their lament had to come from a place it could never have come from on that day, when he had nailed the boards together for their coffins. He had known such sadness in the days that followed, had crossed water, watched sunrises across the plains of America, gone by boat in darkness to find a tiny bay where a man had been buried in his own canoe and then dug up by a pig. A girl had come to him for poetry. A dog had slept at his feet and would have followed him wherever he went, even if it meant losing everything she had known. He had seen the death camas and the healing herb of Achilles. He wept for that, for the memory of a face in lamplight, for the tree frogs that stared at him from window glass, and for the wild roses that beckoned him out of his solitary shack to bury himself in them like a bee might and then lift his face, golden with pollen. And for the men who ferried him over deep water to eat clams and bread salty with the grease of decaying fish, who made him a paddle, slept around him like brothers while wolves howled under stars. For the man, cruel but loved by a tender woman, who had been decapitated through the work of ravens, perhaps the same ravens who had befriended him on that far bay. And when his tears stopped, he embraced Bernadette Feeny and thanked her for bringing the harp back to life.

"Declan, no one could have done so but ye. I could not tune strings that had melted or broken. Ye might have left it as a memory, charred and unusable, but look at it now, polished and whole. And such fine strings, too. They'll last awhile at least."

Chapter Fourteen

"Declan, I have been sorting out the storeroom and found this box of my grandfather's clothing. Why it ended up in the groundskeeper's cabin is a bit of a mystery, but Hugh thinks he perhaps passed along clothing he no longer wore and evidently it didn't suit or fit old Reilly. Hugh doesn't want any of it. You and my grandfather are of a size, if I may say that about you who are alive and my grandfather who has been dead for more than two decades, bless him. Can you use some jerseys and shirts? There are some sturdy corduroy trousers, too, and a nice jacket of Donegal tweed — my mother must have sent that to him, as I recognize the tweed."

"It's very generous of ye, Una, and I will gladly accept them if ye're certain yer father does not need them so. May I leave the carton here until my own place is more ready?"

"You may indeed. And my father certainly does not need them. My grandfather loved the Erriff River and I'd like to think of his clothing going on here, even if he's no longer alive to wear them."

They were planning a sketching and gathering trip up the rough road that led out of Leenane towards Maam Cross. There were mountains, the Maamturks, and a valley between them cut through by the Glengosh River and the Bealanabrack River, and Una wanted to try the wild track which led up to a tiny community called Bunnaviskaun. They were taking lunch and the vasculum as well as an assortment of baskets for transporting living plants with a little clump of earth attached. It was raining lightly as they set out and the road was slick. Una drove carefully, having long since mastered the intricacy of the braking system — a brake for each wheel — and the gears. They went through the quiet centre of Leenane and took the Maam road. Devilsmother loomed to the north, wraithlike in mist, and small cottages hunched under their chimney smoke like sheep, summer forgotten. Una looked over at Declan and smiled. "You might find that the pheasants flee from you in terror when they see you in the jacket. My grandfather was a fearsome shot and was forever shooting at them."

She was indefatigable in the field, even in rain. She strode through the woods near Dereen to a boggy area where once she'd found ragged robin and arrowhead and was lucky enough to find them again, although Declan had to take her word for it that the withered brown leaves belonged to something worth a portrait. She prepared them carefully, shaking excess soil from the roots and placing them in the vasculum. Several plants, including celandine, were taken with a good amount of soil on them so she could plant them at Marshlands in a small marshy area she was slowly populating with likely specimens now that there were no longer horses to trample them; these she wrapped with damp paper and nestled into one of her baskets. She showed Declan how to dig up plants, easing the trowel deeply under them, in a way which brought up the entire root and which didn't disturb adjacent growth too much; he quickly caught on. She sketched the broader view and made small insets of things she found of interest — a variety of wintergreen that she said was too rare to lift and needed to be drawn in situ, with the palette carefully added to the edge of the paper for future painting, and globe flowers in a protected place with a last frail blossom clinging to the stem.

By lunchtime they were parked on the side of a very rugged road and walking over a footbridge that crossed the Bealanabrack River, swollen with winter rain, to eat their kippers and soda bread by the standing stones on the north side of the river. Many small creeks ran down to join the river, their meeting a chilly music. A crowd of dirty sheep wandered among the rocks, hunting for any tussocks they might have missed. Declan and Una ate and talked, examining the pattern of lichens on the standing stones, pondering the possible methods used to raise the stones at the dawn of time. And then they were driving up the track, it could not be called a road, nudging sheep out of the way with the car's bumper, passing farms so isolated that even the dogs forgot to bark in their surprise at seeing a car, passing the remains of a ring fort near Gowlaunlee, and then they were at the end of the road where a few bleak houses huddled together for warmth.

The families spoke no English. Declan told them that Una and he were looking for plants and hoped to walk beyond the end of the road. A man in a pair of homespun trousers with pampooties on his feet told them they were welcome and God be with them and did they know about the mass rock over yonder? They didn't of course, and Declan translated the directions carefully, writing down the names of the townlands in his notebook; they would walk in the direction of Gleniska, where the land would be high and where they might yet see the remains of a farm or two, uninhabited, unworked since the terrible days of the hunger. Then they would come to the spreading rivers, and it was only a short distance to the rock where priests had arrived to say mass as in any church and where the worshippers might feel themselves safe for a time in the eye of the Lord. Two eggs, still warm from the hen, were pressed gently into Una's hands, and a woman told Declan in Irish that he was a lucky man to have found such a lovely woman. He did not translate this for Una but found a place in one of the baskets for the eggs, which he covered with a small bit of moss.

The route the man had described took them to where the first waters of the Glengosh River sprang from the earth and past a ring fort nearly complete, apart from what would have been its roof of rushes. Over a rise to where a spring came up from rock and started its descent down to Killary Harbour, gathering enough momentum to turn itself into a river on the journey. The mass rock came into a view in a small glen between two creeks; the view of it would be hidden from any other approach than the one they used. A long table of rock, which would have served as an altar to Catholics in the area during the time of the Penal Laws and after, Declan explained to Una, when the hope was that the religion would simply die away, with the education and ordination of priests illegal. But as he had learned in his own teaching, the will of the Irish to be educated and to hold and observe their faith was stronger than anyone might have supposed.

"How do people know about these sites?" asked Una. "To me, it could simply be part of one of the dolmens, the usual supports collapsed, or even a natural piece of rock which simply resembles an altar."

"Ah, but ye've underestimated the power of memory, Una. When so much has been taken over the years, or forbidden, when education was denied us, land ownership prohibited, when ye've come through what the Irish have suffered, ye see that survival as a people has meant using every faculty to its utmost, and maybe nothing was more important than memory. In one way, the use of this mass rock is beyond memory — we are talking hundreds of years, after all — but the language itself is congenial to the notion of the present tense. Everything is present, always, so talk of this place would be given to new generations as though its use was in the present tense. I think that makes what happened here harder to forget."

"You talk of the Irish, Declan, as though I am not Irish. And yet the Fitzgeralds have been here since the time of the Normans, our family has memory, too, although not of mass rocks and ruined cottages, I agree. I think one of the saddest things for me about this country is how easily we neglect to include the others — for the Catholics, the Protestants; for the wealthy, those who are not — in the idea of what it is to be Irish, to be connected to this country. Sometimes I have knelt by a bed of wild cress, all foamy with blossom, and wept at the beauty of it, the fact that people have seen such things for longer than we can possibly imagine, and yet I am treated in the village like a foreigner. Everyone goes quiet when I go into the shop and I am always Miss Fitzgerald, even though I have asked to be simply Una."

Declan saw that she was in tears. He moved to her and put his arms around her.

"No one sees me," she cried, "they see what they think my forefathers have done to them, yet my grandmother opened her kitchen to the hungry, my great-aunt died making soup in the workhouse at Killybegs because the fevers didn't distinguish between Catholics or Protestants. Nor did she, which was why she was there; she thought God would expect no less from her. And look what has happened to both our families, for heaven's sake."

She sobbed against his shoulder, which was clothed in the tweed jacket of her grandfather, and he patted her back, stroked her hair. There were so many words to say, and none.

They lived in a country of such wonders and such despair. Declan murmured reassurances that perhaps the tide was changing, that surely her goodness would be recognized in the village for what it was (and sure wasn't that why the Cumann na mBán had asked her to join them). He told her how sorry he was if his actions had made her believe he thought her less than Irish. She pulled away and found a handkerchief in her rucksack, wiped her eyes and blew her nose. Then she smiled at him, the wide, generous smile he had come to take pleasure in, and told him she had never imagined him to be part of the problem.

"And what is this, Declan, this campsite we are standing by without even noticing?"

Looking around, Declan could see the pressed earth of recent use, a ring of stones where a fire had burned, some tins with their jagged lids askew. It was a protected place, the glen, with fresh water, trees for cover, good sight lines. He was not surprised to find some spent bullets at the foot of a tree, which betrayed from indentations in its bark that it had been used for target practise.

"I am thinking, Una, that this site has been used more recently than I supposed. Well, and doesn't it make sense that the hidden places would be where fellas would head to? It is perhaps what I meant when I said talk of such places made them alive to each generation. I am also thinking that the mist has turned to rain and we'd best be on our way so."

By now the sky was very overcast. Gusts of wind were strong at that high elevation as well, tumbling branches of heather and gorse across the wide expanse. With the rain, it was harder to see where they were going and the landmarks they thought they'd recognize were so different coming from the opposite direction. It took them hours to find their way back to Una's car and they were soaked through to the skin. One of the farmers they'd talked to before venturing off to find the mass rock came out of a cottage and insisted they come in for a cup of tea.

They were given old, clean feed sacks to dry their hair and to try to wring some of the water out of their clothing. A bench was drawn very close to the fire and they sat side by side with their feet stretched out gratefully while a group of small children watched from the side of their mother's skirt. Declan spoke to them in Irish but they were too shy to engage in any kind of conversation. They did not go to school, as it was too far to walk, but the master would visit them upon occasion and help with the alphabet and sums. Mugs of tea were brought, and thick slices of bread spread with brambleberry jelly. It was warm in the small house, and dark, with only a single lamp on the table for light. Declan asked the woman of the house whether she used plants for dyeing, and she said yes, they gathered autumn crocus to make a yellow dye for the wool of their sheep, and wild pansies for blue, and foxgloves for green. Nettles, she told him, were a great food, and she made broth for her elderly parents when they ached with the rheumatism. When they finished their tea, they reluctantly said goodbye, thanking the family for their hospitality. The woman replied tartly that it wouldn't be much of a world if you could not open your door to strangers and make them welcome. In Irish she reminded him that a guest should be welcomed no matter the hour since every guest is Christ. As they walked out to the car, she called a blessing, and Declan answered her with a "God save all here," realizing that it ought to have been his greeting.

Driving back down the track from Bunnaviskaun, Una commented quietly that the woman had certainly proved her wrong, hadn't she, with her generosity, not making assumptions about her class.

"Aye, and I'm thinking that there are people like her all over this country but somehow the others have a way of making us remember them. I am minded of the Greek stories where a humble couple take in a stranger, feed him up with the little they have, and he turns out to be a god who grants them a grand wish. Tell me, Una, why the car is suddenly making that noise?"

The car coughed a few times and then stopped. Una was unable to start it again.

"This will be the test of our resourcefulness, Declan! I was told that driving through puddles might cause the car to stall. Would it be that the wiring has become soaked?"

It took them more than an hour to figure out how to dry out the wiring, to check the spark plugs, Una repeating some steps she had been told in the parking area of the Great Southern Hotel, her voice strained as she said the mantra of the plugs over and over. Finally the engine fired. Their hands were cold, their only light from a very dim torch, and the rain streamed down their necks, completing the soaking.

Una drove slowly down the road to Leenane, the visibility terrible. They had to keep stopping to wipe off the windshield for the tiny difference it made, and the rain had caused the surface of the road to become slick and treacherous. The lights of Leenane were never so welcome as they were that night. Without saying a word, Una stopped at one of the public houses and ran inside, her hair drenched and lying flat against her head. She returned with a bottle she handed to Declan to hold.

"Guard that carefully. I think hot whiskeys will be more a necessity than a luxury, Declan. And I'm going to insist that you stop at my house for the night. You can't sleep in a turf shed as wet as you are with no facility for getting dry or warm. We don't want you contracting pneumonia and blaming it on a crazy woman hunting for celandine in January."

He could not contradict her. The prospect of entering his makeshift bed feeling as he did was about as unpleasant as anything he could imagine. Past Leenane, up to the top of the

Harbour where the Delphi road left the main road snaking through the Partry Mountains to Westport, and along a short distance to Marshlands. Parking the car, Una gathered up the baskets and vasculum and let them into her house, immediately lighting the lamps.

"Declan, I'm going to fill the bathtub for you and leave you in the kitchen while I sort out my plants upstairs and begin to press some of them — after I've changed into dry clothing, of course. And I think if you look through the carton of Grandfather's clothes, you'll find a nightshirt. It will be clean, if considerably mended."

She quickly brought the fire to life, put the kettle on her range, and left to change. Returning, she lifted a zinc tub from its hook in the scullery and placed it on a mat near the fire. The reservoir on her stove provided steaming jugs of hot water for the tub, and she kept adding cool until it seemed a comfortable temperature. Opening a cupboard, she brought two towels, which she put on a stool drawn up to the tub along with a bar of soap and a sponge.

"And now, my final act before attending to my plants, will be to make you a hot whiskey to drink while you soak! I have no lemons, I'm afraid, but cloves and a little sugar?"

It sounded wonderful. Once the mug had been placed on the stool with the towels, well within reach of a bather, Una went upstairs. The room was pleasantly warm. Declan removed his wet clothing and draped it over a drying rack lowered from the ceiling by the fire. He eased his body down into the water, sighing as he did so. It had been so long since he'd had the opportunity for a real bath, relying as he did on his basin and cloth. He took a small drink of his whiskey and closed his eyes. The last time he had immersed his body in water was at Oyster Bay when he'd bathed in the sea, sitting on rocks the sun had warmed before the tide came in. His skin tingled as he remembered the chill of that water and the gauzy haze that formed when the heat of the rocks met the cold tide.

Listening, he could almost hear the Neil children laughing over in their cove and the curious ravens *tok, toking* as they watched him from the trees (*for sorrow, for joy*). He saw Rose naked in the tide, and he remembered Eilis bathing their daughters and filling a tub for him too after he'd dug potatoes until his back ached. He could hear her murmuring to the girls in the other room as he soaked his muscles. The room was filled with ghosts! Children far and near, a wife, even the lost men camped by the mass rock in blinding rain ... Opening his eyes, he reached for the sponge and soap and began to wash himself, lathering his neck, what he could reach of his shoulders and back, between his legs, the sad skin of his knees. All the grime and weariness of rebuilding his house, walking back and forth to Leenane for supplies, alone on the road like any beggar, of walking with Una over the hilly shoulders of the Maamturk Mountains, everything was sloughed away by the washing. The layers of his old self, the man who had cursed God for the actions of those soldiers, who had ridden to North America in the hold of a boat, who had travelled by train from the eastern seaboard to the West Coast where he had found a house, a dog, a difficult peace, the self who imagined his heart had become small with bitterness, washed away with sweet soap and water.

He stood up in the tub, surprised at how wrinkled his fingers had become, how pale his flesh. He towelled himself off. The nightshirt had been hung by the fire to air, and Declan pulled it over his head. Despite its mendings, it was very grand: soft white cotton, very full, sheaves of tawny wheat embroidered on the placket. He sat in one of the comfortable armchairs and sipped the remains of his drink.

He heard Una come downstairs and called was there anything he should do with the water?

"Nothing tonight, Declan. In the morning, you can help me drag the tub to the door. Luckily it has a plug in the side to empty it so I drain it out in the yard. Now, was it nice?"

"Ah, Una, like heaven itself. And the whiskey is a fine caution against pneumonia."

She looked at him, smiling. "I remember that nightshirt. My grandmother did the embroidery and my grandfather teased her about it. 'Wheat!' he'd say. 'Was there nothing romantic you could have given me on my nightshirt?' She would just laugh. I loved it, of course, because even then I was happy to discover plants in any manifestation."

They sat by the fire, talking about the day, and drinking their hot whiskeys, and then Una heated some soup, telling him as she stirred it how the plants had survived the drive home from the Bealanabrack River and how she had catalogued them. Declan drank a bowl of the soup and found he could not keep his eyes open. His hostess noticed and showed him to the bed in the box room where the harp was kept. Linen sheets and billowing eiderdown put him to sleep almost immediately.

At first he didn't know why he was awake. He located himself: no, not at World's End, not in the turf shed, alas no longer wrapped in Eilis's arms as he so often dreamed, faint memories as he worked himself backwards in his state of disorientation; then he sat up in bed, listening. Someone was crying. It must be Una. He got out of bed and allowed his eyes to adjust to the dark. Her room was on the other side of the main room, and he made his way to her door. A few coals of turf glowed in the darkness. "Una," he called softly, "are ye all right?"

"Oh, Declan, I'm so sorry to have woken you. Open the door, Declan, and come in. I'll light the lamp. Unless you can't bear to hear a woman weep and want only to return to your bed, and I shall quite understand if you do. There, the lamp is lit.

No, I'm not all right, although I'm not ill or anything. I woke and felt so desperately lonely, as though I might never be happy again. I keep wondering if I've made the right decision, coming back to Marshlands. Seeing you in my grandfather's nightshirt, I was filled with memories of my childhood here when everything was innocent and good."

She looked stricken, her eyes swollen with crying. The room was bathed in soft light, and Declan could see that her bureau was covered in photographs, her walls held framed portraits of her family, including the grandfather who'd owned the nightshirt; Declan remembered him from childhood, a kind man who rode a tall grey hunter. He stood by Una's bed and felt helpless at her sorrow.

"My cousins and I rode our ponies to far lakes and hills without a single worry apart from how to explain that our pony had cast a shoe and we'd never noticed," she said. "We all expected to do grand things. We were raised to expect that, I suppose, so how did I get to be this age without any accomplishments? No child, no real role in my community, not even a pair of wolfhounds to walk with and care for. I can't help but think that my grandparents must be so disappointed in me, wherever they are."

"Disappointed in ye, Una?" asked Declan as he sat on the edge of her bed. "Ye are so alive and so brave! If they could have seen ye encountering the problems of the car on that forsaken road, their hearts would have been bursting with pride. As for accomplishments, well, what are they anyway? Ye think ye have done the things that yer life leads to so, and then it all disappears in the wink of an eye, taken by fire. Aye, and a child …" his voice trailed off in sadness.

"Oh, I'm so sorry, I didn't mean to remind you …"

He looked up. "Of course ye didn't. But the book plan, surely that is something good. Putting down what is known about dyes and cures. Yer grandparents would be mightily proud of ye, particularly if they could see the drawings of all the homely things I walked by a hundred times and never noticed."

He was stroking her head. She was lovely in lamplight, her hair down and curly from its earlier soaking. She reached up to touch his face, her fingers suddenly electric on his skin, and then they were kissing. It was a long kiss, containing the yearning for lost partners, arms emptied of lovers' bodies, one mouth unblessed by another for years, and when Una broke away to ask, "Do you think this is a sin?" Declan could only reply, "I never dreamed kissing ye would be so right."

And then he was holding her fiercely in his arms, not for comfort, as he had held her by the mass rock while she wept. She was not weeping, she was kissing him as though she was hungry for what his mouth contained, and she moved his hands to the inside of her nightdress where her breasts waited, full and soft, their nipples rising to his fingers. She smelled of rain and tasted of cloves and just faintly of whiskey, as he thought he must, too. He could not believe he was being held by her, her hands gently guiding him so that he was entering her, having forgotten the utter sweetness of a woman's body, its rich temperatures, its weathers. Her body was responding as he could not have anticipated, her arms were wrapped around his hips and she was pushing his buttocks forward with her hands so that he was fully within her; they were moving under the coverlet as though they had loved one another for decades. When he could not wait any longer, she suddenly broke her mouth away and shuddered against him, her belly damp with sweat.

When he could breath again, and when his heart had quieted within the cage of his chest, Declan asked, "Una, what have we done?"

"Do you really need me to tell you?" she laughed. "I want to assure you, though, that this is not what I intended when I suggested you stay here for the night, if that is what you're thinking.

But I will confess something to you. When you comforted me on the high rocks this afternoon, I realized that I have fallen in love with you. All my talk about the divisions in our country, and I fall in love with a Catholic man who farms his land. That is an example of practising what I preach, would you not agree?"

"But love, Una? How could a woman like ye, with yer education and yer family, say that ye've fallen in love with a man who has only ever taught country children their sums and dug turf and hoed his potatoes, come summer?"

"You are simple-minded, Declan, if you honestly think that is all you have done. I have fallen in love with a man who is decent and intelligent and who has shown me that he believes in honour in a way most men could never understand. Besides, I have always wanted to learn Greek and I am counting on you to teach me. Tomorrow let's begin with the alphabet!"

"And that collector of lilies, Una? Ye have no plans for him, are ye telling me this?" He would not tell her that he had fervently hoped that she had not given that man a gift at Christmas, that his own book of plants she had wrapped for him was kept under his pillow — for protection, he'd have said if anyone had seen it, but he remembered the sting he had felt when she'd mentioned the fellow in passing.

"Declan, I believe you're jealous! My mother has mentioned him in letters, hinting that he would not say no to an invitation to come to Ireland to look for lilies. Well, I don't imagine he would be satisfied with our simple wild garlic or the three-cornered leek. But do you know, I cannot even remember his name. Higgins, perhaps?"

When he woke again, the body of a woman against his back, he thought he was dreaming. It was like being in the canoe, every nerve ending alive, and the divisions between the living world and the other world blurred. He thought he could hear music, but taking a moment to gather his wits, he realized it was the

Erriff River rushing down to meet Killary Harbour. He began to ease himself out of the bed when Una woke and kissed his neck.

"Will I make us a cup of tea?" he asked, stroking her hand.

"I am perishing for tea," she replied, lifting the weight of her hair from the pillow.

Walking back later that morning to Delphi, in sunshine, for the rain had lifted to show the Mweel Reas in blue air with their white peaks glittering, Declan made up his mind to offer his teaching services to the National School for the next year. He had been adrift, and if not now at anchor, he at least felt that he wanted his feet on dry ground, a reason to rise in the mornings, his days filled with purpose, an occupation. The idea of a book of the townland and beyond had settled into his mind and he saw its potential for bringing together families, generations, village people and those of the outlying farms. He remembered his mother telling him that some women could coax beautiful dyes out of simple plants and that she wished she knew how, for she'd colour the old tea towels something other than grey, there being entirely too much grey in the world. The Kelly children at the school: Declan remembered that their grandmother had worked in the woollen industry in Leenane as a dyer, and he knew the woman was still alive, though she spoke not a word of English. Well, there was the beginning. Perhaps.

News came that Liam Kenny had been wounded and taken by the Civil Guards who had assumed policing duties in Leenane. He was sent to Galway, where he was imprisoned and then released. He wrote to Declan, saying that he had great respect for his teaching and that the young men from his classroom had spoken with some knowledge of Irish history and politics. "I am about to take my degree at the university, though there was some determination to keep all jailbirds out, but those who knew my father have spoken in my favour. I will work against the cursed Treaty but hope, of course, that this might be done in a civilized way. I mind that an Irish winter is a cold time to be camping out around a sizzling fire with only the odd old tune to comfort a man. Erin go bragh, Mr. O'Malley."

One ghost less in the chilly hills, thought Declan. One less song to ring in the clear air, accompanied by the crack of a rifle shot, a circle of stones, the smoke gone out. And he wondered if a girl had loved Liam Kenny and watched for his light across the hills and was waiting yet for him. In years to come, this might form a story for Liam Kenny, something he would tell his grandchildren, of how he had fought with Republican brigades in the Connemara mountains, had been shot in the leg, and had left their grandmother for years not knowing whether he was alive or dead, and here he was, a solicitor in a country town who would meet old mates for a drink from time and time and relive the days of '23. For his sake, Declan hoped the story might go something like that.

One night, sleeping in Una's bed, he heard the soft rap of knuckles at her cabin door. He gently shook her awake.

"Una, there is someone knocking. It might be best if I not answer." Declan helped her out of the bed; she reached for her wrapper and lit a candle to see her way to the door. Declan stood behind the bedroom door, which he left ajar so he could hear if he might be needed; there was no telling what to expect on those dark nights with the Civil Guards in the barracks and the fierce Republicans still in the mountains.

He listened as a boy, he couldn't tell who, told Una that there had been a skirmish and some wounded and the women of the Cumann na mBán were needed for first aid — the doctor, reliable in such emergencies, was away on a difficult maternity case down near Kylemore. They were to go to the designated place, the boy said, and sounded relieved when Una said she would just dress and get her kit. She told the boy to go wait in her car and she would be ready shortly. She returned to the bedroom to quickly put on warm clothing.

"Will I come with ye, Una? I don't like the thought of ye travelling into dangerous ground."

"Declan, I would rather you didn't. We have an arrangement, I have three women to collect to bring along with me, and two of them have revolvers in case we need such things. I am quite certain, though, that first aid is just what we are needed for."

He heard the car engine start, cough a little. The vehicle moved down the driveway, the headlamps casting a path to follow. He drew on his clothing and walked out to the main road and watched the smudge of light make its way towards Leenane, then disappear as the car turned at one of the side tracks leading into the pleated hills. She would be collecting Brigid Tierney, he thought, and it gave him some comfort to stand in the darkness and imagine sensible Brigid joining Una for the task ahead of them.

It was hours until she arrived back, dishevelled, her clothing spattered with blood. Yes, there had been a skirmish near the barracks. The road leading south to Clifden had been trenched by the Republicans and the road leading through the Maam Valley had been barricaded by the Nationals; she'd had to do some fancy talking to get past the latter to the safe house, four women in a private car in the dead of night. They'd said they were attending a birth. There had been a lot of shooting, some dead on each side, sniping from impossible positions in the hills where you'd expect only to find gorse, maybe some hardy sheep. Una was very pale as she recounted the number of wounded who had been spirited away to the designated house — she would not tell him which one, she said, because it was safer that he didn't know in the event she was arrested — where the local Cumann na mBán team arrived with their kits to staunch the bleeding and remove bullets.

"One young man, Declan, whom I will not name but whom you have taught as well as spoken of, he will lose his leg, I'm afraid. The bone was splintered beyond repair and although we gave him opium and then brandy on top of that, he could not keep from screaming in obvious terrible pain."

She was sponging a bloody mark out of her skirt as she talked and Declan noticed that her hands were behaving as though separate from her. They kept dabbing obsessively at the mark with a cloth, without thought, and finally Declan came to her and gently took the cloth from her. She covered her face with her hands for moment, gave a small sob, and then continued.

"The doctor's wife — and you will forget that I told you she was there — was very calm, holding his hand while we tried to clean the wound but privately, once he had been sedated enough to lose consciousness, she told us she was certain the leg could not be saved. The others were less serious, though it was traumatic for them, of course. And for one woman who entered the room to find her own son-in-law on the table, head bandaged and arms riddled with bullet wounds."

Declan finished removing the bloody mark from the skirt and then made tea for Una; he poured in a measure of whiskey, as she had begun to shake in the telling. Neither of them slept at all in the hour remaining of night and in the morning they said reluctant goodbyes. Both had work to do in their individual houses, and Declan declined Una's offer of a ride home, thinking that the morning air would clear both his head and his heart. He had been saddened beyond telling to know that deaths had occurred while he lingered in the protection of Una's cabin, the night spectacular with stars. He tried to find comfort in the poem on his walk home but realized how many deaths were contained in its own sinewy lines.

At the turn north by Tully, the road was barricaded by an armoured car, two other military vehicles, sandbags piled around their tyres. Declan could see no men at all, but as he approached, a voice shouted "Hands up"; he stopped and raised his arms above his head. Two men emerged from the armoured car and advanced towards him, rifles pointed at his chest. To his horror, he noted that the guns were Enfields, the same as those he had found that day in his turf pile. These men were dressed in the uniform of the National Army, and their voices were Irish.

"Why are you on the road so early?" one of them asked.

"I am returning home after a night away," Declan replied, as calmly as he could. He could feel sweat dampening his shirt, and his heart pounded in its cage of chest.

"Away, were you? Can you tell us, please, where you were and what you were up to?"

"I spent the night in a woman's bed," he answered. "I would rather not say her name."

The men laughed, and one of them nudged Declan's arm with his rifle. "You'll have to do better than that, man. These are dangerous times, you must know, and we are charged with protecting the citizenry from the Republican Western Division, what's left of them — you might have heard they attacked the barracks in Leenane last night and there was great bloodshed. Can you say you know nothing about this? You cannot hide behind an anonymous woman, man, when for all we know you might have been one of the men with dynamite. We've found one young lad down by the river trying to hide a rifle and we've got him hog-tied by the lorry. We'll do the same to you if you don't come clean and tell us what you know of the ambush last night."

"I know of it to be sure. This is my community, after all, and people talk of shots being fired in the night, explosions. But I am not part of them, I am only a schoolmaster who has never fired a gun. And I will not harm the name of the woman I was with by identifying her to you." Declan was growing angry at the repeated nudge of the rifle in his ribs, his shoulders. He could see a boy, one of the youths he'd spoken to on their way home from Tawnynoran gap, and the boy was shivering with fear. Declan longed to go to him, to lead him firmly up the Delphi road to his farm and his mother who would scold him but then offer porridge, tea. "Ye have a job to do, I am with ye there, but to threaten a man on his own road, to insult him as ye are doing, this is no way to treat an Irish citizen. Where were ye with those protecting guns when my house was burned to the ground by the Black and Tans in 1921, when my wife and daughters were burned within it? Where were ye then with yer brave words and guns? Take that rifle from me arm and let me pass. And mind ye treat that young lad with respect. There is no need to tie him up like an animal going to be butchered. He has no gun and there are more of ye than him, I'm thinking. He could be yer brother, or yer son. I am going home to plant potatoes."

Another man with the stripes of a sergeant joined the two soldiers, and the three of them conferred for a moment. The sergeant held out his hand to Declan and told him he was free to pass but to mind his step — there were snipers positioned in the hills overlooking the Delphi Road all the way up to Westport.

It was the longest road he'd walked. The blackbirds were silent in the reeds by the Bundorragha River, the sun rose quietly over Ben Gorm, spilling its gold over the rocky flank of the mountain, and there was a smell in the air of cordite and brass — or was that dust washed from the stones by an earlier rain? He did not want to think of explosives as he walked home to his unfinished house and a bucket of shilawns for planting. Cupping his hands around his eyes, he tried to keep the image of all that was sacred to him on this road that his family had walked for generations, a tunnel of rocks and low trees, punctuated by birdsong, a scrabble of badgers in the dense fuchsia. All that he loved was held in that cup of vision, all that he knew of homecoming and leave-taking, the road inward and outward, the long stitches of stone walls securing the fields of Tullaglas to the townland. He was overcome with such contrary emotions — anger at the soldiers, love for Una and this road that also stitched them together, an unlikely quilt, grief at the darkness of war that shadowed these sunlit mountains like the rot that had come to the potatoes in the last century and which caused such endless suffering — so overcome that he sank to his knees as though shot. He wept into his hands, closing the cup so that flat palms covered his eyes. His tears scalded his face, his sobs came from his throat like a sickness, bitter as sloes. When he stood again, the view tilted and he saw only the track leading home. He would stop at the young lad's home and tell them what had happened, hoping by now the ropes had been loosened, a few civil words said.

It was all that was spoken of in the district for some weeks. The boy treated by the women did lose his leg, and his parents mourned that loss as though he had died himself; there would be no great lad to help with the ploughing or to shepherd the lambs. The man with his arm badly wounded was spirited away to Sligo, word had it, where a boat was waiting to take him to France. It appeared he had connections to the bringing in of arms and it was felt loose tongues might jeopardize his safety. Women from a Cumann na mBán branch further south had been arrested and sent to Mountjoy Prison; they had been stopped at a roadblock and guns found in the boot of their car. But still the fighting continued, smaller skirmishes followed, the Republicans emerging from their mountain fastness in the night to blow up a section of road or to fire at sentries. Winds were shifting, the Free State National troops taking over Clifden to the south and restoring bridges, train service, and the Western Division staff was found and arrested.

Declan was reading about the aftermath of the slaughter of the suitors, some of them felled by the bright bow. Odysseus had sent his old nurse, Eurycleia, who had already figured out who he was by the unusual scar on his thigh, left by a wild boar's tusk, to bring Penelope down to greet her husband. All along she had thought him a beggar, though a useful one, willing to take on the men who hung around the palace, hoping to be chosen by her as her new bridegroom; she was unwilling to believe that this man was her husband, having waited for him for nineteen years, raising their son on her own, and sleeping alone in the olive-trunk rooted bed of their marriage. She refused to believe that her husband had returned, thinking it a cruel trick of the gods.

> τῷ δι' ἀτασθαλίας ἔπαθον κακόν· αὐτὰρ
> Ὀδυσσεὺς
> ὤλεσε τηλοῦ νόστον Ἀχαιΐδος, ὤλετο δ'
> αὐτός.

In a far country Odysseus has lost his way to return to the Achaian land, he himself is lost.

Is that the sum of it, then? thought Declan. *A man might think himself returned, but the self he has become is so unrecognizable that both the home and the man might be presumed to be lost or dead. The way itself lost? Sure my home was a shell, and myself too. I have rebuilt the former, but it will not be the home it was, populated by women. And as for myself, I was dead for all purposes, that much is true, and I am no longer dead. In the canoe I met my mother in the other world — a man who has walked among ghosts, who has used stones heavy with memory to rebuild his house, a man who has planted his oar on the graves of his women and made small sacrifices of rabbits for his cooking pot. And he almost could not* bring himself to remember the man in Una's arms, clean from the bath and kissed alive as he would have not thought possible. *Have I lost my true self?* he thought. *It is something to think on.* He wondered if Neil might be thought of as a sort of suitor, a rival, though not for his wife's attentions. Rather he stood in the way of Rose becoming what she might become, in the fullness of time; he used force to keep his wife from following her own instincts with her children. And in an act of extraordinary violence, he had lost his head. *How swift is justice, or what we might want to think justice,* thought Declan. In his mind's eye he was looking at a scene as grisly as any in the *Odyssey* — a ground wet with blood and a head at some remove from its body, bits of tissue and bone mixed with tree branches, the fertile cones of evergreens. Only the boots were worth saving, and in that was a terrible irony. Boots to be worn, to be filled by sons growing up in the absence of such a man.

Una collected him again for jaunts into the Partry mountains or to the hills above Kylemore where new grass was greening and insects were at work in the hazels, male catkins hanging in clusters of yellow. One such trip, up a shoulder of Ben Baun, in weather so warm it might have been summer, saw Una dressed in a frock of flowered lawn, a lace collar soft on her shoulders and a necklace of amber beads around her neck. On her feet, sensible walking shoes, which did not detract from her spring-like appearance but proved her practicality. The same haversack which had carried her iodine and gauze now held a flask of tea, some barmbrack and cheese, bananas. It felt safer in the mountains, although signs would be found of campsites, spent bullets, even a stash of something that might have been dynamite in a natural cave high beyond the road on Devilsmother. They walked a wide circle around this last and decided silence was the better part of valour.

"Old Kathleen O'Meara told me that people carry a hazelnut in their pockets as protection against lumbago and rheumatism. Do you think they'd help against explosives?" Una asked, as she sketched a female catkin, the red styles protruding. "And look, Declan, don't you think those catkins look like lambs' tails? We just need some lambs now to compare them to."

"My mother always said that hazels warded off bad spirits, like the rowans," Declan remembered. He was thinking how pleasant it was to watch Una draw, how it felt like he was drawing her at the same time, paying attention to the shape of her face, the line of her breasts through her jacket. They had made love together in her bed several more times since the day they had driven to Bunnaviskaun and back and the night she had been called to tend the wounded; each time he wondered how it was that a woman like her could desire a man so plainly made as himself. But she would touch him as though his body was a fine fabric to be stroked and smoothed, and she responded to his caresses with joy; this impressed upon him again that there were mysteries in the known world, secrets in the human heart that revealed themselves unexpectedly. He had been beloved once and was again.

Below them, the castle at Kylemore nestled in its grove of trees and the lake was placid in the still morning. The Republicans had taken Kylemore House for a time in '22 and young men from hill farms had seen grand bathrooms for the first time, and rooms as big as potato fields. Declan had been told about a holy well, Tobar Maoilean, along the trail up Benbaun. They had walked up through a tunnel of rhododendron heavily in bud and across a small bridge over the Mweelin River. They could hear water and walked towards the sound, laughing as a group of sheep scattered at the sight of them, the lambs with their tails like catkins. The well was housed in a small stone hut, slate-roofed, with a step down to where water puddled in a depression in the ground. It was dark in the hut, but cress grew on the damp perimeter. Sticks in the earth held tatters of cloth, and some coins glittered in the water.

"What are the bits of cloth, Declan?"

"I am thinking this must be a well for infirmities. Some of them have to do with fertility, I know, but all of them are said to have great healing powers. Ye leave a bit of clothing here and it is thought that your illness or misfortune stays once ye've gone. And as the cloth wears away, so does yer condition. My grandmother knew about the wells, and I wish I'd paid more attention. See the pins there, Una? I mind her saying that ye could make a wish and toss a pin into the well and that was as good as a coin. And sure in many families, a coin is too precious to toss down a well, particularly if there is a person needing a lot of care."

Una reached into her haversack and took out two pennies. She handed one to Declan and tossed the other one to the well. Then she went outside and sat on a rock near the well to sketch the hut and its surrounding vegetation. The wide sky was hung with drifts of cirrus clouds like crinkled banners streaming.

"Mare's tails, we called those in Donegal when I was a girl growing up. So lovely, all of it — this view, the sky, those pretty lambs tucking their noses into their mothers' milk bags! In a few months, the rhododendrons will look spectacular. It's hard to believe that they're considered a pest, isn't it? Will you have a drink of tea?" she asked, bringing out the flask.

There was such comfort in her company, thought Declan. He had made a wish at the well, that … well, he was superstitious enough not to want to actually think it even to himself. She was precious to him, and he wondered what to do with such feeling. The night she had driven off to treat the wounded, he had briefly imagined her lost to him. Falling down into grief again, he had waited and waited, almost not hoping, until the headlamps of her car illuminated the way to her cottage from the main road. There had been such missions since, but she did not speak of them, telling him that it was better he not know. Once he heard her in conversation with a woman at the door and heard her exclaim, "Hunger strike! And what day is she now?" and then the voices lowered as if suddenly aware of his presence.

Declan was walking back from Leenane, a sack of oatmeal over his shoulder, when Una stopped her car at the bottom of her lane.

"Declan, Fintan has brought me a telegram. Who do you suppose has decided to come to favour us with his company but the lily collector I told you about, Edward Higgins. He has wired me to say he will be staying at the Killary Arms and will I show him the choice spots for lilies. He who has been to China and Japan and Nepal — I am fearful that he will not be impressed with our small offerings of wild garlic and those bog asphodels, and in any case it is too early for many of them to be in bloom. So my dear, I will be busy with him for the next week or so. But surely you'll stop in for a meal when you're passing?"

He nodded, shared a few words with her, and then went on his way. He was stung again by jealousy, the same sour note of it that had sounded when she'd mentioned Higgins after her return from London and again during their first night as lovers. A man with a castle and a whole background in common with Una's. A man who knew plants and had the means to travel far in their service and who could offer Una such trips. He could not believe that she would not find the man more suitable in contrast to himself. And he was not sure that his stopping for a meal would be welcomed by such a man.

As it turned out, he did not need to stop in, for one day, as he worked on his house, Una's car stopped again by his gate as it had that day so many months ago when she had taken him to Cregganbaun, but this time a man sat in the passenger seat. Both of them emerged from the car, the man tall enough to duck his head and unfold his arms and legs. He had the look of a man born to plenty — his fair hair was cut and smoothed back with some sort of pomade, his clothing, fine soft tweed, was brushed and tidy, a cravat knotted casually around his neck. When he smiled, his teeth were very large and white.

"Declan, this is Edward Higgins. And Edward, I'd like you to meet my friend Declan O'Malley who is just rebuilding his house as you can see. He is a man of many talents, is Declan. He is also translating the *Odyssey* and has learned to string a harp!"

The two men shook hands. Declan was acutely aware that he must cut an odd picture in his worn trousers from Una's grandfather's box and a jersey which was much in need of a wash. As he was himself, having just planed a door to fit an opening and hoisted flat stones up from Dhulough for his hearth.

Higgins praised the view and then poked his head in the front opening. "And you will live here, will you?" was his only comment, to which Declan nodded yes. It must look so meagre in the eyes of one born in a castle, the small rooms with their single windows, the uneven slates of the floor. Una began to talk about their outing, saying that she was returning to the area where they'd found the orchids. She hoped there would be something to show Edward but wondered if it might be too early.

"There are the ransoms now in the wood near Delphi Lodge," Declan told her. "I'm after picking some to have with potatoes."

"Oh, thank you," Una exclaimed. "We'll stop there on our way back, though ransoms are perhaps too simple for you, Edward! Still, wild garlic in an Irish wood is worth adding to your life-list, if only for its very novelty!"

The man sniffed, then smiled again, though there was something of a sneer to his smile. The little common wild garlic, with its starry blossoms, was not what he had come to Ireland to find, Declan was aware of that, but watched as the pair got into the car, their vasculums on the floor behind the seats. His heart sank down into his boots.

Una had invited him to have dinner with them on the following evening, so Declan washed one of his better shirts and aired out a jersey, not wanting to bring the smell of the turf shed to the table. Fergus Mannion was going to Leenane in his donkey cart in the late afternoon and offered to leave Declan off at Marshlands on his way. There was a sympathy in Fergus's eyes, though he did not say anything about Una or Higgins. But of course everyone knew Declan was courting her, in a manner of speaking, and of course everyone knew that she had a visitor from England, staying at the Arms. He had been seen already, fly-fishing in the Erriff River, with a local boy holding his creel for a few pennies. He had stood the drinkers a pint in the pub of the Arms and held forth briefly on the sunset as viewed through the small-paned window. And Una's car — well, it could not be missed, being one of only three in the immediate area. Fergus talked only of potatoes and the weather until he pulled the donkey in where the Marshlands lane met the road, and then he turned to Declan, grasped his hand, and said, "Yer a better man than him, Declan, and if she is the one for ye, then ye must declare yer heart."

That very heart did leap and sink as he walked to Una's cabin where smoke flowered out of the chimney and the hens clustered near the door. A smell of roasting lamb issued from the door when Una opened it, a wide smile on her face.

It irked Declan to see Higgins so at home in the cabin, his vasculum on the sideboard and his coat hanging on the hook where Declan usually hung his own. He was offered an aperitif—

such a word! — by the man, had joined him by the fire where Higgins held forth on the scarcity of blossom near Cregganbaun, and was beginning to wish he'd never come when Una asked them to be seated at the table, indicating that Declan should sit opposite her at the head.

"May I ask you to carve, Declan?"

And he did, the sharp knife slicing the leg of young lamb into rosy portions after running it along his thumb to test its edge. There were also potatoes boiled in their jackets with a clipping of wild garlic strewn over them in their dish. There was a small unpleasant moment when both men tried to help Una to mint sauce and their hands met on the dish, Higgins recoiling as though his hand had been soiled. More talk about their gathering jaunt ensued, and a few details were settled about the next day, when Una was to collect her guest at his hotel and drive up the Maam road to drop him off so he could make a foray into the wetlands on Joyce's River; she herself was unavailable to accompany him. He wanted to go to Kerry at some point to see the rare *Simethis plan-ifolia*, which grew nowhere else in Ireland. After the meal they sat by the fire with tea and small glasses of a rich port the visitor had brought and Higgins spoke of trips taken in search of elusive lilies — the beautiful *Nomocharis aperta*, which he'd collected in western China in high alpine pastures, and a glorious white lily from Nepal that he'd seen in every variation from green to brown and crimson. It was interesting to listen to his descriptions, but Declan felt that he had nothing to add or to offer in return. When he mentioned the small orange lilies he'd seen on the rocks by Francis Point, he was told that it was almost certainly *columbianum* and very common at that; Kew had both plants and seed in the collection. Declan remembered the scent of oranges, the notion that Indians had eaten the roots in great numbers, and how he had been enchanted by the notion of sustaining one's life with a flower. But it was not something he wanted to talk about with Edward

Higgins, who had perfect posture and who was clearly interested in Una Fitzgerald. She tried to include Declan in the conversation, even directing Higgins's attention to the harp, telling him how Declan had figured out the difficult stringing process himself. That sniff again! And though he looked at it in a cursory way, he showed no interest in how a harp might be strung, how it might be played. He evinced a passion for chamber music himself. By now they were all seated around the fire, which Una had stoked with dry logs from a fallen tree in her woods. A fire so warm, and he so weary after days of lifting stones for his fireplace and hearth, that he found himself dozing off. When he opened his eyes, he realized that Una and Higgins were arguing.

"You can't possibly know, Edward. It is not your country, and who are the English to make these decisions for the Irish?"

"My cousin was here for two years and I don't mind telling you that he thought the Irish very undisciplined indeed. All this talk of independence without a hope of success. He is a captain, you know, and his men were assigned to an area of Cork where they constantly had to take measures against the peasants."

"And was he part of the mob who burned the beautiful centre of Cork, then? The whole of Patrick Street? That was the Black and Tans, and the auxiliary RICs, and they refused to let in the fire brigades to put out the fire. Or the shooting of the Lord Mayor, Tomas MacCurtain? And taking poor Terence McSwiney on such trumped-up charges and letting him starve himself in one of those dreadful prisons ... You will find, Edward, that your cousin doesn't have much cachet in Cork now, nor ever did he."

Una was furious, Declan could tell, as she gathered up the glasses and cups onto a tray.

"Let me take them for ye," he told her as he sprang to his feet. She gratefully handed him the tray, meeting his eyes with a look he could not interpret. He took it to the sink, where a pan of warm water waited, and carefully washed the dishes soaking in the pan, drying them with a clean linen cloth and putting them away in the hutch. He found himself spending a particularly long time polishing the carving knife, briefly imagined plunging it into Higgins's heart, and quickly put it into its sleeve of flannel while the unsuspecting suitor intoned about treason and treaties and the long patience of Lloyd George. It was as though he was talking to children, his tone very deprecating.

"I think we will conclude this discussion now, if you don't mind, Edward," Una said briskly. "I fear our differences might lead to unpleasantness. But I would like to show you some drawings, if you would care to see them. Here, this is a little view of the crow garlic. I love the spathes shielding the flowers! Don't they look just like a monk's cowl?"

Declan heard the man agreeing too fulsomely for comfort and made that his opportunity to depart, taking up his jacket and borrowing Una's torch for the long walk home. It was a pleasant night, and he wanted the chance to gather his thoughts, to examine the sour seed of jealousy which had taken root in his heart. On the one hand, Higgins was a man who inhabited a world well known to Una; she had met him, after all, at a dinner party given by her family in London. They had approved of him and had encouraged her to see more of him. And of course there was the shared love of plants, though when Higgins spoke of a plant, it was as though of a personal conquest, but to be fair to him, there was a lot of trekking about in mountains and so forth to locate the plants in the first place. He was not lazy. But on the other hand, he was so English, so sure of his opinions, and weren't they just rid of the English as an oppressive force? And Declan and Una had an understanding. He thought they did. Didn't they? Now there was a question. Would he dare to ask her? Was it time to ask her?

Just as he was nearing Tullaglas, the beam of his torch scanning the track up to his gate, he heard the sound of wheels, the clip-clop of a donkey's hooves on the hard ground of the road, and then Fergus Mannion called out his name. He turned in surprise.

"I was kept overlong in Leenane, Declan, and then took a few pints to fortify me for the drive home. How was yer evening so?"

"Ah, Fergus, I am just thinking on it now. It was a good meal Una prepared, but the man himself was a source of arrogance and irritation. I'm thinking it's a good thing we've sent them packing altogether."

"Just so. He was in the pub earlier in the day, it seems, boasting about his cousin who served in Cork. And gassing off about our fellas, Griffith and De Valera. He'd be a wiser man if he knew when to hold his tongue."

"Well, tomorrow Una is taking him by motor car to botanize on Joyce's River and leaving him there for the day, so they'll be rid of him for a good stretch anyhow."

The men bade each other goodnight and went their separate ways, Declan up the track to his dark shed and Fergus further along to his snug cottage and the warm sleeping body of Bride. An owl called from the sycamores down by the lake.

Two days later, Declan was walking down to Tully in light rain to arrange for a new blade for his scythe when a car came over the hill towards him and came to an abrupt stop on the road. It was Una. She looked flustered.

"Declan, you know I offered to drive Edward up the Maam road yesterday morning so he could botanize on his own for the day. He was to get himself back to Leenane, by foot or by flagging down a car on the road. Well, it seems he didn't come back at all, the publican has told me this, and now I'm a little concerned. Would you mind coming with me to search for him? I'd feel better if there were two of us in the event he has fallen or God knows what."

"Of course I will come with ye."

It took most of an hour to get to the place near Joyce's River where Una had left Edward Higgins off with his vasculum and a rucksack of lunch. The river was very full with spring run-off and raced along its course, gathering in the waters of other smaller rivers coming down off Rinavore and Munterowen. It was raining quite hard when they parked the car and walked east to where Una had suggested Higgins concentrate his attentions on the early purple orchids and the lesser butterfly orchids which grew in relative abundance on the acid soils of the moorlands there. Recent footprints led them along the riverbank and over the small stone bridge to where the road climbed up to a few farms at Lee.

Una saw the body first. She gave a shriek and ran up the slope, Declan quick at her heels. It was Higgins, sprawled in a pool of mud and blood, his face badly puffed and bruised. The fine tweed jacket was in ruins, the sleeves torn from the body of the garment. Nearby, a vasculum lay broken and crushed, its contents scattered on the muddy ground.

"Oh, dear God, what has happened to him?" Una cried, then: "Who has done this to him?" for it became obvious that the man had been beaten. "Is he alive? Can you tell?"

Declan bent to the body and reached under Higgins's neck, feeling around until there was a place where the pulse made a small slow thump against his fingers. Declan felt his own pulse race as he realized how weak his rival was, how pathetic.

"He's alive, yes, and if ye're able, I think ye must go on yer own to get help. I'll stay here with him so. But hurry, Una. There's nothing I can do for him but cover him with my jacket for the warmth."

Higgins groaned and his eyes fluttered. Una ran down the slope and over the bridge to the car and Declan removed his jacket, arranging it over the man's shoulders, patting them gently as he did so.

"I don't know if ye can hear me or not. I'm not going to move ye in case it does more damage but I'm here and Una has gone for help. She'll be here as soon as she can. We'll do what we can for ye and we'll not leave ye alone."

The man's eyes fluttered again, and he made sounds of pain in his throat. He moved his mouth, but Declan could see that his jaw was damaged, perhaps even broken, and he touched Higgins's arm. "Don't try to talk. All that can come later."

Jackdaws were nesting nearby and made their usual noise. *Tchack, tchack,* they called from a tree at the edge of a wood where a nest hole was visible. In a different country, Declan might have believed they were telling him the story of an attack, naming those who had struck and kicked Edward Higgins and left him for dead on an isolated slope. But try as he might, he could not decode what these birds were voicing, and anyway this was no time for frivolity. If there was a message in their calls, it was a warning to stay away from their eggs in the adjoining sparse woodland. Declan was not proud at that moment to remember how he had imagined pushing Una's carving knife into the heart that was now struggling to keep its owner alive.

When Una returned, it was with the gardai and the doctor in a separate vehicle, the latter's Austin van. An improvised stretcher was brought up the slope, and the doctor made an examination of the body while the two gardai took notes.

"His right arm is broken, as are some fingers, I'm certain. The jaw is dislocated, if not broken. I can't tell just now with all the swelling. That's a nasty gash on the back of his head, which I'm going to just dress quickly and then we'll hoist him onto the board. Time is of the essence here. I'd like at least one of you" — he addressed this to the gardai — "to accompany me to Clifden with him. There's no time to lose, and we can't wait for an ambulance. We'll hope that the road is in good repair because

he has lost a lot of blood, that's evident, and there may be com-
plications along the way."

He reached into his bag and took out cotton for dressing the
head wound. And then the men carefully moved the body onto
the stretcher, wrapped blankets snugly around it, and began the
descent to the road, Higgins groaning as they stumbled with the
weight of him down the hill over rough ground. At the vehicles,
a few words were spoken about contacting the man's family and
then the van carrying the doctor, one garda, and their bloody
cargo sped off towards the Clifden road. The other three got into
Una's car and drove towards Leenane, subdued. The garda asked
a few questions — how long had Una known Higgins, did he
have family in the country, who should be contacted with the
news of his injuries? Una answered in a perfunctory way, naming a brother in London, parents in Sussex, and then said, "I
hardly knew him at all." They dropped the garda at the Killary
Arms. Una was very quiet as they continued on to Marshlands.

"Declan, I couldn't bear to be alone tonight. Tell me
you'll stay?"

"Of course. As long as you need me."

They went in to the cold house and busied themselves with
making a fire, putting the kettle on. Then Una began to cry. She
turned to him, her face very anxious, and wet with tears.

"I feel so responsible, Declan."

"Responsible, Una? How could ye be responsible? Ye were
not even there. Violence was done to the man by other men, ye
saw for yerself how broken up his face was, and how much
blood he'd lost. I think he was left for dead. And he is lucky ye
thought to look for him, that much is sure."

Una took a deep breath, sobbed, and then said, in a soft
voice, "The reason why I didn't accompany Edward in his
botanizing was because I had a Cumann na mBán meeting mid-
morning. I'm afraid I was not discreet in my comments about

him. I mocked him. I even told of his terrible cousin and his problems with Irish 'discipline.'"

"Well, he has been gassing off in the Arms about the cousin, Fergus Mannion told me as much when I left after dinner the other night. So he has not been discreet himself, and him a guest in our country. Do not blame yerself for what happened."

"But Declan, what if one of those women went home — we were finished by noon — and told her husband or son or for goodness' sake anyone at all? It's clear he was beaten by someone who must have known he was there, isn't it? Or do you think he might have strayed upon something he was not meant to see?" Her face actually brightened somewhat as she thought of the latter possibility. But then she broke down crying again, saying she would have to try to call his family and see what they wanted her to do with his things.

Declan comforted her and made the tea, bringing her a cup of it well-sweetened and pale with milk; he was afraid she would not be able to stop crying, that she might go into shock. He too had been indiscreet, he realized, remembering his conversation with Fergus Mannion on the dark track two nights earlier. If he looked into his conscience deeply, would he discover that he had hoped that more might come of that conversation? There was the knife. Had he mentioned his thought about what he wanted to do with the knife to Fergus? He could not remember.

He would say nothing to Una, he decided. He had known Fergus all his life, but does anyone ever truly know another? Fergus had helped him a great deal since his return, as had Bride, but there was the day he had found the rifles in his turf pile and Fergus's counsel that he not tell the Garda. It might have been Fergus, might have been him putting a word in another's ear. A chill ran up his spine and along his shoulders. It did not bear thinking about. That night they made love quietly and at length, wanting the small peace they had begun to find before Edward

Higgins wired to say he was coming to the Killary Arms. Una cried in her sleep, and Declan held her, only falling asleep himself when light began to ease into the room through the soft curtains.

τοὺς δὲ ἴδεν μάλα πάντας ἐν αἵματι καὶ κονίῃσι
πεπτεῶτας πολλούς

He saw all of them then, all slain and fallen
In the dust and blood

As it turned out, Higgins was indeed severely injured but was expected to recover. His jaw had been wired shut to heal, his broken arm set, the gash on his scalp stitched and dressed. He had no memory of the attack but woke after two days' sleep to mumble when he might go home; he was given a pad and a pen to write out his questions because even the mumbling hurt. Una drove to Clifden to visit him and encountered his mother at his bedside. She was polite but chilly, accepting the flowers that Una brought, the basket of sweetmeats, the drawing of crow garlic that he had admired in her home. It was clear she was in Ireland reluctantly and probably would not come again.

Rumours abounded about the attack but nothing clear was determined, no one was arrested, and after a few weeks, the event was tucked away in memory, not forgotten, but not cherished, like the small Republican victories, the spiriting away of wounded men by boat right under the noses of the English. A brief tale might be told in a pub of how a loudmouthed Englishman was dealt with by Joyce's River, but apart from a few smiles that could be thought secretive, that was the extent of its course. Una never heard from Edward Higgins again.

A few weeks later, Una arranged to drive up to Westport and take the train to Donegal to visit her aunt and uncle for a month now that the rail lines were open. She wanted time away from an area redolent with the blood of both sacrifice and revenge; she wanted to sleep in a house where she would not be awakened by a knock that might take her to a boy crying from the pain of his injuries or a telegram advising of a visit. When Declan left her after their final night together before her departure, she told him she would miss him terribly and that he should feel welcome to use her cabin at any time. So he left his papers there and stopped in regularly to light a fire and spend time with Odysseus. His nightshirt hung behind Una's door like a hopeful ghost, the sleeves patient and the placket undone.

He had made a draft of the passages he loved best, the ones that spoke out of the poem to him and his life. He had no son, no father, no bright wife waiting. There had been a suitor, not slain but certainly damaged, perhaps not by him, but he could not completely absolve himself from that possibility. He thought of Rose, wondering if she had been his princess at the river with her dream of a bridegroom, her clean linens drying in the hot sun on rocks, her kindness. No mention had been made of erotic interest on Odysseus's part, yet Declan remembered how he had awoken in the canoe to watch Rose bathe naked in Oyster Bay like a sea-born daughter of Aphrodite, his body responding to the sight of a maiden of the white arms at play in the water. He wanted to do something for her, give something to her, so she would remember their time on Oyster Bay as he now remembered it, softened by distance (he had almost forgotten the loneliness, the days of weeping in the small close cabin, the nights in the skiff by Outer Kelp waiting for dawn so he could drop his spoons with their baits of herring, the unsettling night on the rocky island while he waited out a storm, bones falling from their platforms in the trees), an interlude which had given him back himself, not whole but able to find in the words of a poem something of a map to lead him home. In his best handwriting, he wrote out the first three hundred lines of Book 6, Odysseus's meeting with Nausikaa and his journey to her father's palace. In Greek and English, he made a version of himself and Rose, of a princess and a wanderer, a mother who knew the solace of a fire and good food, a father who made possible the means of return. He reminded her of the sheets she had folded with her mother, patched linen washed on the stones of Anderson Creek. Then he sent the package off to her in brown paper.

One day while he sat with the poem, there was a knock at Una's door. It was Bernadette Feeny.

"I was passing and saw the smoke, Declan, and I thought I'd make sure the harp was keeping in tune."

He invited her in, explained Una's absence and his presence, and she listened to the harp strings, adjusting several to bring the instrument true. He watched her cradle the harp and suddenly wanted to know how it felt to hold it in that way. She turned to him and saw the longing in his eyes.

"Come, Declan, draw up a stool. Ye could try this for yerself so."

The harp was placed between his knees with its shoulder resting on his right shoulder. Then Bernadette took his right hand and showed him how to touch the strings, thumb up and fingers extended, as though holding the knob of a door in readiness to open it

"Keep your hand so that the thumb and first three fingers rest in the middle of the string," she advised him. "Forget about the small finger. Ye'll not need it. Then do the same with the other hand so that the two hands face one another. The right hand plays the melody, Declan, and the left follows with chords or graces. Just so. Yer hands are as they should be. Try to take that string there, yes, that one, with the first finger, and that one there, yes, leaving off the one in between, and stroke it with yer thumb. Pluck them in a motion as a scissor might work, striking up with the thumb. Ah, that's it. But difficult, I'm thinking. So now just put yer nail on the string and pluck."

Surprisingly, a brief note sounded, not unpleasing. Declan was so startled he laughed out loud. He tried it again.

"This harp has a very pretty harmonic curve," Bernadette told him, tracing the line of the harp's neck with her hand. "Yer own hands should echo that."

What he liked was the way the harp rested against his shoulder while his arms supported it, embraced it. How many times had he watched Grainne holding this very harp in the same embrace, her fingers meeting through the strings? He had the sensation, briefly, of holding his daughter, the manageable weight of her body, while his hands sought out her music from strings that had never known her fingers.

Bernadette placed her hand on his right one and helped him to pluck out the opening phrase of the beautiful "Mabel Kelly." Ah, it was sweet, the melody with its lilting notes, the dignified chording. With her left hand she dampened the strings so they didn't ring out so long; Declan remembered her telling him of this when she'd first tuned the instrument. Bernadette sang softly as they played, "Lucky the husband who puts his hand beneath her head ... Music might listen to her least whisper, learn every note, for all are true." And her hand upon his took them through the ancient modal air: "Lamp loses light when placed beside her ... Her beauty is her own and she is not proud."

"There, Declan O'Malley, that's what it's like to play the harp so though 'tis easier for me to guide the smaller hands of a child, I'd say. But ye did well enough. See how ye are holding the shoulder with yer hand. It is like ye've always known it."

Declan saw her to the door and closed it behind her. Her words sounded in his mind, *it is like ye've always known it*, and he thought how it was not quite accurate. It was not the music he had sought, although he would try to play the harp again, perhaps with Bernadette's guidance, and could tell that he would enjoy the challenge of finding the notes within the strings, fitting the shape of his hands to the harmonic curve of the instrument. It was for the moment of embrace, when he held Grainne in his arms, feeling her in the polished wood, his shoulder taking the weight of the harp as hers had.

Walking home, he encountered an old woman on the road, gathering plants. He asked what she had in her basket. She showed him dyer's rocket and a kind of woad, the one giving yellow, she said, and the other a clear blue. She had cress, for a soup, and a stem of hound's tongue against a dog she had to pass on her way back to Gobnamona. She had the clouded eyes of the very old, and yet she bent to the ground and examined the ditch without a complaint. "And this," she said, "is bedstraw, a fine plant for setting the cheese. I've a great old goat these days and the milk makes a fearsome cheese. I'll send some for ye at the school, will I?"

(News travelled like wild seeds or magpies ...)

In May, he was washing the newly plastered walls of his house with lime and water, a little blue added to keep it bright. The roof was sound, the windows kept out the wind. All he owned fit into a small corner, but a fire made in his hearth was warm enough for the whole house. Over the lintel of the main doorway, he painted a proverb in deep green paint from a tube of colour that Una had left behind after a sketching trip: *Ar scath a chéile a mhaireas na daoine, In the shadows of each other we must build our lives.* It looked like a scribble of delicate vine.

One morning he awoke in the turf shed to small drifts of snow that had come in with fierce northerly wind, and he remembered how he had once felt like Suibhne. *The very cold sleep on a whole night, listening to the billowy sea, the multitudinous voices of the birds...* Magpies were beginning to pair up for the season (*two for joy*), and he saw wild swans flying to the great loughs of the midlands. The weather could be so unsettled, first the snow, then fine sunlight.

He looked up from passing his brush over the new wall to see Una coming through his gate where the basalt pillar watched for those arriving as well as those leaving. She was looked beautiful, rested, the dark shadows that had appeared under her eyes after Higgins's beating gone, her skin clear and glowing.

"I am just on my way home from Donegal, Declan, and I came this way so I could stop to see if the asphodel at Cregganbaun was showing itself yet. And doesn't your house look fine! A fire burning, the sound of birds, and look, even a jug of bittersweet on the sill! I'd like to introduce you to Bran, a gift from my uncle."

Reaching into the basket she carried, she lifted out a puppy, brown with odd, wiry hair. "Believe it or not, he is a wolfhound although he has some growing to do yet before we can consider him a dog at all. But he has enjoyed the drive down from Westport and would like to explore, I think, if you don't mind." She put the puppy down on the ground where it immediately peed, then began to run in the direction of the potato bed.

Declan laughed as he watched the young pup follow its nose on the scent of something, obeying some old order. It had something in its movements of Argos on the other shore, bold and awkward. Una smiled and then embraced him, her breath warm against his neck. He was wearing one of her grandfather's shirts and a well-darned gansey which Bride Mannion had given him for the warmth she said he'd need to get through the winter. Here it was, May already, with the weather so unsettled! And yet, in Una's arms, he was fierce with happiness and wouldn't have noticed the cold even if he were out in it naked. She brushed his hair away from his eyes and laughed.

"And what do you think of this, Declan? I am certain we are going to have a child. I thought so before I left but I wanted to be sure before I told you. I will not be a young mother, of course, and my doctor has a few concerns, but I feel wonderful and wanted you to know."

He could only hold her tighter, his heart aching for what was lost and found.

> ἀλλ' ἔρχευ, λέκτρονδ' ἴομεν, γύναι, ὄφρα
> καὶ ἤδη
> Now come to the bed, my woman, that we be
> lulled in pleasure
> ὕπνῳ ὕπο γλυκερῷ ταρπώμεθα κοιμηθέντε
> to a sweet sleep that we will delight in together.

The new rooms of his house glowed, clean and ready. Far away, on Oyster Bay, he imagined the gulls fishing and the ravens talking in the cedars. What were they saying? Old stories, new sightings, even a man asking at the store where a shelter might be found, a boat borrowed, a voyage taken to a campsite where clams were cooked on a beach fire and where wolves made themselves known in the night. Bones had been found in an old canoe and used to frighten children but the soul of the dead man soared up to the heavens like a feather on the wind, cleansed by yarrow. With time, the body of the man who had found the bones might rest also in peace on an island within spitting distance of his farm. The Lurgan boat, put to earth in some forgotten ceremony, and taken from it in wonder ... In the soil, seeds waited for the sun and rain to urge them back to life, while withered roots slept in their own anticipation. Even a harp might be buried in a bog near Limerick, then brought forth to be played again, its strings remembering both joys and sorrows. Even a man in a distant field, keeping alive the means for fire, might be found by a woman at a river, cleaned and robed, and taken home to tell his story.